About the Authors

USA TODAY bestselling author **Julie Miller** writes breathtaking romantic suspense. She has sold millions of copies of her books worldwide, and has earned a National Readers Choice Award, two Daphne du Maurier prizes and an RT BookReviews Career Achievement Award. She is a multiple finalist for the prestigious RITA® Award. For a complete list of her books and more, go to www.juliemiller.org

USA Today bestselling author **Katherine Garbera** is a two-time Maggie winner who has written 108 books. A Florida native who grew up to travel the globe, Katherine now makes her home in the Midlands of the UK with her husband, two children and a very spoiled miniature dachshund. Visit her on the web at http://www.katherinegarbera.com, connect with her on Facebook and follow her on Twitter @katheringarbera.

Cat Schield lives in Minnesota with her daughter, their opiniated Burmese cats and a silly Doberman puppy. Winner of the Romance Writers of America 2010 Golden Heart® for series contemporary romance, when she's not writing sexy, romantic stories for Mills & Boon Desire, she can be found sailing with friends on the St. Croix River or in more exotic locales like the Caribbean and Europe. You can find out more about her books at w̶

Confessions

Confessions of the Nanny

JULIE MILLER

KATHERINE GARBERA

CAT SCHIELD

MILLS & BOON

First Published in Great Britain 2022
By Mills & Boon, an imprint of HarperCollins*Publishers*
1 London Bridge Street, London, SE1 9GF

www.harpercollins.co.uk

HarperCollins*Publishers*
1st Floor, Watermarque Building,
Ringsend Road, Dublin 4, Ireland

CONFESSIONS OF THE NANNY
© 2022 Harlequin Enterprises ULC.

Nanny 911 © 2011 Julie Miller
Billionaire's Baby Bind © 2017 Harlequin Enterprises ULC
Nanny Makes Three © 2016 Harlequin Enterprises ULC

Special thanks and acknowledgement are given to Katherine Garbera for her contribution to the *Texas Cattleman's Club: Blackmail* series.

Special thanks and acknowledgement are given to Cat Schield for her contribution to the *Texas Cattleman's Club: Lies and Lullabies* series.

ISBN: 978-0-263-30494-7

NANNY 911

JULIE MILLER

Thank you to MaryAnn McQuillan.
You opened up your big heart and your busy
schedule to take pity on my sore fingers
and computer frustration. Thanks for
retyping the manuscript for me!

Prologue

"Start the countdown."

The armed driver in the modified camo uniform floored the accelerator, forcing his five passengers to hold on for their lives as they bounced over the ruts and sand and scrub brush of the arid terrain. "I recommend waiting until we get to a safe distance."

The one person not wearing mock military garb clung to the Hummer's passenger seat. "And I recommend you follow my orders to the letter. That's why I'm paying you, isn't it?"

"Part of my job is to protect you. There could be fallout here."

"I didn't come all this way to miss the show. I want to be here at the beginning, just as I'm looking forward to being there at the end—when I see his face and can revel in his failure." The anticipation of seeing that arrogant face downcast in broken sorrow, his eyes filled with tears, his clipped voice perhaps begging for mercy, was enough to make one light-headed. Or maybe it was this bone-jarring ride across the Kalahari that was affecting rational thought. The boss gripped the door handle and dashboard and turned to the driver. "Push the button."

Surrendering to the inevitable winner in this battle of wills, the driver pulled the tiny remote-control switch box from his shirt pocket and activated the countdown. He set the device in his lap, but refused to stop the vehicle. Supposedly, that was the sign of a good leader—putting the safety and well-being of his team first. Too bad not every man in this world believed that.

"Another mile between us and the facility won't make any difference on this terrain." The driver slowed his speed a fraction and handed over a pair of military-grade binoculars, ironically designed by Quinn Gallagher, owner of the facility that was growing smaller and smaller beyond the swirl of dust in the vehicle's side-view mirror. "Here. Take these. You'll be able to watch the sweat beading on their foreheads when they realize they've got no place to run or hide."

"You're certain there are only the guards at the gate?"

"You know, for someone who has planned some seriously scary stuff out to the last detail, you're pretty squeamish about collateral damage."

"I'm not afraid to kill someone if I have to." The raging injustice and bone-deep pain swirling through the passenger's heart made it far easier than even the mercenary driver could imagine to inflict pain without feeling remorse. "But I don't want a high casualty rate. Too many outsiders would get involved then and he'll lock down tighter than one of his vaults. Because I've mapped my strategy down to the last detail, I need to maintain control of the situation. To do that, each task must be completed the way I've directed."

It was a lesson that had been learned the hard way—that there were steps, deadlines, terrible costs for not getting everything just right. It was a lesson that could never be forgotten.

"You're the boss."

"Don't you forget that." The enemy had. That was why he had to pay. "If he thinks I'm going to stand by and let him ruin my life, he's mistaken. I intend to hurt him as badly as he's hurt me. And I intend to strike where it will hurt him the most."

"It's almost time."

"Stop the car."

With the advantage of higher ground on the mesa where they'd stopped, the view of the facility was unobstructed. The boss adjusted the binoculars to watch.

"Five, four, three, two—"

The boss held up a hand, demanding silence, wanting to savor this first triumph.

It started as a rumble, a sound so deep they felt the tremors through the ground, vibrating up through their feet and legs seconds before hearing the first pop. Then there was a flash of light, followed by that distinctive whoosh as the initial ignition in the plant's disposal chamber sucked all the oxygen from the surrounding rooms. There was a split second of silence, the anticipation leaving them all holding their breaths.

And then…*boom. Boom. Boom!* One by one the explosions fired off, each one larger than the last, tearing through the shiny new facility, spewing flames and steel and glass into the air. Thick black smoke coiled upward, forming dense black clouds against the desert's crystal blue sky. In a matter of seconds, there was nothing left of Gallagher Security Systems's newest production facility except mangled webs of steel and burning rubble.

The team of mercenaries watching alongside had done their job well. The boss lowered the binoculars and watched it burn, feeling the heat even at this distance.

The satisfaction was intense.

Payback had begun.

Chapter One

7 Days until Midnight, New Year's Eve

"Someone is trying to destroy me."

Quinn Gallagher touched the temple of his dark-framed glasses, an ingrained habit left over from his youth, when he'd been a four-eyed brainiac from a rural Missouri trailer park who'd learned how to defend himself and his mother from the respective bullies who'd preyed on them. He was no longer poor, no longer had his beloved mother—and up until the murder of his wife, Valeska, nearly three years earlier, he'd believed that he no longer feared anything.

Now three employees that he'd never met, but for whom he certainly felt responsible, were dead in a foreign country. And the office building that he'd closed for the holidays, with paid vacations off for all but the skeleton crew of security guards receiving over-time pay, was being searched from basement to rooftop by a team of black-uniformed cops, armed like the special-ops security details his company outfitted for wealthy individuals and companies across the country. The captain of KCPD's SWAT Team 1, Michael Cutler, often served as a consultant to GSS when they were developing new weapons, protective gear and security technology.

He was also one of the few men in this world Quinn Gallagher trusted without question. He strode into the penthouse office suite with a disturbing yet unsurprising announcement. "Thus far, we've found no sign of forced entry into the building or your office. I've got my team checking the top floor here now. Of course, this place is locked up tighter than Fort Knox. Whoever got in had to have the same kind of talents you possess." It was a wry compliment. An enemy with Quinn's technical skills would be a formidable opponent, indeed. The SWAT captain turned toward the small, unwrapped Christmas present Quinn had left on his desk. "Don't let me or my men interrupt your meeting."

"Come and go as you need, Michael. Thanks." Quinn adjusted the knot of his silk tie and paced the length of his office. The men and woman in suits on the matching sofas waited expectantly for some sign that he was ready for their problem-solving input. But none of them dared offer any personal condolence or sympathetic look. He paid them exceedingly well to be the best at the jobs they'd been hired to do, not to be his friends. That was a bonus he rarely bestowed on the people around him. Caring had cost him dearly— when he'd lost his mother, and three years ago when he'd lost his wife.

He didn't need the distraction of emotional ties to interfere with the efficiency of this Christmas Eve meeting. And his people knew that. Keeping an eye on Michael Cutler and the furtive movements of the rest of his five-man team through the chrome-and-glass partition separating his office from the rest of the floor, Quinn turned his attention back to the executives who'd been able to report on such short notice.

Louis Nolan, his vice president of operations and Quinn's eyes on every aspect of Gallagher Security Systems, was speaking. "I've already been on the phone with Nikolai Titov, our primary investor there. He wants answers."

"He'll know them as soon as I have them," Quinn promised.

"The Kalahari plant hadn't even begun production yet," Louis continued. "We were still in the hiring process with the locals. I know we were building there to save money, but now we're posting a loss on GSS's bottom line and facing speculation from the press. Titov's already putting the pressure on to let him reopen and expand the St. Feodor plant in Lukinburg. The last thing we need right now are nervous stockholders. I think we should entertain his offer before this unfortunate incident turns into a catastrophe."

As Quinn suspected, his security chief, David Damiani, wasted no time pushing to his feet and confronting the older businessman. "Unfortunate? I lost three good men in that explosion. Try making that phone call to their families when Christmas is tomorrow."

"I'm not denigrating the loss of life." Louis was a cagey old salt who had no problem defending himself. "I'm pointing out that this could be an environmental or political attack on GSS's expansion into South Africa. I know our base of operation here in Kansas City is thousands of miles away, but this could snowball into a real tragedy if we don't spin some control over the situation in the next few days, if not the next few hours."

David raked his hands through his hair, the movement exposing the Beretta he wore holstered beneath his left arm. "It's already snowballing, Lou. How do you explain someone breaking into GSS headquarters when we've got the best damn techno-security on the planet? I can't. As far as I can see, we're already under attack."

"Gentlemen," Elise Brown intervened. Quinn knew his executive assistant could be counted on to keep everyone focused and moving forward. "None of us are thrilled to be taken away from our families and vacations at this time of year, and certainly none of us are pleased to hear about sabotage and the murder of GSS employees, but you're missing the point. Quinn said someone was trying to destroy *him,* not GSS." She turned her soft brown eyes up to him. "Isn't that right?"

"Yes." That was the painful distinction he'd made. Going after his business empire was one thing. But the gift-wrapped package he'd received on his desk this morning...

His gaze drifted over to the shiny red paper and white tissue decorated with candy canes, of all things—his daughter's favorite holiday treat. Quinn seethed inside, momentarily experiencing that same helpless fury that had plagued him growing up, before he'd learned to use his brain as a weapon to outsmart the kids who'd picked on him and the men who'd thought his mother didn't have anyone to protect her.

He forced his gaze away from where Michael Cutler was processing the unwanted gift with his gloved fingers. He looked out the floor-to-ceiling windows, over the stone-gray parking lot, highways and wintry fields around the modern building he'd erected near the Kansas City International Airport north of the city center. The isolation he felt made the glass windows, marble tiles and Oriental rugs seem especially cold and sterile today. He'd mistakenly thought he'd left the users and abusers of the world far behind him in that small-town trailer park. Instead, after the destruction of his South African plant two days ago, Quinn realized that he'd simply graduated to a more ruthless, more covert class of users who wanted to hurt what was his.

He wasn't so naive to think he hadn't made a few enemies over the years. At forty, he'd already earned and lost one fortune. But now that he'd established himself and his company as a world leader in high-tech security support and management, he was sitting on an even bigger fortune and had enough influence across several different industries that only a fool—or one very sick, very cruel bastard—would dare to defy him.

Judging by the message he'd received this morning, he was opting for the latter.

"What? Now? I'll be right there." Elise had pulled her cell phone from the coat she'd tossed over the sofa beside her. The distress in her tone was enough to divert Quinn's attention. Her eyes darted to him, then just as quickly looked away. More trouble? "Excuse me."

"Ma'am." An oversize SWAT cop, carrying one of the electronics-scanning devices Quinn himself had invented, stepped aside to let Elise exit the door into the privacy of her office. The big man, who answered to the name Trip, settled in behind the desk to run a check on the phone and computer for any hint that someone had downloaded entry codes to the building and offices.

One by one, the rest of Michael's team filtered in. Quinn traded a nod of recognition with the SWAT team's second in command, Rafe Delgado, whom he had met when he'd offered him the use of a secure safe house for his wife, the witness who'd finally identified the man who'd murdered Quinn's wife. Rafe introduced himself to David Damiani and took the security chief aside to discuss possible incursion scenarios into the building.

A short, muscular cop with curly black hair came through the doorway next and reported in. "Murdock and I have got nothing, Captain. This place is locked down tighter than a tomb. This room and the roof are all that we have left to search. You want us to head on up?"

"Have Murdock check the cameras in here for any signs of tampering. You go on up, Taylor. Stay warm."

"Yes, sir."

Officer Taylor turned his Benelli shotgun and disappeared from the doorway, only to be replaced a moment later by an unexpected colleague. Quinn's eyes narrowed as he found himself studying the last member of Michael Cutler's elite team. He didn't know if the long ponytail, as straight and shiny as a palomino's tail, or the Remington sniper's rifle strapped over her right shoulder surprised him more.

"Captain?" she spoke.

"Front and back, Murdock. If we can't find an unauthorized access point to this room, then we damn well better find where the perp covered his tracks." Michael Cutler pointed to the two cameras at either end of the room, and after her moss-colored eyes took note of every person here, including him, Officer Murdock's long legs carried her to the security camera mounted over the bar/kitchenette at the back of the office.

"Yes, sir."

Quinn watched her climb on top of the counter in her ungainly boots and shimmy around a counter to stand eye to eye with the camera. He couldn't be sure if it was her monkeylike athleticism and disregard for the obstacles in her path or the hint of firm hips and buns in her snug black pants that fascinated him.

Annoyed with his scientist's penchant for observing and explaining conundrums like the well-armed woman, Quinn cursed under his breath and summoned the focused business mogul inside him instead. The momentary diversion of the lady SWAT cop was a distraction he could ill afford today. There was only one female in his life who mattered, and she was the reason Quinn had called Michael Cutler and his team, as well as the leaders of his own staff, into GSS today.

Quinn buttoned his jacket and strode over to stand beside Captain Cutler at his desk. "Did you read it?"

The words Michael read were already branded into Quinn's memory. But the others in the room—his staff, Michael's team—needed to hear this.

"Do I have your attention now? Your daughter will pay the price if you don't make things right by midnight on New Year's Eve. Instructions will be texted to you." Michael carefully slipped the letter into a plastic evidence bag for examination in the KCPD crime lab. "And you received the text?"

"Not yet. I wanted to have a plan in place before he contacted me again."

"Any idea who your enemies are?"

"Any idea who they aren't?" Louis Nolan pushed himself up off the couch to join the conversation. "I'm sorry, Quinn, but we'll be here all day if we start compiling a list of people you've ticked off—employees you've fired—"

"Only with just cause."

"—business rivals, greedy cutthroats after a chunk of your money, maybe even a broken-hearted lover or two?"

Quinn shook his head. "There's been no one since Val."

Louis patted Quinn on the back and raised one eyebrow in a skeptical, paternal look. "Not for lack of trying. On the part of the ladies, I mean. A widowed billionaire makes for a fine catch."

"This reeks of inside information—someone with building schematics, someone with knowledge of my schedule, someone with access codes to this building as well as the plant in South Africa. The fact that I have enemies doesn't bother me as much as not knowing who this particular one is." And he hated to admit that the possible list of suspects Louis referred to was as long as it was.

Quinn had fended off takeover bids, negotiated with foreign governments and endured scathing reviews of his products in the press. He wasn't a warmonger, nor did the upgrades to weapons and protective technology he owned dozens of patents for turn the police patrolling the streets of Kansas City and other towns around the world into a military state. Everything he invented, every product his company produced, from home security systems to bulletproof flak vests, was designed to keep people safe. He protected people. The same way he'd learned to protect himself. And his mother. The way he'd protected his wife, Valeska, from the violence of her past—only to have her die at the hands of an obsessed serial killer in the backyard of the home they'd once shared together. A home he'd since razed to the ground and replaced with a fortress more secure than the government buildings his company sometimes equipped.

Nothing, no one, would ever harm his remaining family again.

That was why he wasn't above calling in favors from KCPD and summoning his most trusted associates to the office on Christmas Eve. "This building is supposedly more secure than the Cattleman's Bank. So how did someone get into my office and put this here without anyone seeing the perp, or capturing the intrusion on one of my cameras?"

Trip Jones, the big guy with the electronics scanner, rose and circled the desk, with David Damiani, the GSS security chief, right behind him. "I can't see anything that's been tampered with on this end, Captain. There's no indication on the key cards that anyone other than Mr. Gallagher has entered this office in the last twenty-four hours. If there's no record of a break-in to leave the present, then the perp found another way in and covered his tracks."

Officer Murdock climbed down from the file cabinet where she'd been inspecting the other camera. "There's no indication that either of these cameras has been compromised."

Trip nodded. "Then the tampering must have occurred at the monitor end of things. Digital recordings can be altered as easily as a videotape."

David Damiani's team had already determined as much. "That means you're accusing one of my people of delivering that threat."

"No one's accusing anyone of anything." Michael Cutler coolly defused the growing tension between the two security forces. "Yet. Let's just get all the intel we can first. Arm ourselves as best we can so we know what we're up against."

"Sounds like a smart strategy," Quinn agreed. He nodded to David. "Check it out."

"Quinn." David Damiani was right to protest. GSS wasn't a billion-dollar corporation because it gave away its secrets to outsiders. "There's classified equipment in my offices."

Michael Cutler refused to back down. "You're obstructing a police investigation?"

"He's obstructing nothing," Quinn counter-manded. When the threat involved his three-year-old daughter, nothing else mattered. "David, go with him. Give Trip full access. Maybe between the two of you, you can spot something your guards missed."

"Yes, sir."

While Quinn impatiently waited for the info that could give him the answers he needed, his gaze strayed once again to the woman with the flak vest, Glock strapped to her right thigh and sniper's rifle secured over her shoulder. She was over at the windows now, trailing her fingers along the chrome trim.

Louis Nolan had followed her to the windows, his bushy silver brows knitted together with the same perplexed interest plaguing Quinn. "They'd have to rappel from the roof and cut a hole in the glass to get through that way."

She nodded, studying the seam of the window from top to bottom. "It could be done. I could do it."

"Unless you had a fear of heights," Louis teased.

"Fortunately, I don't."

"I'll bet you don't fear much, do you, darlin'?"

The blonde officer's cheeks flushed a delicate shade of pink. Carrying numerous deadly weapons and crawling across his furniture didn't fluster her, but a *darlin'* from a good ol' Texas charmer did?

Quinn stopped the conversation. This wasn't the time for Louis's flirting. Or his own scientific observations. "I think we'd see the evidence if someone had come through the window. Beyond the fact that it's tempered, shatterproof glass and the condensation outside from the freezing temperatures would make any kind of traction for your climber almost impossible, there's no way to replace that specific kind of window overnight."

She turned her wide green eyes from Louis, seeming to understand his facts better than his COO's flirting. "Is there another exit to the roof besides the stairwell next to the elevators? Anything with direct access to your office?"

"No."

She tipped her chin up toward the ceiling "What kind of duct work do you have running up there?"

Officer Murdock was definitely an odd sort of woman, certainly nothing like the polished beauty of his executive assistant, Elise, or any of the other poised and tailored belles he escorted to society events. "Standard issue, I suppose. Although the access panels do have sensors to monitor whenever one opens or closes."

Michael Cutler seemed to think she was onto something. He looked up at the air-return grate over Quinn's desk. "Murdock. Call Taylor down and scout it out. Looks like there's more than one way to get into your office, Quinn. The right perp could even lower the package through that grate without ever setting foot in here."

The bothersome blonde paused by the desk on her way out the door. "Couldn't the break-in be something more simple? Like, someone you know—someone who wouldn't raise any suspicions if they were caught on camera walking into your office?"

Quinn bristled at the accusation. "The people who work at GSS are family to me. I surround myself with people I trust without question."

"Well, that's a problem, then, isn't it?" She flipped her ponytail behind her back, looking up at him with an earnest warning. "You may be trusting the wrong guy."

"Randy, go."

Her captain's brusque command finally

moved her out of the room. "Sorry. Climbing into the rafters now, sir."

Apparently, Louis's interest in waiting for answers on the break-in—or for the promised text message—waned once she'd left the room. "I'll be in my office if you need me," he excused himself, "and *do* call as soon as you find out anything."

"Randy?" Quinn asked after they'd both gone and he was alone in the office with Michael.

"Miranda Murdock." The police captain shook his head, as if Quinn's wasn't the first curious reaction the SWAT sharpshooter had garnered from the people she met. "Believe me, what she lacks in tact, she makes up for in sheer determination. There's not a task I've given her yet that she hasn't accomplished."

"Other than successful public relations."

"She's raw talent. Maybe a little too eager to get the job done at times. She matched the highest score for sharpshooting on the KCPD training range."

"You have faith in her."

"She wouldn't be on my team if I didn't."

"Quinn?" The familiar knock at his door told Quinn that his assistant, Elise, had an important message for him.

"What is it?"

Elise tucked her dark hair behind one ear, hesitating as she walked into the room. Quinn braced for whatever unpleasant bit of news she had to share. "The current nanny has gotten wind of the threat against Fiona and wants to quit."

He adjusted his glasses at his temple, snapping before he could contain a flash of temper. "I'm having a Mary Poppins moment here. How many nannies do I have to go through to get one who'll stay?"

"She's afraid, Quinn."

"There's a guard with Fiona at all times," he argued.

"Yes, but not with the nanny," Elise patiently pointed out. "Quinn, she has every right to be concerned for her safety. The guard's first duty would be to Fiona, not her."

Where was the loyalty to his family? The sense of responsibility? The devotion to his daughter? She was the fourth woman he'd hired this year—after firing the one he'd caught drinking at the house, and the one who thought spanking his three-year-old was an option, and filing charges against the one who'd tried to sell pictures of his daughter to a local tabloid. "Where is she now? I'll double her pay if she stays."

"Um…"

"Daddy!" Quinn understood Elise's hesitation when the tiny dark-haired beauty who looked so like her late mother ran into his office.

"Hey, baby." Quinn knelt down to catch Fiona as she launched herself into his arms. He scooped her up and kissed her cool, wind-whipped cheek as her long, thin fingers wound around his neck. "How's my little princess today?"

"'Kay." Even though she couldn't read yet, he turned her away from the hateful note on his desk and bounced her on his hip. Fiona batted away the gloves that were clipped to the sleeves of her coat and held up her well-loved, oft-mended hand-sewn doll. Fiona's bottom lip pouted out as she pointed to the bandage taped to the doll's knee. "Petwa has a boo-boo."

Quinn pulled up the cloth leg and kissed it, suspecting he'd find a similar first-aid job under the knee of Fiona's corduroy pants. Although the initial flush of her cheeks had concerned him, he was relieved to see that Maria, the nanny du jour, had at least taken the time to dress his daughter properly for the winter weather and brush her curling dark locks back into a neat ponytail before abandoning her.

"There. She'll be all fine now." Stealing another kiss from Fiona's sweet, round cheek, Quinn set her down and pulled off her hat and coat. He nodded toward the specially stocked toy box he kept behind the counter of the kitchenette at the far end of his office suite. "Okay, honey. You run and play for a few minutes while I talk to Elise."

"'Kay, Daddy."

He waited until the box was open and the search had begun for a favorite toy before he turned his attention to his assistant. He didn't have to ask for an explanation. "The nanny didn't call," Elise told him. "She dropped Fiona off with me downstairs and left. I couldn't convince her to stay."

Quinn unbuttoned his jacket, unhooked the collar of his starched white shirt and loosened his tie, feeling too trapped from unseen forces and ill-timed inconveniences to maintain his civilized facade. He paced down to see with his own eyes that Fiona was happy and secure, playing doctor on her doll with a plastic stethoscope and thermometer.

He came back, scratching his fingers through his own dark hair. He needed to think. He needed answers. Now. "Can you watch her, Elise? I have work to do. I don't want to leave until I resolve this threat."

Elise's mouth opened and closed twice before her apologetic smile gave him her answer. "For a few hours, maybe. But my parents are in town, Quinn. I'm supposed to be baking pies with my mother, and taking them to the candlelight service at church this evening. Besides, I can't keep her safe. And if that threat is real…"

He had no doubt that it was. Three dead men in the Kalahari proved that. "You could come to the house. You know what kind of security I have there. There's a panic room and armed guards."

"And my parents?" He'd always admired Elise for her ability to gently stand up to him. "It's Christmas Eve, Quinn."

He was already nodding, accepting her answer, knowing it had been too much to ask. "Of course. I understand. I was just hoping I wouldn't have to upset Fiona's routine any more than it already has been."

The vibrating pulse against his chest ended all conversation, blanked out all thought except for one more visual confirmation that Fiona was safe. Then he let the protective anger he felt purge any distraction from his system as he pulled his phone from inside the pocket of his suit jacket.

"Quinn?" Michael prompted, equally on guard.

He nodded, reading the message he'd been promised. "It's the text."

"What does it say?" Elise asked.

Quinn read the skewed nursery rhyme, filling in the abbreviations as he said the words out loud. *"Mary, Mary, Quite Contrary, how does your money grow? With silver bells and 2.5 million shells into 0009357:348821173309. Midnight tonight. Or there'll be another present for your daughter."*

"What the hell?" was Michael's reaction.

"It's a riddle," Elise needlessly pointed out.

"I get it," Quinn assured them. "Mary was my mother. I have a memorial trust in her name. Whoever this coward is wants me to transfer two and a half million dollars into this account by midnight. Or…" He glanced over at Fiona's laugh. He couldn't imagine a world where someone had silenced that glorious sound. "I'll transfer the money."

"I don't recommend that." Michael took the phone from him, calling his tech guru Trip on the radio to get him up here to trace what

Quinn was certain would be an untraceable number.

"What choice do I have, Michael? How can I fight the enemy when I don't know who he is? And until we do find out where the threat is coming from, there's no way to stop him from coming at me again." He turned to his assistant. "Elise, contact my bank. Don't let them close before I get there."

"Yes, sir." She hurried to her office to do his bidding.

Michael copied down the message. "What if you hadn't understood the rhyme?"

"I don't think this bastard is stupid. And he knows I'm not."

Michael pointed toward the letter wrapped in the evidence bag. "This message says to make something right before New Year's Eve. That's a week away. It can't be this simple, and he's gone to too much trouble to have it all be over this soon."

"Agreed." Quinn propped his hands on his hips. "As long as I can keep Fiona out of this, I want to string this guy along until I can get my hands around his neck."

Any further conversation stopped as the grate over Quinn's desk swung open and Miranda Murdock lowered herself down through the opening to plop her combat-style boots on top of his desk. She'd stripped off her Kevlar and rifle and was brushing dust from her black uniform and snaggled hair. And she didn't seem to see anything odd about making such an entrance.

"I think I found the way in, sir," she reported to Michael, jumping down beside him. "Barring the whole 'just walking through the front door' scenario. Of course, the intruder would still have to alter the camera recording—and turn the sensors off for the few seconds it would take to get in and out." She paused in her report, her sharp eyes turning to the side and widening enough that Quinn turned to see what had caught her attention.

Fiona. Standing in the middle of his office, her doll dangling to the floor beside her, looking up at the tall blonde woman as if a dusty angel had just descended from heaven.

Miranda's lips twitched before settling into a smile. "Hey."

The tiny frown that creased Fiona's forehead gave her an expression that was more concerned than afraid, or even curious. "You fell."

The SWAT officer looked up at the open grate, still swinging slightly from the ceiling where Fiona was looking. "Um, no. I crawled. And climbed. And...jumped." She plucked a clump of cobweb from her hair, glancing toward Quinn and her commanding officer with a questioning plea before pointing a finger at his daughter. "But, you shouldn't try that. It's too high. I'm, you know, taller. And a grown-up."

But the explanation had taken too long and Fiona had moved on to her real concern. Quinn's hands curled into fists at his sides as Fiona walked right up to Miranda and held up her doll. "Petwa falled."

"Oh. Um, well..." She snapped her fingers. "That's exactly why you shouldn't crawl through ceilings."

Fiona stared.

Quinn gradually relaxed his protective stance. Not everyone got small children, nor knew how to communicate with them—and he suspected Miranda Murdock was on that list. But he could see she was doing all she could to allay Fiona's worries.

"Not that your dolly—Petra, is it?—would do that. She needs to stay close to you. On the ground." Seemingly as flummoxed by his daughter's fascination as she'd been with

Louis's idle flirtation, she looked to her captain for help. "Sir?"

Michael nodded a dismissal. "Prove to me that you can get back out through that heating duct, and I'll have Trip check the sensors there to see if they've been triggered by anyone else in the last twenty-four hours."

That, apparently, she could do. Needing no more encouragement, the twenty-something female officer climbed up on the desk and pulled herself back up into the ventilation duct in a skilled combination of pull-up champ and gymnast.

"She's...different, isn't she?" Quinn observed.

"Like I said, Murdock is gung ho. She'll get the job done."

"Michael." Quinn usually found his instincts about people to be unerringly accurate. "I have another favor to ask of you. Just how much faith do you have in Miranda Murdock?"

Michael's blue eyes narrowed. Perhaps he'd just had a similar brainstorm. "You've supplied my team with nothing but the best equipment since we first started working together. Your vest design saved my life from a bullet once. I figure I owe you."

"Then I have a proposition for you." Quinn scooped Fiona into his arms, drawing her attention away from the dusty blonde angel and the grate that had closed over their heads. "*We* do."

Chapter Two

Miranda stilled her breathing, calmed the twitchy urge to blink and squeezed the trigger of her Glock 9 mil, landing five shots, center mass, through the paper target's chest. Then just for good measure, and because the accuracy score of her shooting range trials was one thing she could control, she angled the gun and put a hole through the paper target's head.

"You shouldn't be alone at Christmas," Dr. Kate Kilpatrick advised. The police psychologist was always full of advice during their sessions. "If your brother is still over in Afghanistan—"

"He is."

"—then maybe you could volunteer at one of the city mission shelters, visit a shut-in in your neighborhood or invite a friend over for lunch."

And just which of her friends would be

*available on Christmas Day? Certainly none
of the men on her team. They all had families—wives, children, in-laws. They'd be real
gung ho about giving up holiday family time
to keep the "odd man out" on their team from
being alone on Christmas Day. Lonely was
one thing. Pity was another.*

Miranda pulled off her earphones and
pushed the button to bring the hanging target
up to the booth for a closer inspection. Instead
of heeding Dr. K's recommendation to find
some company after her mandated counseling
session that afternoon, Miranda had come to
KCPD's indoor firing range in the basement
of the Fourth Precinct building to blow off
steam.

All that touchy-feely stuff Dr. Kilpatrick
wanted her to talk about got stuck in her
head and left her feeling raw and distracted
when they were done. Randy Murdock was a
woman in a man's world. Her brother, John,
a KCFD firefighter who'd reupped with the
Marines after the love of his life had married someone else, had raised her to understand that when the job was tough—like being
a part of KCPD's SWAT Team 1—that what
she was feeling didn't matter. Four other cops,

and any hostages or innocent bystanders, were counting on her to get the job done. Period.

No warm fuzzies allowed.

Nodding with satisfaction that her kill rate had been 100 percent, Miranda sent the target back and cleared her weapon.

"What are you thinking?" Dr. Kilpatrick asked after a long, uncomfortable silence.

"That I'm not the only person with such a nonexistent home life that I'm available for an appointment the afternoon before Christmas."

"Ouch." Observant though it was, Miranda regretted the smart-aleck remark as soon as she'd said it. But the therapist let it slide right off her back with a poised smile. "There you go deflecting the focus off yourself again. Deftly done, too. I could write an article about your classic avoidance tendencies. Always striving to please someone else instead of working toward your own goals. Using work or physical activities to avoid thinking about your feelings or dealing with the loneliness."

Sharp lady. Miranda hated that the police shrink might be onto something there. "So why are you here at four o'clock on Christmas Eve, Doc?"

"To see you, of course."

"Sorry about that." Miranda pushed herself up out of the cushy seat. "We'd better wrap things up then, hmm?"

"Miranda, sit." Dr. Kilpatrick wore a maternal-looking frown now. And though she'd never known her own mother, or maybe because of that, it made Miranda feel so unsure of how she should respond that she sank back into her chair. "You're just as important as any of the other officers, detectives and support staff here in Kansas City."

"Yeah, that's why I'm the low man on the totem pole on my team."

The maternal vibe became a supportive pep talk. "That's nonsense. You're a highly quali-fied sharpshooter. You passed all the same rigorous physical and mental exams as the other members of your team. Other than chain of command, you know it takes all five of you working together equally and complementing each other's strengths to make SWAT Team 1 the success it is."

Miranda released the magazine from the Glock's handle and pulled out the remaining blanks. Then she reloaded the clip with 9 mm bullets from the ammo box on the shelf in front of her and ensured her gun was in proper working order before returning it to the holster strapped to her right thigh.

She was in the locker room showering when more of the conversation she'd had with the psychologist started replaying in her head.

Dr. Kilpatrick had the patience of a saint. She could ask a question and wait. But the ongoing silence in the psychologist's office finally got to Miranda, and she blurted out one of the few things that scared her. "Holden Kincaid is coming back."

"Kincaid? I know several Kincaids on the force. Which one is he?"

"He's the guy I replaced on SWAT Team 1 when he went on paternity leave. He and the guys are all pretty close." The random confession had sounded like polite conversation to fill the silence at first. But once one insecurity was breached, others came out. "I mean, even if I prove I'm as good at this job as he is, possibly even better, what good does that do me? If Captain Cutler and the guys resent that I'm there instead of him, that messes up our efficiency. I'd feel like a real usurper for being there. But if I transfer off the team, or get cut because Kincaid is a better man..."

She turned off the hot water and hugged her arms around her naked body as the water ran down the drain and the locker room's cool air raised goose bumps across her skin. If Dr. Kilpatrick wasn't so good at her job, then Miranda might not still be shaking from the embarrassing accuracy of the psychologist's next question.

"Do these self-esteem issues go back to that incident this summer when the Rich Girl Killer attacked you?"

"He wasn't after me. He wanted Sergeant Delgado's girlfriend—his wife now—because she could ID him."

"I read Delgado's report myself. He said you slowed down the RGK long enough for him to get there to save his wife from being murdered."

Backhanded praise was no better than a reprimand. *"My job wasn't to slow him down. It was my job to stop him. I failed. He got the drop on me, bashed my head in and I failed."*

"There's a reason it's called a team. It takes all of you, working together, to complete your mission. You're there to complement each other's strengths, and, on certain days, compensate for a weakness. Every man on that team knows that. Every man has been where you are. No one blames you for having an off day."

That indulgent, don't-be-so-hard-on-yourself tone only made the self-doubts whispering inside Miranda's head shout out loud. "You know it's different when you're a woman, Doc. 'Good' isn't good enough. If I can't perform when my team needs me to, then why the hell should Captain Cutler keep me around?"

The psychologist jotted something on her notepad, then leaned forward in her chair. "SWAT Team 1 is your family, aren't they? That's why you're being so hard on yourself, why you're so afraid of making a mistake. You don't want to lose your family again."

Stupid, intuitive psychologist! That was why the session with Dr. Kilpatrick had upset her so much today. She'd gotten Miranda to reveal a truth she hadn't even admitted to herself yet.

With her parents both gone and her older brother stationed in Afghanistan, Miranda had no one in Kansas City. No one, period. All she had was this job. Being a cop—a highly select SWAT cop—was her identity. It gave her goals, satisfaction, a sense of community and worth. If she screwed it up, then she'd really be up a creek. Of course, the holidays only exacerbated that reeling sense of loneliness she normally kept at bay.

And she'd actually revealed all that to the doctor?

"Ow!" The pinch of sanity on her scalp told her that (a), she was tugging too hard with the hairbrush, and (b), she needed to get a grip. If she wanted to make the claim that she was a strong woman who deserved to have the job she did, then she needed to quit wallowing in these weak, feminine emotions that felt so foreign to her, and get her head on straight.

Decision made. Time to act. Emotions off.

"Now get out of here, Murdock," she advised her reflection in the mirror.

After pulling her long, straight hair back into a ponytail, Miranda dressed in her civvies and bundled up in her stocking cap and coat to face the wintry air blowing outside. Night had fallen by the time she hurried down the steps toward the crosswalk that would lead her to the parking garage across the street.

Heading south for half a block, she jammed her hands into the pockets of her navy wool peacoat and hunched her shoulders against the wind hitting her back. When she reached the crosswalk and waited for the light to change, she pulled her cell phone from her pocket to check the time. Great. By this hour on Christmas Eve, none of the usual restaurants where she liked to pick up a quick dinner would be open. She tried to picture her freezer and wondered what microwave choices she had on hand that she could zap for dinner, or if she'd be eating a bowl of cereal again. Why couldn't she remember these things before she got hungry and the stores had closed?

The light changed. She jumped over the slushy gray snow that had accumulated against the curb, and hurried across the street. That was another thing she missed with John being over in Afghanistan. Besides the bear hugs and patient advice, the man could cook. She'd never really had to learn because he had the gourmet talents and interest in the family. Miranda could easily recall the ham, mashed potatoes, baby asparagus, fruit salad and thick chocolate cake John had fixed for Christmas dinner last year. Her mouth watered at the memory of silky, semisweet frosting and light, moist layers of pure fudge heaven.

Her bowl of cereal was sounding pretty sad right about now.

She entered the parking garage and jogged up the ramp to the second level, where she'd parked her red pickup that morning, long before they'd gotten the call to the Gallagher Security Systems building. As the morning's

events passed through her mind, her thoughts
took a left turn and landed on the image of
GSS's boss, Quinn Gallagher, running the
show in his poshly furnished, high-tech penthouse office.

The tailored suit and way he spoke, straightforward and concise, as though he was used to
people jumping at his word, were clear indi-
cators of his wealth and power. But the short
dark hair with that one shaggy lock falling out
of place onto his forehead, and those Clark
Kent–ish black glasses said science geek. Surprisingly, there'd been muscles under that suit
coat. She'd seen them flex and push at the
seams of his jacket when he picked up his
little girl. Quinn Gallagher was an odd combination of a man—a nearsighted nerd with
guns and pecs hidden beneath his suit and tie.

Miranda grinned at the inside joke of her
own making. Did Mr. Gallagher even know
that he resembled a famous comic book character?

"What's so funny?"

Stifling the startled gasp that tried to
escape, Miranda halted at the big man climbing out of a truck parked in the row across
from hers. The black KCPD sweats marked
him as a friend, but recognition made it diffi-

cult to keep her feet from dashing to her own vehicle. Talk about lousy timing.

"Hey." Lame greeting, but sufficient. Holden Kincaid needed no introduction. She shrugged off the sappy grin that had caught his attention. "Private joke. About a comic book."

"It's Murdock, right?" He pointed to the proportionately sized silvery malamute circling the bed of his truck. "Yukon, stay." Amazingly, the dog sat on his haunches as his master crossed the driving lane to extend his hand. "Holden Kincaid."

"I know who you are, Officer Kincaid." There was nothing but polite friendliness in his demeanor, so running away from the man whose return to duty was giving her such fits about her job would only broadcast the insecurity she needed to hide. With the workout sweats, stocking cap and scarf tucked around his neck, she could guess he wasn't here to take her job this evening. "Going for a run?"

He nodded, thumbing over his shoulder at the dog. "Ol' Yukon there loves the snow, so any chance we can do a winter run, we go for it."

Keep it natural and conversational. "Even on Christmas Eve?"

His laugh clouded the chilly air. "Liza said I needed to get out of the house for a couple of hours. I take it there's some Santa Claus stuff in the works with her and my son. So I took the dog out for a run, then came here to lift weights in the fitness center. I figure they need about another thirty minutes before it's safe for me to go home."

Liza must be the wife. Friendly man. Obedient dog. Family at home. Miranda's isolation burned like a giant hole opening up in her belly.

"Well, I won't keep you from Santa Claus."

"Wait a sec. Murdock?"

"Yeah?"

When she turned to face him again, his smile had turned into a wry frown. "I'm glad we ran into each other."

Right. So she was naive to think she was the only one who felt there was a competition between them. He was trying to make the best of an awkward situation. She should be mature enough—confident enough—to do the same. She pulled her ponytail from the collar of her coat and tossed it down the middle of her back, busying her hands for a moment to calm her nerves. "Yeah, well, it was bound to happen. I mean, you're back from leave, and I'm...always here, apparently."

With something like a sigh of relief, Kincaid's smile returned. "Captain Cutler said you were a bit of a workaholic."

Guilty as charged. "I like the rush of the job, I guess. I feel useful. I'm in my element."

"I know what you mean. I love being home with my wife and the baby, but I'm anxious to get back to it."

Great. So she and Holden Kincaid were kindred spirits with similar talents. They might have been friends under other circumstances—if he wasn't gunning for her job; if she hadn't taken his in the first place.

She glanced around the nearly deserted garage and tried to make an exit again. "Well, um...Merry Christmas."

"Murdock." This time Miranda kept walking. "Look, I just wanted to say this isn't how I wanted it to happen."

She opened her truck door, but stopped at the odd remark. "Wanted what to happen?"

Her cell phone rang in her pocket, but she was more concerned about deciphering the apology stamped on Holden's expression.

He nodded toward her coat pocket. "You'd better take that."

"What are you talking about?"

"Your phone. It may be Captain Cutler." He started backing away. "If so, it's important."

"How do you know…?" An ingrained sense of duty pushed aside the ominous vibe that this *chance* meeting with Holden Kincaid had nothing to do with coincidence. Too many phone calls in her life meant a summons to an emergency, and seeing Michael Cutler's name on the screen of her phone indicated this was a call she couldn't ignore. She climbed into her truck, closing the door as she hit the answer button. "Yes, sir?"

With a "Merry Christmas, Murdock," Kincaid turned and jogged down the ramp and disappeared around the garage's front gate into the night.

"I didn't catch you in the middle of dinner, did I?" her commanding officer asked. The friendly greeting told her this wasn't an emergency.

So Miranda took the time to start her truck and get the heater running before answering. "This is a good time to talk. What's up?"

"We've had a situation develop over the course of the day at Gallagher Security Systems that requires your… unique expertise."

"A situation?"

With a muffled curse, the captain cut the chitchat and got straight to the details. "I talked to Sergeant Wheeler about your schedule this week. She said you volunteered to take some extra patrol shifts over the holidays so that some other officers could spend more time with their families."

He was calling her on Christmas Eve over this? "I've already cleared it with the desk sergeant. It won't count as overtime. I'm just trading my vacation days for another time."

"It's an admirable gesture, but I took the liberty of clearing your schedule for the next week. I've already talked to Holden Kincaid, and he'll take the shifts you were going to cover so no one else has to change their plans. The team is on On Call status this week—if something comes up, he'll fill in for you."

A bolt of icy electricity rippled down Miranda's spine and her gaze shot to the black pickup in her rearview mirror. *This isn't how I wanted it to happen.* Kincaid's words made sense now. He'd already known he was replacing her—not on SWAT 1, not yet—but that was what the preemptive apology was about. Cutler had already made the arrangements to get her out of the picture.

The gray dog sat in the back of the truck,

watching her. He'd probably known his master was here to take her place, too.

She clenched her fist around the steering wheel as those insecurities that had plagued her since the Rich Girl Killer screwup shivered through her. She was losing the job she loved, losing her *family,* as Dr. Kilpatrick had put it. Only a girly-girl would sit here and cry about it. Still, the inevitable feelings of loss, betrayal and failure burned beneath her eyelids.

"Randy?" Captain Cutler was speaking in her ear. "You still there?"

Tearing her gaze away from the dog and turning off those self-sabotaging emotions, she managed to keep an even tone as she answered. "I'm here, sir. Why don't you want me to work over the holiday?"

"I don't want you to work patrol," he clarified. "Since you're not traveling out of town, I'm recruiting you for a dedicated assignment this week. And you *will* be receiving overtime pay for the extra hours."

Pay was the last thing on her mind at the moment. "What's the team going to do at Gallagher Security?"

"Not the team, Randy. You."

"Well, can't Holden take the assignment instead of covering for me?"

"No. He can't." The normal clip of authority in his tone softened to something slightly more paternal. "I'd consider it a personal favor if you do this for me. Can you meet me tomorrow? After you're done with whatever plans you have for Christmas morning?"

Miranda's sigh filled up the cab of the truck. She was available after a bowl of cereal tonight if he wanted. Besides, doing a personal favor for the captain couldn't hurt her chances of staying on SWAT Team 1 now that Holden Kincaid was back in the picture. "I'll be there."

She jotted down the address he gave her and promised to meet him at noon.

What kind of assignment was she good enough for, but Holden wasn't? Or was it a case of what assignment was Kincaid too good for, but she was adequate enough to fit the bill?

Stop it, Murdock. Miranda willfully shut down that negative voice in her head and disconnected the call. Dr. Kilpatrick might have her pegged better than she'd given the psychologist credit for. Her confidence really had been rattled by recent events.

Miranda shifted the truck into Reverse and pulled out of her parking space. When she braked to shift into Drive, she took a moment to scan her surroundings. There might be skeleton crews working over the holidays at KCPD, but none of them had parked up here. There wasn't a soul to be seen. It was just her and the unblinking malamute who watched her drive past. And the dog didn't count.

She was alone on Christmas Eve. No one was here to see her drive away; no one was at her apartment to welcome her home. Her boss had some sort of mysterious assignment that would separate her from the rest of the team for a week.

One might think she'd have gotten used to going solo through life by now.

But she hadn't.

It stank.

Chapter Three

6 Days until Midnight, New Year's Eve

What was she doing out here in the middle of this ritzy new subdivision on the northern edge of Kansas City on Christmas Day?

The homes were spread out on tracts of land, each one big enough to be a city park, with tall, old trees lining the road, and well-established landscaping, despite the newness of the construction of the multistory, sprawling mansions she could see from the road. Her whole apartment could probably fit into the garage of one of these places. Heck, it could probably fit into one closet. She was a long way from her home in downtown Kansas City in more ways than one.

Miranda checked the address in her hand one more time before turning her truck into the short driveway that marked the entry to

Quinn Gallagher's estate. Unlike the other estates she'd passed, there was no part of the house visible from the street until she pulled right up to the front entrance. Taking note of the cameras set on either side of the front gates, she peeked through the wrought-iron bars. There was a secondary set of gates recessed behind the decorative entrance. They looked solid, like steel doors that could come together to completely close off the front entrance. And from this vantage point she could see that the masking effect from the street had more to do with the height of the brick walls surrounding the property rather than the mansion being smaller than any of the others in the area.

Almost austere in its offset, multitiered design, the white house was set well back from the road, with a frozen creek that acted almost like a moat circling around it. The only thing breaking up the lines and angles of the numerous windows and long porches were the ropes of colored lights and greenery decorating it for the holidays. With a foot of snow on the ground, the undisturbed lawn on either side of the long, curving driveway created a sea of white. Approaching the house without being seen would be nearly impossible. It was probably an architect's dream home, or, more likely, the brain child of a man obsessed with security for himself and his family. Snow drifted three feet deep at the base of the tall brick walls on either side of her, and nestled on every leaf of the thick ivy covering the barricade, completing the illusion of an impenetrable ice palace.

"The Fortress of Solitude," she mused out loud, wondering if Quinn Gallagher had read the same comic books she had growing up. Either he was clueless about the whole steely-man-hidden-beneath-the-nerdy-exterior persona he projected, or he possessed a tongue-in-cheek sense of humor and was actually playing up the similarities to the incognito superhero.

Then again, maybe she was the only one in a five-mile radius who noticed that the gazillionaire inventor turned businessman resembled an icon from her youth.

Ignoring the random thought, Miranda rolled down her window to press the call button on the intercom system outside the gate. As she leaned out, her eyes went to the black BMW parked in front of a giant evergreen wreath at another set of estate gates farther down the road. It wasn't unexpected to see an expensive car with a driver in this part of the city. It wasn't unusual to even see the tinted windows that masked whoever was riding in the backseat.

But it was Christmas Day and she'd been the only traffic moving through the neighborhood since she'd turned off of I-435 near the airport. And if that was someone visiting a family member, why park in the street? Why not pull up to the gate as she had?

Maybe they were lost and stopping to read a map or check a GPS. It was a plausible explanation.

"Yes?" The unidentified voice over the intercom demanded her attention.

Apparently, friendly greetings weren't standard procedure here. Miranda followed suit. "Officer Murdock from KCPD. I'm here to meet with Captain Cutler and Mr. Gallagher."

"You're expected."

She heard a metallic snap, a motor firing up and then the distinctive sound of gears grinding against each other. Retreating from the cold, she rolled up her window and watched the heavy gates slowly slide apart.

She might have shifted into Drive and readied her truck to drive on through if some little sixth sense hadn't pricked the hairs at the nape of her neck. Never one to ignore such a cosmic warning, Miranda subtly angled her head to check her mirrors and windows.

A woman so used to being alone had fine-tuned the instinct to notice when she wasn't. Her gaze went back to the black BMW.

They weren't lost.

They were watching her.

Or maybe watching the Gallagher estate?

As soon as she turned in her seat to look head-on at the lurking car, the backseat window rolled up and closed, giving her a glimpse of silver hair and pale eyes staring in her direction. The window hadn't been cracked open before. Someone was definitely checking her out.

And there was no excusing the passenger's curiosity as an effort to decide whether or not to approach her. The car with its unseen occupant suddenly sped up and drove past.

Instinctively, Miranda kept her truck in Park and blocked the entrance to the Gallagher estate. It wouldn't be the first time an opportunistic thief or terrorist or whatever threat waited inside that car seized the opportunity to enter a locked-down area by tagging along when someone else opened the door. But the BMW never slowed. In a matter of seconds, it had turned the next corner and disappeared over a hill leading back to the highway.

But not before she'd pulled a notepad and pen from the center console of her truck and copied down the license plate number.

"You coming?" the voice from the intercom asked. "Drive forward so we can lock the gates."

"Yes, sir."

Tucking the plate number into her coat pocket, Miranda shifted into gear and pulled forward. She steered around the first curve of the driveway and headed toward the bridge decorated with multicolored lights and garland that spanned the frozen creek. A mysterious car with a curious passenger might be nothing important.

But a SWAT officer left nothing to chance.

"BABYSITTING?"

Quinn finished the calculation he was figuring and typed the variables into the laptop on the desk between him and the leggy blonde sitting beside his good friend Michael Cutler. He adjusted his glasses as he glanced from Michael to Miranda Murdock. Had he not explained himself clearly?

He zeroed in on the curious mix of shock

and resentment darkening the mossy-green irises of Officer Murdock's eyes. She looked intelligent enough to understand the situation. This wasn't going to work if the woman had an attitude, either. Surely Michael wouldn't recommend her or have her on his team if she was a problem. "There's a distinction, Miss Murdock."

"It's *Officer* Murdock."

"My mistake, *Officer.*" He wished he had options besides Blondie here right about now. "I'm hiring you to protect my daughter until the threats against us have been resolved."

"Wait a minute." Her booted feet hit the carpet and she leaned forward in her chair. "I work for KCPD. You can't just hire me away."

For a split second, Quinn's multitasking mind wandered away from both his calculations and the irritating need to clarify himself. For that split second, his brain filled with observations about Miranda Murdock's black uniform and how not even the mannish turtleneck or starched collar could detract from the natural blush staining those sculpted cheekbones. And her long hair, pulled back with an eye toward practicality rather than style, was more than just blond. He detected variations of honey and wheat and sunshine in the strands framing her face. Very pretty coloring all round.

A pesky voice cleared its throat inside his head. Why was he noticing a woman all of a sudden? Why was he noticing this one? He had a wife. So the key word was *had,* since Valeska had been killed three years ago, shortly after Fiona's birth. His New Year's resolution in January had been to finally put away the wedding ring he hadn't been able to take off. He hadn't made any resolutions yet for the upcoming year about starting a new relationship, or even considering candidates who'd be eligible for one. This argumentative tomboy certainly wouldn't be suitable.

Move on.

Just like that, the moment passed. Thoughts of his wife's murder and the veiled threats against his daughter and company negated any fanciful observations about a woman's subtle beauty and focused him firmly on the business at hand. He nodded toward the SWAT emblem embroidered above her chest pocket and returned to his calculations. "You can't wear that outfit around Fiona."

"I earned the right to wear this uniform."

"And you should be commended for that. But my donation to the KCPD Widows & Orphans Fund gives me the right to decide how you dress around my daughter. I don't want her frightened or put off by the military-looking attire." Quinn completed his calculations and plugged them into the new parameters he'd been texted this morning. "She likes jewel-tone colors. Do you have anything like that you could wear? Jeans or slacks are acceptable over the holidays."

"Jewel-tone…?" Her unadorned cheeks were blushing again. Temper, he suspected, not embarrassment. "Do you want me to paint my gun fuchsia pink?"

Quinn swung his gaze over to his friend for help. "Michael?"

This conversation had already taken more of his time than it should have. He had a deadline he needed to meet here. Hours after he'd transferred the money from his mother's trust fund into the unmarked Swiss bank account, he'd received the next threat. Rework the blueprints on a remote-access lock he'd designed several years ago. It was an old system that was no longer in use with any of GSS's customers, so it didn't pose a security breach to GSS or any of its production facilities. But Quinn didn't ask why the unidentified caller wanted him to waste his time on this today. It was enough that the caller had threatened to deliver another present for Fiona by the end of the day if Quinn didn't comply.

Complete the task or it will be Fiona's last Christmas.

Protests or not, refitting the old design by 5:00 p.m. made gaining Miranda Murdock's cooperation of the utmost importance.

Michael Cutler had seen the text. He understood the threat. Maybe he could get Officer Attitude there to understand. "This *is* a police matter, Randy. Quinn and Fiona are Kansas City citizens whose lives and livelihood have been threatened. With GSS's connections to KCPD, as well as to global security, the commissioner has asked us to form a protection detail to stay with the family 24/7 until we get this straightened out."

"Through New Year's Eve," Quinn added, prepping the design for an online trial. "24/7 until January 1. And then…" His stomach somersaulted as he thought of his beautiful little princess playing with her presents in the adjoining family room. He prayed he'd be able to right whatever perceived wrong this bastard was accusing him of by New Year's Eve. He wished his unseen enemy had come straight for him instead of involving Fiona in this sick countdown game. But then the creep must have known that there was only one way to get Quinn to do exactly what he wanted— threaten the love of his life.

He felt the moss-green eyes on him as he watched the dark-haired little girl putting stickers over all of her green velvet dress, and on most of the furniture in the room.

"A protection detail I get." He detected a softness in Officer Murdock's voice that hadn't been there a moment ago. But when he turned to meet her curious gaze, she looked away to speak directly to Michael. "I'm happy to watch the premises or assist his security staff. Maybe we could start by putting a live guard on the front gate. With the way the security cameras are positioned, there was no way for the man inside at the monitors to spot the BMW parked in the next block and scoping out the place."

"What?" Quinn's alert level ratcheted up another notch. "You saw a car watching the estate?"

"I couldn't see much of who or how many were inside—other than an older man in the backseat. They drove away as soon as I showed an interest in them." She turned to

Michael again. "I've got the plate number if you think I should run it."

Michael took the paper she pulled from her pocket. "I'll handle that. Quinn, do you want me to…?"

Quinn had already dialed David Damiani's number at the estate's security office. "David. I need you to run an ownership and identification check for me on a…" He pointed to Officer Murdock.

"Black BMW."

"…on a black BMW." He signaled Michael for the license number. "Missouri plates C3K-49F. It's not one of your guys, is it?"

"In a Beemer? No, sir."

"Then get one of your men out to the front gate. My KCPD guests spotted the car watching the estate earlier."

"Will do, boss." Damiani was brusque, but thorough. "I'll put Hansen on it and get out there to check it myself."

Quinn hung up. He pulled off his glasses for a moment and rubbed at the headache forming between his eyes. Then he slipped them back on and looked directly at the woman who might just be exactly what he needed, after all. "Now do you see why I need you to be a part of my household this week? I can't afford to miss anything that could impact my daughter's safety."

"You want me to go undercover as the nanny for your little girl."

"I want you to *be* her nanny. That means staying with her 24/7, seeing to her needs and doing whatever it takes to keep her safe."

She fidgeted in her seat. "I'm happy to volunteer to provide extra security. I've had some experience with bodyguard assignments."

Quinn shook his head. "A bodyguard isn't good enough. Fiona's only three. It's not like a stranger can tell her to keep her head down and expect her to comply, or reason with her. She needs someone she trusts, someone she'll bond with. I don't want the split second it takes one of my security men to react or get her attention to be the split second that gets her killed." Quinn stood, emphasizing his point and ending the conversation. "She needs a nanny."

Miranda stood to boldly match his stance. "Then she needs someone besides me. I'm not good with kids. I've never had any experience with them."

Bravo for Michael Cutler's diplomacy. He stood, as well, diffusing the tension radiating off Miranda. "Then how do you know you're not good with them?"

Quinn followed up on the logic of Michael's lead. "I don't have time to take one of my bodyguards and teach him how not to frighten my little girl. Nor do I have time to train a nanny with the skills you already possess."

Her proud shoulders sagged for a moment, then stiffened again. "All right, Mr. Gallagher. You have yourself a nanny. I need to go home and pack some gear." She turned to Michael. "I'm assuming I can use my police-issue equipment and weaponry?"

Michael nodded. "And I've got SWAT Team 1 on call to back you up if you need anything."

"Thank you, sir." She gathered her gloves and stocking cap off the desk and reached for her coat on the back of her chair. "When I get back I'd like to meet whatever security you have on staff so I can learn their names, recognize faces, get a handle on procedure here. I'll want a tour of the entire estate, as well. I don't want any hidden gates or staff-only entrances to surprise me. I'll need pass codes or keys to whatever type of physical locks you have on the place."

"I'll make the arrangements." Quinn picked

up the phone to call David again. "I'd like you back here by seven. Fiona's bedtime is at eight, and that's strictly observed—even on holidays. Maybe especially on holidays with all the excitement. It's important to maintain her routine."

Miranda nodded, then pulled her black cap on, camouflaging the femininity of her beautiful hair. "I'll see myself out. Make sure security locks up after me."

She paused to look at Fiona, lying on her belly with a water marker and drawing mat, with something like disbelief or even dread on her face. Then she shook it off and hurried into the hallway toward the front door.

"Michael…" Quinn's heart squeezed in his chest as he watched Fiona arrange her doll beside her and tuck another marker beneath the stuffed hand so that they could draw together. There'd be a hell of a price to pay once he found out who had threatened to take that precious life away from him. "You're certain Officer Murdock is capable of being a nanny to Fiona?"

Michael was a wise man who knew how to choose his words well. "She'll keep your daughter safe."

Chapter Four

Something wasn't right.

Miranda doused her headlights and climbed out of her truck as soon as she was through the front gates of the Gallagher estate. Pulling her stocking cap low around her ears, she tucked her ponytail into the back of her navy blue coat so that there was nothing to reflect in the lights from the flood lamps mounted over the security cameras there. With a bit of nimble timing, she slipped through the gates before they clanged shut and locked behind her, and she slipped into the shadows of the moonless night.

She stopped behind a towering pin oak to peer up and down the line of walls and ivy. The car was back. Well, *a* black sedan was parked against the sidewalk about an eighth of a mile from the gate. Without proper streetlamps out here, it was impossible to make out if it was the same car from this afternoon.

And where was the guard? Hadn't Quinn Gallagher ordered his security chief to place a man at the front entrance?

If so, where was he? She'd come in exactly the same way she had that afternoon, punching a button and being cleared over the intercom system. Even though she was now technically a member of the household staff, someone should have stopped her.

She inhaled deeply, then slowly released her breath so that she didn't create a telltale cloud in the cold air that might reveal her presence. Calming her pulse rate the way she had at the shooting range last night, Miranda reached up beneath her coat and pulled her gun from the holster clipped inside the back of her dark jeans.

Rule 1 of SWAT was reconnaissance. Know your enemy. Know his location. Know his intention. Action was pointless unless you had a plan.

Of course, she'd been checking out a similar hunch about suspicious activity that day the Rich Girl Killer had clocked her in the head and left her for dead so that he could go after his real target. She'd been so intent on proving her worth and saving the day that she hadn't seen him coming until it was too late to use her weapon, too late to get the jump on him. She'd fought him off, but she was so woozy from the initial blow that she passed out before she could stop him. She'd failed.

Tonight there were some niggling doubts that she could handle this similar situation on her own. But without Captain Cutler, Sergeant Delgado and the others, she was a team of one. She didn't have the luxury of second-guessing herself. Michael Cutler and Quinn Gallagher were counting on her to do this job. Time to get some answers.

Sticking close to the trees, she crept several yards through the snow, past the parked car. Crouching low, she raised her Glock between two steady hands and approached the car from the rear blind spot. Jeans or not, she still wore her service boots. The composite soles had picked up some melt-away salt and now she was crunching across the cleared pavement.

But she could hear the radio music rocking out from here. No way could they hear her approach. She could make out two silhouettes inside—the driver and a passenger in the front seat. Not the same setup as before. But if one of them had silver hair, then they had a lot of questions to answer.

"KCPD! Open up! Get out of the car. Get out of the car now!" She slipped her fingers beneath the passenger-side handle and lifted, quickly returning her grip to the Glock. "Hands on your head. Get out!"

The sudden blare of music faded into background noise in her head. "What the hell…?"

Both men were wearing GSS Security uniform jackets. And both were slumped in their seats.

Miranda quickly shucked a glove and pressed her fingers against the side of the passenger's neck. He had a pulse, faint but steady.

She leaned in to turn off the radio and shut down the engine. As she reached across, she took note of the coffee spilled across the driver's lap, and of the cup tipped over in the passenger's lax fingers and dripping onto the floor mat at his feet.

Surging adrenaline sparked through Miranda's senses. The guards had been drugged. Why? She glanced up at the gates. The man in the command center had spoken to her before *un*locking the gates. Was the danger already inside? Were the Gallaghers under attack?

Ah, hell. Her team of one suddenly seemed

awfully small and outnumbered. She needed to get help. She needed to sound the alarm.

"Hey!" She shook the man closest to her. Dark hair. The driver was a blond. Neither had been the man watching the estate earlier today. She lightly smacked his cheek. "Wake up!"

He groaned and leaned back, his head lolling against the headrest. But he didn't wake up. Glancing up and down the street, she saw no sign of anything. No vehicle. No pedestrians. No lights beyond the holiday decorations adorning a couple of the neighboring driveways. Isolated. Alone. Again.

Her breath came hard and fast in her chest. She hadn't seen anyone when the RGK had blindsided her, either. No, no, no. She couldn't let those self-doubts get inside her head.

Miranda's toes danced inside her boots. Treat this like she was on the firing range. Take control. "Think, Murdock. Think."

She tried to wake the driver, but both men were out for the count. Her instinct was to reach for the radio on her shoulder and call in backup. Only, her hand tapped nothing but wool. She was in her civvies now. She had her cell phone in her pocket. But did she call 911 or Captain Cutler? She had no clue about

Quinn Gallagher's number or his chief of security or…

Her gaze alighted on the dashboard radio. Of course. They'd be connected to the estate's security office.

But as she pushed the snoozing driver aside to get to the radio, something tumbled from the inside of his coat and landed at her feet. "What's this?"

She picked it up.

The damp wind whipped at her cheeks, but she was turning cold from the inside out.

It was a little doll. A roughly made, voodoo-like miniature of the rag doll Fiona Gallagher always had with her. Only this one was covered in something red and sticky. And instead of beautifully embroidered eyes, this one had two tiny slashes drawn across its face.

A dead doll.

Miranda pulled out a piece of paper that had been tucked inside the doll's dress. She unrolled the stained note and read the message typed inside.

And then the anger kicked in, casting out self-doubts and second-guessing.

See how easily I can get to you? Make it right, Gallagher, or this is your little girl.

Uh-uh. Not on Miranda Murdock's watch.

She put the note back where she'd found it and pushed the drugged driver aside to grab the radio. She had no idea about GSS procedures, so as soon as she had a clear channel and a stern "Who is this?" she went with the whole get-your-butt-out-here-now protocol.

"Hey, whoever's in the command center, this is Randy Murdock, KCPD. I'm one of you now, and I need backup. You've got a situation with your guards here at the front gate. Someone in charge will want to see this. Oh, and you may want to call an ambulance."

"Whatever they spiked the coffee with will have to wait until we can get it to a lab," Quinn declared. "But this is gelatin. Red gelatin and food coloring." He tossed his plastic gloves into the trash can beside his desk—resisting the urge to toss the gruesome doll in there, as well. "Probably made with corn syrup instead of water to keep it from setting completely. It's an old kid's trick to make fake blood."

"This isn't any kid's joke." Miranda stopped her pacing on the far side of his desk and came up between his security chief, David Damiani, and her own boss, Michael Cutler.

"It's a very calculated, very sick way to make you feel threatened."

"It's working." Quinn's gaze skipped from her slender curves to David's bulk and steaming temper, to Michael's lanky height and piercingly intelligent eyes, and back to the unblinking intensity of Miranda's mossy gaze. Was that concern he saw written there? Temper? Fear?

Beyond his own intellect and drive to succeed, one of the things that had aided Quinn in his rise to the top of his field was his ability to read people. David was ticked off that his men had gotten hurt and that all his preventive measures and training hadn't been able to stop the attack. Michael was thinking, evaluating possible plans of action, trying to come up with a scenario where everyone came out unharmed.

But Miranda? She was a complete mystery to him.

With her gun and plain talk, she was as tough as any man in the room. Yet there was something curiously vulnerable about that tumble of emotions alternately darkening and brightening her eyes. Her blue jeans and plain brown sweater did little to highlight her femininity, yet his body had hummed with a distinctly masculine energy from the moment she'd entered the room—peeling off her stocking cap and shaking that golden ponytail down her back, removing her coat and tossing it onto a chair with that effortlessly sinuous grace of hers.

Miranda Murdock was a baffling conundrum he wanted to figure out.

But analyzing that fascination was a distraction he didn't need right now.

The clock is ticking. The text he'd received while watching Fiona open up her gifts this morning had been perfectly clear.

"The only way an enemy could get under my skin *is* to threaten my daughter." Quinn took his eyes off the distraction in the room and paced off the walls of books surrounding them. "The question is why? Who did I step on? What offense did I commit? I paid the money he wanted."

"Into a Swiss account we're working on tracing," David reported. "Thus far, we've dead-ended at a dummy corporation called United Lithographers of Southern Europe."

"U LOSE?" Miranda's eyes went dark again as she pieced together the acronym that was a mocking message in itself. "That's cold."

David's expression was almost a sneer as he

glanced down at her. "We're still investigating."

"Have you found out where the text messages are coming from?"

The follow-up question didn't improve David's mood. "Disposable cell phones. A different one each time. Impossible to trace."

"Apparently, I've really ticked someone off." Quinn didn't need bickering children in the room right now, each trying to prove he or she was the better security expert. "I spent today updating that old patent of mine, which is still practically worthless on the market, and I sent it to the generic email account specified. Now I have to run a simulation to prove that it works by noon tomorrow. I've got a couple of techs in the GSS lab working to trace it in the meantime." He sank onto a black leather sofa, then shot to his feet again. He wasn't used to being a man without answers. He didn't like it. "What is it I have to 'make right' by the start of the New Year?"

"That could be a long list," Michael suggested. Add guilt to the list of problems Quinn needed to fix. He'd taken his friend from his new wife and baby, and teenage son, on their first Christmas together as a family. But Michael hadn't complained. "You don't become as rich as you are without someone else being jealous of what you have. A competitor might think he got the short end of a business deal. You fired an employee who feels he or she didn't deserve it. Someone thinks you took credit for an invention he or she worked on."

"I didn't," Quinn argued. "I came from nothing. I worked hard and used my brains to earn every last penny I have."

Michael shrugged. "This perp we're looking for doesn't have to think logically, the way you do, Quinn. He may be fueled by emotions and misconceptions. What matters is that, in his mind—or hers—you've done him wrong."

"So this guy could just be some lunatic?" Nobody in the room argued the possibility. Quinn raked his fingers through his hair. "Ah, hell."

"Could it be something personal?" David asked.

Quinn stopped at the mantel over the empty fireplace and studied the collection of family pictures there. Growing up, he and his mother had had so little. Now he had so much. But none of it mattered. Only one thing mattered. "I have no personal life beyond Fiona."

"What about Valeska?"

Quinn's gaze snapped across the room to

David's dark eyes at the mention of his late wife. "Val worked her way up through my company. She earned her vice presidency before I ever married her. If somebody resents that…"

David averted his gaze for a moment, knowing he'd hit a hot button. But Quinn hadn't hired the former military man because he shied away from a potential confrontation. The GSS security chief crossed the study to meet him at the fireplace. "What about Valeska's father? Vasily Gordeeva? He spent a lot of years in that political prison. Supposedly, the U.S. was supposed to be a safe place for his family. Does he blame you for Valeska's murder?"

"Three years after the fact?" Tilting his head to the ceiling, Quinn vented his frustration on a sigh before answering. "The Rich Girl Killer murdered my wife in the backyard of our own house that day—leaving my infant daughter in the stroller right beside her. And this bastard thinks I need to pay a higher price than that?"

Miranda's soft gasp reminded him that not everyone knew the story as well as he did. She turned away when he tried to meet her stricken stare and apologize for his bluntness.

But he could flush the anger and grief from his voice. That was a skill he'd learned long ago, back with the bullies in the Shoemaker Trailer Court. "I've never even met my father-in-law. Val grew up here in the States without him. Even when I did business in St. Feodor, she never went there. It wasn't safe for her to return to the country. How could Vasily hold me responsible for her murder if the two of them never had a relationship? And now the plant in St. Feodor is closed. Other than a few investors there—who made a tidy profit through GSS, I might add—I have no ties."

He was surprisingly relieved to see Miranda face him again. "Your father-in-law is in prison?"

"In the Eastern European country of Lukinburg." Quinn scratched his fingers through his hair and moved back toward his desk. "He's a political dissident, accused of financing a failed rebellion there. I don't know much more of the story than that. For their own protection, he severed his relationship to Valeska and her mother, and they emigrated to the U.S. She never talked about him."

"That sounds like heavy stuff."

"We're talking about *my* enemies here, Miranda. Not Vasily Gordeeva's. This enemy is right here at home."

"With all due respect, sir, we don't know where your enemy is."

Why was she arguing this? "This isn't about politics in a foreign country. This is about greed or payback or both." Quinn stopped and turned right in front of her. "I'm guessing I'll receive another task to complete tomorrow— something every day until the end of the year. Let's try to get some answers sooner rather than later, shall we?"

She propped her hands at her hips and tilted her eyes up to his. "Well, I think you're asking the wrong question."

He opened his mouth to reply to the provocative taunt, but for once in his life, the right words wouldn't come to him. He had to move away before he could speak again. "Michael, isn't there some chain of command you teach your people to follow?"

"I also teach them to think on their feet." Not a yes man in the room tonight. "What is it, Randy?"

Her cheeks heated with color and her expression animated at her captain's encouragement to share her opinion. "Why drug the guards? Why not kill them outright?

They didn't hesitate to kill those men at the plant overseas. If you're going to take the risk of them being able to identify you, why give them the chance to wake up and point a finger?"

Sound reasoning. Hell, why hadn't he thought of that? More irritatingly, Quinn wondered why he hadn't expected that from her. Why couldn't he get a read on Miranda Murdock? She was antagonistic yet insecure. She was a physical woman, yet she also showed a keen intellect.

Michael, fortunately, wasn't wasting any time of the puzzle of Miranda Murdock. "So whoever served them that coffee is either someone they know and trust, or it was done by someone they never saw at all."

David thundered back across the room. "If you're suggesting that one of my men is behind this—"

"Check them out," Quinn ordered.

"—after I've personally and thoroughly screened every last one of them."

Damn it, this was *his* company, *his* family that was being threatened. He paid Damiani a lot of money to follow his commands. "Screen them again."

Michael was a little more diplomatic. "It'd

narrow down our list of suspects. Your men were drugged outside the gate because the perp couldn't get inside. Security's still good here."

No wonder he was one of KCPD's top negotiators. A deep breath heaved through David's barrel chest and his burst of defensive temper dissipated. "But if they can figure out how to get to them out there, it's only a matter of time before they figure out how to get past my men and the protocols here. I'd better not have a mole on my team."

"Let's change up the protocols," Quinn suggested, thankful that someone in the room could keep his head. "I want your best men on this, David. And find out who the hell drugged those guards."

"Daddy?" A soft voice from the hallway turned all four adults toward the open door. Fiona hugged her doll against her chest, her blue eyes wide as they sought out Quinn's. "Why you angwy?"

Quinn glared at the guard lurking behind her in the hallway. A grown man couldn't keep a little girl in her room for an hour?

"She insisted we come down here," the man apologized.

Condemning his own raised voice, Quinn

dismissed the guard and scooped Fiona up into his arms, turning her so she wouldn't get a glimpse of the mutilated doll on his desk. "What are you doing here, sweetie? I thought you were watching the new movie Santa brought you up in your room."

Her small fingers splayed across his cheek. "Petwa wants more cookies."

Quinn shifted his gaze to the fraying embroidery of the doll's blue eyes. "I think Petra has had enough sweets for one day." He pressed a kiss against the delicate fingers on his cheek. "So have you, young lady."

Her tiny mouth stretched with a yawn and Quinn checked his watch. As much as he loved the sweet weight of her in his arms, he had work to do. Above anything else, it was his job to protect her. And that required changing security codes and talking revised strategies with David Damiani and Michael.

So he handed Fiona over to the new nanny. "It's after seven now. It's time to get Fiona to bed."

"Wha—?" Quinn held on a moment longer, worried for a moment that she wasn't even going to wrap her arms around his daughter. "But we haven't finished debriefing. What's our next plan of action? I won't know the new security protocols. I don't know the old ones yet." Miranda's hands finally closed around Fiona's back and thigh, and she shifted her onto one hip. "I don't even know where her bedroom is."

Miranda's eyes were dark like a pine forest now, yet wide with panic. The woman should never play poker. Definitely a puzzle.

"Fiona can show you."

Given a mission to do, Fiona sat up straight, excitement chasing away her fatigue. "I know." She squiggled down to the floor, catching Miranda's hand along the way. "Come on."

Quinn exchanged a glance with Miranda as Fiona led her out of the room. *Do your job,* he warned silently.

If he wasn't mistaken, Miranda's arched brow read something like *What do you think I've been doing?* Or maybe it was *Help!* as she disappeared around the corner.

The need to go after them, to make sure his decision to hire Miranda to protect his daughter wasn't a mistake, jolted through his legs. But what harm could come to a three-year-old and an armed SWAT cop going upstairs to Fiona's bedroom?

Ignoring the tension that refused to go away, Quinn forced himself to return to the two men at his desk. "Do we have any leads at all on who took out the guards and left this vile message?"

David shook his head. "Holmes and Rowley couldn't have been out for too long because they made their thirty-minute check-in."

"Increase it to fifteen-minute reports. Go through the security camera footage to find out when they got that coffee, if they stopped anyone at the gate, or if anyone walked up to the car." Quinn pulled off his glasses to rub at his tired eyes. "We need to find out who's behind this. First, a foreign base of operation. Then the GSS offices here in KC. Now my home. He's getting way too close for my comfort."

"Permission to speak freely, sir?"

Quinn put his glasses back on to bring the security chief into focus. "Of course."

"I know your judgment is a little skewed right now with the threat against Fiona." David thumbed over his shoulder toward the empty doorway. "But Dirty Harriet there is a loose cannon. She pulled a gun on my men."

"They were unconscious."

"What if they weren't? We'd have had a fire fight in the middle of the street on Christmas night." He pulled back the front of his jacket to prop his hands near the holster at his waist. "Do you really want someone like that around your daughter?"

"Considering *she* detected the threat against this home when your men couldn't, yes."

Chapter Five

"Is that choking you, sweetie?" Miranda frowned at the neckline of the long pink underwear-looking pajamas she'd put on Fiona as she tucked the quilt around her in the canopy bed. She'd spent too much time familiarizing herself with the layout of the bedroom suite, complete with retractable steel window shields and a panic room she could access inside the walk-in closet. She should have given a little more thought to pajama etiquette. "Maybe they snap in the front." She tossed the covers back and smiled an apology to the little girl. "Will you stand up for me?"

They ought to put directions on these things for first-timers like her. But Fiona was more than happy to jump to her feet on the bed. She weighed next to nothing as she braced a hand on Miranda's shoulder and dutifully picked up each foot so that she could turn the pajamas around and get them back on the right way.

Miranda fastened the last snap up beneath the girl's chin and slid her fingers inside the neckline to make sure they fit more comfortably this time. "All righty. Down you go."

With a giggle that made Miranda smile, Fiona plopped down on her bottom and then leaned back into the pillows.

"Good night, Fiona."

But a small hand grabbed the cover before she could pull it up to her young charge's chin. The quizzical narrowing of Fiona's round blue eyes reminded Miranda of another Gallagher who seemed to find fault with a lot of the things she said or did. "We didn't bwush my teeth."

"Oh." Duh. Even though she wasn't familiar with the needs of three-year-old girls, at the very least Miranda should have been thinking about her own nighttime routine. "We'd better go take care of that. We don't want all your teeth to fall out of your head."

The joke must have needed an older audience.

Miranda shrugged off the confused response and kept smiling.

"Show me where you keep your tooth-brush."

Using one of the posts at the foot of the bed, Fiona climbed over the safety railing to the floor, then reached back for that ever-present doll. With "Petra" in one hand, and Miranda's fingers in the other, Fiona led her into the connecting bathroom.

It was almost a reversal of roles as Fiona showed Miranda each step of her routine. First, she climbed onto a stool just inside the bathroom to turn on the light. Then there was another step stool in front of the sink. There, she filled a plastic cup with water and wet the brush herself before squeezing a fistful of toothpaste onto the bristles. Miranda arched an eyebrow at her reflection in the mirror over the sink. She was on a steep learning curve here. *Pj's close in front. Prep the toothbrush for her. Watch out where and how high this one climbs.*

After the task was done, and Miranda had wiped away the extra foam from Fiona's face and hands and the countertop, she tried putting her to bed again. Pajamas on the right way. Teeth brushed. Doll and girl tucked in. Head for the light switch. She'd already spotted the night-light in the plug beside the bathroom door, but she knew some children had a fear of the darkness. So she paused a moment to ask, "Is it okay if I turn the big light off?"

The blue eyes blinked, but never looked away.

"What?"

"What about my stowy?"

"You like a bedtime story?"

Fiona beamed with a smile and nodded.

Miranda located the white bookshelf nestled between the windows overlooking the second-story porch and crossed to it. Picture books. Beginning readers. Classic chapter books. Alphabet books. *Overload.* "What do you like to read?"

Fiona giggled again. "I can't wead."

"No, I mean, what do you want me to...?" That laugh was a delightfully musical sound. Maybe the jokes all had to do with her own incompetence in the bedtime arena, but Fiona's giggle went a long way toward easing Miranda's fears that she was going to warp the child for life as long as she was in charge of her care. "What shall *we* read this evening?"

"The pink pwincess one."

It took a search through five different princess books to find the right adventure Fiona was looking for. "Okay. Here we go."

Miranda started the story in the rocking chair beside the bed. But two pages in and Fiona was up on her knees with the covers thrown back, twirling around like the princess in her ball gown. By page five, they were both growling like the dragon who wanted to eat all the flowers in the kingdom.

Miranda was on her feet, playing the part of the prince, dueling the bedpost with a toy broomstick sword while Fiona giggled and roared away, when she realized there was another presence in the room. A tall, bespectacled, steely-eyed presence filling the doorway. As much as Fiona's laugh delighted, Quinn Gallagher's scowl sobered her up.

"Uh-oh." Miranda stopped mid–dragon growl and tossed the chubby-handled broom back into the toy chest before closing the book with her finger marking the place. She wished she didn't feel quite so much like a little girl who'd been caught making too much noise at a slumber party. She hugged the book to her chest, subconsciously turning it into a shield between her and Quinn. "Fiona said she needed a story."

"A story, yes. Not a live reenactment."

"We were using our imaginations and

having a little silly fun. You do allow your
daughter to have fun, don't you?"

He stood with his arms crossed over his
chest, the corded strength of his forearms
straining beneath the rolled-up sleeves of his
button-down shirt. No, perhaps he was a man
who didn't do *silly.* "Her bedtime routine is
supposed to be a quiet time to help her relax
and go to sleep."

Lois Lane had it all wrong. Clark Kent was
the hottie. Or maybe Miranda was the one
who was all wrong. *Get it together, Murdock.*
It must be the late hour, or those extra lone-
some working-on-a-holiday genes, kicking in.
She was here to protect this family, here to
do a favor for the captain. Lusting after her
cranky boss wasn't part of the job description.

She exhaled a sigh of frustration and returned the book to the bookshelf. "I told you
I wasn't any good at this."

"Let's go, sweetie." Quinn picked up Fiona
and smoothed the dark curls off her flushed
face before laying her in the bed and pulling
up the covers. "Daddy will tuck you in."

"The dwagon goes *grrrr,*" Fiona roared
with high-pitched enthusiasm, curling her
fingers into a little claw the way Miranda
had. "And the pwince and pwincess... e-yah,

e-yah." She thrust out her fist into Quinn's chest, mimicking Miranda's rebel charge perfectly.

"I'll 'e-yah' you, young lady." Quinn caught her little fist and kissed it before tucking it under the cover, as well. "And the dragon and the prince and princess became friends and planted a garden and lived happily ever after."

"Wandy tells it better."

"Maybe that's a story you should read during playtime, not when it's bedtime."

"I'm not sleepy…" Fiona's big yawn was Miranda's cue to exit. Fiona turned her face into the soft cotton of her doll. "'Night, Daddy. 'Night, Wandy."

Being included in the three-year-old's goodbye warmed Miranda like a gentle squeeze of her hand, chasing away some of the loneliness and inadequacy she'd been feeling. "Good night, Fiona."

Miranda was in the hallway, almost to her room next door, when a real hand snagged her wrist. Instinctively, she twisted free and spun around to face her opponent. But she had no place to go when Quinn closed in on her. She had to flatten her back against the wall and stay put, ignoring the poke of her gun and holster at her waist. Either that, or she could shove her boss's best friend in the chest or disable him in some other, considerably more painful, way. Miranda opted for standing tall and staying put.

Quinn braced his hand on the wall beside her head and leaned in. "I do not need you to question me in front of my people. Or my daughter. We have routines in this household for a reason."

"Control freak much?"

"You're the damn nanny. Not my conscience. I need you to do what I say when I say it."

Their voices were charged, hushed, intimate, as they kept their argument beyond the earshot of anyone else in the house. "I'm here to protect your daughter, not to be bullied by you."

"Bullied?"

"You have all the money, all the power—you're used to people jumping to do your bidding." His eyes were blue, blue, blue, up close like this. Even the refraction of his lenses couldn't distort their color. Miranda felt like a specimen under a microscope as they evaluated every nuance of her words and expression. "Maybe that's how this crazy countdown to New Year's got inside all your state-of-the-art security—because *you* haven't thought of every possible threat. Smart as you are, Mr. Gallagher, you don't know everything."

"Are you always this much trouble, Officer Murdock?"

"Pretty much."

They weren't touching, but they were both breathing hard as the furtive exchange of tempers and opinions mutated into a different kind of heat. Their breaths mingled and their chests nearly brushed against each other with every inhale. Her head filled with the spicy scent of shaving cream or soap on his skin. Her body warmed with the proximity of his body lined up with hers. She wasn't even aware of the holster poking into her backside anymore. Quinn's gaze fixated on her lips, and Miranda couldn't look away from those laser-blue eyes.

This was crazy. *She* was crazy. She was the bodyguard and he was the boss and they butted heads, and she really shouldn't be wondering what it would be like if he kissed her right now.

She wrapped her fingers around the chair rail on the wall behind her to conquer the urge to brush that stray lock of hair off his forehead. But she couldn't. She shouldn't. Finally, in a breathy voice, she summoned the will to whisper, "You're in my personal space."

"I am." There was something bold and sexy about the statement of fact and the idea that he must be feeling this, too, or he would have retreated by now. "I don't get you, Miranda."

"I *am* a little different from the average woman," she conceded wryly.

It was the opening those niggling self-doubts needed to sneak inside her head. But when she lowered her gaze and looked away, Quinn's hand was there, gently pinching her chin between his thumb and forefinger and tilting her face back up to his. "One way or another, I'm going to figure you out."

It sounded like a vow.

Any sensible reply lodged in her throat. As little as she knew about raising little girls, she knew even less about healthy romantic relationships with grown men.

Fortunately, she was granted a reprieve from those shortcomings piling on the growing confusion inside her.

"Daddy?" a soft voice called from the bedroom.

Just like that, Quinn's touch was gone. He took his uniquely masculine scent with him as he shoved his fingers through his already mussed hair and put the width of the hallway between them.

"That shouldn't have happened."

Miranda hugged her arms around her middle, feeling strangely chilled. "Nothing did."

Technically, that was true.

Quinn's jerky nod indicated that he didn't quite believe that a sensual awareness hadn't just erupted and continued to simmer between them, either. But she understood the signs of dismissal in his posture, and the need to return to the business at hand.

"I'll sit with Fiona for a few minutes and get her settled. David Damiani and the guards on duty at the house this evening are gathered in the command center to meet with you. He'll get you a card for the electronic locks and explain the pass codes, panic rooms and security lockdown procedure." Fiona called out again, and Quinn moved toward his daughter's door. "The command center is down on the basement level. I'll join you as soon as she's asleep."

"Quinn?"

"Please. Do not argue with me this one time."

"I was just going to say that I'll do better with Fiona. I can get online tonight, or go to the library tomorrow. There have to be some tips and tricks somewhere to teach me how to do the nanny gig."

His eyes narrowed into that quizzical frown. "You're doing just fine. I haven't heard that kind of laughter from her for a long time. I'm the idiot who's being too critical of too many things right now. I'm just…" His broad shoulders rose and fell with a weary sigh, letting her know that she wasn't the only one plagued by self-doubt in this house. "I want to know who the hell has the nerve to threaten my daughter."

"We'll find him," Miranda promised. Although whether she was talking as a cop or a woman, she wasn't sure. She checked her gun at her back and offered Quinn a smile. "Captain Cutler always says we have to trust the team. So let us all do our jobs. No one is going to hurt Fiona. Not on my watch."

Miranda just prayed that, for this overwhelmed father and his sweet little girl, she wasn't the member of the team who let everyone down. Again.

THE IMAGE OF THE BLOND-HAIRED woman in the black uniform on the computer screen went dark at the punch of a button.

This was an interesting new development. Imagine GSS, a global force in personal security technology, bringing in outside help to keep its own CEO and his daughter safe. It was ironic, really. So the king of Gallagher Security Systems was feeling *insecure.*

That was satisfaction to take to the bank.

Of course, having the woman on the premises would make it a little harder to get to Fiona Gallagher. But it wouldn't be impossible, not by a long shot. It simply meant adding one more tally to the body count.

A trail of dead bodies, from the Kalahari Desert to Kansas City, Missouri, would certainly put a crimp in the almighty Quinn Gallagher's sterling reputation. If the man behind GSS couldn't keep his own people safe, then why would anyone trust his company to protect them? He'd be ruined.

It was something worth smiling about.

Taking his daughter would destroy him. She was the only thing meaningful enough to Quinn Gallagher to ultimately be worth taking. It was the only thing meaningful enough to count as payback for what Quinn Gallagher had done.

Gallagher had exacted too great a price on his way to the top of his field. Hearts had been broken, dreams shattered. He hadn't protected everyone who should have mattered. An unjust price had been paid for his success. It was time to take back a little—make that *all*—of what he owed.

The boss leaned back in the office chair and placed a call to the man who'd required the tidy sum of two and a half million dollars for his team to carry out the necessary work for the rest of the week. Two and a half million was chicken feed to a man like Quinn Gallagher. Imagine how much would be taken from him by the time this was all said and done.

A split second passed before the man answered. "Yes?"

"Is everything in place?" His hesitation wasn't the best way to begin a report. The boss demanded an explanation. "What is it?"

"We couldn't get the doll placed where you wanted it, but Gallagher has it now."

Good enough. The bloody doll had been more about shock and diversion and making Gallagher squirm. Quinn Gallagher thought he was smart enough to plan for every contingency. But there was one he would never see coming. "And the other?"

"Soon. You were right. My guy piggybacked right off Gallagher's design file when he emailed it to us." First his business, then his family. Step by step, Gallagher would go down. "As soon as he starts running the software simulation, we'll have access to the entire computer system. Once we're in, the building will be ours. You can deliver the next message whenever you're ready."

"Good." Time to initiate the next phase of the plan.

Chapter Six

5 days until Midnight, New Year's Eve

"Hey, John. Sorry to get you up so early." Miranda beamed inside and out at the gritty image of her brother in his desert camouflage uniform on the screen of her laptop. "Merry Christmas, big guy."

"Merry Christmas, kiddo. Sorry to keep you up so late."

"That's okay. I'm on duty, anyway."

"In your pajamas? Where's your gun stashed?"

Miranda curled her legs beneath her in the chair in the Gallagher estate's security command center and grinned. At least one perk to working the holidays for a man who was as wealthy and techno-savvy as he was unsettling and opinionated was access to a pretty sophisticated computer setup. This was the best satellite link she'd had with her brother since he'd been deployed. "Long story. So tell me, what did you do to celebrate?"

John's hair was a few shades darker than her blond locks, but the same green eyes looked back at her and smiled. "Well, I just stuffed my belly with a ridiculous amount of food. They went all out for the holiday meal—ham, turkey, prime rib. Baked potatoes. Mashed potatoes. Sweet potatoes. Cherry pie. Pecan pie. Chocolate cake. Ice cream…"

"Stop. I'm gaining weight just listening to all that." Although his deep, indulgent tone was familiar, she couldn't help but notice the tight lines bracketing his smile. "You look tired."

"I just came off the front line today."

The time difference between the States and the Middle Eastern region where his marine unit was stationed required these rare face-to-face hookups to take place at odd hours. But she didn't think a lack of sleep fully accounted for the gaunt look of his handsome face. "John? You do remember that I'm a twenty-eight-year-old grown-up now, right? You don't have to protect me the way you used to. Did something happen?"

He looked away from the camera for a

second, then tried a little harder to make his smile stick. "Did I tell you I got that care package you sent? Loved the books and the sports drinks. Not sure what I'm going to do with the red-and-green socks, though."

"Nice dodge, big brother." John Murdock avoiding a straight answer raised her concern another notch. "But you didn't answer my question. Is it really that horrible there?"

She and John had been a family unto themselves since the time she'd been a teen and he'd been in his early twenties and their parents had died in a car accident. She could read her brother's moods and expressions like he could read hers—and they didn't keep secrets from each other.

"I'm in a war zone, kiddo. It's rough."

"John…"

His tension eased on a wry laugh. "Fine. I was never able to outlast your stubborn streak." Miranda's heart squeezed in her chest at the pain that passed over his features. "We had a bad encounter on one of our last sorties. I lost a good friend. I asked the CO if I could write a letter to his family. It was tough."

"Oh, John. I'm so sorry." His pain became her own. She was so far away, so helpless to do anything for him. Was there any job she was going to be able to successfully accomplish anymore? *No. Don't go there.* This wasn't about her. She swiped at the tears stinging her eyes and smiled for his benefit. "What can I do to help?"

"Give me a present," John answered, the shift of his wide shoulders making the effort to lighten the mood. "Tell me what you did to celebrate the holiday."

"I worked."

"That's a lousy present. I'm going to have to have a talk with your captain when I get home. At least tell me you have fun plans for New Year's Eve."

"As far as I know, I'm working then, too."

John shook his head. "Can't the criminals let you celebrate at least one holiday?"

"I'm trying to earn some brownie points with Captain Cutler. So I volunteered for a special assignment with one of his friends, Quinn Gallagher." She gestured to the wall of computer towers, wires and monitors behind her. "That's why we've got such a great link this time. Mr. Gallagher is letting me use the computer lab in his security offices."

"That explains why it looks like you're sitting in a bunker. You've got plenty of ventilation there, right?"

"There's a huge cooling system here with all these electronics." She glanced up. "I'm staring at a vent now that leads up to the main floor and is bigger than my closet."

"Maybe I should be there instead of this tent."

"I wish you were. It's hard to feel like celebrating the holidays without you." Miranda patted the belly of her red plaid flannel pants and pouted. "There was no one to bake me a caramel apple pie."

John laughed. It was a good sound to hear, and eased her worry about him just a bit. "You're really roughing it, aren't you?"

"Hey, you haven't had to butt heads with Quinn Gallagher." Her body tingled at the memory of that heated encounter in the upstairs hallway. She hugged her knees up to her chest, trying to dispel the prickly aftershocks of sexual awareness before her brother picked up on any of her unplanned and inappropriate fascination with her temporary boss. "He's like something out of a comic book—a driven, brainiac, his-way-or-the-highway kind of a guy. Although, I haven't decided whether he's more the hero or the villain yet."

"A comic-book character?" John scoffed. "I knew I should have gotten you to read more

Austen and Brontë than that fantasy adventure stuff you ate up in school. You're talking about the guy who created Gallagher Security Systems, right?"

"You've heard of him?"

John thumbed the collar of his captain's uniform. "GSS doesn't make flak vests just for cops."

"I can imagine his company making only the best for our troops. Even his house here in Kansas City is a fortress. I've had a crash course in keyless remotes, motion-activated sensors, panic room protocols and redundant armor systems to close off windows and doors in the event of an attack. I swear, if there's a security technology out there, Quinn Gallagher has it installed here. The whole estate is like a model home for security technology."

"So what are you doing for GSS?"

"It's for Quinn, specifically. There have been threats against the family, and he has this adorable little girl." Who, despite Miranda's screwed-up efforts thus far, seemed to like her, as well. "I'm working as a nanny for a week."

John snorted a laugh. "You? I never pictured you as the domestic type. This Gallagher does know you can't cook, and you've never changed a diaper, or—"

"Give it a rest," she chided with a grin. "I'm the girl's bodyguard. I tried to tell Quinn that we weren't playing to my strengths here. But I met the most important requirement."

"What's that?"

"I was available."

John's deep-voiced chuckle made Miranda smile, as well. "Is there a mother in the picture?"

"Quinn's a widower. Why?"

"Because you've mentioned him by name at least three times in the past thirty seconds. Somebody's got a crush."

Despite the refrigerated temperature of the basement office, Miranda felt her cheeks heat with embarrassment. "I do not. I mean, can you imagine someone like me together with someone like him? There are so many reasons why it would never—"

John's image disappeared off the screen and an odd image blipped into its place. Long tables. Equipment, knobs, wires. A blurry glimpse of a figure whose face was above the angle of the camera shot. There was no marine, no khaki tent wall in the background.

For one second, maybe two, she was looking at a different place, a different person.

Miranda's mouth was still open, midprotest, when snowy static blurred the picture on the screen and John suddenly reappeared.

"John?"

"Did we lose the connection?" he asked. "We were supposed to have the feed for twenty minutes."

She unwound her legs and dropped her feet to the floor. "You saw it, too?"

He was sitting up straighter, too. "I lost the signal for a few seconds. Instead of looking at you, I was looking at—" he shrugged "—someplace else."

"Like a visual party line. I don't know what it was."

"Who knows how many satellites we're bouncing off of to make this connection? A line's bound to cross somewhere."

"Yeah." But wouldn't the monitor just go blank or fuzzy if they lost the satellite connection? "I need to go report this."

"Randy?"

"A lot of weird things have been happening here." It had been the weird behavior of a suspect near the witness SWAT Team 1 had been assigned to protect that had diverted her focus, allowing the Rich Girl Killer to sneak up from behind and attack her. Was this a diversion that could take her attention away from protecting Fiona Gallagher? "Do you remember me telling you about the RGK?"

"Yeah. He cracked your head open and you think that means you failed your team. The guy's dead, Randy. He's got nothing to do with a computer glitch."

"I know." Maybe she could confess to her brother the secret self-doubts the police psychologist had had to pry from her. "But I nearly blew that mission to hell, John. And now I second-guess everything. Every thought, every action. Everything I see. I can't let anything happen to that little girl. But I don't know that I'm the best person for this job."

"Nobody trains harder than you. Nobody understands responsibility and wanting to do the right thing more than you. You're smart. You've got good instincts. Hell, I taught you everything I know about staying safe." And he'd done it very well. "I'm the one fighting a war. I do not want to get a telegram that says something happened to my baby sister while I was away."

Her heart lurched in her chest. "Thanks for the pep talk. I'll be careful if you will."

"Deal."

"Swear?"

"I swear." He nodded toward her. "Now trust those instincts and go find out what just happened here."

They each touched their hands to their respective screens. It was as close to a hug as either one of them was going to get. "I love you, John."

"I love you, too, sis."

Miranda's fingers were still there when the satellite feed ended and the monitor returned to its screensaver image.

And then she was on her feet, searching for anyone else on the estate who was still up at this hour.

"WHAT ARE YOU DOING OUT here?" Miranda's footsteps had been noiseless on the stairs, and yet Quinn had known he was no longer alone the moment she reached the landing. Some switch of hyperawareness had been turned on in his brain, specifically tuning his radar to alert to her presence. "Is something wrong?"

He pulled back from the door frame where

he'd been watching Fiona sleep and quietly closed the door to her room.

"Quinn?" She'd come up beside him, the point of her chin tilted toward him, those green eyes sharp with concern as they tried to read his expression.

"She's fine." He tightened his robe around his bare chest and the sweatpants he'd worn to bed. He adjusted his glasses at the temple to buy him another second to wipe the depth of his worry from his face before turning to her. "I'm the one who can't sleep. I keep thinking that if I drop my guard for even one moment, if I let her out of my sight…"

"That's what I'm here for, right?" She pointed to her bedroom door. "I can take the comforter off my bed and bunk on the floor in here if you like. I grew up doing lots of camping with my family, so it's no problem."

Keeping the fact that he'd been tempted to do that very thing to himself, Quinn shook his head. The one person innocently unaware of all the dangers swirling around his daughter was Fiona herself. But if she woke up to find one of them in there with her, that sharp little brain of hers would quickly realize that something was wrong. It was one thing for him to be afraid, but seeing that fear tainting his daughter's eyes would tear him in two. "She'll be fine. Father's prerogative to worry, you know."

"Sounds like my big brother." She gently splayed her fingers against the door. "Fiona's a lucky girl. It's a secure feeling to know someone's looking out for you."

Miranda's serene smile when she spoke of her family eased an answering smile onto his own mouth. "Did you make the connection to your brother?"

She nodded, curling her fingers into her palm. "Thank you." In the dim light of the hallway, Miranda seemed shorter, not quite up to Quinn's nose where she'd been earlier in the evening. A more observant glance up and down the red and white of her pajamas revealed that she'd been running around the estate in her socks, adding a younger, inexplicably vulnerable air to the tough chick who'd been armed and dangerous and argumentative from nearly the first moment they'd met. "Talking to John is the best present I could have asked for."

So why wasn't she still smiling? "But…?"

Her shoulders lifted with a deep breath. "Something hinky happened to the link while I was talking to him. John disappeared for a couple of seconds, and I was looking at something else, some*where* else. Kind of like someone switching the channel on the TV, and then switching it back. I asked the guard on duty, O'Brien, about it. But he seemed to know less about computers than I do."

"Hinky, hmm? Let me check." Her confusion was cause enough to trigger his own concern. And since he wasn't sleeping, anyway, Quinn headed down the stairs to his office study, with Miranda following on quick, silent footsteps. He sat at his desk, turned on a lamp and pulled up the estate's mainframe access, typing in code after code to get into the secure server that constituted the brain for all of the estate's electronic activity.

He felt her lean against the back of the leather chair to look over his shoulder. "You know how to do that?"

"I know my way around lots of different technology. I designed this system myself." Once he was in, he scrolled through all the recent online activity. "I didn't make my millions by being a pretty face."

"No, you couldn't do that."

What? Quinn stopped midtype and turned in his chair to question the taunt.

She slapped her hand over her mouth, her

face blushing rosy pink all around at the stray thought she'd spoken out loud. The hand came down and she backed away from the chair. "That didn't come out right. You aren't pretty. Not with the chest and the arms and the... I mean, you've got that whole hero-beneath-the-nerdy-black-glasses thing going for you..." Her hands came forward, imploring him to understand her embarrassed rambling. "You're Clark Kent on the outside. But underneath, you're really..." Her posture withered as she hugged her arms around her waist. "Shutting up now."

Maybe this woman would never make sense to him. Still, Quinn appreciated the round-about stroke to a male ego that hadn't really cared about such things since his wife's death. So Miranda had noticed something beneath the button-down suits and glasses that had long defined him to the world. Nice to know he wasn't the only one in the room battling a little bit of ill-timed lust.

He grinned as he went back to his search. "I always fancied myself more of a Batman type." The grateful laugh behind him touched something a little deeper than his ego and warmed him inside. Going head-to-head with Miranda Murdock was invigorating, but this quieter, friendlier detente between them was waking parts of him that had been dormant for a long time. "All our computers here are on a server that goes through the mainframe at GSS. I'm just double-checking to see if there was a—"

That shouldn't be there.

Quinn pulled off his glasses and got right up to the monitor to verify what he was seeing. Son of a bitch. So brilliant. So simple.

He sat back and punched in another command. "Here. Look at this."

Miranda's arm came right in beside him, pointing to the computer screen. "That's what I saw. My brother saw it, too. For a couple of seconds, maybe."

"You saw this image?" The mainframe room, the brain center, of the GSS office building in the northern section of Kansas City stared back at them.

"Yes. There was a person there when I saw it. Could have been a man or woman, but it was just a glimpse. White coat. I couldn't see a face."

Quinn put on his glasses and picked up the phone on his desk. The late hour didn't matter. He paid his people good money to be roused at any time of day or night if there was an emergency. And this could be a big one.

He stared hard at the camera shot captured by the computer until a drowsy voice picked up. "Hello?"

"Ozzie? Quinn here. I need you to run a diagnostic on our computer system. I'll meet you at the lab first thing in the morning. I think somebody tapped into our mainframe."

"We've been hacked?" He could hear Ozzie Chang waking up. Sitting up. Going on alert. "Impossible."

"At the very least, somebody tried. I need you to get to the lab and run a full diagnostic on the system. Find out how deep it goes into our design work and programming. Bring in whatever help you need."

"I'm on it, boss."

After hanging up, Quinn took Miranda by the elbow and walked her to the door. "I'm going to be on the phone awhile longer. But you'd better get some sleep. It's already morning and I want you well rested for Fiona."

She planted her stockinged feet and turned in the doorway. "Is this something major?"

Quinn shrugged. "It's not the first time someone's tried to get into the GSS network. A good hacker could get his hands on

some very sensitive, very costly information." Someone had gotten into GSS, but had
they gotten beyond all the firewalls and pass-
words and layers of security code they'd built
into the system? "I need to find out what programs, if any, were actually accessed."

"Do you think it's related to the threats?"

"There's no way to tell yet. It could be a diversion. Or, threatening my daughter could
be the diversion that kept me occupied while
someone tried to break in. It could be unre-
lated altogether." He touched the soft cotton of
her sleeve again, dismissing her into the hallway. "There's no way to tell until my staff and
I get in there and look."

"Mr. Gallagher—"

"Quinn. If we're going to be working together, living together, we might as well be
on a first-name basis."

"Then I'm Randy."

"No, you're not." Quinn deliberately
dropped his gaze to the tiny nips beading beneath her long-sleeve T-shirt, and the decadent flare of her backside in those soft flannel
pants. And then he sought out the intriguing
beauty of her eyes. There was nothing boyish
about that strong body of hers, or his reaction

to it. "Is it all right if I call you Miranda instead?"

"No one calls me…" Her lips parted on a heated breath and bowed out in a tempting curve the way they had earlier in the evening. He'd be kissing her before this week together was done, Quinn was certain of it. It might be a damn fool move, and he wished he had the strength to ignore the attraction arcing between them. When her tongue darted out to moisten the curve, and an answering heat sparked inside him, he was doubly certain it was going to happen. "Miranda's good."

"Thank you for bringing the computer malfunction to my attention." He brushed his fingers over the back of her hand, intrigued by the contrast of velvety softness and sinewy strength. He gently caught her in his grip and squeezed. "Good night, Miranda."

Her fingers tangled with his and squeezed back. "Good night, Quinn. Don't worry about Fiona. Do your job. And I'll do mine. I'll stay with her tonight."

He couldn't wait any longer for the inevitable. Cautious of any sign that he'd read this draw between them all wrong, Quinn dipped his head and pressed his lips against hers.

They were warm, soft, as lushly tempting to the taste and touch as they'd been to the eye.

Her mouth opened slightly, moved beneath his, and he adjusted his stance to claim what she offered. Miranda braced her fist against his chest and rose onto her toes, sealing the bond between them more fully.

He thanked her for caring about his daughter, encouraged her to care a little about him, too. He caught her bottom lip between his, pulled on it gently, dabbed his tongue along the sleek, warm curve of it. Quinn shifted on his feet, instinctively wanting to move closer. He angled his mouth one way. She turned her mouth to fit his. Her tongue brushed his lips, darted to meet the tip of his. Her throat hummed with a breathy moan when he took command of the kiss again.

Their hands touched, their lips touched, and little more. It was just a kiss. A simple, tender, leisurely, getting-acquainted kind of kiss.

Yet Quinn sensed the low-burning flame kindling deep inside him, stirring in his blood. This kiss crossed the barriers of boss and employee, father and protector, professional and personal—clarifying them into basic man and basic woman, linking him to Miranda in ways that were too new and delicate and unexpected for him to process right now.

And he needed to be able to process. He needed to be in control of his thoughts and actions right now, especially when he wanted nothing more than to loosen that golden ponytail and tunnel his fingers into the silky cascade of Miranda's hair. He wanted to drive her back against that door frame and deepen the kiss, to feel that taut, slender body pressed against his. He wanted to fill his hands with that beautiful bottom and drag her up against the undeniable interest of his body.

Instead, Quinn ended the kiss, resting his forehead against hers. For a moment, he savored the gentle caresses of each stuttering breath against his cheek and lost himself in the drowsy passion in her eyes. "Wh-why did you kiss me?" she whispered.

Still looking to question him? Quinn smiled down at her. "Why did you kiss me back?"

Then he retreated a step, released her hand, let the cool night air of the house move between them. This wasn't the time for investigating just how far this attraction between them would go. It wasn't the time for giving in to wants. He had to leave if she wouldn't.

"We each have a job to do." He nudged her into the hallway and closed the door on temptation. "Good night."

Chapter Seven

4 Days until Midnight, New Year's Eve

Miranda sat across the breakfast table watching Fiona sticking the fruit-ring cereal she wasn't eating onto her fingers and onto her doll's nonexistent fingers, subsequently dropping most of them into her lap or onto the floor.

Miranda's own oatmeal and sliced bananas were eaten, the bowl and spoon washed. The second mug of coffee she'd poured herself had cooled. She wondered how many more bites of cereal could possibly be in that bowl, and just how long she was supposed to wait for the easily entertained little girl to either become full or tire of her creative jewelry making.

And while she sat and waited, Miranda noted how easily Fiona Gallagher smiled and laughed. Although the rich color of blue in her eyes was the same, their expression bore a marked contrast to her father.

Quinn Gallagher was more like Jekyll and Hyde than the comic-book alter egos he resembled physically. He was bossy and arrogant, used to people not questioning his orders. He was clever and stubborn and demanding. Yet he was heartsick and unsure about his daughter's safety. He was a vigilant protector of his home and family. He commanded a small staff and hundreds of employees and half the world's law enforcement and military supply lines, if the press about GSS was to be believed. Yet he seemed isolated and alone high in his ultramodern office and behind the tall, thick walls surrounding his home.

She was alone because her brother was overseas and she had no other family. She hadn't been able to develop really close relationships with the men she worked with because she was the newest member of the team, she was a woman, and she was the only member who wasn't at least married and starting a family. And she was so busy with work or training for work or worrying about work that she hadn't had much luck developing female friendships beyond the tentative bond she shared with Sergeant Delgado's wife, Josie. But Josie had a new baby, a new marriage and a new job as a trauma nurse. Miranda wasn't about to impose herself on Josie's time and put a strain on that one woman-to-woman bond. She'd become a pro at avoiding those fragile relationships that she seemed to have a talent for messing up in any number of ways.

Quinn Gallagher was alone because he'd lost the woman he'd loved to violence, and he wasn't about to care about anyone so deeply that it was worth the risk of losing someone else. He was alone because, like Miranda, he didn't quite fit in with the people around him. They deferred to him. They served him. They might even fear him. He was up on such a pedestal of wealth and power that people avoided getting too personal with him.

And yet, last night, in the silent shadows of a doorway warmed only by the lights of the Christmas tree in his study, two lonely people from two different worlds had connected. She and Quinn had created their own little world filled with hushed words and secret vows and a kiss.

A purple cereal ring bounced across the table and Miranda absently popped the sugary bite into her mouth, touching her lips and re-membering that kiss.

In some ways, she supposed, it had been just a casual kiss. Other than her hand on the soft flannel of his robe and their lips, their bodies hadn't touched. Yet she'd been tempted to splay her fingers against the wall of his chest, to slide her palm inside to find the warmth of the skin she could feel through the velvety cotton.

No one had groped anything. Although even now, she could remember the pulsing grip of his hand around hers, as though his fingers were anxious to explore but unsure if they'd be welcome on her body.

His tongue had lightly tasted the tip of hers. His supple mouth had squeezed and pressed and gently suckled. The grip of Quinn's hand had been sure around hers—a support, a com-fort, a connection.

Miranda couldn't remember ever being kissed like that—so gently, so thoroughly, so perfectly. Even now, in the wintry morning sunlight shining through the bank of windows in a cereal-studded kitchen, she could feel that kiss.

She'd gone all melty and gooey inside in a way that was totally at odds with the man and her mission. She'd sensed a power in Quinn, a potent male need held in check by the sheer strength of his will. And if that will had surrendered for even one moment, she suspected the warmth inside her would have exploded in a wild conflagration.

Remembering that kiss this morning made her temperature rise and her chest ache and parts of her body that had rarely been a priority ache to touch and be touched, to hold and be held, to kiss and be kissed again.

Quinn strode into the kitchen, startling Miranda from her thoughts. "I'm going into the office to meet with my chief software designer to make sure the computer simulation for that patent..." The remembered heat flooded her cheeks and she hid her face behind a sip of tepid coffee. Quinn pulled his leather gloves back off and tossed them onto the breakfast bar. "What is she doing?"

"Eating breakfast."

"She's making a mess."

Miranda rose to defend herself at the subtle accusation she heard in his voice. "Yes, but I figured I would wait until she was done and then clean everything up just one time."

Definitely Jekyll and Hyde. And there was no sign of the needy, passionate loner she'd connected with last night in the kitchen with her this morning. This was the GSS mogul, the brilliant eccentric, the man who gave orders—not the frightened father and tender lover who'd reached out to her in the shadows of the night.

He was dressed in a black wool coat, a suit and tie. Still, he reached for Fiona, lifted her from her booster seat and sat her in a clean chair at the side of the table to brush the bits and crumbs off her pajamas. "She was probably done twenty minutes ago. Get a washrag out of the drawer next to the sink and wet it."

Fiona held up her long, tiny fingers while Miranda found a cloth to clean her. "See my wings, Daddy?"

"I see them, sweetie." He nibbled one of the cereal rings off her finger and she chortled with delight. Quinn ate another bite from her hand, and another. By the time he'd polished them all off, she was belly-laughing and hugging him around the neck. He was a handsome man when he smiled and, frankly, a little intimidating when he didn't. Miranda wasn't feeling the love when he took the damp cloth from her fingers and started cleaning Fiona's face and fingers. "You really don't know anything about raising children, do you?" he said over the little girl's head.

Miranda bristled at the unfair attack. She'd been up front with him about her skill set when she'd agreed to this job. "I'm not on loan from KCPD because I have a way with kids."

He did not just roll his eyes, did he? "Are you at least armed?"

She tapped the back of her jeans and the weapon secured there. "24/7 this week. I'm keeping track of my Glock at all times since she's going to be around it."

"Good."

"Petwa?" Fiona reached for her doll in the messy chair.

In a surprising maneuver of multitasking efficiency, Quinn dabbed at the doll's face, then handed the doll to Fiona before giving Miranda the rag and some advice. "Fiona's a little girl. She doesn't eat all that much at a sitting. Try smaller portions and snacks throughout the day rather than three big meals. When she starts playing with her food, that's usually a sign that she's done."

"Thanks." So maybe a little bit of Dr. Jekyll had shown up this morning, after all. "I'll remember that."

"She can be taught."

Was that a joke? Even if it was at her expense, it was worth a smile. "Don't worry about the mess," she promised. "I'll clean up."

"Make sure you dress her warmly today. I'd like her to get some fresh air."

A brief moment of panic set in the moment he turned away. "What kind of games does she play outside?"

Quinn's eyes narrowed in that quizzical expression. "There's a foot of snow on the ground. What would *you* play?"

"Okay. I can do that." She breathed a little easier. Building snowmen and forts wouldn't be nearly as hard as figuring out the nighttime routine had been.

Cereal crunched beneath Quinn's shoe as he went back to the counter for his gloves and pulled his keys from his pocket. "Make sure you grab a radio from the command center and let them know when you go out and come back in. You've got a key card and understand the security codes?"

"Yes, sir." She patted the rear pocket of her jeans.

She wondered if Quinn's gaze had lingered an extra moment on the spot where she'd patted her hand. He adjusted the corner of his glasses, masking the exact angle of his eyes.

"I should be home early this afternoon unless there's an issue with the simulation. And there won't be. I have to prove it works by noon."

That was a sobering reminder of the real reason she was here. "What happens if you can't do everything this guy asks?"

Quinn looked down at Fiona, who'd kicked off a slipper and was now picking up cereal with her toes. He bent over to kiss the crown of his daughter's hair. "I'm not giving him the chance to find out."

MIRANDA WAS FEELING LIKE a little girl herself as she ducked down behind the wall of the snow fort she and Fiona had built. It was an easy game of hide-and-seek, where they hid in the same place every time, and finding each other was all about the squeals of laughter and loud *Aha!*s of discovering a new friend.

Fiona's laughter was like a tonic to Miranda's doubting soul. In that little girl's eyes, the lopsided snowman and leaning fort wall were works of art. Conversations were simple and didn't always include words the other one understood, but there was real communication taking place. And despite the ever-present Petra and girly garb of pink on pink, from the topknot of her stocking cap to the toes of her tiny insulated boots, there were definite signs of a fellow tomboy lurking inside Fiona Gallagher.

Miranda held her breath as she heard the pink boots crunching in the snow and the breathy exertion of her companion scrambling over the top of the wall. She hunkered down in the icy snow, knowing there was no place for Fiona to land but on top of her.

"Aha! Found you."

Miranda rolled over, catching Fiona in her lap and laughing with her. "You found me. Yay!"

Obeying an unexpected impulse, Miranda hugged Fiona tight and kissed her cold, rosy cheek. When Fiona yanked her doll up between them, Miranda gladly kissed Petra's damp face, too.

It was so easy to fall in love with Fiona's sweet laugh and beautiful spirit, and Miranda was well on her way there. Her time outside with Quinn's daughter this morning was the best celebration of the winter holidays Miranda had enjoyed in a long time. She was relaxed, having fun, in delightful company.

But she wasn't about to forget her responsibilities. She pulled back the cuff of her coat to check the time. They'd been outside for almost

an hour now. And though she'd bundled up
Fiona in enough layers to resemble a small
blimp in her snowsuit, she wasn't going to risk
the chance of her getting chilled. Besides, Miranda's own stomach was beginning to grum-
ble for a bite of lunch.

Using a newly acquired skill to encourage
Fiona's cooperation, Miranda peeled off her
glove to check the doll's muslin cheeks. "I
think Petra's getting cold. Should we get her
inside for some hot soup?"

Fiona mimicked the same touch with her
pink mittens on the doll's face and agreed.
"Petwa's cold."

"Okay. Let's go in." Miranda put her glove
back on and dusted the snow from her jeans
as she stood. Then she dusted the snow off
Fiona's suit while Fiona brushed the snow off
her doll.

A flash of light in the corner of her eye
stopped Miranda from taking Fiona's hand.
She turned her head, wondering what she'd
seen. Scanning the wide expanse of the Gallagher acreage, though, she saw nothing but
the creek, the tall white wall covered in ivy,
the tops of the trees beyond and lots of undisturbed snow between them and the front gate.
"Hmm."

Must have been the sun glinting off the snow, or the reflection from a windshield of a car along the street on the other side of the wall. She waited several seconds, spotting nothing unusual. And when she felt the grasp of Fiona's hand tugging at her fingers, she turned toward the house and headed for the mud room entrance off the kitchen.

Until she saw it again. Reflected in the glass of the outer storm door. Another flash of light.

Miranda spun around, pinpointing some kind of movement in the distance. She picked Fiona up in her arms and jutted out her right hip to carry her toward the house while she pulled the walkie-talkie David Damiani's men had assigned to her out of her pocket.

She was moving quickly across the snow toward the cleared sidewalk. She was hanging on to Fiona with one arm now, and the little girl was struggling to climb down. Miranda hitched her up against her side again and pressed the call button. "Holmes? You there? This is Officer Murdock."

The man stationed at the monitors in the command center this morning answered. "I'm here, Murdock. What's up?"

The radio communication amongst Damiani's crew wasn't as precise and polished as what Captain Cutler had drilled into her, but it was functional enough to serve its purpose. "I just saw a light, or reflection of one, on top of the north wall, west of the gate. I swear it looked like a camera flash. Or someone sending signals with a mirror." Fiona was squirming again. "I need you to sit tight, sweetie." The words meant nothing to the three-year-old and she squiggled free. "Fiona."

Where was she going?

Fiona waddled back to the fort and Miranda changed course to hurry after her.

"West of the gate, you said?" Holmes asked. Although she'd met the dark-haired man Christmas Day passed out in the car with another guard and the bloody doll, they really hadn't had a chance to get acquainted beyond basic introductions. Maybe the guy was hard of hearing.

"Yes. Approximately thirty yards. Can't tell if it's from the top of the wall or in one of the trees on the other side." Something up there was definitely moving. And then the light flashed again. Son of a gun. Some perp was spying on them. Oh, for a pair of binoculars right about now. "I just saw it again. You want me to investigate?"

"I'll have Rowley walk the perimeter and check it out."

"Tell him to get there fast. This guy's on the move. Murdock out." Fiona was back at the fort, climbing over the wall again. "Fiona. Come here!"

"Petwa find me."

"No." It was time for the game to stop. "You need to listen to me."

Fiona dived into the snow just as Miranda reached for her.

Just as a man stood up on top of the wall fifty yards away.

Miranda's internal alarm kicked into overdrive. She glanced down at Fiona, half-buried in the snow. She glanced up at the man who was bundled up enough from head to toe to make it impossible to get a read on his face at this distance. Ah, hell. Was he climbing down inside the property?

Giving one more look to assure herself that Fiona was hidden from sight behind the wall of the fort, Miranda followed the urgency to meet the threat head-on that sparked through every nerve ending. "You stay here with Petra, sweetie. You hide and I'll come find you."

The man was scrambling to cling to the top of the bricks now. He must have slipped in the snow on top and was desperately trying to find a toehold and pull himself back up. But what was he doing here in the first place?

Miranda reached beneath her coat and pulled her gun. She clasped it firmly between her hands, barrel pointed down as she ran through the snow to the driveway. She crossed the creek and stopped at the last pylon of the bridge over it, raising her gun with a steady aim and raising her voice. "KCPD! You're trespassing on private property! Put your hands up and identify yourself."

With a heave that was all muscle, the man swung a leg up on top of the wall and pulled himself over. But something he was wearing caught in the ivy vines and pulled him off balance. He swore, a low, muffled sound.

"KCPD!" she shouted again. She fished the walkie-talkie out of her pocket and hit the call button. "Holmes! He's getting away! Holmes! Rowley! Is anybody out front? Somebody talk to me."

Miranda sprang to her feet as he jerked free and dropped down on the opposite side of the wall. The thing around his neck—the camera, maybe?—hit the bricks and tumbled down through the ivy on the wall. The instinct to pursue jolted through her legs, but he was already out of sight. She pointed her gun up above the treetops and fired a warning shot. "KCPD! Stop!"

As soon as the loud pop of her gun rent the air, a high-pitched squeal sounded behind her. Miranda lowered her weapon and turned as Fiona, startled by the loud noise, burst into tears.

"Oh, sweetie." Miranda tucked her gun in the back of her jeans. "Oh, no." What had she done? She squatted down and reached for the girl. "Don't. Don't do that." She scooped her up in a tight hug and the girl wrapped her arms around Miranda's neck and bawled into her ear. "What are you doing here, sweetie? I thought you were hiding."

Now she was tired of playing the game?

She stood with Fiona in her arms, cradling her head against her neck and rocking her from side to side. "That was a gun, sweetie. See why you should never play with one? It's loud and scary and it could hurt you." Fiona squealed again and clung even tighter. Miranda didn't understand. "Do you think I'm hurt? I'm not hurt." Then she turned her face away from the girl and shouted her frustration. "Somebody talk to me!"

"Who fired that shot?" Holmes's voice

buzzed over the walkie-talkie. "Do I need to lock it down?"

"What?" There was a loud thunk of metal on metal at the front gate, followed by smooth whirring noises, like the pulsing chirp of a million grasshoppers, from the entrance to the estate and the house behind her. "No!" They were engaging the reinforced steel gate while steel shutters were coming down over every door and window of the house. "Fiona will be stranded out here in the open. Stop what you're doing and go after that guy!"

Over a second thunk and the whirring noises of the steel barriers disengaging, Miranda heard the snapping of twigs, a thump and a curse in the distance. And then she heard the distinctive sound of a door slamming and a car speeding away.

"I missed him." Finally, Rowley reported in, after a punch of static from the walkie-talkie in her pocket. "The guy fell about halfway down the wall. He's hurt, but I couldn't catch him. The car came up out of nowhere."

Miranda stepped into the snow on the far side of the creek and headed for the ivy wall as she pulled out the walkie-talkie. "Did you get a plate number?"

"A partial. He was already in the car by

the time I reached him. He's long gone now." Fiona seemed to like the bumpy trip of being carried across the deep, undisturbed snow. Her cries had quieted to whimpers and sniffles, although her hold on Miranda's neck was as snug as ever. "It's not the same car you saw," Rowley added. "It's another black Beemer, but the first digits on the license I saw were different."

Miranda was blind to events from this side of the wall, and she wasn't sure she trusted the report. She would have given chase, shot out a tire, scaled that wall, if she didn't have Fiona with her. Just what kind of incompetents did Quinn have working for him here? They'd gotten drugged. They let a suspect escape. They'd nearly locked her and Fiona out of the house. At least he'd gotten the make of the car and a partial plate.

She was at the wall now. She paused for a moment to wipe away the tears freezing on Fiona's cheeks, and smiled. "Can I set you down now?"

Fiona shook her head and thrust herself against Miranda's chest.

Miranda hugged her, stroked her back…and got an idea.

"Do you want to help me?" she asked. She

made it sound like the adventure of a lifetime. "I need you to climb the wall."

Boom. Just like that, the whimpers stopped and Fiona leaned back.

"That's my girl." Miranda pointed to the camera hanging in the torn ivy, just above her reach. "Can you get that for me?"

With an enthusiastic nod, Fiona let Miranda turn her in her arms and lift her onto her shoulders. Then she leaned against the cushion of ivy and pushed Fiona up. "Can you reach it?"

Like the closet monkey she was, Fiona braced one hand against the wall and grabbed the camera. When she tugged it loose, it crashed into the snow and popped open.

In spite of her tear-chapped cheeks, Fiona was all smiles when Miranda set her down. "I climb," she said proudly.

Squatting down, Miranda hugged her to her side. "You sure did, sweetie. You did a good job."

Miranda dug the broken camera out of the snow. It was an older model, one that made instant snapshots. She pulled out the last photo that had gotten stuck in the mechanism and shook the snow off it. Moisture dotted and smeared the image, but the subject was clear—it was a picture of her and Fiona playing in the snow.

The guy must have been watching them for at least twenty minutes. And the guard at the gate hadn't noticed him?

"Murdock?" Holmes was calling her on the walkie-talkie again. "You there? Are you and Fiona safe?"

She pushed the button to answer. "We're safe. Go ahead and call Captain Cutler—and your chief, Damiani—to report the guy taking pictures. Ask if there's any follow-up we need to do."

"I've already got Damiani on the line. Say, Murdock?"

"Yes?"

"You know, you didn't have to panic like that."

Panic? Miranda steamed. That nincompoop of a snail was accusing her of panicking at the intruder?

"If you get locked out of the house, there's an override on the second-story windows. The boss designed it that way in case there was a fire, so no one would get trapped inside. The steel shutters up there are built on a flexible hinge. Just jimmy it with something small like a screwdriver, and the shutter will pop open."

"Jimmy it with a screwdriver. Got it." It might have been nice to let her know that before this place locked down like a prison. Weren't they all on the same team, trying to protect this family? "Murdock out."

She looped the camera strap over her shoulder and picked up Fiona, taking care to hold the picture so it didn't sustain any further damage and there was some chance the crime lab could analyze it. With each step back to the house, her pace slowed as her protective temper abated and those familiar doubts crept back into her head. Did she really have room to complain about the quality of Gallagher's security force?

She hadn't noticed the spy until he'd already taken several pictures, either.

"WORKS LIKE A DREAM, BOSS." Ozzie Chang hit the print command and rocked back in his chair in the GSS computer lab. "In theory, anyway." He pulled a pen from his spiky black hair and marked a couple of reference points on the printout. "Although, I still don't get why you wanted to run a simulation program on the old electronic locks. Are we really going to start building these again? This is like two models and a whole bunch of out-of-date source codes ago."

Quinn squeezed Ozzie's thin shoulder as he checked the time on the clock. 11:32. Just in time before the noon deadline. He needed to get someplace private and send the updated design to the anonymous email address. "Thanks, Oz. I'm just feeling sentimental," he lied. There was no need to involve anyone else in this game he'd been forced to play. "I wanted to see if there was any value in revitalizing the old program."

"Yeah, but over Christmas? I figured you were a workaholic, man, but even I took the day off to play a marathon of 'Zombie Apocalypse' with my buds online."

To each their own way of celebrating the holidays. Although he was anxious to be on his way and get the job completed by the deadline, Quinn grinned at the young man. "Did you win?"

"Kicked their butts into the New Age, sir."

Quinn breathed out a reluctant sigh and pushed his glasses onto the bridge of his nose. Had he ever been that young and carefree? Growing up had been about working to help his mom make ends meet. It was about learning to outrun the bullies, then learning to outwit them as he got older. A few times, it had been about a four-eyed kid learning how to fight—to defend himself, and to defend his mother from some of the desperate choices she had made.

It had rarely been about holiday celebrations and playing games where the biggest consequence was developing sore thumbs from too many hours at the game controller.

There was a lot to envy about Ozzie's young-at-heart attitude. He was glad to have that kind of young energy working at GSS. "Would you email the data to my office address?"

"Sure thing, boss." With a spin of his chair, Ozzie was typing at the keyboard again. "Email sent. Anything else?"

Quinn swiped his key card and punched in the code to leave the lab. But he paused at the open door. "Yeah. Go home. Call your folks. Call your friends. Do whatever it is you do that makes you happy. I don't want to see you again until after the New Year. And look for a bonus in next month's paycheck."

"Sweet."

"Can you lock up the shop?"

Ozzie grinned. "Yes, sir. Happy New Year."

"Happy New Year to you."

Quinn didn't wait for the door to close behind him. He jogged to the bank of elevators and got inside to press the penthouse office button.

As soon as he was in his office, he logged into the company server and pulled up the email from Ozzie. Then, with a grim sense of foreboding, he emailed the file to the anonymous email address he'd been given and waited.

He wasn't quite sure how updating the design specs on an old security system, and proving it still worked, would make things "right" for his tormentor. He had a feeling the task had been more about busywork, a diversion of some kind. But he wasn't going to argue the inanity of the task. He was simply going to do it and pray it would be enough to remove Fiona as a target in this anonymous bastard's scheme.

His phone vibrated in his chest pocket and he inhaled a deep, steadying breath before answering it. There were still four days to go until the New Year. He'd been threatened by too many bullies growing up to believe this was actually going to stop without some kind of major fight.

He read the text message on his phone screen.

Nicely done, Mr. G. Your daughter gets to live for another day. You will be hearing from me tomorrow. And trust me, the message will be loud and clear.

Chapter Eight

3 Days until Midnight, New Year's Eve

Louis Nolan paced the sitting area of Quinn's office. The receding points of his hairline wrinkled with the tension radiating off him. "Nervous investors are bad for business, especially when we're about to start a new fiscal year. We're talking millions of dollars here, Quinn. He's come all the way from Europe. The least you can do is hear him out."

"I'm a little busy right now, Louis." Quinn glanced up from the printout where he'd been reviewing the simulation data provided by Ozzie Chang. He'd been an idiot—a full-fledged, too-smart-for-his-own-good-so-he'd-overlooked-the-obvious idiot. The reason for the busywork and the noon deadline yesterday was hidden right here, in the thousands of lines of code that ran the program. He and

Ozzie had provided the means for a talented hacker to get into the GSS network.

It was impossible to tell how successful the break-in had been from this printout. He'd already made certain that the thousands of home security systems they monitored hadn't been compromised, so this wasn't about a spree of pending burglaries. And it would be a long, painstaking process to go through all of GSS's data files and employees' personal computers to see if any of them had been tapped into, downloaded or stolen.

This was his own damn fault. He'd been so distracted by the Kalahari explosion and the trespasser taking pictures of his daughter and the sick threats against his family that he'd made an amateur mistake. The hacker had tapped into the GSS mainframe through the trapdoor created when he'd run that simulation program. Now he needed a way to backtrack to the source and eliminate any other inroads into GSS and its systems.

You will be hearing from me tomorrow. And trust me, the message will be loud and clear.

Tomorrow was now today, and Quinn didn't want any more surprises. If he could figure out the target inside the GSS mainframe, then maybe he could finally get ahead of this creep and stop him. "This is where my talents are best put to use today. I trust you to handle the situation with Titov."

His attention drifted to the tiny brunette playing at the far end of his office, and the tall blonde sitting dutifully still while Fiona listened to her heart with a plastic stethoscope and put bandages all over Miranda's dark blue sweater. He'd hired the best security in the city—heck, he'd invented and developed some of the best security technology in the world. And yet he couldn't shake the irrational fear that letting Fiona out of his sight meant not being able to protect her.

Finding out who'd dared to threaten his family, and stopping him, were the only things on Quinn's to-do list right now.

Louis slapped his palm on Quinn's desk the moment he returned his attention to the printout. "That's what I'm trying to tell you. I don't know that I *can* handle it. I've reassured him every way I know how, but Nikolai insists on talking directly to you."

"You're the one who has the rapport with him. You're the one who brokered the deal to keep his money in GSS after we closed the plant in Lukinburg." No matter how influential an investor was, or how much clout he carried in the European market, nothing was more important than his daughter's safety. Until Quinn could determine whether or not the attack on the GSS security network was part of that threat, or another distraction that was diverting his attention from his daughter, his focus needed to be right here. He summoned up a reassurance for his COO. "You're my right hand in this company, Louis. I know you can handle Nikolai Titov."

"As your right hand, you've always trusted me to take care of the business side of things—no matter what else is going on with your life. I kept things running for months while you dealt with Valeska's murder. I've helped you weather wars and economic crashes. I know you're worried about Fiona right now." Louis's bushy silver brows lifted with a friendly beseechment. "But this company is her future, too. A short meeting to alleviate the concerns of one of our most important partners is all I'm asking from you right now. Ten minutes of your time this morning, and I'll be able to keep the European market afloat for us while you see to the needs of your family."

It was Louis's job to put the company first. As much as the timing stank, Quinn was a smart enough man to listen to the experts he'd hired.

"You know, Louis, anyone else talking to me like this would be downright irritating. But I know you're thinking of the bigger picture when I can't. All right. Ten minutes." He slipped the printout into the top right drawer of his desk and called his assistant. "Elise? Show Mr. Titov and his associates into my office."

"Yes, Quinn. Right away."

Pushing back his chair as he stood, Quinn rolled down his sleeves and buttoned his cuffs. He circled around his desk to grab his suit jacket off the back of one of the sofas and kept on walking until he reached Miranda and Fiona. He buttoned his collar and tightened his tie before squatting down to Fiona's level. "Hey, sweetie. Daddy has to do a little work now. Why don't you and Miranda go check out the break room and get a snack? Do you remember the way?"

Fiona grinned from ear to ear. "Soda pop."

"That's right. It's where the soda pop machine is." Quinn shook his head and directed his wishes to Miranda, who was on her knees peeling off bandages. "Make sure she drinks juice. Go to the elevator and follow the hallway around."

"I saw the room during our search on Christmas Eve." Miranda stood, her expression concerned behind Fiona's back. "Trouble?"

Quinn hugged his daughter and set her on her feet before standing. "Business."

When he took Fiona's hand and pressed it into Miranda's, his fingers brushed against hers. His sensitive fingertips tingled at the brief contact, remembering where a simple holding of hands had led them the night before last. Just as quickly, he pulled away before he could get sucked into a distraction like that again. He needed a clear head to deal with Titov and Louis's concerns so he could be done with them and get back to his investigation into the hacked computer system.

Still, when a woman had a green mermaid bandage stuck to her shoulder, it was a gentleman's duty to remove it for her. He peeled the strip of plastic off Miranda's sweater. The movement brought him close enough to look over her shoulder to see the bulge of her gun at the back of her waist. Right. Tingling skin and remembered kisses had no place between them. As much as he hated the idea of a gun being so close to his daughter, the idea of a three-year-old being completely defenseless against an unseen threat frightened him even more. "Don't let her out of your sight."

"I won't."

"Right this way, gentlemen." The office door opened before Miranda and Fiona reached it. Elise Brown, who'd interrupted her visit with her parents to come in this morning, made Quinn think this was any other day at the GSS offices—for a moment. The last few days had left his brain in perpetual turmoil— solving riddles, being stymied by Miranda's sexy quirks and, unpredictability, protecting his daughter. Elise's stylish suit, cordial smile and efficient manner added a touch of normalcy to the room that Quinn needed in order to deal with a man like Titov. Nikolai and two of his associates came in, and Elise gestured to the seating area in the middle of the office suite. "Make yourselves comfortable wherever you like."

Quinn was shaking hands and being introduced to Nikolai's accountant and a Lukinburger stock analyst when a dark-haired dynamo dashed back into the room.

"Petwa!" Fiona darted through the middle

of the gathering to retrieve her doll from the box of toys where they'd been playing.

"Sorry, sir," Miranda apologized from the doorway. "We forgot her sidekick."

"She doesn't go anywhere without Petra. Her mother made it for her when she was born." Quinn passed his hand over the silky crown of Fiona's dark waves as she zigzagged back through the towers of amused adults in her path.

Before she reached Miranda, Nikolai Titov picked Fiona up in his arms. Quinn was more startled than his daughter seemed to be, but Louis's calming hand on his arm stopped him from taking more than half a step toward them. Miranda was moving right up behind Titov. Quinn still had her in his sight. Despite the emotional jolt that quickened his heart rate, logically he knew his daughter was safe.

"What a beauty you are." Nikolai offered Fiona a fatherly sort of smile as he tucked a curl behind the little girl's ear. His accented voice trilled the *r*'s and punctuated each consonant. "She looks so like your Valeska, does she not, Quinn?"

Quinn met the sincere appreciation in Nikolai's gaze and nodded. Had it been that long since he and Nikolai had met face-to-face?

That last dinner together on the Plaza, when Val had been pregnant with Fiona? No wonder Louis was worried about Titov and his foreign investors losing faith in GSS.

"Fortunately, Fiona takes after the better-looking parent."

Fiona poked at Nikolai's silver-and-black goatee. "Are you a gwandpa?"

"No. Unfortunately, I never will be. I have no children." He gave her a noisy kiss on the cheek.

Everyone in the room laughed except for Miranda, who lifted Fiona from Nikolai's arms and caught her by the hand. "She gets her smarts and curiosity from her father." Her warm smile included each of the guests in the room. "You all have business to discuss, so we'll, um, go do some exploring."

Quinn wondered at the lack of a smile when her eyes reached him. The double shifting of her gaze toward the door sent a clearer message, however. "Excuse me a moment, gentlemen. Elise? If you'd be so good as to pour our guests some coffee?"

"Of course. Mr. Titov…" Elise took over the meeting for a moment as Quinn slipped away to meet Miranda at the door.

"What is it?" he asked in a whisper.

Miranda pulled her ponytail from the front of her shoulder and flicked it down the middle of her back. She answered in an equally hushed yet urgent voice. "Mr. Titov's *accountant* is wearing a gun in an ankle holster."

An armed man in his office? Quinn stiffened his neck against the impulse to turn and confirm her observation. But the more rational side of his brain wouldn't let him panic. "He wouldn't be the first wealthy man to hire a bodyguard."

Her eyes blanched wide as she remembered her own position, then narrowed. "Once we're out of here, I'm calling Mr. Damiani down in the security office to make sure he checked these guys out thoroughly."

"Get her out of here." Quinn hurried them out the door and readied to close it behind them. "Don't stray too far," he called after them for the benefit of the others in the room.

He appreciated her firm grip on Fiona. "We won't."

Quinn adjusted his glasses at the temple, giving himself a moment to blank the suspicion from his face before returning to his guests. Putting out fires with a primary investor was not how he wanted to be spending the day. But Nikolai Titov was worth millions to

GSS. And he'd only be separated from Fiona for the ten minutes it took to reassure him of his importance to the company.

"Nikolai, please." He strolled back to the center of the room, positioning himself to verify the gun on the beefy accountant's leg, and to see if he could spot whether anyone else was armed. "You've been on a flight for twenty hours. Sit and relax. We have plenty of time to talk." He smiled as Elise carried a tray of coffee cups and a pot to the long table between the sofas. "You remember my executive assistant, Elise, don't you?"

"Yes." Nikolai actually took the tray and set it down for her. "You are looking as beautiful as ever, is she not, Quinn?"

Huh? Oh, yeah. Elise was a pretty woman. Talented. Skilled. Loyal. But she was, well, Elise. He'd never thought of her as anything but the boon she was to the company. She'd worked for him for ten years now. Elise he understood. Quinn's gaze slid over to the door Miranda had just exited. Understanding that one, on the other hand…?

"Thank you, Mr. Titov." Elise was blushing under the continental charm of their guest. "Well, if you need anything else…"

Nikolai frowned as she handed him the

china cup and saucer. "You are not joining us for the meeting, Miss Brown?"

"Quinn?"

What the hell? Was Nikolai thinking of stealing his top assistant? Or did he just have a thing for brunettes? He had no reason to question Elise's loyalty. And since she was privy to pretty much everything at the company, anyway... "That's fine with me." Perhaps Louis was right, and he needed to give their guests his full attention in order to stave off a different sort of threat to everything he'd built. Quinn refused a cup of coffee for himself and gestured to the sofas and chairs. "Please. Have a seat."

"How was your holiday?" Elise asked, joining Nikolai on the sofa across from the men who'd accompanied him from Lukinburg.

Nikolai sipped his coffee and sighed. "I cannot celebrate at a time like this."

"What's wrong, Mr. Titov?" she asked.

"Nikolai, please."

Quinn went to the window and looked out at the snowy white landscape, and the airport control tower and hotels on the horizon. "You should have called before flying all the way to the States, Nikolai."

"This cannot wait. I do not like what I am hearing, half a world away."

"What are you hearing in St. Feodor?" Louis asked.

Quinn heard the rattle of a cup and saucer behind him, and saw Nikolai's reflection in the window as he approached. "I heard about the Kalahari plant being destroyed. Is it the work of terrorists?"

"No way to know yet. No factions I know of have taken credit for it."

"I gave you a million dollars for that and pledged ten more. We were going to make military-grade drones. And now we have nothing."

"My insurance will cover your lost investment, Nikolai."

"But what about the future profit I have lost? Who will pay the millions you promised me?"

Quinn slipped his hands into the pockets of his slacks and faced the shorter man. "Other than the tragic loss of life in the explosion and fire, this is something GSS will recover from."

"But when?" Nikolai pointed a stubby finger at Quinn's chin. "If you do not get that plant up and running soon, my investors in Lukinburg will be very disappointed." He dropped his voice to a whisper. "And these are not the type of men you want to disappoint."

Did that explain the armed accountant? Had Nikolai received some sort of threat, as well?

Quinn shook his head and turned away, flattening his palm against the cool glass, struggling to maintain an equally cool, unemotional facade when everything inside him was arguing to end this discussion and get back to the work of tracking down the enemy who wanted to destroy him.

"It's not like I can get the plant up and running again in a matter of days. Or even weeks." The glimmer of an idea popped into his head. Days. Time line. *Make it right.* Had he offended somebody? Shortchanged anyone by green-lighting the Kalahari project? *Do I have your attention now?* Why wouldn't destroying the plant be enough? Why come after his daughter? Why not just ask for more money?

Maybe it was just the countdown to New Year's weighing on his mind and getting mixed up with Nikolai's visit that made him think he was onto finding an answer here.

A little of that frustration crept into Quinn's voice. "Whoever planted those bombs razed it to the ground. We're talking about months of rebuilding."

"My partners in Lukinburg were expecting to see results in a few months." The strain of remaining civil raised the volume in Nikolai's voice. "Now we are talking about delaying profits for a year or more."

"You knew the risks."

Louis joined them at the window and tried to play peacemaker. "Nikolai, your investors aren't the only ones who lost money. Some of us here at GSS put our own funds into that project. We took a hit, too."

"Then I have a solution for you, Mr. Nolan." But Nikolai's answer was aimed squarely at Quinn. "The GSS plant in St. Feodor that you closed last year. Move the drone-assembly operation there. The building and assembly lines are still in place. We have the rail lines and a small airport nearby. It could work."

"We closed the St. Feodor plant because it was too small. And the cost for refitting it for a new product—"

"—would be offset because you would not have to rebuild the entire facility. And you know we have the skilled workers there." Nikolai must have been planning this speech all the way from Lukinburg. "Many are still out of work since the plant closed. I think I could convince my investors to put up the money again if they know they are investing in the benefit of their homeland."

Ten minutes and making nice was done. "I'll consider it, Nikolai. But just now I have another issue that is quite urgent I must attend to. Let me call you after the New Year. Perhaps Louis could take a trip to Lukinburg to look over the condition of the plant and discuss it further." He nodded toward Elise, who could read him well enough to know when he wanted to end a meeting and began ushering their guests toward the door. "He could take my assistant with him."

Elise and Nikolai made some eye contact at the door. To Quinn's surprise, but apparently to Elise's pleasure, Nikolai raised her knuckles to his lips and kissed her hand. "That would be most agreeable."

"I'd look forward to it," Elise agreed.

Nikolai released her to hold a hand out to Quinn. "Do not wait too long, my friend. The investors I speak of are not patient men."

The questionable nature of some of Titov's investors had been another reason to close the St. Feodor plant. But Quinn didn't have the time, nor was he in the right frame of mind, to bring up that topic or make any major business decisions right now.

He was reaching out to shake Nikolai's hand when the elevator doors opened on the far side of Elise's office and David Damiani came charging out. "Quinn? Quinn!"

"What the...?"

David was a linebacker, running straight at the quarterback. "I couldn't risk calling your cell. We need to evacuate the building."

"What's wrong?"

Going on instant alert, Quinn wondered if Miranda would hear the shouting or feel the tension multiplying on the top floor. Was she drawing her gun? Getting Fiona as far away from the security chief's alarm as she could?

"Everyone needs to turn off their cell phones. Landlines only if you need to make a call." The big man pushed past their guests, and ran to Quinn's desk. "Have you checked your emails? We need to get these people out of here."

"David. Answers. Now."

"We've been monitoring all computer activity since that...glitch yesterday." David flipped on the computer and pulled Quinn behind the desk, urging him to type in his password and pull up his files. "Phones off?" he prompted to the others in the room.

One by one, everyone but Elise pulled out cell phones and complied. "Mine's in my purse at my desk," she said.

"Get it," David ordered.

"Quinn?" Miranda shouted from the hallway.

David saw her at the elevator now, too. "Elise, tell the nanny to turn off her phone."

"Ah, hell." Quinn looked through the glass walls of his office. No, no, no, no, no. Miranda was running toward them. She had her phone in one hand and Fiona in the other. "David, talk to me."

"Here." David highlighted an email and opened it. He turned the monitor to Quinn and pointed to the screen. "Ozzie Chang found this encrypted in the system. I verified it myself and evacuated the lab."

Quinn frowned. "What's Ozzie doing here? I told him to take a vacation."

"Does it matter?" David tapped the monitor. "Look."

"Son of a bitch."

Another day of this nightmare. Another threat.

As promised, the message was a hauntingly

clear photo of the GSS computer lab. And the open briefcase with the wires and timer and C-4 sitting on the table in the middle of the lab had nothing to do with computers at all. The picture was framed by a rotating word stream that read, *See? I can get to everything that belongs to you. Make it right. Tick. Tock. Tick. Tock...*

"Make it...?" The blood in Quinn's brain drained to his toes before adrenaline pumped his heart into overtime. "What the hell do you want from me?" He swung around to the others. "There's a bomb in the building. Everybody out of here! Now!"

"That's the same picture I saw when I was talking to my brother."

"Damn it, Miranda." She was right beside him, looking at the same picture, reading the same threat. "Your job is to protect my daughter. Get out of here."

"I sent her with Elise. She'll be safe. That's enough plastique to take out a couple of floors." She picked up the corded telephone on Quinn's desk. "Damiani, take those people down the stairs. We can't risk anyone getting stuck in the elevator. Is there anyone else in the building?"

"Sir?" David was questioning who was in charge here.

Quinn plucked the phone from Miranda's fingers and handed it to David as he pushed her toward the door. "You stay with my daughter."

With a twist of her body, she freed her arm from Quinn's grasp and hurried back to the desk. "Get real, Quinn. This is exactly the type of situation I'm trained for. *You* need to get out of here with Fiona and let me work." She turned to David. "Is everyone out of the building?" she repeated.

The big man nodded. "Every person who signed in at the front desk has been accounted for now. There's hardly anyone here over the holidays, but I've got my men doing a floor-by-floor search, just in case."

"Have you called the police?"

"Already spoke to your friend Cutler. His team is on the way. Local cops are clearing a perimeter around the nearby businesses."

She picked up the phone again and punched in a number. "Where is the lab located?" she asked.

"Fourth floor," David answered.

Her call picked up. "Yes, sir, this is Murdock. I'm at GSS headquarters now." Michael

Cutler must be on the line. She was all business, all focus now, as she pointed to the computer screen. "Can we print this out?"

David hit the print command while *Officer* Murdock answered another question. "Nine souls on the top floor." She stretched over the desk to see through the glass wall. "Four men, a woman and a child are coming down the northeast stairwell."

Quinn remained a step behind her, unheeded, fuming. "What about Fiona?"

"You don't think I can do more good for her dealing with the bomb than holding her hand?"

"What if that bomb's a dummy and this is all a ruse to get Fiona outside, unprotected?"

She glanced up at David. He muttered a curse and shook his head, understanding the silent request. "My job is to protect this man and this company."

As much as Quinn wanted Miranda out of here with Fiona, he knew what needed to be done. He motioned David to the door. "Your job is to do what I say. She's right."

"I don't like leaving you up here."

"We'll be right behind you in a few minutes. I won't have any other deaths on my conscience. My daughter is your top priority. Get her someplace safe. Go."

"Don't let Dirty Harriet here screw up our protocols. If I don't see you outside in fifteen minutes, I'm coming back in."

As far as Quinn could tell, security was already screwed up if someone had gotten inside GSS to place a bomb. The idea that anyone could get past all the systems he'd invented and put to use smacked of an inside job. But with the clock ticking and people in danger, he didn't have the luxury of speculation right now. With a nod from his boss, the security chief, David, hustled out the door as quickly as he'd barged in.

Quinn pulled the photo from the printer and tried to make out the bomb's schematics while Miranda glared at him across the desk. "You should go, too."

"You stay," he challenged, "I stay."

All at once her posture changed. She was talking on the phone again. "No. I can't, sir." She squeezed her eyes shut and mouthed a curse. "My gear's in my truck, back at the estate. I rode in with Quinn and Fiona. All I have on me is my sidearm."

"Miranda?"

"But—" Whatever Michael Cutler was

saying transformed the bullheaded cop into a woman far less sure of herself. "Understood, sir. Yes, I will. Murdock out."

She hung up the phone. "Captain Cutler will be here in ten minutes to take charge of the scene. He wants the building clear by that time, too. In the meantime, I don't suppose you have an extra flak vest lying around?"

"Come with me." Quinn reached across the desk and grabbed her hand, pulling her into a jog out the door with him. Finally, something he had an answer for. "GSS makes them." A few seconds later, he unlocked a storage closet beside the break room and shoved aside a box marked Gas Masks and one labeled Flash Bangs before opening a third crate and pulling out two vests. "We keep samples of these and other nonlethal products in the building. We use them as visual aids in our sales presentations."

"I can only wear one."

"I'm coming with you." He pulled off his jacket and tie and strapped on the vest. "I'm guessing Michael told you to get the hell out of the building, and you plan to go take a look at that bomb, anyway, before you leave."

At least she didn't bother denying her intent. She secured the Velcro straps beneath each arm, then checked her gun to make sure she could still easily access it with the vest on. "I need to get eyes on that device so I can describe it to the bomb squad when they arrive. Why are you still here?"

She ran to the stairwell and Quinn chased after her. "I'm the bomb squad."

"What?" She stopped in her tracks on the stairwell's concrete landing, and Quinn plowed into her back. He got a brief imprint of sleek curves and heat against his harder thighs before he grabbed her arms and pulled her back from the steel railing. She turned to face him. "You think you're going to defuse that bomb?"

"I build bomb components in one of my GSS divisions. I've designed half the electronics in that picture myself. Chances are I can defuse it before any of KCPD's experts can get here."

Miranda's hand came to the middle of his chest and pushed him back to arm's length. "We are not leaving this to chance."

He leaned forward, pressing into her hand. "I'm not arguing with you on this."

"Rule 2 of my job is to get eyes on the threat. As officer on the scene, that's *my* responsibility." She slid her hand up the vest and cupped his cheek. "Rule 1 is to protect civilians and prevent casualties. You need to be outside, out of harm's way."

Quinn reached up to cover her hand with his, wondering if she was aware of just how much concern was shining from her eyes, and just how afraid he was for her and Fiona, in return. "*My* building. *My* people. I'm the captain of this ship. You don't think I can do more good for my daughter dealing with the bomb than holding her hand?" Her eyes widened when he threw her own words back at her. He leaned in, stopping up her protest with a quick kiss to ease the sting and trade a bit of reassurance. Now to toss some infallible logic into a debate he refused to lose. "Do you know where the lab is located?"

"Fourth floor. I can find it on my own. You need to leave."

"Do you know the code to get inside?"

With a sigh of resignation and a squeeze of his hand, she pulled away. "Fine. Lead the way, Captain."

Chapter Nine

Miranda clipped the spare radio Sergeant Rafe Delgado had brought her from the SWAT van to her collar, and adjusted the earpiece before testing it. "Captain Cutler, this is Murdock. Can you hear me?"

Michael Cutler's voice buzzed over the connection. "Loud and clear, Murdock. Now give me eyes on what you're seeing."

She went back into the sterile white computer lab to find both Quinn and the sergeant examining the briefcase bomb with flashlights and an assortment of tools. A lump of worry caught in her throat to see the contrasts between the two men. Rafe, the team's explosives expert, was suited up from head to toe in protective armor. But Quinn had only whatever protection the flak vest and his tailored wool trousers could provide. He wasn't wearing a helmet. Heck, he wasn't even wearing his glasses. Instead, they lay on the tabletop beside the case while he leaned over, his face mere inches from the bomb itself.

But none of that was what the captain wanted to hear. She swallowed the lump and relied on her training to get her through this. "Sarge and Mr. Gallagher think they can disarm it. They're removing the firing pins from the C-4 blocks." She moved in close enough to look over Quinn's shoulder. "I think the trick is going to be removing the firing mechanisms from the briefcase itself. It's tangled up pretty good in there, with several redundant systems. They're going through them one by one, but the timer's down to—" she read the thin red numbers counting down on the digital clock in a beat more steady than her own heart "—seventeen minutes. Even an accidental connection with the electrical current might set off a chain reaction that could still blow everything."

"Are we all clear on the time?" the captain asked, including the rest of the team. "Everyone is out of the building in fifteen minutes. No exceptions."

"Captain?" Rafe tapped his mike and added to the report. "I can safely remove about half of the C-4 without disturbing anything. But if Gallagher can't turn this off, there'll still be enough explosive left to take out this room. I recommend bringing in the box."

"Roger that." The "box" was a heavily reinforced metal container with specially designed baffles inside. It was used to detonate a theoretically controlled explosion so that no shrapnel would be thrown out to cause injury or damage. Still, an explosion was an explosion, a wild mess of forced air and flying debris, a potentially deadly risk to everyone in the area. The captain called another member of the team. "Trip, what's your twenty?"

Trip Jones's deep voice came over the line. "Ninth-floor stairwell. The floors above me are clear. No sign of another bomb or any civilians or suspects in the building."

"Roger that. Continue your search." Captain Cutler wasted neither time nor words to keep his team moving in its symbiotic fashion. "Taylor, what's your twenty?"

Alex Taylor chimed in. "Third floor, working my way down, sir. Three through six are clear."

"All right, Murdock, I'm putting you to work."

Miranda snapped to attention at her captain's summons.

"I need you to leave your position and take over the search of the last two floors."

"Yes, sir."

"Here. Take this." Rafe handed her his big metal flashlight, then pulled a smaller spare from one of the pockets in his utility vest and stuck it between his teeth to free up his hands.

"Thanks, Sarge."

While she pulled her gun and checked the clip, the sergeant opened the carryall bag he'd brought with him and started gently packing the blocks of C-4 he could safely remove.

Captain Cutler was still issuing directions from the command center in the van. "Taylor, you're with me right now. I need you to take the box in to Sergeant Delgado."

"Roger that. Taylor out."

Quinn's steady voice sounded behind her. "Cutting the blue wire in three, two, one…"

Miranda held her breath and heard the tiny snip. No boom. Always a good sign. She exhaled and headed for the door. "You two okay here?"

"Wait." She glanced back as Quinn put on his glasses and straightened. His laser-blue gaze reached her clear across the room and jolted through her. "Check on my daughter again."

She nodded and tapped her radio, beginning to understand the depths of how much a father could love his child, and just how much he would risk to keep her safe. "Captain? Do you have eyes on Fiona Gallagher?"

"She's right here in the van with me and Elise Brown." He chuckled, a rare sound. "I gave her a walkie-talkie without batteries to play with, and she's running her own op, copying nearly everything I say. Tell Quinn not to worry. She's occupied."

"Thank you, sir. Murdock out." She never took her eyes off Quinn. "Fiona's with the captain. She's just fine. I'll check her myself once I get out there, and radio in to the sergeant."

"Be safe," Quinn warned.

Miranda smiled. "Don't either of you blow up."

And then she was out the door and down the stairs to the second floor. The offices were smaller and more numerous here, belonging to paper pushers rather than researchers or executives. Leading with her flashlight and gun, hand over fist, she moved quickly along each hallway, meticulously checking in each and every door on the floor. She nudged open the door to the stairwell landing, looking up and down before venturing out. "Second floor clear."

She made her way down to the first floor, tuning out most of the chatter on her headset. "KCPD," she announced with each new room she entered. Door open, light on, check behind desk, look inside closet. Close doors and move on. She ignored Christmas trees and Hanukkah decorations, paid little heed to whether the decor of each space was flashy or homey or modern. She was simply searching for bombs and bodies and hidden bad guys, making sure the citizens of Kansas City were out of harm's way.

She was doing her job, doing it well.

Until one of the captain's commands resonated loudly in her ear. "Kincaid, you're my eyes in the sky. Have you spotted anyone showing a particular interest in what's going on?"

Miranda pulled up short behind the reception desk in the GSS lobby. Eye in the sky. That was codespeak for when the sniper on the team found a high vantage point where she could take a clean shot or provide intel as needed for the rest of the team. *That* was *her* job. And Holden Kincaid was doing it.

You're not good enough.

The team can get the job done without you.
They don't really need you.

"Shut up." Miranda silently cursed that voice denigrating her in her head. She still had the same badge, the same skills she'd possessed when she joined SWAT. Had she been blind to her shortcomings before the RGK's blitz attack? Or had something in her truly changed that day?

"Murdock?" the captain questioned.

Oh, hell. Her mike was on. "Nothing, sir." *Shake it off.* She literally shook her ponytail down her back and straightened her shoulders. "First floor clear."

"We've got your usual looky-loos, press vans and reporters lined up on the outer road leading to the interstate. It's pretty wide-open countryside to the west and south of the building." Holden Kincaid was back on the line. "Wait. I've got a black car parked in front of that trucking company about half a mile to the north beyond the cordoned-off perimeter. I count three men inside. They're separated from the rest of the crowd."

Black car? A different voice spoke inside Miranda's head. "Can you make out the plate number?" she asked.

Holden must be adjusting his binoculars because several seconds passed before he rattled it off.

Captain Cutler recognized the license number as soon as Miranda did. "The first three digits match the plate of that car with the camera creep outside Quinn's estate."

She remembered the name on the car rental agreement, too. It was the second black BMW an Alex Mostek had taken from one of the airport rental places. A man was entitled to like a certain kind of car, but she wasn't buying the coincidence of the same cars showing up near Quinn at two different locations three times in the same week, either.

Thank God he wasn't on a radio to hear of the suspect in the area. Quinn was working with enough C-4 to kill him, Sergeant Delgado and maybe the two other SWAT cops in the building if he got distracted and made a mistake.

The need to do her part to put an end to this nightmare got her moving. "I'm checking it out."

She was reluctantly grateful for Holden's next report. "Be advised you need to use the east exit and stick to the parking lots or he'll see you coming."

"Roger that."

Captain Cutler, of course, always had the last word. "We've got five minutes until I want that building clear, and I expect a roll call from every one of you, so make it fast."

"Yes, sir." Miranda raced to the side door leading out into the parking lot and pocketed the flashlight before stepping outside. A brisk wind chapped her cheeks, reminding her that her winter coat was still upstairs in Quinn's office. But five minutes, twelve flights of stairs and their first real lead on whoever was behind the threats to Fiona, Quinn and GSS forced her to ignore the cold and hunker down a bit to move forward at a good pace along the side of the building.

Once she left the shade of the building, she had to squint against the afternoon sunlight reflecting off the snowy hills around her. Once her eyes had adjusted to the brightness outside, she covered the distance across the parking lot and ran along the fenced lots between GSS and the next set of buildings in this industrial-park area. Her boots kept her feet warm and dry as she crunched through the snow, but her jeans were soaking in the moist cold and chilling the skin around her knees and calves.

"You're headed right for them," Holden

advised. He was probably on the roof of one of these buildings already. "If you circle the truck company offices—the yellow brick facade—you'll come up on the car's backside."

"Roger that."

The cold was making her fingers stiff and she wished she'd at least stopped by the SWAT van to bag a pair of gloves. But determination was fueling her and the clock was ticking. If she could find out who was in the car, she might be able to put a stop to this dangerous game. She could protect the Gallaghers the way she knew how and prove to herself that she still had the mojo she needed to make it as a SWAT cop.

"Kincaid, I want you on the ground now to provide backup," the captain ordered.

Miranda paused at the corner of the building and leaned back against the bricks. Great. Just what she needed—the man poised to replace her on the team swooping down to save the day because Cutler didn't think she could do the job herself. While the rational part of her knew SWAT was all about teamwork, that raw need to prove she was worthy tried to get inside her head again.

She gritted her teeth to silence the voices of

doubt and tried to fill her head with images of the dark-haired little girl who was depending on her, and the dark-haired father who was risking his own life to take a bomb apart so they could all be safe. Flexing her fingers around the grip of her Glock, Miranda took in one last steadying breath, nodded her own readiness and spun around the corner.

She spotted the target vehicle almost immediately and darted between the semitruck trailers parked on the outer road behind it. She peeked out the far side to make sure she was in the car's blind spot and then crept up behind it, sticking close to the trucks and bending her legs to keep herself low to the ground. The plume of exhaust coming from the tailpipe told her the engine was running.

Were they curiosity seekers just trying to stay warm? Or was someone much more sinister preparing to make a quick getaway after seeing the results of his handiwork? Either way, she doubted Quinn would appreciate the obsession with him and his company.

"The briefcase is in the box," Sergeant Delgado reported in her ear. "Quinn got it down to a safer payload. We're moving it outside now to blow it."

"The parking lot is clear." The captain indicated they should bring the reinforced bomb box out to the deserted parking lot east of the building. "SWAT 1, sound off your twenty."

One by one, they reported by rank, ensuring every man on the team was safely accounted for before detonation. "Delgado, first floor. Exiting the building now."

"Jones, north entrance. Civilians are clear of the blast zone."

"Taylor, exiting the building now. Gallagher's with us."

Miranda opened her mouth to report in last, but another voice beat her to it.

"Kincaid. North of GSS, approaching Murdock on her three."

Was she part of this team or not?

"Murdock?" the captain prompted.

"Murdock here," she whispered, feeling her confidence sink like a stone. Maybe she should be grateful the captain had included her at all. *Keep it together.* This time she kept her voice low, since the wind would blow the sound straight at the car she was approaching. "I'm twenty yards behind the black car. Two men in the front seat. One in the back. I'm going in to get a look."

Determined to ignore Holden Kincaid's imminent arrival and deal with the potential threat herself, Miranda moved up onto the asphalt behind the car and silently angled herself around to get a look in the open window before she was spotted in one of the mirrors. Closer, closer. The man in the backseat was leaning toward the half-open window, clearly intent on the SWAT van, yellow cordon tape and news reporters and cameras gathered around the GSS building.

She quickly processed the details. Gray hair. Gaunt features. Curly gray beard. For a split second she envisioned an older, shaggier version of Nikolai Titov. But the man turned and saw her. Pale eyes. Not Nikolai.

"KCPD," she announced. "I need you to step out of the car. I just need to question you. Do it now."

The man thumped the seat in front of him and shouted in a foreign language. His window went up as the front window went down and a hand came out.

"Gun!" she shouted.

The car shifted into gear as the driver popped off two rounds in Miranda's direction. The engine growled and the back tires spun on the wet pavement.

Miranda quickly aimed as the car lurched forward. Her first shot took off the driver's side mirror. The front wheels found traction and the car fishtailed into a U-turn.

"Murdock!"

She stood her ground in the middle of the road and took out the right headlight. The passenger-side window went down and a second gun came out. She heard men shouting gibberish from the car—to her? To each other?—in a language she didn't understand.

More bullets peppered the pavement at her feet.

Miranda aimed for the front tire.

"Fire in the hole!"

The command in her ear distracted her for a split second and her shot pinged off the bumper.

The car picked up speed.

"Murdock! Move!"

Boom! The muffled report of the exploding box thundered through the cold air and shivered right down her spine. "Quinn?"

He'd better have been clear of that bomb.

"Murdock!" Holden Kincaid's voice dragged her back to the black car barreling toward her.

She raised her gun. But it was too close. It was too late to get off the shot.

The heat from the engine glanced off her

body as she leaped out of the way. She landed hip first in the snow and rolled down into the ditch as the BMW blew past her. Pain burned along her forearm and throbbed in her knees and elbow by the time she cracked the ice at the bottom of the ditch and crashed to a stop.

Miranda heard two more shots, but they hadn't come from her. Somewhere in that roll down the hill, she'd lost her earpiece and weapon. The world of snow, trash and dead field grass reeled through her spinning vision as she pushed herself up to her hands and knees. And then two large hands were helping her to her feet and dragging her up to the road.

"Crazy lady." Holden Kincaid sat her down on the pavement and knelt in front of her "Cutler said you were fearless."

"Huh?" She blinked several times and breathed in the cold, crisp air, clearing her head and settling the queasy aftermath in her topsy-turvy stomach.

"Are you hit?" Kincaid's hands probed her arms and legs, searching for injuries.

"Ow!" Okay, so she must have scraped up her arm pretty good. But the vest had protected everything vital, and neither the bullets nor the car had actually struck her. "I'm fine."

Her cheek was burning now, too. Maybe that was just the cold, wet glop from the ditch clinging to her.

"How many fingers am I holding up?"

She pushed all three fingers away. "Enough to annoy me. Where's my gun?"

Holden put her Glock into her hand and then helped her to her feet. Miranda brushed aside any further assistance and surveyed the area. She didn't need to hear Holden reporting in to know the suspects were long gone. "The car got away, sir. Better call a bus. I think she's okay, but Murdock needs to be checked out." He covered his mike with a leather-gloved hand. "Can you walk?"

She batted his hand aside and stretched up on tiptoe to speak into his radio. "Cancel the ambulance, Captain. I'm scraped up, but I'm fine."

Holden grinned. "I'll take that as a yes. We're heading in, sir."

In a way, Holden Kincaid reminded Miranda a lot of her brother, John. Big man. Easy smile. Dry sense of humor. But she pressed her lips tight to hide the traitorous smile that wanted to answer him. She should not like this guy. He was the competition.

Besides, there was another man on her

mind. A handsome father who'd kissed her in the midst of danger, who'd stuck by her side despite every effort to isolate herself with the danger of the bomb. A man whose image had gotten inside her head when she should have been focused on the car that tried to run her down. "Is everyone okay?" she asked.

"If you mean the bomb, yeah. The threat is neutralized and everyone's safe." Holden gestured down the road, and she fell into step beside him as they rejoined the team at the van. "I think you're the only one we need to worry about."

Miranda wiped the moisture and mud off her gun with shaky, numbing fingers before holstering it at her back. She'd missed her shot, gotten a stupid minor injury and was being escorted back to command by her replacement. Quinn and Sergeant Delgado had taken care of the bomb. Captain Cutler and Quinn's assistant had taken care of Fiona.

She'd fallen into the snow and mud and let the suspects shooting at her get away.

Way to shine, Murdock. Way to shine.

MIRANDA WAS BLEEDING.

Quinn tried to concentrate on the debriefing with Michael and his team up in his office, but all his brain could see at the moment was the blood oozing from the scrape on her cheek. Trip Jones had cut off the shredded sleeve of her sweater and blouse and packed a pressure bandage on the long gash on her forearm and elbow. But there were still broken and muddy reeds of grass stuck in her hair, and the graze on her cheek was bleeding.

This was *his* building, *his* problem. The threats were against *him*—destroy his company, take his daughter. He should be the one getting hurt—no one else. If he had known Miranda was going to be playing chicken with cars and guns, he would have insisted she stay with Fiona in the SWAT van. He would have kept her in his sight while he and Rafe cut apart that bomb and detonated what was left of it outside the building. He would have…

…not done any of those things, he admitted. He'd hired Miranda Murdock specifically because she was a woman who could handle bombs and bad guys and guns. She could think on her feet. Hell, she could think clearly enough when the pressure was on that she still had the time and energy to argue with him. Even now, while she was shivering in her damp clothes, just thirty minutes after the bomb had been detonated and the mystery car had sped off to the interstate and disappeared, she was clear-eyed and contributing to the sharing of facts after the incident. Michael Cutler expected her to be tough. *He* expected her to be tough, or he never would have hired her.

But that was the logic in his head talking. Something else, closer to his heart, something primal that was almost painful to acknowledge, wanted to do something about her getting hurt.

"I got a good look at the man in the backseat," she said.

Michael sat on the sofa across from Miranda. "Good. I'll have you sit down with a sketch artist at the Fourth Precinct. Today, if possible."

"The sooner, the better," she insisted. "I don't want to forget anything."

"You said they were speaking a foreign language? Any idea what it was?"

She twisted her hands together, trying to hide the way she was shivering. "Russian, maybe? Slavic? Like I said, there was a lot of noise and distraction."

All these grown men around the room, treating her like she was one of the guys, like she was just as impervious to pain as they had to be. Quinn had never considered himself particularly chivalric, but it made good common sense to drape his suit jacket around her shoulders to add an extra layer of warmth. He ignored her startled "Thank you." But he could feel the verdant gaze that tilted up and followed him all the way across the room to the bar sink where he wet a couple of paper towels with cool water.

Fiona was there in the kitchenette area at her little table and chairs, playing happily away with the walkie-talkie Michael had given her. "Woger that," she spoke into the mouthpiece, then held it up to Petra's ear, fortunately oblivious to the details of the adults' conversation and just what kind of danger she'd been in. "Mudock out."

Inwardly, he smiled. He was pretty fascinated by the nanny, too. Outwardly? He tried to keep it all cool, calm and collected. But he was quickly failing. He couldn't keep his eyes off the wound or her hair or the vulnerable extra tilt of her chin as she continued to answer questions.

Miranda clutched the jacket together at her neck when he returned. Seeing her in his coat, on his furniture, in his office—especially with other men in the room—tapped into something slightly more possessive than protective, and eased some of that raw, unsettling need to take care of her. Quinn perched on the edge of the sofa beside her. "Here." He dabbed away some of the mud and grit from around the scrape on her cheek, then pressed it against the seeping wound. "Did the men sound like Nikolai Titov?" he asked.

She hissed a breath of pain through her teeth before answering. "It was similar. I didn't understand what he and his associates were saying when they spoke in their native language here, either." Still stubbornly showing that streak of independence, she took the towels from his fingers and held them against her cheek herself. She turned the rest of her answer back to Michael. "Mr. Titov isn't the man I saw."

But Michael was looking at Quinn. "Where are Titov and his associates now?"

"I don't know. Once David came in, my only concern was the bomb and getting Fiona and the others out of the building. Where they went after that…?"

Quinn didn't realize that Elise had been tracking his movements across the office, too, until he caught her watching him with a curious frown from across the coffee table.

She quickly looked away and crossed to where David Damiani stood near Quinn's desk. "They're gone. Nikolai took off with Louis pretty much as soon as David got us outside. I'm assuming he took them to their hotel. Would you like me to find out where they're staying?"

"Please," Michael answered. He gestured to Holden Kincaid, who opened the door for Elise and followed her out to her office.

Odd that Titov and his men had skipped out so quickly. Quinn had been certain that they'd had more argument to give about reopening the St. Feodor plant. Maybe, with their Eastern European background, they were cautious about the gathering of reporters outside, and being associated with any kind of attack that could be construed as a terrorist event.

Quinn was still thinking about the curious timing of men with foreign accents watching the building in crisis and shooting at Miranda, and the unexpected visit from Titov, when Rafe Delgado handed Michael a copy of the email Miranda had printed out. "We've got this photo and message about the bomb. But who was the first person to find the device? To actually put eyes on it? You, Quinn?"

David straightened from the back of the

couch where he'd been sitting. "I can answer that." He circled around the end of the couch to face the senior officer. "Ozzie Chang, one of our computer geeks, found the email and called me in. I went into the lab myself and discovered it shortly after noon. That's when I called 911 and ordered the building evacuation."

"Where was Ozzie?" Quinn asked, rising to his feet. "He wasn't supposed to be working in the lab today."

David shook his head. "He was in his office when he called me."

"He called you because of the email, not because he'd found the bomb itself?"

"I guess." David's square jaw clenched before he cursed. "You think he could have put it there?"

"I'm not accusing one of my own people. With the holidays and a nearly deserted building, someone with the right skills could get inside." Although Quinn couldn't fathom how an outsider could get into one of GSS's most secure rooms, he didn't want to think that the easiest answer was that someone he knew and trusted was behind these threats. Still, Ozzie did have the know-how to hack into GSS from a remote location. The question was why. "I'm just trying to make sense of something that doesn't make sense to me. He did come in to help me yesterday, but I sent him on vacation for the rest of the week. What was he doing here?"

Miranda huddled inside his jacket as she stood beside Quinn. "Does Ozzie know how to build a bomb?"

"I hire very smart people to work for me. Anything's possible." He still wasn't buying it. "But what's his motive?"

"Two and a half million dollars?" David suggested.

"The money's already been paid. Why risk killing more innocent people and doing millions of dollars' worth of damage?"

"Maybe he was covering his tracks."

Quinn raked his fingers through his hair and rubbed at the headache forming at the base of his skull. "This feels personal, not like it's about the money."

"I wouldn't write off the computer geek yet." David braced his hands at his hips and puffed up, refusing to have his idea dismissed. "There's one more thing, boss. Whoever put the bomb there used an authorized access code. Nothing was flagged to security when the door opened."

"Could that code be what the hacker was after?" Miranda asked.

"Or maybe Ozzie punched it in himself." David's point was made, even if Quinn didn't like the idea of a traitor working for him.

Michael Cutler stood and signaled to his men. "Taylor. Trip. Grab Kincaid and go find this Ozzie Chang. And let's get some detectives to look into his financials. Mr. Damiani, can you get us an address?"

"I can take you there myself." David nodded and headed out the door with the uniformed cops on his heels.

"Rafe and I will make sure your assistant and the three of you get home safely." SWAT Team 1 was on the move again. "Chang either saw that bomb and lied to your security chief, or someone used the code to get in after he left and we need him to narrow down the time frame when that could have happened—"

"—or Ozzie has a lot of explaining to do about his loyalty to me and GSS." Quinn was running through the same possibilities Michael was, and was ready to find some answers. He went to the kitchenette and scooped Fiona up into his arms.

Miranda was already gathering up their coats. "No matter what, I have a feeling there are a couple of detectives who'll want to question Ozzie."

"Forget the detectives." Quinn intended to take the women home and then accompany Michael and his men. "I want to talk to him myself."

"I AM ONE STEP AHEAD OF YOU, Quinn Gallagher." The figure sitting in the car laughed. The brilliant self-made man thought he could plan for every situation, that he could control every outcome with his brains or money or business savvy. "Look who has control now."

The child would have been so easy to take while the big boss of Gallagher Security Systems was playing hero. As suspected, Quinn wouldn't be able to resist tackling the bomb himself, once he recognized bits and pieces of his own designs all set into place to topple his empire. Quinn was the type of man to step up and take responsibility, to look out for those around him, to notice who needed him and who deserved his help.

He was a born leader, a consummate protector—in every single facet of his life and work. Except one.

And that one mistake, that one oversight—that one glaring example of Quinn Gallagher

not giving a damn about the right person—
was the reason for being here.

The figure sitting behind the wheel clutched
at the pain stabbing straight through the heart.
No one should have to suffer that kind of loss.
No one should have to feel that helpless—to
know everything one tried to get noticed, to
make things right, wasn't enough.

There was only one way to make things
right now.

Quinn Gallagher had to suffer in the very
same way.

Remembering the success of the day, the
driver sat up squarely behind the wheel.
Everyone was packing up now. Catching their breaths. Escorting people home.
Crisis averted. Now Quinn would go back
to his mansion and seclude himself with his
thoughts. He'd reflect on every misstep and
close call of the past four days, wondering
what he'd missed, whom he'd offended, where
he'd gone wrong. He thought he could fix this
if he surrounded himself with the right people
and thought about the game long enough and
hard enough.

It was a delight to watch him be confused,
angry—to watch the great Quinn Gallagher
not have all the answers.

There were so many delicious ways this afternoon could have gone. Property damage. Destruction of the GSS mainframe computer. Loss of lives. Losing the young life most important to Quinn.

But the timing wasn't right. The game had to be played a certain way, on a certain schedule—mimicking the time frame of the driver's own suffering—or the satisfaction that was so long overdue wouldn't be gratifying enough.

It was the only way to make things right.

Paying little heed to the police officers still working around the GSS building, the figure behind the wheel speed-dialed the mercenary who'd been paid very well to do exactly as ordered. "Is it done?"

"It's done."

"Good." The boss picked up the disposable phone on the dashboard and ripped open the package. "Then I'll send my next message."

Chapter Ten

"Did he have family?" Michael Cutler asked.

Quinn's eyes burned as he tore his gaze away from the neat bullet hole in the middle of Ozzie Chang's forehead and looked across the body on the floor to his friend. "Parents in San Francisco. I'd better call them."

"Let the detectives handle it." Michael braced his hands on his knees and pushed himself away from the puddle of blood on the entryway's hardwood floor. "Why don't you take Randy and Fiona home? You all need some rest."

"I can't rest until I find out who's behind this, Michael." He curled his fingers into fists at his side. "Ozzie was barely out of college. Those guards at the Kalahari plant had no clue what hit them. Men are watching my house and my daughter and shooting at Miranda. I need to figure this out. I need to get ahead of this guy and stop him." He raked his fingers through his hair in frustration and came back shaking another fist. "That's what I do, Michael. I find solutions to problems. I solve puzzles that other people can't. I figure things out."

"Don't beat yourself up, buddy." Michael literally took Quinn by the arm and led him to the front door. "That's part of what this guy wants from you. He wants you out of your element. He wants you to suffer."

"He's doing a damn fine job. My God..." A horrendous thought hit him, one that almost made him gag as he turned back to the grisly murder. "What if that was Fiona?" He sought out Michael's steady gaze, needing someone, anyone, to understand. "I will die—I will kill—before I let something like this happen to my little girl."

He circled around the body to look into the sparsely furnished living room of Ozzie's small white house. A beat-up sofa, a new recliner and a wall full of electronics— gaming systems, a large flat-screen TV, computer towers. Not a lot to show for twenty-some years of life. Yet Quinn had envied the young man just yesterday.

Ozzie Chang had been young and full of

fun and possibilities. He'd come in to GSS during his vacation at Quinn's request. A bullet to the head was his punishment for helping him.

Or was it his payment for helping someone else?

Quinn scrubbed his fingers over the five o'clock shadow on his jaw. "How soon before the detectives and CSIs get here and get us some answers?" The rage and grief cleared a small corner of his brain and gave him a chance to observe and think. "Oz must have known whoever he let in the door—or else didn't feel threatened by his killer. There's no sign of a struggle."

"Quinn—"

"Do you think the people who paid him to hack into GSS and deliver a bomb betrayed him to cover the connection to them? Didn't he know how much money I have? How much money I'd pay to ensure the safety of the people I care about?"

"You think Chang hacked your system? That he was a mole in your company?"

"It sure seems like somebody is." Quinn tamped down on the emotions raging through his blood and tried to present a logical argument. "Or is Ozzie the innocent kid I thought he was, and he stumbled onto something he shouldn't in the lab? He saw something in the computers, or he saw someone place that bomb—and now he's another innocent victim in this retribution game."

Betrayal or a friend caught in the cross fire? He didn't like either option.

Quinn faced Michael again, counting off options on his fingers. "I've been racking my brain, trying to come up with suspects—people who might hold a serious grudge against me. Mom's live-in boyfriend, who I threw out of the house once I was big enough and tough enough to get him to stop hitting her. Business competitors. I've absorbed several companies around the world into GSS and have put others completely out of business."

"Quinn, stop. You're grasping at straws."

"I have to grasp at something! I can't stand not being in control. I hate it."

"I know where you're coming from. When my Jillian had a stalker, before I married her, I was… When he had her tied up with a gun to her head, I…" Quinn saw the first crack of emotion in Michael's stern facade. "It was the first time in a long time that I was truly scared. And I didn't like it. It threw me off my game and I almost lost her." He swallowed hard, glanced away for a moment, then looked him right in the eyes. "You and I are a lot alike, my friend. The bad guys don't get to win. But you're in no shape to do battle right now. You're exhausted. Your anger is getting in the way. And this is not the place where you want to do your thinking." Michael went to the front door and opened it. "So go home and get some rest."

Quinn glanced down at the injustice of the body at their feet. "And give that bastard the chance to do this to somebody else because of me?"

"Think of it this way—a few hours' sleep will clear your mind so you *can* figure it out." Michael rarely talked about the man who had stalked and kidnapped his wife. The glimpse of deep, conflicted emotion from his normally unflappable friend made Quinn understand that Michael truly got what he was going through.

It also gave him hope that he could get through this crisis, too. As long as he kept his head. "I guess I'll wind up with a cranky toddler if I don't get Fiona to bed."

"And, I've entrusted you with one of my team, Quinn. Randy's not as tough on the inside as she is on the outside. I need you to take good care of her."

Quinn looked through the open doorway to see a battered Miranda standing guard over the car where his daughter slept. Her eyes were sharp as she paced up and down the sidewalk. But the mark on her face was already bruising, and she hugged her arms around her middle as she walked, as though not even the hat and coat she wore were enough to keep her warm.

Those same possessive, protective instincts he'd discovered in his office this afternoon heated his blood. Yeah, he could take care of Miranda, too. If she'd let him.

"All right." Maybe he could do more good for the cops, his company and those two women outside if he could get some rest and some rational thoughts in his head. He extended his hand to Michael to thank him for all he and his team had done for him today. "But call me the minute KCPD has anything to report."

"Will do."

"Captain?" Trip Jones called them back into the living room. "I pulled this up on Chang's computer. You're going to want to see this."

Quinn should have walked on out the door.

The words typed on the screen were in big, bold print. The taunting promise in the words was even bigger.

I am one step ahead of you. Now Mr. Chang will never reveal the favor he did for me. Now you see I can get to you at work. I will require another 2.5 million in the Swiss account or I will strike much closer to home.

"YOU GOT THIS, DAVID?" The pictures on the wall of monitors in the estate's security command center were blurring.

Quinn was a weary man. He pulled off his glasses and scrubbed his hand over his entire face, from his aching eyes down to the sandpapery stubble of late-night beard growth on his jaw.

"Yes, sir." David Damiani's tie was loose, his suit jacket was draped over the back of the chair beside Quinn's and his coffee mug was nearly empty. "Between my men at the gate and Cutler's men doing periodic drive-bys, as well as me in the security office and Murdock upstairs, we're completely secure. I've got eyes on the front door, back door, side entrance and more. If our presence and technology aren't deterrent enough, at least there's no way we won't see this guy coming."

Quinn slipped his glasses back on to get a good look at the camera shots where David was pointing. He knew David's ego had probably taken a few dings the past few days. GSS employees had been killed. A bomb had been rigged in GSS headquarters. Quinn had called on his friend Michael Cutler and SWAT Team 1 in addition to David's private security team—not because Quinn doubted David could handle the threats, but because Quinn could never feel secure enough where Fiona was concerned.

It was hard to fight an enemy you couldn't see or identify, and Quinn knew the situation would be even more impossible if his security chief wasn't on the payroll. "I appreciate you coming in to take charge of watching over the house tonight. I know it's not your primary responsibility, but—"

"*You* are my responsibility, sir. Without you, GSS falls apart." His big shoulders lifted with a shrug and a grin. "I'm thinking I'd be out of a job if something happened to you."

Quinn managed half a laugh at the wry humor. He motioned David to stay seated when he stood, then reached over to shake his hand. "Thanks. I'm turning in. If you need anything..."

"I won't. Good night, sir."

"Good night, David."

Quinn climbed the stairs to the main floor, taking note of every locked window and hallway camera in the silent house. Even though David had done the same an hour ago, Quinn checked the front door, the garage exit and mud room door before dragging his feet up the next set of carpeted stairs to the living quarters there.

More than the promise of his own bed and a few hours of sleep, the dim light shining into the hallway from Fiona's room drew him like a guiding beacon.

He paused in the doorway, leaned his head against the jamb and smiled at the scene inside. He wasn't the only one exhausted by the day.

Fiona sat in Miranda's lap in the rocking chair. Her cheek was smushed against Miranda's red pajama top, her bow-shaped mouth was slightly parted and her eyes were closed in sleep.

But what caught his heart and made him smile was the beautiful contrast of Miranda's golden hair hanging straight and loose and tangling with Fiona's dark curls. The book they'd been reading had fallen to the floor. Miranda's undamaged cheek rested against the crown of Fiona's hair and she was softly snoring right along with her.

Michael had charged him with taking care of both of these girls, but it was a task nobody had to ask of him. Feeling oddly energized and renewed by the endearing sight, despite the fatigue screaming from every cell of his body, Quinn tiptoed into the room. He picked up the book and set it aside, then slid his arms beneath Miranda's knees and around her back.

Miranda startled awake at his touch. "I should go..."

"Shh." Quinn whispered a reassurance and lifted them both from the chair. "Let me. Got her?"

Nodding, she tightened her arms around Fiona, who never stirred. With Miranda's help, he pulled back the covers and laid them both on the bed.

"She's content with you holding her." Quinn pulled the sheet and comforter up over them both and tucked them in. He caressed Fiona's hair, then bent to give her a kiss. "I don't want to wake her."

"I'll stay with her," Miranda promised,

gently stroking Fiona's dark hair off her rosy cheeks.

He stayed where he was, hovering over the bed. He mimicked the same tender gesture, brushing Miranda's hair, still damp from her shower, away from her bruised cheek. Her green eyes were hooded, drowsy, fixed on his as he leaned in to kiss her temple, as well. "Good night, Miranda."

But her hand snaked out from beneath the covers to capture his jaw and guide his mouth down to hers instead. He gladly obliged the bold request, covering her lips with his, parting them. He slipped his tongue inside for a taste of her heat. He welcomed the answering pull of her lips beneath his, braced his hand against the headboard and leaned over farther to angle his mouth more completely over hers. A slow, liquid warmth ignited in his chest and seeped into his blood, giving life to his tired body, reminding him he was a strong, healthy man. But the hour was late, and with his daughter here there was little he could do about the aching needs this woman kindled inside him.

So with a deep breath and a troubled heart, he pulled away. But as long as those beautiful eyes were on him, he couldn't completely retreat. He'd wanted Miranda to bond with his daughter, and she had. But he was forming a bond with her, too. Her fingers brushed across his jaw; her thumb stroked his lips. She blinked her eyes and smiled. "Good night, Quinn."

When her eyes blinked shut with fatigue and didn't open again, he finally moved away. He set the storybook back in its place on the bookshelf, turned off the lamp and headed for the door. But he couldn't leave.

Everything he loved—everything he wanted—everything that truly mattered was sleeping in that bed behind him.

Even with guards and cameras and the holstered gun on top of the bookshelf, he couldn't be sure they were safe. His bedroom at the end of the hall was too far away. With Fiona and Miranda out of his sight, he wouldn't be able to relax.

So he kicked off his shoes and settled into the rocking chair beside the bed to watch them sleep. He wasn't leaving Miranda and Fiona tonight, not even for a moment.

But after half an hour of dozing fits and starts, Quinn woke again. Even this chair was too far away to assuage his loneliness and his need to protect this makeshift family. In his mind, there was only one logical thing he could do.

He got up and circled the double bed, pulling off his belt and untucking his shirt. And then he climbed into bed with them, stretching out on top of the covers behind Miranda.

Her back and bottom fit perfectly against his chest and groin. When she nestled against him in her sleep, he buried his nose in Miranda's thick, damp hair, filling his head up with the smells of sweet coconut and tangy citrus. She was warmth and health and life and every good thing he wanted in this world.

Quinn wrapped his arms around both of them and finally drifted off to sleep.

Chapter Eleven

Miranda wiped Fiona's sticky fingers and held the chair while the little girl climbed down and hurried to the end of the table to get Petra down from her seat.

After popping the last uneaten bite of Fiona's peanut-butter sandwich into her mouth, Miranda carried her cup and plate to the sink, where she rinsed them and stacked them in the dishwasher. Two successful meals under her belt now without trashing the kitchen. She sincerely hoped Quinn didn't mind ordering take-out pizza for dinner because the cook wasn't scheduled to be back until after the New Year, and she'd already discovered a dearth of anything microwaveable in this house except for popcorn.

She wondered if the Marines would mind

if she called her brother again to get a recipe for dinner. Thinking of John and how amused he'd be at her quandary made her smile. "Probably not."

It was amazing how a little success in the nannying department, a fresh bandage for the cut on her forearm and a good night's sleep could refresh her energy and boost her confidence in her responsibilities here. Miranda had never considered herself a domestic-bliss kind of woman before, but waking up with an aroused man hugged tightly to her backside and a little girl sprawled with innocent abandon on the pillow next to hers gave her ideas about wanting to give the cooking and cleaning and "welcome home, honey" routine a try.

This morning, for the first time in months, she hadn't felt alone when she woke up. And it wasn't just the physical closeness of having an extra body in the bed. There was something incredibly sensuous and equally tender about waking with Quinn's hand splayed possessively on the flat of her stomach, then feeling his lips nuzzle the sensitive skin at her nape before he whispered, "Good morning."

"Good morning. Sleep well?"

The sandpapery stubble of his beard was like the caress of a cat's tongue when he nodded against her neck and answered, "Best sleep I've had in years." His hold around her tightened like a hug and she knew he was looking beyond her to the child sleeping several inches away. "They're perfect angels when they're asleep, aren't they?"

Miranda had laced her fingers with Quinn's and marveled at how well their hands fit together, how well their bodies fit, how well their thoughts meshed. She was warm, contented. She had the idea that this was where she belonged, *this* was where she finally fit in. And if she was only dreaming it, she didn't want to wake up. It had been easy to agree on Fiona's beauty and so much more. "Perfect."

"Petwa and I help."

And then there was reality and the bright sunlight of a cold winter's day.

Miranda heard the scratch of a step stool sliding across the tile floor and felt the tug at the sleeve of her insulated henley shirt. Quinn had sequestered himself in his home office right after breakfast and she hadn't seen him since. And, once again, she had a dark-haired girl at her elbow. As had quickly become a habit with nearly every task, Fiona joined her at the sink, wanting to help with the grown-up's job.

"Okay. Set Petra down so she doesn't get wet." The doll dropped to the floor immediately and Fiona reached for the glass Miranda had used. In a deft move she hoped the girl was still too young to notice, she pulled her plastic cup back out of the dishwasher and switched it with the breakable glass.

They were both wet to their elbows and kneeling in front of the open dishwasher door to load the cube of dishwasher soap when the kitchen door swung open and Quinn strode inside. "Hello?"

"Over here." Miranda popped up from behind the counter.

Fiona batted her hand away when Miranda automatically reached back to start the machine. "I push the button," she insisted.

"This one here," Miranda pointed out. Fiona pushed the button and smiled from pigtail to pigtail when the wash cycle started right up.

"Look what I did, Daddy." Fiona hugged her father's leg and tilted her face all the way back to look up at him. "I did the dishes. And Wandy helped."

Miranda grinned at the mention. The five-minute task had taken fifteen, but she'd stayed busy and Fiona had been entertained. Quinn cupped her head and congratulated her before sending her off to play on her own for a few minutes. "Good job, sweetie. Why don't you go up to your room and help Petra try on some of the new outfits she got for Christmas? I need to talk to Miranda, okay?"

"Okay."

Quinn turned to watch her push through the swinging door and listen for the light rhythm of footsteps going up the stairs, giving Miranda the chance to notice the scuffs of dust on the sleeve of his navy blue sweater and the knees of his corduroy slacks. When he faced her again, she plucked a cobweb from his hair and took the liberty of smoothing that stray lock on his forehead back into place. "Where have you been?"

He adjusted his glasses in that adorably nerdy habit of his. "Up in the attic, going through some boxes of Val's things."

Oh. The late wife. Nothing like the mention of the woman he'd loved and married and started a family with to put a crimp in that silly dream of belonging here. She was the nanny. The bodyguard. Not the future Mrs. Gallagher. Miranda brushed away the cobweb and the feel of his silky hair against her fingers on the leg of her jeans.

"Looking for something in particular?" she asked, matching her posture to the business-like tone of his voice.

He spread a piece of paper with a computer-generated picture on top of the center island. "This is the police artist's rendering of the guy in the backseat of that black BMW that Michael faxed over from KCPD this morning." He set an old black-and-white photograph on the counter beside it and tapped at the faded image. "Is this the man you saw in the car that tried to run you down?"

Miranda picked up the photograph. She didn't need to see the drawing because those pale eyes and gaunt features shouting some kind of warning to the men in the front seat of the car bearing down on her were embedded clearly in her memory.

She studied the image of a young man in his late twenties. His hair was curly, dark. The swim trunks he wore revealed a muscular upper body. But the eyes looking straight into the camera were the same.

"Gray up his hair, put some wrinkles on him and shave off about fifty pounds, and yes, that's the man I saw." She set the picture back on the counter and frowned. "Who is it?"

"Vasily Gordeeva. My father-in-law."

The silence that filled the kitchen following that announcement left Miranda fidgeting inside her skin. Quinn could stand there and bore holes into the photograph with those laser-blue eyes for as long as he wanted to process whatever thoughts were going on inside his head. But she needed to move.

Spying the coffeemaker, and inhaling a whiff of the fragrant roasted liquid, she went to the cabinet above it and pulled down a mug to pour herself a cup. She held up the pot toward Quinn and he looked up long enough to nod.

Some of the tension in him had eased by the time she rejoined him at the island and handed him his drink. "Thanks."

Miranda cradled her mug between her hands to warm her fingers. "Do you and your wife's family not get along?"

"I've never met the man." Another cryptic statement, punctuated with a swallow of coffee. "Val left Lukinburg when she was six or seven. Neither she nor her mother ever had contact with him again."

Now she was getting an idea of where his thoughts had been. "So why would your father-in-law be spying on you?"

"And why would he want to hurt the grand-child he's never even met?"

More to the point, "How could he? I thought he was in prison."

"So did I."

Miranda set down her mug and lined up the two images side by side on the counter. "You know, there's a big difference between this strapping young man and the elderly gentle-man I saw."

"A gentleman wouldn't plant bombs or take potshots at you."

"Technically, he wasn't the one doing the shooting."

"Small comfort."

Miranda appreciated the sarcasm on her behalf. But there had to be an explanation somewhere. "What if he's ill? He wouldn't be the first long-term prisoner to be released near the end of his sentence because of health issues."

Quinn shot his fingers through his hair, destroying the tidying up she'd done earlier. "And his first wish as a free man is to come after me? He doesn't need the money. I'm guessing he had to pay a hefty fee to some-body to leave the country, maybe even to get out of prison. He's rented multiple luxury cars here."

"All three men were wearing suits and ties and nice wool coats," she added.

"And goons with guns and cameras don't come cheap."

"You said he was imprisoned for his politics?"

Quinn picked up her mug and carried both of them to the sink. "Specifically, he was put away for raising funds and running the campaign for a presidential candidate who turned out to be the front man for a Lukinburger mob boss. According to Val, the guy won. But shortly after, there was a revolution and the mob-influenced government was overthrown, and Vasily went to prison."

"And neither you nor your wife were ever any part of that?"

Quinn shook his head. "Val was embarrassed by his criminal connections, I think. They certainly put her and her mother in danger after the revolution there. So no, once they became American citizens, they were never part of anything there."

Great. So they could finally name a suspect, but he lacked a motive.

They stood side by side at the counter,

staring at the contrasting images of Vasily Gordeeva.

"I was thinking," she started, reaching up to lift her ponytail and play with it for a few moments while her idea settled into place.

"About what?"

"The threat at Ozzie Chang's house."

Quinn pulled her ponytail from her fingers and smoothed it down the center of her back. "Let's try to forget it for a few hours, okay?"

As much as she wanted to savor the comforting caress, she turned to face him instead. "You think that message means he's coming here to the house, too, right?"

"Yes. He wants more money or 'I will strike much closer to home,'" he quoted.

Miranda narrowed her gaze on Quinn. "Well, hasn't he already been here?"

"Hmm?" For a smart man, this particular puzzle wasn't yet falling into place.

"The men in the car watching the house. The guy who took pictures of Fiona." Miranda reached for his hands, squeezing them between hers, willing him to understand. "If he's already been here, then a note like that doesn't make sense."

Quinn connected the dots with her, and maybe deduced a little something more.

"There are two things going on here. And, just maybe, they're related."

"You've figured out who's behind this?"

"Partly." He pulled her hands to his lips and kissed her fingers. He was energized again, moving, on his way out the door. "I want to put in a call to my father-in-law first."

"WHY DON'T YOU BAKE COOKIES together?" Such an innocent suggestion for a wintry vacation evening.

But Miranda would rather run a timed simulation at the KCPD firing range.

Still, fearful of taking Fiona outside again in the darkness of twilight, even with lights blazing all around the house, she'd needed something to do to keep the little girl entertained. The last nanny, or maybe two or three nannies ago—the exact details had been blanked out by the momentary panic attack she'd had at Quinn's suggestion—had made great strides teaching Fiona the child-appropriate basics of cookie making. Cutting out shapes. Decorating them with sprinkles. Eating them.

Unfortunately, those were the same skills Miranda was familiar with when it came to baking.

And now their first batch was coming out of the oven. The edges were burned, the middles were doughy. Fiona waited on her step stool, ready to shake the colored-sugar bottles and chocolatey bits over their creations. Miranda checked the picture in the cookbook one more time to confirm that what she had in her oven mitt was a tray full of chewy hockey pucks rather than anything resembling sugar cookies.

But hopefully, as she scraped them off the cookie sheet and set them on the cooling rack, this exercise in frustration was more about the fun Fiona was having and less about Miranda's ability to produce something edible and appetizing.

"There you go, sweetie." She tested some of the hockey pucks that were cool enough to handle and set them on the plate in front of Fiona. "Have at it. Make them pretty."

While sugar and sprinkles flew, Miranda scooped up more cookie dough, trying to make the second tray more even in size. She double-checked the temperature of the oven one more time and slipped them inside.

The kitchen door swung open behind her. "Mmm. Smells good in here."

"Daddy! Look what we made."

Miranda wondered at her own little flutter of excitement at seeing Quinn walk into the room. Fiona jumped down from her step stool and trotted over to greet him, leaving a trail of green and red sugar in her wake.

She might as well admit the disaster this was right now. "Well, cleaning up this mess will certainly give us plenty to do between now and bedtime." She tossed her oven mitts on the counter. "Fair warning."

"About what?" Quinn scooped Fiona up in his arms and took a bite of the cookie she stuffed into his mouth. But it was clearly a struggle to get down. "I see. Got a glass of milk?"

"Coming right up."

Quinn set Fiona on the far edge of the counter and did his duty as a good father to eat the entire cookie and give her a wink as though he was enjoying it. Once he'd cleared his throat by downing half a glass of milk, he placed three cookies on a plastic plate and sent his daughter on a mission.

As soon as she was out the door and marching down the hallway, Quinn pressed the intercom button to call down to the men in the security command room. "David?"

"Sir?" the security answered back through a buzz of static.

"No emergency," Quinn assured him. "I'm sending my daughter down to you with a plate of cookies." Miranda laughed at the helpless face he made before speaking again. "Be nice and try one before you send her back. And remember, I pay you a lot of money."

"Okay...? I'll keep an eye out for her. Damiani out."

Quinn laughed with her as he came back to the center island to finish off his milk. "You weren't kidding when you said baking wasn't a strength of yours." He nodded toward the swinging door. "But that's one happy little girl."

"I guess I had fun, too. Can't say I'm proud of the results, but it's like a science experiment. And I liked my chemistry class in high school." Miranda gathered up the bowls and measuring cups scattered over the counter and carried them to the sink. "So how did your phone call with Elise Brown go? Did she get a hold of Nikolai Titov?"

Quinn joined her at the sink with another

load of dirty dishes. "Yeah, I guess he took her out to dinner. I can't tell if Titov is trying to steal away the most organized member of my staff or if they're actually sweet on each other."

"Really?" Miranda ran the water until it got hot, and then she squirted in some liquid soap to wash the items by hand. "I'm no expert on such things, but I got the idea that Elise was sweet on you. She didn't seem real thrilled that you gave me your jacket and took care of me after the shooting outside your office."

"You noticed I was trying to take care of you, hmm?"

"I notice everything you do." Like the tender caresses he gave his daughter. The quizzical frowns he often gave her. The heated debates. The subtle, certain touches of his fingers or lips against her skin. The way he generated a heat that leaped between them whenever they were close, even standing side by side in front of the kitchen sink.

Quinn cleared his throat beside her, as if he still had a bite of that cookie stuck there. She had no such excuse for the difficulty she suddenly seemed to have catching her breath.

"Let me." Quinn nodded at the bandage on her arm and rolled up his shirtsleeves to plunge his hands into the sudsy water himself. "I think Elise is just protective of me. More mother hen than sweetheart. I count on her to make me look good to my clients and the people who work for me, especially when I'm stuck in my head with an idea or a business plan. She apparently smoothed things over with Titov. At least for the time being. Those kinds of people skills are invaluable to me as a businessman."

"She's a pretty woman, too." Miranda wet a second dishrag to wipe down the counters and put some clear-thinking space between them while he washed.

"You're the second person to tell me that this week. I guess I've noticed in some part of my mind that she's attractive. But she must not be my type."

"So…" The bell on the oven went off and Miranda took out the last batch of cookies and set them on the cooling rack. At least they weren't burned. It was enough of a victory that she dared to ask, "What is your type?"

When she turned around, Quinn was right there, his thighs crowding hers back against the island as he set his soapy hands on the countertop on either side of her. "I think you know."

She definitely noticed the heat between them.

And the laser focus of those deep blue eyes skimming over her face.

She noticed the enticing wave of dark hair tumbling over his forehead, and the breadth of those shoulders straining beneath blue-striped oxford cloth as he leaned in.

She noticed the simple, masculine smells of soap and spice on his skin.

And she noticed the warm, gentle pressure of his fingertip brushing across her cheek-bone.

"Me?" she uttered on a breathless whisper.

He held up the white-tipped finger.

Her hand flew to her cheek, which felt ridiculously hot. Oh, no. She had flour on her face.

Instead of answering with a word, he dropped his gaze lower, to her left breast and the smudge of flour smeared there. He liked klutzy incompetents?

But the joke sounded lame, even inside her own head.

Quinn wasn't laughing. He looked serious, intent…hungry.

Her breath hissed when he brushed that same finger across the streak of flour—deliberately caressing the nubby weave of her shirt, the smooth satin of her bra, the shallow curve of her breast.

Miranda noticed the rapid tempo of her heart, racing beneath his touch. She noticed the way her tender nipple beaded to attention, straining to feel his touch there, as well.

She noticed his mouth moving toward hers, her lips parting in anticipation. His deep-pitched whisper was a husky caress against her ear. "You."

And then he was kissing her. Wanting her. Claiming her. His tongue swept along the needy swell of her lower lip and plunged inside her mouth to brand her with his sugar-cookie flavor and his abundant heat.

Miranda wound her arms around his neck, rubbing the aching tips of her breasts against the wall of his chest as she pulled herself up onto her toes to take everything he would give her. "Quinn." She clutched at the silk of his hair, nipped at his chin. "Quinn." She dragged her sensitive palms along the stubble of his jaw and down the column of his neck. She slipped her fingers beneath his collar, un-hooked a button and slid her fingers beneath the crisp material to find warm, sleek skin. "Quinn."

"I know." He lifted her onto the countertop, spread her thighs and pulled her to the edge, holding her taut and open against his swelling desire. "I know."

Miranda's legs convulsed around his hips at the hard, intimate contact. She felt heavy, molten, weepy inside. She tried to think of reasons why they should stop. Fiona, others in the house. She worked for Quinn. He was the boss. A frustrating, intriguing, compassionate, sexy boss. "Are we crazy?"

"Yes." He slid his palms beneath the hem of her shirt, his strong hands sweeping hot and needy over the cool skin of her back. "It makes no sense." He yanked her shirt up, exposing her torso to the chilly air. "This makes no sense." He dipped his head and closed his hot mouth over the distended peak of her breast, wetting her through the thin material of her bra, laving her, catching the tip between his teeth and tongue until she let out a breathless gasp of torture and joy. "It's never been like this for me." He slid his fingers beneath her bottom and squeezed, lifted, showed her exactly what he wanted if there weren't layers of clothes between them. "I haven't figured you out yet."

Miranda clung to his shoulders and gasped against his neck. "Is that important?"

"It's a—"

The loud *whoop-whoop* of an alarm stopped Quinn midsentence, and Miranda froze against him. Emergency lights at the mud room door flashed on and off. For the longest of seconds she couldn't make out anything but the thundering of her pulse inside her ears.

Fiona shrieked from somewhere in the house.

"Loud noises." Miranda was pushing even as Quinn was pulling away.

"Fiona!" he shouted.

"She hates loud noises." She was jumping as Quinn lifted her off the counter. They straightened their clothes, ran toward the swinging door, forgot their own unanswered desires because a terrified little girl needed them right now. "Fiona!"

Like a chain-reaction crash on the highway, Miranda's senses slammed into place one by one. Security alarm. Intruders on the premises. Draw gun. Find Fiona.

Quinn saw her first, standing in the hallway—screaming, crying. He scooped her up in his arms and hugged her tight to his chest. "It's okay, baby. Daddy's got you. It's okay."

Another light flashed on and off at the front door. The alarm blared its warning.

Her own heart crying at Fiona's terror, Miranda brushed a dark curl off the little girl's cheek. "You'll be fine, sweetie. Daddy won't let go and I'll keep you safe."

Just as quickly as the compassion had welled up inside her, Miranda squashed it back down. She had one job to do, and this was it. She moved her hand from Fiona's head to Quinn's shoulder and urged him to come with her. "We need to get to one of the panic rooms."

He nodded, cradled Fiona's head against his shoulder and hurried toward the stairs.

A stampede of footsteps charged up the stairs from the lower level behind them.

"Keep moving," she ordered, pushing Quinn up the stairs. Miranda whirled around, her Glock gripped between her hands, and changed course to meet the approaching threat head-on.

She saw the end of a rifle first, appearing around the corner. She ducked into the nearest doorway and shouted, "KCPD! Halt right there!"

"Whoa!" A man in a dark uniform threw up his hands before he ever reached the hallway.

A second man stumbled into him. He pointed his gun up into the air and raised his hands, as well. "Murdock?"

"Holmes? Rowley?" These two bozos were running through the house, armed with assault rifles? She lowered her gun to a less lethal angle, but refused to lower her guard. "What's going on?"

"The black Beemer's here again," Holmes reported. "Three men inside."

"Here?"

"Two of your SWAT guys caught them at the gate and are bringing them in."

All at once the alarm stopped and David Damiani came up the stairs, speaking into his walkie-talkie. "Make sure you disarm them. Check for ankle holsters, knives and any other easy-to-hide weapons."

"Roger that." She recognized Sergeant Delgado's voice on the radio.

"Quinn!" Ignoring her gun and her authority and shouting for the boss, David pushed Rowley aside and glared down at her as he walked past. "Loose cannon," he muttered, signaling his men to fall in behind them. Then, in a louder voice, he announced, "Dirty Harriet here almost shot my boys."

"What?" She spun around to find Quinn standing on the bottom step. Wasn't this her op? Wasn't she the one charged with keeping Fiona Gallagher safe? Wasn't she good enough to get the job done without Damiani's interference?

"It's all right, Miranda. I know who the three men in the black car are now." Fiona had a white-knuckled grip around his neck, but her sobs had quieted to deep, stuttering whimpers. "Tell your men to put their guns away around my daughter, Damiani."

David pointed a finger and the two men complied.

Quinn stepped down to the main floor and stood nose to nose with the big man. "And if you ever speak to Miranda in that tone again, you'll answer to me."

"I can take care of myself," she argued weakly, heartened by his defense of her, yet a little ticked that he thought she couldn't stand up for herself.

"This is my fault," Quinn apologized. "I shouldn't have expected them to simply go away."

Sergeant Delgado's voice buzzed over the radio again. "We're ready to come in."

"Get the door," David told his men.

"What is going on?" she demanded. "We have intruders and nobody's getting you and Fiona out of here?"

"Holster your weapon," Quinn ordered.

Miranda opened her mouth to protest being spoken to with the same superior disdain that he'd addressed David with. But she snapped her lips shut. Right. Make-out session in the kitchen didn't happen. Tender looks and cuddling in bed meant nothing. She was the hired help. The nanny. She took orders from Quinn Gallagher just like everyone else around here.

Fine. If he wanted a cop, she could be a cop. She secured her gun at the back of her waist. "I'm still waiting for an explanation about the alarm."

"Take Fiona upstairs."

That was his answer? She willingly took Fiona's slight weight when he placed her in Miranda's arms. "Quinn?"

"I didn't think he'd come to the house when I called."

"Who?"

"They're here, sir," Holmes reported.

"Open the door." David pulled the front of his jacket back behind the grip of his Beretta and let his hand rest on the weapon holstered on his belt. "Slowly."

Resigned to the role of protecting the daughter, even though the father was making that difficult to do, Miranda carried Fiona up the stairs. She stopped halfway up when the front door opened at her feet and Rafe Delgado stepped in. He had a hodgepodge of confiscated weapons tucked into his flak vest and utility belt.

Two men in suits and coats walked in behind him with their hands folded on top of their heads. One of them was limping. Holden Kincaid came in, his hand beneath the elbow of a frail gray-haired gentleman.

The older man glanced up as soon as the door was closed and locked behind him, giving her a glimpse of pale gray eyes. Recognition jolted through her. Instinctively, she turned Fiona away from the captured intruders. But Miranda couldn't take her eyes off the haunted paleness of an obviously ill man. "That's him. That's the man I saw in the black BMW out front."

Vasily Gordeeva.

"May I see her?" he asked, his voice thickly accented and sad. "May I see my granddaughter?"

Chapter Twelve

1 Day until Midnight, New Year's Eve

"Why would you threaten her? She's your own flesh and blood."

Quinn had sat up most of the night in his office study, getting to know Vasily Gordeeva, learning a lesson in Lukinburg history and avoiding the occasional accusatory glare from Miranda. She sat on one of the black leather couches with Fiona and Petra wrapped up in a throw blanket and sleeping in her lap. Vasily's two "extended family" members had agreed to retire to the kitchen where they shared coffee, a snack and a lack of scintillating conversation with David Damiani and the two other men assigned to guard them. Rafe Delgado and Holden Kincaid stood in the hallway, waiting to escort Vasily and his associates straight to the airport to put them on a plane back to Lukinburg.

Quinn adjusted the pictures of Val and Fiona and himself on the mantel, then moved each frame back into its original place before turning to his father-in-law. "I can understand you having a vendetta against me, because my wealth made Val a target, and that got her killed. But Fiona—"

"I would never harm my granddaughter. I came to America specifically to see her, to perhaps spend a few hours with her— my last remaining blood relative—before I die of this cancer." Vasily sat at the opposite end of the sofa from Miranda, his fingertips touching the edge of the blanket that covered Fiona. He barely looked strong enough to sit upright, much less strike fear into the heart of the Lukinburg government and its citizens after spending nearly two decades in prison. "I am sad, yes, that Valeska did not live long enough to see me out of prison. And I read the papers. I know about the Rich Girl Killer and that he blamed my daughter—your wife—for his failures. I do not hold you responsible." He stroked the fringe on the blanket without ever once touching or disturbing Fiona. "But I am gravely concerned that you believe I would harm the child."

"Somebody wants to."

Vasily stroked his thinning beard, thinking for a moment. "Nikolai."

"Nikolai Titov? Why? I do business with him. There's nothing personal between us."

"This could be my fault," Vasily admitted. "When I was released from prison, I asked my associates to find out all they could about you and my daughter in the States. Choices I made as a young man took the people I loved from me. I had money, power. But after so many years alone in a cell, I realized I had nothing. In these last days, I wanted to find my family again."

"I'm sorry you're dying, Vasily. But you and your *associates* aren't exactly people I want around my daughter." Quinn sat in the wing chair across from the couch. "But tell me about Nikolai."

"My inquiries may have, as you say, put you on his radar."

"I've made millions of dollars for that man. How can he have a grudge against me that would justify threatening Fiona?"

Vasily shook his head sadly. "There are

other things in this world of far more value than money, Quinn. Family. Freedom."

"Nikolai," Quinn prompted. If Vasily had answers, he needed them. "Why would I be on his radar?"

Vasily stroked the blanket again, his gaze lingering over his sleeping granddaughter. When he looked at Quinn again, there was nothing wistful nor ailing in those sharp gray eyes. "You do not know about Nikolai's son?"

"I didn't know he had a son."

"I do not suppose our newspapers are as common reading across the ocean as yours are for us." The old man slowly pushed to his feet. He buttoned his suit coat and straightened his tie before crossing to the mantel to see the pictures of the family he barely knew. "I have heard from a reliable source that Nikolai Titov used your plant in St. Feodor for more than the production of the munitions you created there."

"I suspected as much. The shipping numbers never did add up for a facility that size. That's one reason I closed the plant, though we could never prove anything. What was he funneling through there—drugs?"

"He contracted with arms dealers to move their illegal arms along with your shipments.

Very easy to get through customs with your clearance."

Quinn gripped the arms of the chair and channeled his rage into the leather upholstery. Fiona's life was in danger because of some greedy bastard in a foreign country? And he had the nerve to show up in his office? To wine and dine his assistant? "The clock is ticking, Vasily," Quinn urged. "Whatever it is, get to the point. Why would Nikolai Titov want to play this crazy game of 'make it right' with me? What do I have to make right?"

Vasily traced his finger along a photograph of Valeska holding their infant daughter. "The men Nikolai worked with blamed him for the five million dollars they lost when the plant closed. They kidnapped his son and demanded he repay them."

"Five million dollars?" The extortion numbers added up. Quinn rose and joined him at the fireplace. "So Titov takes my five million and gets his son back."

"Not exactly."

A softer voice entered the conversation, the voice of a woman who seemed able to figure out the pieces to a puzzle when Quinn could not. "What happened to Nikolai's son?" Miranda asked.

Vasily nodded at her perception. "Your plant closed more than a year ago, Quinn. Nikolai could not make the restitution they wanted. So, after seven days…they killed his son."

Miranda's gaze shifted to Quinn. The fear he read there matched his own. "There are seven days from Christmas to New Year's. This game, these threats…he's making everything match the same time line he went through with his son. Maybe the bomb, the threats he's sending, are the same things he went through."

"And Ozzie Chang was the inside man he used to get the access to me and GSS he needed."

Miranda scooted out from beneath Fiona's sleeping head and pulled out her cell after carefully tucking the blanket around her again. "We need to get on the phone with KCPD or the FBI. They need to find Titov and arrest him or deport him."

"That son of a bitch." Quinn hurried to his phone to place a call that would wake up Elise Brown. She was the last person he knew to see Titov in Kansas City. He had twenty-four hours to track him down and stop him before he did to Fiona what he'd done to Ozzie Chang and those guards at the Kalahari plant. "I ran a legal business there. He used my company for his illegal activities, but he blames *me* for his son's murder?"

Vasily Gordeeva might be the only person in the room who truly understood that kind of retribution. "An eye for an eye. A child for a child."

THE SNOW WAS BLINDING IN THE afternoon sun as Quinn stood in the concourse at the Kansas City International Airport and watched the plane carrying Vasily and his associates back to Lukinburg take off. The FBI agents who'd processed them and put the three men on the plane were talking on their phones while Quinn watched, until it was just a speck in the clear blue sky.

Taking pity on a dying man, he'd given Vasily the picture of Valeska and Fiona from the mantel. The old man had kissed him on each cheek, and promised that the hours he'd spent with his granddaughter in Kansas City were a true gift that would not be forgotten.

Fine. Quinn could use the good karma, judging by the icy looks he'd gotten from Miranda since the security alarms had cut short that fiery encounter in the kitchen. What a hell of a time for his emotions and libido to take over his rational thinking. As much as they both seemed to be willing to explore whatever was happening between them, it wouldn't have been fair to her to have let it go all the way. Quinn's emotions were a jumble right now, and the fear he felt for Fiona's safety was as potent as the need he felt for Miranda. His anger at Nikolai Titov and his resentment of Vasily for asking questions about Fiona that had given Titov this sick idea of payback in the first place were mixed in there, too. How was that fair to make love to a woman, to think about having a real relationship with someone besides his wife, when Quinn wasn't sure what he was feeling at any given moment?

He needed Miranda to focus on protecting Fiona just as much as he did. Any hurt feelings or misunderstandings or errant hormones sparking between them didn't matter—couldn't matter—until this nightmarish game was over and he knew his daughter was safe.

He'd given a picture and been given a promise in return.

He'd met a unique, fascinating, wonderful woman who just might be crazy enough to feel something for him, too—and he had to let her go. He had to put his daughter first and ignore the ache in his chest and the hurt in her beautiful green eyes.

One threat down. Vasily's spying explained the recurring appearance of the BMWs. His former father-in-law had apologized profusely for drugging the guards in an attempt to get inside the gates, and he had promised Miranda that his men would be severely chastised for shooting at her and running her down with the car. Apparently, he'd had nothing to do with the mysterious package and the bloody doll and the bomb. His search into locating his granddaughter had caught the attention of the man who did, though.

One threat to go.

Quinn's security team was on full alert. Every system had been checked and re-checked. Michael's SWAT team was positioned around the outside walls of the estate. And Miranda was with Fiona.

No one on the planet was safer than his daughter.

He was going to have to disappoint his enemy. Titov could drain Quinn's bank account if he wanted. But no way was he going to *make things right* by tomorrow. Or ever. No way was he sacrificing Fiona to assuage another man's grief and rage for his murdered son.

Now he had to get home and hold his daughter in his arms until the danger outside their home had passed.

Both the FBI agents paused in their conversations on their phones. "Are you sure?" one asked.

"There's no record of him getting on a plane or a boat? Or slipping over one of the borders?"

Feeling a dread as cold as the marble floor beneath his feet, Quinn demanded answers from the two men. "You don't know where Titov is?"

The first one disconnected his call. "If he left the country, he was using an alias. We haven't been able to track him."

The second agent took Quinn by the arm and led him toward their car, parked outside on the circular curb. "We need to get you to a secure location, Mr. Gallagher."

"You need to get me home."

As soon as they were on their way, Quinn called the house.

David Damiani answered. "Sir?"

"You keep eyes on my daughter at all times. Tell Miranda and Michael Cutler and your men. The Feds can't find Nikolai. He could be anywhere."

24 Minutes until Midnight, New Year's Eve

THE FIRST POP SOUNDED LIKE the illegal fireworks the neighbors down the block were setting off to celebrate the coming New Year. Miranda blinked her eyes open to make sure Fiona was still sleeping soundly and checked the time. She wondered if the game would truly end in twenty-four minutes—or, if Nikolai Titov's idea of making things right wasn't met, the New Year was when the real nightmare would begin.

Miranda shifted in the rocking chair, crossed her booted feet and pulled the afghan up around her neck before dozing off again. Why was she so sleepy? Sure, she'd had some late nights this week, and some emotional ups and downs that had drained her. But she was the last line of defense between Fiona and the horrible thing Titov wanted to do to her. She needed to get on her feet and shake off this terrible fatigue.

Miranda sat bolt upright at the second pop and immediately paid the price for the rapid movement with the pinball machine playing inside her skull. "What the hell?"

She could smell it now—the faint tinge of something sulfuric in the air. She squinted at the yellowish mist swirling beneath the hallway door. Oh, my God. This was some kind of gas attack, an airborne sleeping drug that was slowly stealing her consciousness from her.

"Miranda?"

She heard Quinn's voice calling from the hallway. Then she heard a couple of thumps before something big crashed onto the carpet outside the door.

"Quinn?" She pushed to her feet and stumbled to the bed to hold her hand beneath Fiona's nose. Good. She was still breathing. So far it was just a sleeping gas and not something more deadly.

Her legs felt like putty, her feet like lead weights as she grabbed on to the bedposts and pulled herself around the bed. Quinn was in trouble out there, but they all would be if she passed out, too. She changed direction and headed toward the windows on either side of the bookshelf.

"Miranda?" The door swung open and Quinn collapsed to the floor. He was wearing nothing but his glasses and the sweatpants he slept in. He pushed the door shut and stuffed his robe into the opening at the base of the door. "Gas…coming…from downstairs. Is she…okay?"

"We need air." She fell against the bookshelf, hitting her injured arm. The sting of pain shooting up her arm and down into her fingers revived her for a moment. "We need to get a window open."

"Fiona?" Quinn was crawling across the carpet now, pulling himself toward his daughter.

Miranda unlatched the first window and tried to raise it. But she was so weak. Her knees buckled before she could reach the second window. They were all alone. She was alone. Always alone.

As the blackness threatened to overtake her, she heard a sharp voice. "Miranda!" Quinn's voice. Quinn needed her. "You can do this, sweetheart. Save her."

Fiona needed her.

"Save her."

She wasn't failing the people who needed her again.

Reaching up, Miranda grabbed the edge of the bookshelf. She pulled herself up high enough to grab the window ledge. She got her feet beneath her and pushed with her legs to stand. But the window was so heavy.

In a burst of strength that came from determination alone, Miranda pulled herself up higher, climbing the shelves with her hands, one by one, reaching up to the top of the shelf and feeling around until her fingers closed over the grip of her Glock. *Tick. Tock,* the cruel voice inside her head warned. Time was running out.

Air. They needed air. They were passing out. Maybe dying.

Her hands, trained by the best, trained to be the best, knew what to do even when her eyes refused to focus. Miranda unhooked the holster and dropped it. Her palms folded around the grip, her finger slid against the trigger. She raised the heavy gun and fired three shots at the window, shattering the glass.

Cold night air rushed into the room, clearing her head as she breathed it in. She tucked her gun into the back of her jeans and found the strength to slide over to the other window and open it. The curtains fanned out into the room, telling her the sweet, fresh air from outside was filling the room.

She heard another pop. Her ear jerked to

the sound. From somewhere inside the house. With her head clearing, she identified the three pops immediately.

Gunshots.

They were in trouble. Big trouble.

And she'd just announced to whoever was in the house that he wasn't the only one here armed with a weapon.

"Quinn? Quinn!" Growing stronger with every breath, she stumbled back into the room and knelt down beside his still form. She rolled him onto his back and spread her hand over his chest. "Thank God."

There was still a strong heartbeat.

"Quinn?" She tapped his cheeks, tried to rouse him. "Quinn, wake up. We have to get out of here. Someone's in the house."

She rose to her feet and pulled on his arm. But all she managed to do was turn him sideways. He was too big for her to drag outside. And away from the windows, she was falling under the influence of the knockout gas again.

"I'll come back for you." She stooped down and pressed a kiss to his mouth. "It's my job, right? I'm going to take Fiona outside. I need you to breathe in the fresh air and wake up while I'm gone, okay?"

He moaned something unintelligible.

She leaned in closer. "What's that?"

"Go. Save her."

"I will. I promise I will."

She could hear footsteps all the way down in the basement level. How had Titov or one of his men gotten into the house? There were guards, gates, cops, codes.

"Come on, sweetie." Miranda wrapped Fiona up in the afghan from the rocking chair and carried her sleeping body to the open window. She kicked out the screen onto the second-story porch.

The footsteps were in the hallway now. Anyone who could move that quickly had to be immune to the gas. A standard-issue gas mask would suffice.

"Quinn!" She turned and whispered desperately. "He's coming."

He was on his hands and knees now. "Go."

"He has a gun."

He pushed himself to his feet and leaned against the bedpost. "Systems must be…offline." He lurched to the next bedpost. "No lights. No alarms."

That was right. The house was deathly quiet. There was no movement outside. She'd fired three shots straight out the front window. This place should have been locking down like Fort Knox. Guards from the front gate should have been storming the house. But it seemed every technical gadget Quinn had put into place was dead.

And then she understood what he intended to do. "No. You come with me. When we get outside we can call for backup."

The footstep hit the first stair.

"Come with me," she begged, panic clearing her head now. "We can run to the gate. Climb over it somehow. Forget your security system."

"I can fix it."

She stepped back into the room. "Then I'm staying with you."

He pushed her right back to the window. He bent his head to kiss Fiona. "You save my daughter. That's why you're here." His blue eyes were clear as he captured her face in his hands and kissed her hard on the mouth. "I'm sorry our timing was off. I didn't know I was ready for another relationship until I met you."

Footsteps. "Quinn."

He freed her ponytail from where it was wedged between Fiona and her chest, and smoothed it down her back. "I owe you a proper New Year's kiss," he promised. "But first I'm going to take this bastard down."

He lifted her out onto the porch and disappeared inside Fiona's closet just as a shadowy figure filled the doorway.

Miranda ran through the snow, shutting down her emotions, allowing herself no opportunity to think about Quinn trying to be a superhero when he just needed to be Fiona's daddy.

She was across the bridge before Fiona stirred in her arms. "Wandy?"

"Thank God." She kissed her soft forehead. "Randy loves you, sweetie. Be still. Be quiet."

Where were the lights of the front gate?

"I'm cold."

If she thought about it too much, Miranda was, too. But she had to get Fiona to safety. Nothing else mattered.

Except getting back into that house to help Quinn.

She saw a large, dark shadow moving behind the bars of the gate and she instinctively zigzagged off the driveway and plunged into the snow again, making it tough for a potential enemy to get a straight shot at her.

"KCPD!"

The shadow called out at the same time Miranda shouted, "Identify yourself!"

There was a huff of relief and then the beam of a flashlight hit her in the face. "Murdock?" The light instantly lowered. "It's Holden Kincaid and Trip Jones."

She saw the second figure, an even bigger shadow in the darkness, working with a flashlight over by the thick brick wall. "I can't get anything to work," Trip groused. "What the hell is going on? We heard gunshots."

Looping Fiona's arms around her neck, Miranda jumped to her feet again and met the two SWAT cops at the gate. "How many?"

"Three."

She shook her head. "That was me." The house must be soundproofed. "I had to bust out a window. There's some kind of sleeping gas inside."

"The gate's locked up tight." Holden wrapped a black-gloved hand around one of the unyielding bars of the gate. "We can't get in unless we scale the wall or cut through these with a torch. The sarge is coming with the van and some rope."

"Do either of you guys have a spare radio and a gear bag?" There was no way either of the big men could squeeze through the bars, but she had a little three-year-old who could. "Here. Take her."

"Wandy?" she whined.

"You're fine, sweetie. I need you to be a big girl for me." She handed Fiona through to Holden on the other side. "Got her?" Funny, trusting this most precious gift to the man she'd feared was back at KCPD to replace her. Maybe he still was. But tonight, that didn't matter. Tonight, they needed to work together as a team. "I have to go back in and help your daddy."

"Hold up. You don't go anywhere without a sit-rep," Trip chided. He thrust a radio and earbud through the gate. "Alex and the captain are on their way. Captain said all of Damiani's guards missed their check-in. They went to find them."

Intel. Routine. Communication. Training. They were all part of being on SWAT. It was the only way to get the job done quickly and safely, and Miranda intended to do both. She gave a quick situation report while she clipped on her radio and tested it. "Somebody's hacked into the security system here. Everything's offline. Quinn's trying to fix it."

"Here you go." Trip unzipped a gear bag and started passing equipment through the gate. Flak vest. Flashlight. Gloves. Watch cap. Spare clips. Second weapon. Gas mask.

Miranda suited up. "There's someone in the house. He's armed. I heard three shots besides my own. I'm going back in."

"Wait for backup," Trip insisted. "We'll get the gate open."

"There isn't time."

"Murdock," Kincaid warned.

She swung back around and pointed a finger at him. "If anything happens to that little girl, I will come back and kick your ass."

And then she was running, retracing her steps through the snow and across the bridge.

"Can she do that?" She heard Kincaid's voice in her ear.

"Oh, yeah." There wasn't a doubt in the world in Trip's tone.

Now she just had to believe it, too.

MIRANDA CLIMBED BACK UP the railings and decorative posts to reach the second-story porch. Moving as silently as the breeze itself, she sidled up beside the broken window and held her breath, listening for any signs of movement inside. Nothing. Then she stooped down and lightly sniffed the air around the window. She couldn't detect the sleeping gas.

She tapped her radio and whispered, "I'm going in."

"Roger that." Captain Cutler's deep voice startled her. Then reassured her just as quickly. "You'd better be coming out, too. Delgado's here with the climbing gear now. Jones and Taylor will be there to back you up in two minutes."

"Yes, sir." She inhaled a deep breath. Two minutes was an eternity when an officer was storming a building in search of a hostage. This was all on her. Saving the man she'd fallen in love with was all on her now. She couldn't fail. "Going to radio silence. Now."

She turned off the radio and climbed inside.

Fiona's bedroom was empty. Miranda checked the closet and the panic room located inside. That must have been where Quinn had been headed. The door stood open, as if he'd tried to take refuge there. But a quick check showed it to be empty, too.

Miranda fought off the fear that tried to take hold. She needed to think clearly right now, for her own survival as well as his. An empty room meant there was every chance Quinn was still alive, that the man who'd been at the door when she'd escaped with Fiona hadn't killed him. Maybe he hadn't even intended to kill him. Maybe that man had been one of David Damiani's security guards, or

Damiani himself, who'd managed to get a gas mask on so that he could find the occupants of the house and get them safely to breathable air.

Yes, think like that. Be positive. Damiani's men were here and—she shined the flashlight on her watch—her own team would be here to back her up in a minute and a half, give or take.

Moving to the door, she checked the hallway for any signs of movement. *Clear,* she sounded off inside her head. She made quick work of the upstairs rooms. *All clear.* Wherever the shadow had taken Quinn, wherever he had gone, it wasn't up here.

She moved quickly down the stairs to the first floor to do a methodical room-by-room search. It didn't take long before she found her first body. She saw the legs sticking out on the far side of the kitchen table. "Quinn?"

Her heart plummeted to her toes as she raced forward. She took a breath of relief. Shirt. No sweats. Not Quinn. She took another breath and frowned in apprehension. This was Rowley, the blond-haired guard, murdered execution-style with a bullet in the middle of his forehead.

She found Holmes at the garage door entrance. Same bullet hole. Same kind of dead. They'd definitely missed their check-in.

But still no Quinn. There was no way out of this house, no way off the grounds with her team closing in.

Miranda checked her watch. Four minutes till midnight. Trip and Alex should be over the wall by now, coming in to back her up. She needed to brief them on what to expect. The sleeping gas had dissipated. There was a dead guard at each exit. No live bodies and one floor left to check.

She tapped her radio, then just as quickly tapped it off when she heard voices coming from the security command center downstairs. She covered her mouth and swallowed her cry of relief. Quinn.

"I knew there had to be a mole in GSS somewhere. Nikolai had the motive, but he didn't have the means to get into my personal systems to send those messages or plant the bomb or take down the security of this house." She tried to pinpoint the source of the sound and finally looked down. She was hearing him through the ventilation duct in the floor. Was there an alternative way to get into the command center without going straight down the stairs and possibly walking into an ambush?

"You didn't answer me. And I don't like un-answered questions. I get why Titov wants me dead, why he wants to kill my daughter. I don't like it, but I get it. Why are *you* doing this?"

She heard another voice, infinitely more troubling, as it answered. "Because he's paying me an obscene amount of money. And," David Damiani added, before Quinn could interrupt, "I wanted to prove I was better than you."

QUINN HADN'T MADE IT TO THE panic room as he'd briefly intended. But he'd provided enough of a distraction when he'd tackled David Damiani and knocked that gas mask off his face that Miranda had been able to get Fiona safely out of the house and beyond David's reach before he even realized they were gone.

Now he had a cracked lens in his glasses, a swollen black eye and a few other bruises to remind him just how long it had been since he'd taken down a bully with his bare fists. Despite his broken nose, Damiani had hauled him straight down to the estate's command center, as he'd hoped, and tied him to the chair farthest from the security monitors, but closest to the satellite feed station.

Quinn prayed that David was so caught up in his own ego that he'd forgotten who'd built this room in the first place, and that Miranda was as good a SWAT cop as Michael Cutler—as *he*—believed her to be.

He eyed the clock on the wall. He had a minute left to play this game. "What happens if you don't finish the job by midnight? You're never getting your hands on my daughter. Is Titov going to let you get away with that?"

"What makes you think I still can't get to Fiona?" he taunted. The man's skull was about as thick as that bulletproof vest he wore. "In a few minutes, you'll be dead and I'll be the last, lone survivor of a terrible home invasion that destroyed the great Quinn Gallagher. It'll be in all the papers. People will pity me or think I'm a hero. But I'm going to walk out of here. And you're not. I've planned for every contingency. Even your mouthy loose cannon of a girlfriend will be taken care of." He edged closer with the Beretta in his hand pointed at Quinn's head. "You think I don't know she's coming for you? I'm banking on it. No way can she get to you without coming down those stairs and coming through me first. And I'll be waiting for her."

"Are you sure the five million dollars is for you, David? Where is Nikolai, anyway? Still in the country? At the Swiss bank, counting his cash?"

"Seriously? He's already in St. Feodor, watching this all on TV. A whole ocean away is a pretty good alibi, don't you think?" His denasal laugh as he reached over to turn on the satellite feed was more pitiful than intimidating. "Nikolai, my friend." The blur of Titov's black-and-silver goatee came into focus on the screen. "I have your prize." He pressed the muzzle of his gun against Quinn's forehead. "Shall I do him now?"

"You must wait." Nikolai pulled up the sleeve of his jacket to count off the seconds on his watch. "My son was killed at midnight. It will be the same for Mr. Gallagher."

"Whatever."

Despite the deadly risk of his current position, Quinn had to bite down on the urge to laugh. "I'm glad you were smart enough to figure out that the satellite link is on an individual feed from the rest of my systems."

"Thirty seconds, David," Nikolai announced. "I have been waiting a long time for this moment, Quinn. I have enjoyed watching you suffer. You took my factory, my money, my influence in Lukinburg—so my associates took my son. Know this. Once you are dead, your daughter will be easy prey."

"You go to hell, Titov."

"Now, Nikolai?"

"Twenty seconds."

David began to pace, counting off the seconds with every step. "I always wanted to prove I was better than you, Quinn. I'm the security expert that *you* hired. I take care of GSS, which takes care of all those cops and soldiers and little old ladies in the neighborhood. *I* do that. And yet, people bow down to you. They call *you* the brilliant one. Well, let me tell you something, boss." He got right in Quinn's face. "I can outthink you when it comes to security. Maybe I should start my own security empire. I can afford to now, you know. I planned it all out. I was ahead of you every step of the way. I took your money. I took out your computer codes at GSS and here."

"Ozzie did that—"

"—I got Ozzie to do it. I put a bomb in your building." He waved his gun toward the floors above them. "I took out Holmes and Rowley because, well, I just want their share of the money. It's just you and me, boss. And when the clock strikes midnight, it'll be just me."

"Ten seconds." Nikolai was enjoying this more than he should.

"Congratulations, David." Quinn wanted to keep him talking, wanted the man to confess every little part of their plan since the government monitored all foreign satellite feeds, and somewhere in the country, someone was watching this little show right now. "You came up with a plan to outsmart me, to take out every single device and protocol I've devised. Is that about right?"

"It's eating you up inside, isn't it?"

Quinn shrugged. "You forgot one thing."

"What's that?"

A dusty angel crawled out of the ventilation duct and dropped to the floor behind him. She put her gun to David's skull, and Quinn smiled.

"You forgot to take out the nanny."

Chapter Thirteen

New Year's Day

Miranda wrapped the hotel's fluffy white towel around her and tucked it in above her breasts. She combed out her damp hair and let it fall loosely down her back and shoulders.

"You're a looker," she joked with her reflection in the mirror. "If you're a prize fighter."

She touched the red-and-purple mark on her cheekbone and studied the stitched-up gash in her arm. She started counting all the tinier bumps and abrasions she'd earned while *celebrating* the holidays this week, but lost interest after number twenty.

Now, what exactly was it she had to offer a man again? Besides her heart?

She wasn't sure if it was a case of opposites attracting, or two lonely souls finding each other at a time of crisis, or because he was her comic-book hero come to life, but she'd fallen for Quinn Gallagher in the short span of a week, and had fallen hard.

Work was settling into place for her, she hoped, as long as she could keep those self-doubts in the past where they belonged. Captain Cutler was writing up a proposal to the commissioner to make KCPD SWAT teams six-man units because it had required *every man and woman on the team to bring everyone safely home*. And she was beginning to think that making Holden Kincaid a surrogate big brother like the rest of the men of SWAT Team 1 might be better than treating him as her enemy. Dr. Kilpatrick was going to have a field day with all the changes going on in Miranda's life the next time she sat down to talk with the police psychologist.

David Damiani had been arrested for multiple counts of murder, including the deaths of his accomplices, Holmes and Rowley. Elise Brown, suffering from an unfounded guilt that Miranda could relate to, had asked for a leave of absence from GSS. Apparently Nikolai Titov's flirtations that she'd found so charming had been a ruse to keep a close eye on Quinn's actions and reactions to each and every threat against GSS and Fiona. And now that there was an FBI and Interpol warrant for Nikolai's arrest, maybe Miranda could take her badge off for a few days to see if she could be the woman Quinn wanted and the friend Fiona needed.

She supposed that new mission started right now.

She opened the bathroom door and walked right into the middle of Quinn's chest. He wore a new pair of sweatpants from the hotel gift shop and nothing else but smooth skin and a dangerous smile. Singed by the contact, her cheeks hot with color, her words stuck in her throat, Miranda retreated a step.

But he followed her right through the doorway, leaning in to capture her mouth in a kiss. "Happy New Year."

Miranda teased him as he pulled away. "You're supposed to do that at midnight."

He shrugged those beautiful shoulders. "I was a little preoccupied at the time." He laced his fingers with hers and pulled her into the main room, where Fiona was stretched out with Petra in one of the room's two queen-size beds. "What do you think?"

Her eyes were on Fiona's sweet face. Oh, to be so young and innocent and to willingly move on from the things that could scare a body right down to her toes. "Is she asleep?"

"She's zonked." He tugged her another step. "I meant this bed."

"Quinn!" she gasped as he pushed her onto the covers and followed her down. His thigh landed between hers, nudging the towel up to an indecent position. Her breast pillowed against his chest as he moved in right beside her. His hands were on her shoulders and face and in her hair. And he was kissing her. And, oh, how this man could kiss. Leisurely. Hungrily. He teased. He took. He lavished. He tenderly invited her to be an equal in every brush of his lips, every foray of his tongue, every gentle nip of his teeth. She was a clinging, grasping puddle of hot, gooey need before she could catch a breath and find her voice again.

"We can't do this here."

"Where do you suggest? My house is closed off as a crime scene. My office has glass walls. This hotel is the perfect place. A locked door. Privacy. Some good friends from SWAT 1 keeping watch outside so we can catch up on our…rest."

"No, I meant…we shouldn't…"

He discovered a sensitive bundle of nerves at the juncture of her neck and shoulder and he teased it with his lips again and again, enjoying how it made her squirm and stammer. He licked the spot and blew warm air across it, raising dozens of goose bumps and making her shiver.

"Damn it, Quinn." She caught his face between her hands and demanded he look into her eyes and listen. "We can't do this here with Fiona sleeping in the next bed."

"You mean, what if you cry out and wake her?"

Miranda caught a taut male nipple between her thumb and forefinger, and grinned as the pectoral muscles bunched beneath her hand and a breath hissed through his teeth. "What if you cry out?" she challenged.

"You are... I can't..." Was the mighty Quinn Gallagher actually at a loss for words?

But he wasn't at a loss for action. As smoothly as they'd fallen onto the bed together, he pulled her to her feet and led her back to the bathroom.

He locked the door behind him and lifted her up onto the granite sink countertop. It was a cold shock to her bottom and thighs at first, but only for a moment. With a sweep of his hands, the towel was gone and his mouth was on her breast, teasing, tormenting. He caught the tip with his tongue and coaxed it to eager attention. His fingers kneaded her hips, her back, her bottom, until they slipped down to her thighs and went suddenly still.

He lifted his mouth from the hard rise and fall of her deep, stuttering chest and looked into her eyes. "I'm finishing what we started in the kitchen last night. Unless you tell me to stop."

Miranda pulled off his spare pair of glasses and gently kissed the puffy bruise beneath his eye. Then she kissed another mark. And another. She kissed his chin. His pulse was beating along his jaw. She laved her tongue around his nipples until he was gripping the edge of the counter and moaning her name.

And then she found his mouth and kissed him there.

She opened her lips to him.

She squeezed a palmful of his butt and pulled herself into his heat, opening her body to him.

He sheathed himself and entered her slowly, filling her, completing her.

He reached over and turned on the shower, but made no move to get either of them wet.

"I don't..." she gasped, clinging to his

shoulders, balancing on a precipice of desire and vulnerability, of need and want. "Quinn?"

He grinned. "We'll see which one of us cries out first."

Then, with those blue eyes never leaving hers, he rocked against her and she gasped. She tongued the base of his throat and he spasmed. He flicked his thumb over her nipple and she moaned. She hugged him with her legs and he grabbed up handfuls of her hair as he plunged in deeper and deeper, faster and faster. Their duel found a rhythm, and a pure molten heat gathered in the tips of her breasts and weighed heavy at her core.

He kissed her, lifted her, plunged into her slick warmth, and she cried her pleasure into his mouth as she crested on wave after wave of aftershocks. And when she started to tumble over, he stiffened between her legs and groaned his release against her neck.

And when she was spent and weak and truly sated, he wrapped her in his arms and she opened her heart to him.

QUINN SAW MIRANDA GO INTO protector mode one more time when the bellman knocked at the door to deliver a mysterious letter attached to a stuffed teddy bear that was as big as Fiona.

It was difficult to conceal a gun in the pocket of her red flannel pajamas. And there was no hiding the protective mama posture she had when she inspected the unmarked gift before letting an eagerly curious Fiona play with it. Miranda turned her back to the room and carefully opened the letter as though it might contain something poisonous or explosive.

When her shoulders sagged after reading the note, Quinn was instantly at her side. He thought she needed to sit, but she shook off attention and handed him the card and a photograph instead. "I'm so glad we didn't let her see this."

The card itself was brief, but the picture of Nikolai Titov with a bullet hole in his head and a knife stabbed into his heart spoke volumes.

Quinn was the one who sank into a chair and needed Miranda's comforting arm around him as he read the message again.

Quinn—
I am a man whose health is failing and whose history has not always been some-

thing a family would be proud of. But I still have some influence in Lukinburg.

I give you this gift.

I will not make further contact with Fiona, as I do not wish for any of my troubles here in St. Feodor to endanger her as they did my daughter. But know that she is safe, and that my enemies, and yours, here in Lukinburg, will never trouble her again.

Someday, tell her that her grandfather loved her. Be well, my son. And be good to the beautiful blonde who looks at you both with such love in her eyes.

Vasily

The three of them had breakfast in bed at about four in the afternoon. It was a messy business involving pancakes and dolls and laughter, flannel pajamas and a newspaper that these two women were never going to let him read.

It was a perfect way to celebrate the New Year, a perfect way to celebrate the terror of the past week finally ending, a perfect way to celebrate the beginning of…what?

Quinn watched the contrast of gold and dark hair bent together as they plotted some silly plan that probably involved him eating a pancake with his hands clasped behind his back again. He listened to the whispers and laughter. He drank in the smiles.

He couldn't ask Miranda to be his new chief of security. Michael had called her less than half an hour ago with some news that had made her throw her arms around his neck and kiss him. Apparently, no amount of money or charm or personal persuasion on the nearest countertop could lure her away from her job at KCPD.

He couldn't ask her to stay on as Fiona's nanny. He hoped there would never be another call for someone as fearlessly determined as she to step up and protect his child.

And clearly, unless there were some lessons involved somewhere along the line, he couldn't ask her to be the cook.

Fiona needed a mother.

And he needed…Miranda.

If he could just figure out what sort of proposition would appeal to her, then he'd do it. A week wasn't a long time to get to know someone. But he felt more sooner, deeper, differently, with Miranda Murdock than with anyone since his dear Valeska. And it was different than the innocent, rosy-eyed feeling he'd had for his wife. He felt alive, energized, sometimes a little frustrated, but always lucky to be with Miranda.

After Miranda set the tray aside, and Quinn had the chance to sit back and read his paper while they sat together with Petra and read the television listings, he found himself staring.

"What?" Miranda looked up from the grand adventure of a cooking show and tucked that silky fall of hair behind her ear.

"How do you feel about my daughter?" The direct approach might just work with this puzzle of a woman.

Miranda hugged the child at her side. "I've fallen in love with her."

"And her father?"

He'd negotiated million-dollar deals, invented technology on the fly and dealt with people from nations all over the world. But there was no question he'd ever asked where he was this nervous about the answer before.

Miranda smiled. "You're the smart guy, Quinn. Figure it out."

Finally, an answer he understood.

He reached for her hand and they hugged Fiona between them.

"I love you, too."

* * * * *

BILLIONAIRE'S
BABY BIND

KATHERINE GARBERA

Thank you to all of the Mills & Boon Desire
authors, editors and readers who have welcomed
me as part of this wonderful reading family.

One

Amberley Holbrook wasn't too keen on meeting new people; she preferred the company of her horses and keeping an eye on the stables where she worked. Normally her boss, Clay Everett of the Flying E, was happy to let her do what she wanted. But they had a guest on the property who had told Clay that he liked to ride. So as a courtesy Clay had suggested she stop by and introduce herself and offer to take the guest for a ride.

This held little appeal for Amberley. First of all, the dude was from Seattle, and the last time she checked there weren't any real cowboys from there, so that meant he was some kind of city slicker. Second…she and city slickers didn't get along. She would be the first to admit that was all down to her and her lousy attitude, which was something her fa-

ther had advised her to keep in check if she wanted
to keep this job.

Third…well, there wasn't any third. Digging in
her heels and refusing to do as Clay had asked certainly wasn't an option. Amberley had packed more
into her twenty-four years than most of her peers. She
knew she needed to keep her job because she loved
the horses she took care of and she certainly didn't
want to go back to her family's ranch in Tyler, Texas.

That was something her daddy had been sure to
remind her of when she'd called him earlier and told
him about Clay's guest. She and her father were close.
Her mom had died when Amberley was thirteen and
she'd had four younger siblings to watch over. She and
her dad had worked as a team to make sure everything on the ranch got done and her younger siblings,
ranging in ages from four to ten, were taken care of.
Sometimes her dad would say he cheated her out of
a childhood, but Amberley never felt that way. She
had her horse, Montgomery, and her family, and until
she'd turned eighteen, that was all that had mattered.

Amberley understood why she was nervous about
this new guest. The city guy had rented a danged Ford
Mustang to drive around in this rugged Texas landscape. She could see the sports car parked next to the
guest house that Clay had assigned him.

The Flying E was a sprawling ranch built in the
heyday of Clay Everett's Professional Bull Riding
career. He'd been at the top of his game until a bull
named Iron Heart had thrown him. Clay had had a
few ups and downs, but landed back on his feet and
started a new career as CEO of Everest, a company
that provided ironclad cloud infrastructure to com-

panies. Amberley was the first to admit she had no idea what that really was, but it made Clay a nice fortune and enabled him to employ her as his full-time horse master.

She took care of the stables on the Flying E, provided lessons to locals from Royal and the surrounding county and made sure any guest of the Everetts had access to horses. The ranch itself was sprawling, with a large mansion for the main house and several smaller guest houses. Amberley lived in a cottage that suited her to a T. She'd always wanted her own place and lots of ranch land, something that was beyond the budget of a simple barrel racer like herself. So living on the Flying E and working for Clay gave her the best of both worlds.

She took another look at the sports car.

City guy.

As a teen, she'd watched shows like *Gossip Girl* and longed to be in Manhattan, though she'd have stuck out like…well, a sore thumb, but she had liked the fantasy of it.

So perhaps it wasn't quite so surprising that this man was making her curious before she'd even met him.

"Are you going to knock or just stand here all day?" Cara asked as she stood in front of the guest cabin that had been assigned to Will. The cabin itself was really a sprawling three-bedroom cottage that was all natural wood and glass.

Cara was seventeen and also worked on the ranch with Amberley, as her apprentice. She'd brought the teenager with her to meet Clay's new guest to be sure Amberley didn't do anything…well, stupid.

"Yeah. I was just waiting for the music to die down a little."

"I don't think it's going to," Cara said. "I thought he had a baby. You'd think the old dude would put on some headphones."

"You think he's old?"

Cara raised both eyebrows at Amberley. "Most def. He's got a kid, right? So, I'm guessing he must be old—"

"Geez, kid, back in my day we had to boot up a big old DOS machine and wait half a day for our computers to start working."

The voice was deep and rich, like the faux bass line in White Stripes' "Seven Nation Army," and Amberley felt a blush starting at her chest and working up over her cheeks as she turned to look at him. Their eyes met. His were forest green and made her think of the meadow she rode past each morning on her dawn ride on Montgomery.

There was a sardonic note in his voice that she totally got.

He wasn't old.

He wasn't old at all.

He wore a faded MIT T-shirt that clung to his shoulders and lean stomach. He had on a pair of faded jeans that hung low on his hips, and as she glanced down at his feet she noticed he had on Converse sneakers.

He was exactly what she'd been fearing and, if she was honest, secretly hoping he would be.

"You don't look too bad for your age," Amberley said. "I'm Amberley Holbrook, horse master, and this is my apprentice, Cara. Clay asked me to introduce myself and let you know that the stables are available for your use."

"Thanks," he said, holding out his hand to Cara. "Will Brady. Ancient one."

"Geez, dude, I'm sorry. I was just being mouthy. My mom has been warning me about that forever," Cara said.

"It's all right. I probably do seem ancient to a high schooler."

Cara shook his hand. Amberley wiped her hands on the sides of her jeans and took a deep breath and then their hands met. His skin wasn't dry and rough, the way so many of the hands of the men on the ranch were. They were soft, and as she looked down she noticed that his nails were neat and intact, not split from accidentally smashing one with a hammer.

She rubbed her thumb over his knuckles and then realized what she was doing and dropped his hand.

"Anyway... Come over to the stables anytime. I'll have to observe you riding before I can clear you to ride alone."

"No problem. I'll probably stop by this afternoon," he said. "I have a conference call with the sheriff this morning."

"Is this about Maverick?" Cara asked. "I heard you were in town to stop him."

Will shrugged and gave her a self-deprecating smile. "Just going to see what I can find on the internet to track that SOB down."

"I know we will all be glad for that," Amberley said. "I'm pretty much always at the stables, so stop by anytime."

Cara arched one eyebrow at Amberley but kept

her mouth shut, and they turned and walked back toward the stables. She tried to tell herself that he was just a guy…but she knew that he was so much more than that.

Amberley wasn't the kind of woman who had time for gossip or staring at hot guys. Yet she'd found herself riding by his place for the last two mornings hoping for a glimpse of him. Instead she'd had a conversation with Erin Sinclair, Will's nanny, and she'd even cuddled his cute daughter, eleven-month-old Faye.

Will had called down to the stables earlier to say he was going to come by for a ride, but he wasn't sure when the computer program he'd been running would be done. So it could be anytime between now and sunset. She was trying to focus on the work she had to do. There were horses to tame to the saddle, and she liked it that way. She'd always preferred animals over people. They were easy to predict, she thought. She'd grown up in a very large family, and the thought of having her own, well… She liked kids and men, but having to take care of her own brood made her break out in hives.

"You have to admit he's hot," Cara said. "Not old at all."

"He's a city slicker who probably can't tell a horse from steer. Who has time for that?" Amberley asked.

She and Cara were both grooming horses for the newcomers so they'd be able to take a ride around Clay Everett's ranch and get the lay of the land. When Cara had asked Amberley if she could help her out at the ranch, her gut instinct had been to say no. After all, what exactly did she have to teach the high school girl, but Cara had been insistent and one thing had led to another, and now she was in the barn grooming horses with a chatty seventeen-year-old.

"I'm just saying if a guy like that looked at me—"

"Your boyfriend would be jealous," Amberley said. Cara was dating one of the varsity football players.

"Yeah, he would be. For now. Next year he'll be gone and I'll be…I don't know where I'll be. Did you ever wish you'd gone to college?" Cara asked.

Amberley thought about it. At seventeen she'd wanted to get as far away from Texas, her siblings and the ranching life as she could. She'd wanted a chance to be on her own. But her family hadn't had the money for college and, to be honest, Amberley had only been an okay student. No one had been offering her any money for school and this job with Clay had come along at the right time. She'd met his foreman when she'd been rodeoing during her early teens and he'd offered the job.

It hadn't been her dream, but it had meant she'd be out of her dad's house and away from the siblings she'd had to babysit, and that had seemed like a dream.

At times, it was easy to forget she'd once wanted something else from life. She wasn't a whiner and didn't have time to listen to herself think of things that might have been. It was what it was.

"Not really. I have my horses and Clay pretty much lets me have the freedom to run the barn the way I want to. What more could a gal ask for?" Amberley said, hoping that some of her ennui wasn't obvious to Cara.

"I hope I feel like that someday."

"You will. You're seventeen, you're not supposed to have it all figured out," she said.

"I hope so," Cara said. Her phone pinged.

"Go on and chat with your friends. I can finish up the other horse. You know he mentioned he didn't know when he'd be down here."

"Here I am," a masculine voice said. "I hope I'm not interrupting."

Amberley felt the heat on her face and knew she was blushing. She could blame it on her redhead complexion, but she knew it was embarrassment. She could only be glad he hadn't arrived any earlier.

"Not disappointed at all," she said, reaching for her straw cowboy hat before stepping out of the stall and into the main aisle of the barn.

She'd sort of hoped that he wouldn't be as good-looking as she remembered. But that wasn't the case. In fact, his thick blond-brown hair looked even thicker today and his jaw was strong and clean-shaven. His green eyes were intense and she couldn't look away from him.

She told herself her interest in him was just because he was so different than the other men around the ranch.

If he had a pair of Wrangler jeans and some worn ranch boots she wouldn't be interested in him at all. But the fact that he had a Pearl Jam T-shirt on and a pair of faded jeans that clung to all the right spots was the only reason she was even vaguely attracted to him.

She noticed his mouth was moving and she thought she wouldn't mind it moving against hers. But then she realized he was speaking when Cara, who'd come out of her stall as well, looked at her oddly.

"Sorry about that. What did you say?"

"I was just saying that I'm sorry if just showing up messed up your schedule. I do appreciate you being available on my timetable," he said. "If you need more time to get ready I can wait over there."

She shook her head. He was being so reasonable. But she just had a bee in her bonnet when it came to this guy. Well, to all men who came from the city. She wished he wasn't so darn appealing. That maybe his voice would be soft or odd, but of course, he didn't have some silly city voice. Instead, his words were like a deep timbre brushing over her ears and her senses like a warm breeze on a summer's day. Since it was Texas, October wasn't too cool, but it was fall and she missed summer.

But with him… Dammit. She had to stop this.

"I'm ready. Cara, will you show Mr. Brady to his horse?" she asked her apprentice, who was watching her with one of those smirks only a teenager could manage.

"Sure thing, Ms. Holbrook," Cara said sarcastically.

"You can call me Will," he told Cara.

"Ms. Holbrook, can Will call you Amberley?"

That girl. She was pushing Amberley because she knew she could. "Of course."

"Thanks, Amberley," he said.

She told herself that there was nothing special about the way he said her name, but it sent shivers— the good kind—down her spine. She had to nip this attraction in the bud. Will was going to be here for a while helping Max St. Cloud investigate the cyber-bully and blackmailer Maverick, who'd been wreaking havoc on the local residents, particularly the members of the Texas Cattleman's Club, releasing videos and other damning stories on the internet. Will was the CTO of the company, so he was more of a partner to Max than an employee, and rumor had it they were old friends.

"No prob," she said. "How'd you end up here in Royal?" Amberley asked Will while Cara went to get his horse.

"Chelsea Hunt and Max go way back. So she asked for our help to try to find the identity of Maverick."

Maverick had been doing his best to make life hell for the members of the Texas Cattleman's Club. He'd been revealing secrets gleaned from hacking into smartphones and other internet connected devices. He'd made things uncomfortable for everyone in Royal.

"I like Chelsea. She's smart as a whip," Amberley said. And she seemed to really have her stuff together. No shrinking violet, Chelsea was one of the women that Amberley looked up to in Royal. She lived her life on her own terms, and Amberley was pretty sure that if Chelsea liked a guy she didn't have to come up with reasons to avoid him…the way that Amberley herself had been doing.

Cara came back with Will's mount and Amberley went back into the stall and saw her faithful horse, Montgomery, waiting for her. She went to the animal and rested her forehead against the horse's neck. Montgomery curved her head around Amberley's and she felt a little bit better. She had always been better with horses than people.

And normally that wouldn't bother her. But it would be nice not to screw up around men as much as she just had with Will. She didn't enjoy feeling like an awkward country bumpkin.

Will hadn't expected to feel so out of place in Texas. He'd been to Dallas before and thought that the stereotype of boots, cowboy hats and horses was something from the past or in the imagination of television producers. But being here on the Flying E had shown him otherwise.

Amberley was cute and a distraction. Something—hell, someone—to take his mind off Seattle and all that he'd left behind there. All that he'd lost. To be honest, coming out here might have been what he needed. His baby girl was sleeping with her nanny watching over her, and he was someplace new.

Max hadn't batted an eye when Will had told him he needed to bring his daughter and her nanny along with him to Royal. His friend had known that Will was a dedicated single dad.

He had work to do, of course, but he'd ridden a long time ago and thought getting back on a horse might be the first step to moving on. From his wife's death.

It was funny, but after Lucy's death everyone had been comforting and left him to process his grief. But now that so many months had gone by and he was still in the same routine, they were starting to talk, and his mom and Lucy's mom weren't as subtle as they both liked to think they were, with their encouragement to "live again" and reminders that he still had a long life ahead of him.

Lucy had had a brain hemorrhage a few weeks before she was due. The doctors had kept her alive until she gave birth to Faye. Then they took her off the machines that had been keeping her alive and she'd faded away. He'd asked them to wait a week after Faye's birth because he hadn't wanted his daughter's birthday to also be the day she'd lost her mom.

"You okay?"

"Yeah. Sorry. Just distracted," he said.

"It happens," she said. She spoke with a distinctive Texan drawl. It was so different from Lucy's Northwestern accent that he... Hell, he needed to stop thinking about her. He was getting away for a while, helping out a friend and having a ride to clear his head. He knew he should let that be enough.

"It does. Sorry, I'm really bad company right now. I thought..."

"Hey. You don't have to entertain me. Whenever I'm in a bad place mentally—not saying you are—but when I am, I love to get out of the barn, take Montgomery here for a run. There's no time to think about anything except the terrain and my horse—it clears away the cobwebs in my mind."

He had just noticed how pretty her lips were. A shell-pink color. And when she smiled at him her entire face seemed to light up. "Just what I need. Let's do this."

"Well, before we get started I need to know what your horsemanship level is," she said. "We'll pick our route based on that."

"Summer camp and college polo team," he said.

"I stopped playing about three years ago. I'm a pretty decent rider and keep a horse at a stable near my home. But haven't been riding much since my daughter was born."

"Sounds like you might be a bit rusty but you've got some skills," she said. "I'll start ya out easy and see how it goes."

"I'm yours to command," he said.

"Mine to command? Not sure I've ever had anything with two legs under my command."

He threw his head back and laughed. She was funny, this one. He wasn't sure if she'd meant that to be a come-on, but there was something sort of innocent about her so he guessed not. She was very different from Lucy, his late wife. That twinge he always experienced at the thought of her colored the moment.

"Let's start with a ride," he said.

She nodded. "There's a mounting block over there if you need a leg up. I'll let you go first."

"Thanks," he said, leading his horse to the block and mounting easily. He shifted around in the saddle until he was comfortable. The horse she had him on was easily controlled and led and seemed comfortable with him as a rider.

"So why are you here?" she asked as she mounted her own horse.

He told himself to look away but didn't. Her jeans hugged the curve of her butt and as she climbed on the horse there was something very natural about how she moved. As she put both feet in the stirrups and sat up, he realized she looked more at home on horseback than she had talking to him.

"Ah, I'm here to investigate all the trouble that Maverick is causing. I'm really good at tracking someone's cyber footprint."

She shook her head and then gently brushed her heels against her horse and made a clicking sound. "I don't even know what a cyber footprint is."

He laughed a little at her comment. "Most people don't think about it, but with smartphones and social media apps, we all are leaving a trail that can be followed."

"That makes sense," she said. "You ready for a run or do you just want to take it slow and steady?" she asked as they left the barn area and reached the open plains.

The land stretched out as far as he could see. It was October, so in Seattle it was rainy and growing colder, but the sun was shining down on them today in Texas and the weather was warm. He lifted his face to the sun, taking a deep breath. It was a good day to be alive.

As the thought crossed his mind, he remembered Lucy again and shook his head. He wasn't going to cry for the wife he'd lost or the family that had been broken. Not now and not in front of this strong, sunny cowgirl.

"Run," he said.

"Just the answer I was hoping for. Follow me. I'm going to start slow and then build. This part of the ranch is safe enough for a run."

She took off and he sat there for a moment stuck in the past until she glanced over her shoulder, her long braid flying out to the side, and smiled at him.

"You coming?"

This ride was just the thing he needed to draw him out of the gloom of the past.

"Hell, yes."

Riding had always been Amberley's escape. But with Will riding by her side, she felt more fenced-in than free. Clay had asked everyone at the Flying E to make Will feel welcome and she tried to tell herself that was all she was doing now. He was just another guest, a city boy, at that. He was here temporarily. She didn't like to think about her past or about the guy she'd fallen too hard and too quickly for. But there was something about Will that brought that all up.

Mostly, she realized it was superficial. They were both outsiders to her way of life. But where Sam Pascal had been looking for some sort of Western fantasy, it seemed to her that Will was looking...well, for a cyberbully but also for some sort of escape. There was a sadness that lingered in his eyes and when he thought no one was looking she could see that he was battling with his own demons.

Something she battled herself.

She heard him thundering along behind her and glanced over her shoulder. He sat in the saddle well and moved like he'd been born to ride. It was hard to keep him shoved in the city-slicker box when she saw him on horseback. She turned to face the field in front of them, taking a moment just to be glad for this sunny October day.

It was good to be alive.

The air had the nip of fall to it and the sky was so

big it seemed to stretch forever. She slowed her horse and waited for Will to catch up to her.

He did in a moment and she glanced over to see a big smile on his face.

"I needed this."

Two

"Not bad for a city boy," Amberley told him as they allowed their horses to walk and cool down after their run. "I'm sorry I was judgmental about your skills."

Will couldn't help but like his riding guide. She was blunt and honest and it was refreshing. At work everyone treated him like he was the walking wounded and, of course, at home his nanny only discussed Faye. Rightly so. But Amberley didn't. She'd been treating him like a regular guy.

He hadn't realized how much he needed to get away and be with people who didn't know the personal details of his life. There was something freeing about being with Amberley on this sunny October afternoon. He felt for a moment like his old self. Before Lucy.

He felt a pang. Shook his head to shove the feeling from his mind.

"I didn't realize you were judging me," he said.

She tipped her cowboy hat back on her head and turned to gaze at him with a sardonic look. Her face was in shadows beneath the straw cowboy hat, but he could read her body language. She was sassy and funny, this cowgirl.

Distracting.

"I was judging you and it wasn't fair. It's just the last time I was around city folk was when I worked on this dude ranch in Tyler and a lot of them were… well, not very good riders. So I lumped you in with them. I should have known Clay wouldn't have told me to give you free rein if you didn't know what you were doing," she said. She held the reins loosely in one hand, and pushed the brim of her hat back on her forehead with the other.

Her eyes were a deep brown that reminded him of the color of his mocha in the morning. They were pretty and direct and he was almost certain when she was angry they'd show her temper. Will wondered how they'd look when she made love.

Then he shook his head.

This was the first time lust had come on so strongly since Lucy's death. And it took him by surprise.

He shook his head again. "To be fair, I'm not sure he knew my skill level. I think Max asked him to make sure I get the full Texas experience."

"The full Texas? That's funny. Well, this might be about it," she said, gesturing to the pastures.

He skimmed his gaze over the landscape and then settled back in the saddle. It reminded him of some of the places he'd visited growing up. His family had some property in Montana and there was a similar feeling of freedom from the real world here.

"I'm sure riding across the open plain isn't the only thing that's unique to Texas," he said. "You mentioned Tyler—did you just visit that dude ranch?"

"Nah," she said, looking away from him. But before she did he noticed a hint of sadness in her eyes.

"I worked there when I was in high school in the summers. Clay offered me this job after…well, when I was ready to leave my family's ranch. My daddy said I was losing myself by mothering my brothers and sisters and he wanted me to have a chance to have my own life. I'm pretty good with horses. My daddy has a nice-sized ranch in Tyler. What about you? Where are you from? The Northwest, right?"

"Yes. Seattle area. Bellevue, actually. It's a suburb," he said. He'd never wanted to live anywhere else growing up. He loved the mountains and his waterfront property, but after Lucy…well, he'd been struggling to make Bellevue feel like home again.

"I've heard of it. I think Bill Gates lives there."

"We're not neighbors," Will said with a laugh.

She shook her head and laughed. "I'll jot that down. You ready for a ride back or you want to see some more?"

"What's left to see?"

She rocked back in her saddle, shifting to extend her arm. "Out that way is the south pasture—there's a creek that runs through it. Down that way is the—"

"Let me guess—north pasture."

"Ha. I was going to say castration shed. We do that in the spring," she said.

He shook his head. "I'll skip that."

"Guys always say that."

She was teasing him and he observed that her entire countenance had changed. Her relaxed smile made him realize how full and lush her mouth was, and the way she tipped her head to the side, waiting for his response, made him want to do something impulsive.

Like lean over and kiss her.

He slammed the door on that idea and sat back in his saddle to be a little farther away from her. There was just something about her easy smile and the wind stirring around them. And he was on horseback in Texas, so far away from his normal world, that he wanted to pretend he was someone different. A man who wasn't so tired from not sleeping and hoping he was making the right choices all the time.

He knew that nothing would come of kissing Amberley. He wasn't here to hook up. He was here to do a job. Besides that, he wasn't ready for anything else. He knew that. But for a moment, he wished he were.

"Back to the ranch."

She didn't move, but just stared at him—there was a closed expression on her face now. "Sorry, sir, didn't mean to be inappropriate. Follow me. You want to run back or walk?"

"Amberley—"

"I was out of line. I guess I forgot you were a guest for a second."

"Who did you think I was?" he asked.

"Just a guy," she said, turning her horse and making a clicking sound. Then she took off back the way they'd come.

* * *

He galloped after her and reached over to take her reins, drawing both of their rides to a stop.

She took back her reins and gave him a good hard glare. "Don't do that again."

"Well, I couldn't figure out another way to stop you," he yelled. He wasn't sure what he'd stepped into, but he could tell something had changed and he was pretty damn sure he was the cause.

"Why would you want to?" she asked. "I'm pretty sure you want to get back to the ranch and I'm taking you there."

"Don't act that way," he said. "I'm sorry. My life is complicated."

She nodded and then looked away. "Everyone's life is complicated. We're not simple hicks out here on the ranch."

He hadn't meant to hurt or offend her.

And all of a sudden he felt ancient. Not twenty-eight. Not like a new father should feel, but like Methuselah. And he hated that. He'd always been…a different man. His father had said he was lucky and someday his luck would wear thin. But he knew his father wouldn't rejoice in the way his luck had run out. Losing Lucy had changed him, and some people would say not for the better.

"I'm sorry," he said. The words sounded rusty and forced but they weren't. She didn't deserve to be treated the way he'd treated her, because he wanted her and he knew he wasn't going to do anything about it. He wasn't about to invite another person into the chaos that his life was right now.

"What for?"

"That sounded…jerky, didn't it? Like I'm trying to imply that your life isn't complicated," he said. "That's not at all what I meant. I just meant I'm a mess and this ride was nice and you are wonderful…"

He trailed off. What else could he say? He thought she was cute. Maybe he'd like to kiss her, if he wasn't so stuck in that morass of guilt and grief. And then more guilt because his grief was starting to wane. And it's not like Lucy would have expected him to grieve forever, but moving on was like saying goodbye again.

"I wouldn't go that far," she said.

"What?"

"Saying I'm wonderful. I mean, I have faults like everyone else," she said. Her words were light and obviously meant to give him a way back from the dark place he'd wondered into. But in her eyes he saw weariness and he knew that she wasn't as…well, un-damaged as he had believed she was.

"You seem like it from here," he said at last.

"Then I better keep up the illusion."

But now that she'd brought it up he was trying to see what there was to the young horsewoman. She seemed uncomplicated. He thought about how when he was her age, life had been pretty damned sweet.

"Tell me," he prompted.

"Tell you what?" she asked.

"Something that isn't wonderful about you," he said.

"Ah, well, I think that would be easy enough. I have a short temper. I believe I gave you a glimpse of that a moment ago."

"You sure did," he said with a laugh. "But that could also be called spunk. I like feisty women."

"You do?" she asked, then shook her head. "What about you? What's one of your faults?"

"Hell, I'm not even sure where to begin," he said. And he knew that he didn't want to open that can of worms. His life was littered with regrets lately. Only spending time with Faye or sitting in the dark working on the computer tracking down code seemed to get him out of his own head space.

"I'm not as clever as I once believed I was."

She started laughing. "Well, I think that's the same for all of us. Race you back to the barn?"

"Sure, but since I haven't ridden in a while I think I deserve a handicap."

"Really?" she asked. "That is such a load of crap. If I hadn't seen you ride out here I might have fallen for it."

"It was worth a try," he said.

The fall breeze blew, stirring the air, and a strand of her red hair slipped from her braid and brushed against her cheek. He leaned forward in his saddle and gripped the reins to keep from reaching out and touching her.

He'd just shoved a big wedge between them. A smart man would leave it in place. A smart man would remember that Amberley wasn't a woman to mess with and he had never been the kind of man who screwed around with anyone.

But he didn't feel smart.

He felt lonely and like it had been too long since he'd been able to breathe and not catch the faint scent of hospital disinfectant. He wanted to sit here until night fell and then maybe he'd think about heading back to the life he had. He wanted...

Something he wasn't in a position to take.

He knew that.

"Hey, Will?"

He looked up, realizing that she'd been staring at him the entire time.

"Yeah?"

"Don't sweat it. I've got a beef with city dudes and it's clear that you have something with your baby's mama to deal with. You're hot and the way you ride a horse makes me feel things I'd rather not admit to, but that's it. You're on the Flying E to work and as a guest and I'm going to treat you like that. So don't think…"

"What do you feel?" he asked.

Will knew he felt reckless and dangerous and he wasn't going to stop now. He wanted to kiss her. He wanted to pull her off the horse and into his arms and see where that led.

"Like I said, I'm not going there."

He shifted in the saddle and dismounted his horse, dropping the reins on the ground to check that the horse would stay, and it did.

Will walked over to her and stood there next to her horse, looking up at her. He was closer now, and he could see her eyes, and he wasn't sure what he read in her expression. He was going to tell himself it was desire and need. The same things he was feeling, but he was afraid he might be projecting.

"Come on down here," he said. "Just for this afternoon let's pretend we aren't those people. I'm not a guest and you're not a ranch hand. We're just a guy and his girl and we've got this beautiful after-noon to spend together."

* * *

Never in her life had Amberley wanted to get off a horse more. But her gut said no. That this wasn't going to be sweet or uncomplicated. And the last time she'd been sweet-talked by a guy it hadn't ended well. It didn't matter that she was older and wiser now. She didn't feel as if she was either.

Riding hadn't helped to chase away her demons back then, when she'd found herself pregnant and alone at eighteen, and it wasn't helping now. He stood there in his clothes, not fake-cowboy duded up the way some city guys dressed when they came to Texas, and to be fair he looked like he fit in. He wasn't chasing a Wild West fantasy, he was here to do a job.

And her job was to make him feel comfortable.

What could be more comfortable than hanging out together?

Dumb.

Stupid.

His hair was thick and wavy and he wasn't wearing a hat, so she could see the way he'd tousled it when he'd run his fingers through it. She wasn't getting off her horse. She was going to be sensible.

Please, Amberley, be sensible.

But she never had been.

She suspected it was because she'd had to be so responsible so young. She'd always had to take care of her younger brothers and sisters. But that was in Tyler, and she was away from there now, with no one to worry about but herself.

And this was safe. He just wanted to spend the afternoon together.

One afternoon.

Surely even she could manage that without having it go to hell.

She shifted and started to turn to swing her leg over the saddle and dismount, then she saw the smile on his face and the look of relief.

He was unsure.

Just like her.

Except he wasn't like her. He had ties. And she hadn't asked about them earlier. There was so much she didn't know. Where was his baby's mother? That baby was pretty damn young to be living with a nanny and her father. Was there any way this could be just an afternoon?

If it was...then the mom didn't matter... Unless they were still together. That would be—

"Hey, before we do this. Where is your baby's mother? I don't want to pry but you're not still with her, right?" she asked.

He stepped back—stumbled was more like it— and she suddenly wished she'd kept her mouth shut.

There was no denying the way all the color left his face, or how he turned away from her and cursed under his breath.

"No," he said, walking back over to his horse and taking his saddle with much skill and finesse.

"We're not still together. She's dead." He made a clicking sound and took off across the field as if the hounds of hell were chasing him, and Amberley guessed maybe they were.

She stood there, a wave of sadness rolling over her. A part of her had died when she'd miscarried. Seeing Will...had made her realize that they were two sides of the same coin. She had no baby and no family and he had a baby and no wife or mother for the child. He was trying to deal with the loss the same way she had been.

She knew that riding helped at times but she'd never been able to outrun the pain. Those memories and the truth of her life were always waiting when she'd gotten off the horse.

She clicked her mare and followed Will close enough to call out if he took a path that wasn't safe, but he had watched their trail on the way out and he made no mistakes on the way back.

She slowed her own horse to a walk as Will entered the stable area and decided that maybe she should just let him go. Give him some space to dismount and leave before she entered the barn again.

She saw the ring that she'd set up earlier to practice barrel racing and rode over that way. Montgomery and she had been partners for the last year or so. And when the Flying E could spare her she took the horse and went and competed in rodeos.

Three

Will had just spent the last ten minutes in the barn trying to avoid a confrontation with Amberley—the woman he'd practically run away from. But he had no doubt she would be avoiding him after his foolish reaction to her harmless question about Faye's mother.

It was hard to think that at twenty-eight he was turning into his father, but it seemed that way more and more. And it wasn't Faye who was forcing the change. It was him. It was as if he'd lost that spark that had always driven him. And the therapist he'd seen for two sessions at his mom's insistence had said that grief took time.

But as he left the barn and spotted Amberley exercising her horse in the ring, he felt that stirring again.

It was lust, because even though he was grieving he wasn't dead, and the feeling was laced with something more. Something much more. She was one with the horse as she raced around the barrels, her braid flying out behind her as she leaned into the curves and got low over the horse's neck, whispering encouragement, he imagined.

He watched her and wanted her.

She stopped at the end of her run and looked over toward the barn. Their eyes met and he felt stupid just standing there.

He clapped.

But that felt dumb, too.

It seemed that he'd left his smarts behind in Seattle, he thought. Everything was different here. He tried to justify his feelings—like he needed an excuse to find a woman pretty or be turned on by her. Yet in a way he felt he did.

But that was his issue, not Amberley's. And it wasn't fair to her to bring her into the swirling whirlpool that his emotions were at this moment.

She nodded and then turned away from him.

Dismissing him.

He'd had his chance and he'd ruined it.

Maybe it was for the best. He had Faye to take care of and a criminal to catch. In fact, he needed to get back to work. Without another glance at her he turned and walked to the golf cart that had been allocated for his use during his stay on the Flying E. He put it in gear and drove to the house that Clay Everett had been generous enough to provide. To be honest, he knew that Clay had a stake in Will finding Maverick, as did most of Royal.

He shifted gears as he drove farther and farther away from the barn and the cowgirl that he'd left there, but a part of his mind was still fantasizing about the way his afternoon could have gone.

His nanny, Erin Sinclair, was waiting for him at the door when he got back.

"Faye's asleep and I need to run to town to pick up some more baby food and formula. Are you okay if I go now?" she asked.

He had hired Erin to help with the baby even before Lucy's untimely death. His late wife had been a product rep for a large pharmaceutical company and traveled a lot for work. Though Will spent a lot of time in his home office, he tended to have a single-minded focus, so he knew that by the time Faye was born, both he and Lucy would have needed help with the baby.

"Yes, go," he said.

He went into the bedroom they used as a nursery and looked down at Faye's sleeping face. He tried to see Lucy in her features but he was starting to forget what she looked like. Of course he had pictures of her but he was starting to lose that feeling of what she'd looked like as she smiled at him. The different feeling she'd stirred in him with one of her expressions that a mere photo couldn't capture.

Dammit.

He turned away from the crib and walked out of the room. He had a monitor app on his phone and had a window that he could keep open on one of the many monitors in his office so he could keep an eye on her.

He walked into the darkened large bedroom that he'd turned into his office for the duration of his stay in Royal. He had four large computer monitors that were hooked up to different hard drives and were all running multiple programs that would determine where Maverick was basing himself online.

Almost all of the attacks had been cyber-based, so Chelsea was working on the theory that he was very internet savvy. In a way that worked in their favor because there weren't many top computer experts in Royal. But then hackers wouldn't be known to many.

One of Will's skills was the ability to look at code and see a digital fingerprint in it. Maverick had habits just like everyone and Will was searching for those, looking for a trail back to the creep's identity.

He opened his laptop after he checked the progress on the different computers and made sure all of his scripts were still running.

He launched his internet browser and searched for information on Amberley Holbrook. He wasn't surprised to see her listed in a bunch of small-town rodeos, stretching from Texas to Oklahoma to Arkansas, as a winner or a top-three finisher in barrel-racing competitions. There was a photo of her winning run in a recent event and he clicked to open it larger in his photo application so he could zoom in on her face. There was concentration but also the biggest damn grin he'd ever seen.

That girl was happiest on the back of a horse.

Why?

He noticed how she was when she was off her horse. On her guard and waiting to see how everyone around her reacted. Given that he was starting to behave that way, he wondered what had happened to force her to build those kinds of walls. She definitely had them.

Why?

And why the hell did he care?

Because she intrigued him. She was different. Funny, sexy, sassy. She made him think of things he hadn't in a really long time.

And he'd just walked away from her. He'd decided he had too much baggage to dally with a woman who was tied to Texas and this ranch. He wasn't here for longer than it took to find the cyber coward Maverick, then he was out of here. And back in the Pacific Northwest, where he could slowly rot from guilt and grief.

That sounded damn pitiful. He had never been that kind of man and he wasn't too sure that Faye was going to want a father who was like that.

He knew he had to move on.

Will had come here in part because Max had asked and also because he knew he had to get away from the memories, get away from the guilt and the grief. But he was in no position to move on. He had to keep moving forward until he figured out what he wanted next. Amberley had been a distraction but also something more. She was honest and forthright. He liked that.

He liked her.

If he were in a different place in his life then the zing of attraction that had arced between them…well, he would feel better about acting on it.

But he wasn't.

And that wasn't fair to her.

Who said life was fair… The words of his therapist drifted through his mind. He'd been lamenting the fact that Faye would never know Lucy and that it wasn't fair.

Well, life might not be, but he knew he couldn't just use Amberley for himself and then leave. That wasn't right.

And he hadn't changed at his core.

But she intrigued him…

Amberley blasted My Chemical Romance as she got ready to go out. It was Friday night and two days had passed since…whatever the hell that had been with Will. She tried to remind herself he was a city dude and she should have known better than to be attracted to him, but that hadn't kept him out of her dreams for the last two nights.

So when her cousin from Midland had called and said she'd be driving through Royal on Friday and did Amberley want to go out, she'd said yes. Normally she was all for comfy jammies and binge-watching one of her favorite TV shows on Netflix, but tonight she needed to get out of her own head.

She was ready to dance to some rowdy country music, drink too much tequila and flirt with some small-town boys who wouldn't walk away from her without a word. It had been a long time since she had blown off steam and it was the weekend. Even though she sometimes acted like she was ready for the retirement home, she was still young.

But she didn't feel it.

There was a weight in her heart that made her feel older than her years. And when Will had said his life was complicated she'd…well, she'd ached because she knew complicated.

She knew what it was like to be a big, fat, red-hot mess masquerading as normal. She'd done that for a year after she'd lost the baby and then gotten the devastating news that she'd never be able to have a child. A part of her should have rejoiced that he'd only seen what she had wanted him to—a cowgirl who was damn good with horses.

But that connection she'd felt with him had made her want him to see more.

And he hadn't.

He hadn't.

She was wearing her good jeans—a dark wash that fit like a second skin—and a pair of hand-tooled boots that her brothers and sisters had given her for Christmas. They had a fancy design featuring turquoise and she'd completed her outfit with a flirty peasant top. She'd taken the time to blow-dry her hair and not just pull it back in a braid, so it fell around her shoulders.

She finished her makeup and put a dash of lip gloss on before grabbing her purse and heading out. She was halfway to her truck when she realized someone was in her yard. Not that it was really her yard, since Clay owned all the property, but that little area in front of her place.

Amberley glanced over and realized the someone was a dog. A ragged stray that was making mewling sounds that she couldn't ignore. He was a rather sad-looking animal with a matted coat. She tossed her purse on the hood of her truck and turned toward the dog, careful not to spook it as she walked toward it. She crouched low and held out her hand for it to sniff once she was close enough.

The animal whimpered and then slowly moved closer to her. She held her ground, noticing that it limped. One of his legs was injured. Just the distraction she needed. Animals were the one thing on this planet that she was actually good with.

She waited until the dog came closer and noticed that there were some briars wrapped around his hind leg, and when she reached for the leg he moaned and moved away from her.

"All right, boy. I'll let it be. But we are going to have to take you to get that looked at," she said. She stood up, pulled her phone from her back pocket and texted her cousin that she'd be a little late. Then she went back into her place, got a blanket, a bowl and bottle of water. Then she grabbed a carrot from the fridge and went back outside.

The dog was exactly where she'd left him. Waiting for her.

"Good boy. You're a boy, right?" she asked.

The dog didn't answer—not that she expected him to. She put the bowl down in front of him and gave him some water and stood to watch him as he drank, then texted the small animal vet that Clay used to let him know she'd be bringing in an injured dog. Though it was after hours, Clay had an agreement for the ranch that included 24/7 coverage.

She spent the next hour getting the dog settled at the vet. He had a chip and the vet contacted his owners, who were very glad to find him. Amberley waited until they arrived before leaving to meet her cousin. But the truth was she no longer wanted to go out.

The dog—Barney—reminded her of how alone she was. Even the stray had someone to go home to. His owners had been really nice and so happy she'd found him and Amberley was gracious to them, but a part of her had wanted the stray to be a loner. To maybe need her.

She hated that she was feeling down about her life. She'd finally gotten past everything that had happened when she was eighteen and now some dude was making her question her situation. She'd never been this knocked on her butt for some guy. Yet there was something about him that had made her want to be more. Want to be someone she hadn't thought about being in a long time.

But there it was.

She wanted to see him again.

Her cousin was waiting in the parking lot of the Wild Boar, a roadhouse that served food and drinks and had a small dance floor with live music on the weekends. There were pool tables in the back and a mechanical bull. If you weren't in the upper echelon of Royal and weren't a member of the Texas Cattleman's Club, then this was the place to hang out.

"Hey, girl. You ready to blow off some steam?"

She nodded. Maybe a night out with Royal's rowdy crowd was what she needed to remind her of where she belonged and whom she belonged with…and it wasn't a hot guy from Seattle.

Midnight was his favorite time of night and when he found the most clarity when he was working—tonight wasn't any different. Faye was a little night owl like he was, so the baby was playing on the floor at his feet while he watched the scripts that were running and tracking down Maverick on the monitor nearest to him.

She'd woken up crying. Erin was worn out from

a long day of dealing with Faye teething, and since Will was up at night working anyway, they'd established that he would take the night shift.

Maverick wasn't the cleverest hacker, but whoever he was, the man was running his internet through a few connections. It would have fooled someone who didn't have Will's experience, but he'd been a pirate hunter in high school for a large software company that his dad had helped found and he'd spent a lot of years learning how to follow and find people who didn't want to be found.

"Dada."

"Yes?" He looked down at Faye. Her face was so sweet and she was holding a large round plastic toy up to him.

He took it from her.

She immediately reached for one a size smaller and held it up to him. This was one of her favorite new games. She gave him all the toys around her and then he had to sit still while she took them back and put them in a seemingly random order in front of him.

But this time she was done handing them all to him, so she crawled over to where he sat on the floor next to her and crawled onto his lap. He scooped her up and hugged her close.

His heart was so full when he held his daughter. She smelled of baby powder and sweetness. He knew sweetness wasn't a scent, but when he held Faye it was what he always felt.

He stood up and walked around the house with her while she babbled at him. He set a notification on the computers to alert his phone when the scripts were finished running and then put Faye's jacket on her so they could go for a walk. He'd grown up in Bellevue, near the water, and some of his earliest memories were of being outside with his mom at night looking at the sky.

He knew that many people would expect Faye to be in bed at midnight, but she wasn't looking sleepy at all. It was probably his fault for having a long nap with her in the afternoon. He'd been keeping odd hours since they had arrived in Royal.

He walked toward the barn, telling Faye the stories his mom had told him. Will's mom's people had been sailors and the sky and the water were a big part of their history.

He heard the rumble of a truck engine and turned as a large pickup rounded the corner. He stepped off the dirt track to make sure he wasn't in the path of the vehicle.

The truck slowed and the passenger-side window rolled down. He walked over and was pretty sure it was Clay Everett. But Will knew if he had a woman like Sophie waiting for him at home, he'd have a better way to spend his night than patrolling his ranch.

"Hey, Will. You okay?" Amberley asked.

He was surprised to see her. She had obviously been out, as she smelled faintly of smoke. Her hair was thick and fell around her shoulders. The tousled tresses, so different from her neat braid, made his fingers tingle with the need to touch her hair.

He regretted leaving her the other afternoon. One kiss. Would that have been so bad? Even Lucy wouldn't begrudge him that. But he hadn't taken it.

So instead a need was growing in him fast and large. Each day it seemed to expand and he knew he was losing control.

"Yeah. Faye's a night owl like me so I thought I'd take her for a walk."

Faye heard her name and started babbling again.

"Want some company?" Amberley asked.

"Sure," he said.

She turned off the engine of her truck and climbed out, coming around by him. Her perfume hit him then—it was sweet like spring flowers. There was a slight breeze tonight and Amberley tipped her head back and looked up at the sky.

"When I was little, my dad told us that if we were really good we'd see a special angel in the sky."

"Did you ever see one?"

"Yeah," Amberley said. She stretched out her arm and pointed to Venus. "There she is."

"That's Venus."

"Show some imagination, Brady. That's my special angel. She watches over me at night."

"Does she?"

Amberley nodded. But she wasn't looking up anymore—she was staring at Faye. "She'll watch over you, too, little lady."

Faye answered with one of her babbles. And Amberley listened until Faye was done and then she nodded. "I know. It's hard to believe that someone up there is looking out for you, but she is."

Faye babbled some more.

"Your mama?" Amberley asked when she was done.

Faye babbled and then ended with "Mamamam."

"Mine, too. They are probably friends," Amberley said.

Faye shifted toward Amberley and Amberley looked over at him for permission before reaching for the baby. Will let Faye go to Amberley and watched the two of them talking to each other. She was good with the baby. He was surprised that Faye had wanted to go to her. She was usually pretty shy with strangers.

He noticed that both of the girls were looking at him.

"She's usually not so eager to go to strangers."

"Well, we're not strangers," Amberley said. "We chatted up a storm while you were holding her."

"You sure did," Will said.

Something shifted and settled inside of him. It was a tightness he wasn't even aware of until that moment. And then he realized that he wanted Faye to like Amberley because it didn't matter how guilty he may feel afterward, he wanted to get to know her better.

Four

The night sky was clear, filled with stars and the waning moon. Amberley tipped her head back, feeling the emotions of the week fall away. The baby in her arms was sweet and soft. She had been cooing and pointing to things as they walked and Amberley fought against the pain in her heart she'd thought she'd finally gotten over.

She loved babies. Loved their smiles and their laughter. The way that they communicated if you just took the time to listen to them.

Her dad had told her that she shouldn't give up on a family, but the hysterectomy she'd had at eighteen had pretty much put paid to that. She couldn't have a baby of her own. So she tended to spoil any kiddos she met.

"You're awfully quiet over there," she said, realizing that Will hadn't said much in the last few minutes. She'd suggested they lie in the bed of her pickup truck and watch the night sky. Will had agreed but only, he'd said, until Faye got sleepy.

"Just trying to get this app to work," he said.

He'd mentioned having an app that could show meteor and comet activity in the night sky and was trying to get it to work. Amberley had spread a blanket she kept for picnics on the bed of the truck and she and Faye had been playing together while he tried.

"If it doesn't work we can just make up stories," she said.

"Like what?" he asked.

"That star over there is Lucky."

"As in it brings luck?" he asked.

"No, its name is Lucky. Sometimes the star falls to earth and takes on the persona of a rock superstar during the day, and at dusk it's drawn back up into the night sky, where she stays steady and true so that little cowgirls and cowboys who are out late on the range can find their way home," Amberley said.

She'd been a huge Britney Spears fan when she'd been about ten and her dad had made up that story about one of the pop star's songs.

"Okay, let me give it a try," Will said. He shifted his shoulders and leaned back against the cab of her truck. Faye crawled over to him and he lifted her onto his lap. The baby shifted around and settled with her back against his chest.

They were so cute together, Amberley thought. She ached for little Faye because even though she had her daddy's love and attention, Amberley knew that one day Faye was going to need her momma.

She just felt close to them because she saw herself in the two of them.

"See that constellation?" he asked, pointing to Sirius.

"Yes."

"That's Lobo and he is really good at catching the people who skunk around in the shadows. Every night he looks down on the earth for clues and then during the day he turns into computer code and helps track down the bad guys."

She smiled. "Like you."

"Yeah. Like me."

"How's that going? Is it okay to ask?"

Faye turned in his arms and he rubbed his hand over her back. He lifted her higher on his chest and she settled into the crook of his neck.

"It's going pretty well," he said, his voice pitched low so as not to disturb his daughter.

"I'm glad. Will you be here for long?" she asked.

"Probably a month."

A month…not enough time for anything serious.

"I'd love to know more about what you do," she said. Sometime between the dancing and talking with her cousin tonight she'd realized that no cowboy or Royal guy could make her stop thinking about Will. Probably not her wisest idea, but she had decided she wasn't going to just walk away unless he pushed her to.

"Stop by anytime and I'll show you. It sounds more exciting than it is. Usually it's me in a dark room with my computers running programs or tracking scripts."

"That is so foreign to me. I spend all my time outside and with animals. I mean, I have my phone, which keeps me connected, but I don't even own a computer."

"I don't see why you should need one," Will said. "Smartphones can do just about everything you'd need a computer for."

"Want me to drive you guys back home?" she asked.

"I don't have a car seat so we probably shouldn't," he said.

She felt silly because she'd been used to riding in the back of the truck from the time she'd been a child. She guessed it wasn't that safe, but there wasn't much out here to cause an accident. It underscored to her the many ways they were different.

But he was only here for a month.

Why was she trying to make it acceptable to get involved with him?

She knew why.

She was lonely. It had been a year since her last boyfriend and she was using that term loosely. She and Pete had hooked up at a rodeo and then gone their separate ways. But she felt something stirring inside of her.

Maybe it was just lust.

She sighed and then realized that he'd been staring at her.

Crap.

"Sorry. I guess I'm getting tired. What did you say?"

He shook his head and shifted around, setting Faye on the blanket next to him. The little girl curled onto her side and cooed contentedly as she drifted to sleep.

"I didn't say anything. I was only watching you,

regretting that I didn't kiss you when we were on our ride," he said.

Kiss her.

"Uh…"

Great. He'd rendered her speechless.

No. He hadn't. She wouldn't let him.

"I thought we both decided that was a bad idea."

"I like bad ideas," he said, leaning in closer. He wasn't touching her at all, but he'd tipped his head and she knew he was going to kiss her.

She licked her lips, tilted her head to the side and met him halfway. His lips were firm but soft and he tasted…good. There was something right in the way he tasted as his tongue brushed over hers. She closed her eyes and forgot about everything except this moment.

Will had tried avoiding kissing her, but with the certainty that the moon would rise every night, he knew he really couldn't keep from falling for Amberley. Tonight, sitting in the back of her pickup truck with Faye, had been one of the first times he'd been able to just enjoy being with his daughter and not think of all she'd lost.

He hadn't felt that gnawing guilt-and-grief combination. And now, when his lips met Amberley's, he'd stopped thinking altogether.

God, he'd needed this.

Just to feel and not think of anything but the way her lips had softened under his.

He lifted his head and looked down at her. By the light of the moon he could tell that her lips were wet from their kiss and her eyes were heavy-lidded. She lifted her hand and rubbed her finger over her mouth.

"Damn. I wish you didn't kiss like that," she said.

Surprised, he tilted his head to the side.

She shrugged. "Just would have been easier to write you off as a city slicker if you didn't know what you were doing."

He threw his head back and laughed at that statement. "Glad to know I didn't disappoint."

Faye stirred at the sound of his laughter and he realized it was getting late, even for two night owls.

"You didn't disappoint... Did I?"

The woman who'd fiercely ridden her horse around the barrels and who walked with a confidence that made him think she could conquer mountains was asking him if he liked her kiss. He patted Faye on the back and she settled down before he looked back over at Amberley.

Her hair was tousled, her lips swollen from his kiss, and he knew that later tonight, when he was alone in his bed, he was probably going to fantasize about doing much more with her.

"You were fantastic," he said. "If we were alone one kiss wouldn't be enough."

She nodded.

"For me, either."

"Good," he said. "Now I hate to do this but I really should be getting Faye back home. But maybe I can see you tomorrow?"

She nibbled her lower lip and he moaned.

"What?" she asked.

"You are making it damn hard for me to resist kissing you again," he said, but Faye had begun to wake up. He needed to get her back and into her comfortable crib.

"Sorry. It's just I like the taste of you."

He groaned.

"I could do with a little less honesty from you, cowgirl," he said.

"I'm not made that way," she admitted.

"I'm glad. I'll see you tomorrow afternoon."

"Okay. I'm giving a riding lesson from one until three, so after that, okay?"

"Perfect," he said. He leaned over and stole a quick kiss because he liked the way she tasted, too, and then he stood up with Faye in his arms and hopped down from the bed of the truck. He glanced back over his shoulder and noticed that Amberley had moved to the tailgate and sat there watching him walk away. It was pretty dark, but he was using the flashlight on his phone. And the moon was full, a big harvest moon that lit up the land around them.

He waved at her and she waved back.

"Good night, Will," she said, and there was a smile in her voice.

"'Night," he returned and then cuddled his daughter closer as he walked back to the guest house.

He kept the image of Amberley watching him walk away until he entered the house and saw the photo of Lucy on the hall table.

He took Faye to her room. He removed her coat and then changed her diaper before laying her in the bed. He turned on the mobile that Lucy had picked out for her and that guilt that he'd thought he'd shaken free of was back.

When Will first came to the guest house on the

Flying E, he'd asked if Clay would allow him to set up Faye's room as it had been in Seattle. He wanted her to feel at home and little things like the mobile and her crib and her toys were important. Clay hadn't minded at all and told Will to make the guest house into his home, which he had. And Erin had been instrumental in making sure everything was set up the way they liked it.

Lucy had been so excited when she'd seen it in a magazine. It was a version of the cow jumping over the moon, similar to one that Lucy remembered from her own childhood. They'd had to search all over to find it. Will had scoured the internet—exhausting every avenue—to find it. He remembered how thrilled Lucy had been when she'd opened the package.

He touched the cow as it spun and instead of thinking of Lucy he remembered Amberley and the way she'd played with Faye while he'd been on his phone trying to get technology to work in the middle of the night.

She hadn't gotten impatient with him the way the nanny sometimes did. He liked how easily Amberley got along with his daughter, but a part of him also knew that Lucy should have been the one holding her daughter.

But she was gone.

This job out here in Texas was supposed to give him perspective and help him finally realize that Faye needed him. It was easier here in Texas to shake off the gloom of the last year. And he was moving forward. Slowly. He hadn't realized how isolated he'd let himself become. His world had shrunk to just his work, and then Faye and Erin.

It had been a while since he'd just had a normal conversation. He and Erin mainly just talked about the baby and her eating habits or how teething was going.

He'd never felt like he would be raising his daughter alone.

He had no idea how to do it.

As much as he enjoyed being with Amberley, she wasn't his forever woman. Will had had that. Faye drifted off to sleep and Will went to his own room to shower away the scent of Amberley and then he brushed his teeth and used mouthwash to try to forget the way her kiss had tasted.

But he remembered.

And he still wanted her. His arms felt empty through the night and when he dreamed he was making love to a woman and he looked at her face, it was Amberley's and not Lucy's.

And the dream left him wide-awake, tortured with lust and need and the kind of guilt that felt like he was never going to be normal again.

When Will had been a no-show for their afternoon ride, Amberley chalked it up to him needing to do his job. Clay had told her that Maverick had struck again. Clay had even been a victim of Maverick. The hacker had made it seem as if Everest's cloud encryption software had been compromised, causing clients to panic. But luckily that had all been cleared up.

So Will was probably deep into his investigation. At least that's what she told herself.

Except he hadn't come around the next day, or the day after. A week later she was beginning to believe he might be more like Sam, the guy she'd hooked up with nearly six years ago, than she'd wanted to believe.

Amberley finally went by Will's place one afternoon only to be met at the door by Erin, holding Faye on her hip.

"Hi, there, Amberley," Will's nanny said.

"Hey. Sorry to bother you. I was stopping by to see if Will wanted to go for a ride," she said.

Erin stepped out onto the porch. "He's not here. He had to go into town to meet with Max and Chelsea. Something about Maverick."

"Clay told me he might have struck again," Amberley said. "I've never really had much patience for bullies. Especially ones like Maverick. If I have beef with someone I take it to them. I don't attack from a hiding place in the bushes, you know?"

Erin laughed. "I do know."

Erin's phone beeped. "That's my timer. I was making some teething biscuits for little Miss Faye here. Want to come in and chat? It's kind of lonely out here."

"It is. I'm used to it, though," Amberley said as she stood up. She glanced at her watch, that old battered Timex she'd been wearing for as long as she could remember. "I could stay for about thirty minutes."

"Good. Come on in," Erin said.

As soon as they stepped into the kitchen, Erin put Faye in her bouncy chair on the counter and went to the oven to check on her biscuits. Amberley went over to play with the baby, who was making her nonsensical sounds again.

She looked into the little girl's eyes and wondered what had happened to her mother. Without really thinking about what she was doing, she turned to Erin, who was putting the biscuits on a wire rack.

"What happened to Will's wife?" she asked.

Erin finished moving all the biscuits to the rack before she took off her pot holder and turned to face Amberley. "She had a brain hemorrhage before Faye was born. They kept her alive until about a week after Faye was delivered. It was heartbreaking."

"I can imagine. Is that when he hired you?" she asked.

"No. Lucy was planning to go back to work so I'd already been hired. They wanted the baby to be familiar with the nanny so the thought was Lucy, Will and I would all be in place from the moment Faye was born," Erin said.

That just broke her heart a little bit more. It sounded like Lucy had been ready for motherhood. That their family was getting settled and then bam, the unexpected. Her daddy had always said that change was inevitable, but Amberley thought it would be nice once in a while if things just stayed on course. Like they should have for Faye's family.

Erin offered her a glass of iced tea. She accepted and stayed to chat with her about the Fall Festival, but she felt uncomfortable in the house now that she knew a little bit more about Will's wife. Lucy. She had a name now, and when Amberley left a few minutes later, she saw the photo on the hall table. Lucy had been beautiful.

It was the kind of classic beauty that Amberley, with her tomboyish looks, could never pull off. She wasn't down on herself; it was simply that Lucy was really different from her. And Amberley wondered if she'd been fooling herself to think the man she'd sat under the stars with could see her as anything other than a distraction from his real life.

She wasn't sure she could see herself as anything other than that.

Determined to remember what she was good at and how great her life was, she spent the next few days with the horses and deliberately tried to shove Will Brady out of her mind.

The following weekend, Amberley went into town for the Fall Festival at the Royal elementary school. It was way past time for her to start decorating for the season. She pulled into the parking lot at the elementary school and realized the mistake she'd made.

There were families everywhere. Why wouldn't there be? This was a family event. Perfect for a Saturday.

She'd come after she'd finished her morning routine with the horses and now she wished she'd stayed on the Flying E with her animals. Instead she was watching everything that she would never have and she hated that.

She'd been devastated when she'd had the hysterectomy. But as her father had pointed out in his sanguine way it was better than the alternative, which in her case would have been death.

But she'd never expected to feel this alone.

She'd always thought when she'd been growing up that she'd one day have a family of her own. And holding Faye a week ago had just reminded her of all that she was missing.

She was twenty-four—too young to feel like this.

She got out of the truck because she felt silly just sitting there. She needed pumpkins. Some to carve, some for making pies and muffins, and some just to use as decorations that she'd keep out until Thanksgiving.

She walked through the playground, which had been turned into the Fall Festival, and tried to make a beeline to the pumpkin patch, but Cara was working at the caramel-apple booth and waved her over.

"Hey, Amberley! I'm glad you showed up."

"You know I need a pumpkin," Amberley said. The booth Cara was using was staffed by high school kids from the Future Farmers of America. They still wore the same jackets they had when Amberley had been a member in high school. She'd also done 4-H. She bought a couple of caramel apples and met Cara's boyfriend, who was clearly smitten. They were cute. It seemed easy for them to be together.

Unlike Amberley, who always seemed to find the rockiest path to happiness with a man. Whatever that was about.

"See you on Monday, Cara," Amberley said leaving the booth and carrying her bag of goodies with her.

The pumpkin patch had an area at the front set up for pictures and she saw the kids lined up for photos. She walked past them, head down and focused on getting what she needed and getting home. She was going to give herself the rest of the day off. Maybe stop at the diner in town and grab some junk food and then go home, sit on the couch and binge-watch something on Netflix. Anything that would take her mind off the place where she kept going back to.

The missing family that she craved.

Will.

Screw Will.

He was clearly messed up from his wife's death. She got that. She could even understand what he must be going through. She was pretty damn sure he hadn't married a woman and had a kid with her if he didn't love her. That just didn't strike her as the kind of man he was. It was going to take him time to get over it. Obviously more than a year and she didn't begrudge him that.

She was angry at herself. She'd spent way too much time thinking about him. She should be thinking about one of the guys she'd met at the Wild Boar, or maybe one of the guys she'd met at the rodeo. Or no guy.

Maybe she'd just start collecting cats and build herself a nice life surrounded by animals and friends. Sure she'd miss having a man in her bed, but she could deal with that. Eventually.

She picked out five pumpkins to decorate her porch and two for the house—she had two windows that would look good with jack-o'-lanterns in them. And then she paid for a large bag of mini gourds and accepted the help of a pumpkin-patch employee to carry them all to her truck.

She carried the last pumpkin herself after three trips to the truck and was feeling much better about her day as she pulled into the diner. She'd phoned in her order so all she had to do was go in and grab it. She hopped out of her truck and walked straight to the counter to pick up her order when she heard someone call her name.

Will.

She turned to see him sitting at a corner table with Max St. Cloud. Though she'd only seen him in town, she knew Max on sight. And she tried to smile and wave, but she was just still so pissed.

She hadn't realized how much she'd been counting on him to be different from every other city guy she'd ever met. She settled for a little wave as the girl at the register called her name. She walked over and paid for her patty melt, fries and onion rings and then turned to walk out of the diner without looking over at Will.

One of them had to be smart and no matter how country she was, she knew it was up to her.

Five

"What was that about?" Max asked Will as they watched Amberley walk out of the diner.

"Nothing."

"Will, talk to me," Max said. "Did I make a mistake when I asked you to come to Royal?"

"No. It is not affecting my work. In fact, I think I am getting close to finding the hub that Maverick is using to run most of the cyberbullying he's doing. He uses a bunch of different accounts, but they are all fed from the same source…or at least that's what I'm starting to suspect."

Max sat back in the bench and nodded. "Good. But I wasn't referring to your work. You have been sending me reports at all hours of the day with updates."

"Then what are you asking?" Will was trying to focus on the conversation with his boss, but he couldn't keep his mind from wandering to Amberley.

"We're friends, right?" Max asked.

"Yeah. But unless you want to hear about what a sad mess I've become you should lay off this questioning right now," Will warned his friend. Max had known him before he'd married Lucy. He was one of the few people who really knew him well enough to understand what he'd gone through when he'd lost Lucy. How marriage had changed him and how her death had sent him to a darker place.

"What's up?"

"Nothing. Just the mix of pretty girl, messed-up guy and trying to do the right thing," Will said.

He took a sip of his coffee and leaned forward because he didn't need everyone in the diner to hear his business. "For the love of me, Max, every damn time I try to do what I know is right it backfires."

"Then stop trying," Max said.

"If it was that easy," Will said.

"It is. You said that you tried to do the right thing and it backfired. Maybe it was the wrong action," Max said. "All I know is that life isn't like a program. You fix the code and make it work, but there is always something unexpected. You know?"

Will leaned back. Like Lucy dying in the hospital after Faye's birth. "Yeah. I do know. Thanks, Max."

Max nodded. "People are getting more tense as this Maverick remains at large. I know you are doing all you can, but right now, because no one knows who Maverick is, everyone suspects each other. If you can get me something…well, the sooner the better."

"I will. Like I mentioned I think I have a lead on something that should lead to Maverick. I just needed to understand the server set up at the Texas Cattleman's Club."

"I put you on the guest list so you can go check it out."

"Thanks. I want to add the access tracking to the main terminal and the server. I'm pretty sure it's got to be an inside job."

"I think there is a connection there, too," Max said. "So you don't want anyone to know why you are there."

"Yeah."

"A date would be good camouflage."

"Of course it would," Will said.

"Just trying to help a buddy out. You look like you need a nudge toward her."

"Thanks… Not a nudge. I need to get out of my own way. Every time I'm around her I forget things… Lucy. And then when I'm alone I'm not sure that's what I should have done."

"Only you can answer that for yourself, but you can't keep punishing yourself for living," Max said. "I'm going to ask Chelsea to make you a dinner reservation at the club for tonight. Get a date or not—it's up to you."

They discussed how Will would deploy the tracker physically on the server. They didn't want to do it remotely, in case Maverick was able to see the code in the program. Max and he parted company and instead of heading back to the Flying E, Will went to one of the boutiques in town and bought a gauzy dress in a small flower print for Amberley. The dress had a skirt that he suspected would end just above her knee and a scooped neckline. He also purchased a pretty necklace that had a large amber gemstone pendant in the center that would rest nicely above the neckline of the dress.

He had it wrapped and then wrote a note of apology on the card and asked for it to be delivered to her.

He checked his watch and then went to the Fall Festival to meet Erin and Faye. Faye looked cute as could be in her denim overalls and brown undershirt. He held his daughter and knew that he'd be mad as hell if he'd been the one to die and Lucy was hesitating to get on with her life.

But it was harder on the heart than it was on the head. And as much as he knew what he needed to do, it was like Max had said—this wasn't code that he could correct with a few strokes of the keyboard. It was so much easier and conversely more complicated than that. He had no idea what he was really going to do about Amberley, but he'd made a move today. No more backing away.

If Amberley gave him this third chance, he wasn't going to waste it.

When he got back to the ranch, he dropped off Erin and Faye at the guest house since it was Faye's nap time and then he got in the golf cart and drove over to the stables to look for Amberley.

She was running the barrels when he got there and he watched her move with the horse and knew that she was worth the risk he was taking. He had spent a lot of time pretending that he could walk away from her, but the truth was he knew he couldn't.

He wanted her.

Not just physically, though that was a big part of

it. He also wanted that joie de vivre that she seemed to bring to him when he was around her.

He liked the man he could be when he thought of spending time with her.

She noticed him and drew her horse to a stop. She dismounted and walked over to the fence around the barrels, and he went to meet her.

"What's your deal?"

She hadn't meant to sound so confrontational. She'd gone back to the ranch and intended to waste away the rest of the day in front of the television. But instead she'd felt trapped in her house. She'd felt restless and edgy and just as she was about to leave, that package from Will had arrived.

With a handwritten apology note and a gorgeous dress and necklace. Who did something like that?

It was safe to say that no man she'd dated before had made such a gesture. But Will was different. And they had never dated. What had possessed him to do such a thing?

She was tired of playing games. It didn't suit her.

"My deal?"

"Yeah. We shared a great kiss and I started to think I could really like this guy and then you just up and disappear, not even a word about not showing up for our scheduled ride. You must think all country girls are just looking for a big-city man to marry them and take them away from all this, but you're wrong. I like this life. I like it just the way it is, and when I kissed you it was because I thought we had a real connection," she said, opening the gate and stepping out of the ring. "And it's clear to me that we have absolutely no connection at all by the way you keep backing out of stuff, but then you send me that dress and necklace and that apology. It sounds heartfelt, Will. And I'm tired of feeling stupid because I think one thing and your actions say something else. So what's your deal?"

He rocked back on his heels, as if he was trying to absorb the force of her aggression. She knew she was being hostile right now but she was tired of feeling the fool. The way he had treated her, the way she'd interpreted his actions…well, she wasn't having it anymore. She'd been nice and if he went to Clay and complained, she knew Clay well enough that she'd be honest with him and she was pretty sure he'd side with her.

"I am sorry. The note was meant to be heartfelt," he said, holding his hands up to his shoulders. "I like you, Amberley. When we are together I forget about the emptiness that I usually feel when I step away from my computer. But then I hold Faye and it comes back. I'm trying to get out of the swamp that I've been trapped in since Lucy died. And I can't figure it out. I'm not playing a game with you. I promise. I was going to invite you to dinner, but on second thought—"

"Do you really want to have dinner with me?" she asked, cutting him off. His explanation made her sad for him. She could feel his pain when he spoke. She, of all people, understood how hard it was to move on after a tragic loss. She could be his friend. Just his friend. That was something she could handle.

"Yes. I do."

"Okay, then let's have dinner. But as friends. We

can be friends, right?" she asked. "You can tell me about Lucy and maybe we can figure out a way to get you free of your swamp. It doesn't have to be anything more than that."

She could be his friend. Sure, she had wanted more, but the last few days had convinced her that wasn't wise. The anger and the despair from his rejection hadn't been what she'd expected. She had uncovered something buried deep inside her that she didn't like.

She wanted to celebrate being young and alive. Not feel old and bitter. She'd never been bitter about the hand that life had dealt her and she hated that this thing she felt for Will was eliciting that response in her.

"Friends?"

"Yes. Seems like a good place to start."

"Okay. Friends. Then I should tell you that I need a date for cover. I want to install a program on the server at the Texas Cattleman's Club, and in case it's an inside job, I don't really want anyone to know what I'm doing."

"So I'm your cover?"

"That's the plan, but I would also like it to be a date," he said. "I am tired of where I am and would like to get to a better place."

Sure, he would. As friends, she reminded herself. "I can do that. And I can provide some cover for you. What time is dinner?"

"Eight. That gives me time to spend with Faye before she goes to bed," he said.

"That works for me. How is she? I really enjoyed playing with her the other night."

"She's good. A little cranky earlier today, but that's just from teething. She's already got one tooth so this is another new one. She bit me last night when we were playing. She's been drooling a lot, so I was letting her chew on my finger and then *ouch*."

Amberley smiled at him like she would if he was a friend. She could do this. Keep her feelings on neutral terms. If only he wasn't so darn cute when he talked about his daughter.

He walked away and she turned her attention to her horse, brushing Montgomery and talking to the animal. He listened to her the way she suspected she'd listened to Faye. Montgomery lowered his head and butted her in the chest when she was done and she hugged him back, wishing she could understand men half as well as she understood horses.

Will took his time getting dressed for dinner after Erin and he had put Faye to bed. Erin was video chatting with her boyfriend back in Seattle, so he knew that she was set for the evening. He went into his office to check his computers again and took the small USB flash drive that he'd loaded his tracker program onto and put it in his pocket.

He was nervous.

He wasn't sure if that was a good thing or a bad thing. Faye always made him feel pretty okay…well, a little sad and bad that she didn't have her mom, but she had that sweet smile, which kind of helped to center him at times.

This was different. He went to the mirror in the guest bathroom and checked his tie again. He favored skinny ties no matter if they were in fashion or not.

He didn't think of himself as a slave to trends and preferred a look he thought worked for him. He'd spiked up his hair on the top and traded his Converse for some loafers his mom had sent him after her last trip to Italy.

He went in to check on Faye and kissed her on the top of her head before letting Erin know he was leaving for the evening.

He walked out of the house, took a deep breath of the fall evening air and realized how much he liked Texas. To be fair, October was a far cry from July, when he knew the temperature would be unbearable. But right now, this cool, dry night was exactly what he wanted.

He drove over to Amberley's house, having texted her earlier to tell her he'd pick her up. There was a bunch of pumpkins on her front step and a bale of hay with a scarecrow holding a sign that said Happy Fall, Y'all on it. He smiled as he saw it. He leaped up the stairs to her front porch and knocked on the door.

"It's open. Come in."

He did as she asked and stepped into the hallway of her place. The house smelled like apples and cinnamon, which reminded him of his parents' place. There was a thick carpeted runner in the foyer that led to the living room.

"I'll be right there. Sorry, I'm trying to curl my hair but it's being stubborn," she called out from the back of the house. "I am almost done."

"No problem," he said, following the sound of her voice. He found her standing in front of a mirror at the end of the hallway off the living room. He stopped when he saw her as his breath caught in his throat.

She was beautiful.

She'd looked pretty the other week after she'd been out, but this was different. Her hair had been pulled up into a chignon and that tendril she was messing with was curling against her cheek.

"Sorry. But in magazines this always looks so perfect and, of course, the reality is my stubborn hair won't curl the right way."

"I don't think it's a problem," he said.

She turned to face him and he had to swallow. The dress he'd picked out was fitted on the top and then flared out from her waist ending just above her knees. And she'd paired the dress with a pair of strappy sandals. The amber pendant fell on her chest, drawing his eyes to the V-neck of the dress.

"You are gorgeous," he said.

She blushed.

"Don't be embarrassed, it's just the truth," he said.

"Thanks for saying that. I don't get dressed up often, which is why I was trying this new updo. I figured I should at least make the effort. Plus, the folks of Royal aren't used to seeing me in anything but jeans and a straw cowboy hat. Do you think Maverick is working in the club or even a member…? Oh, that would really stink if he was a member, wouldn't it?"

"It would. I'm not a member, as you know, but I am aware of how close-knit the members are," Will said. "Are you ready to go?"

"Yes. Let me grab my purse and shawl. I figured that would be nicer than my jean jacket."

He smiled at the way she said it. She looked sophisticated and polished, almost out of his league, but she was still Amberley.

She disappeared into the doorway next to the hall mirror and reappeared a minute later. "Let's go."

He followed her through her home. It was small and neat, but very much Amberley. Not like the guest house, which was almost too perfectly decorated—this place had a more lived-in quality. It was her home. "How long have you lived here?"

"I got the job when I was nineteen…so that's five years."

"Wow, you were young. Were you worried about moving away from home?" he asked.

"Not really. Dad and Clay have known each other for a while. And it's not like it's that far if I want to go home for a visit," she said. "Plus Clay has an excellent stable and he lets me have time off to rodeo when I want to—it's the best place for me."

She was animated when she spoke of her father and her job and her life, and he realized he wanted to see her like this always.

She'd suggested they be friends and he knew now that was the only route for the two of them. Because he wanted her to stay the way she was just now. With her skin glowing, her eyes animated as she talked about the things in her life she loved. Getting involved with him could only bring her down. And even though he knew he felt like he was missing out on something special, her smile and her happiness was worth it.

Six

The Texas Cattleman's Club dining room was busy when they arrived. Since Maverick had started his assault on members of the club, and on Royal, some of the friendliness that Amberley had always associated with the town was gone. Everyone was a little bit on edge. She wasn't going to pretend she understood what Will was doing with the computer, but she'd Googled him and read up on him.

They were dining as guests of Chelsea Hunt and she'd met them early at the bar.

If anyone could unearth Maverick it was Will Brady. He was a whiz at tracking down cyber criminals and had made millions selling the code he had designed to the US government. He was gaining a reputation for keeping secrets safe as well, having successfully blocked an all-out assault on one government database by a foreign entity intent on doing harm to the US. Obviously, Will was a well-respected expert in his field.

One of the articles had been accompanied by a picture of him and his late wife dressed up to go to the White House, where Will had been given a commendation.

Seeing that picture of Will's late wife had made the woman very real to Amberley. And she was even more glad she'd decided just to be friends with Will. She liked him. She wasn't going to pretend otherwise. As she went to the bar while he excused himself to go do whatever he had to do in the computer room, she thought more about all Will had lost.

She wanted to be a good friend to Will. He needed a friend.

She remembered how he'd made up a story for her while they'd sat under the stars. No one had done that for her since she was a girl. The men she had dated…they saw the tough cowgirl and they didn't always realize she was vulnerable. But Will treated her differently.

"What'll it be?" the bartender asked her.

"Strawberry margarita, frozen, please," she said.

"Should I open a tab?" the bartender asked.

"No. I'll pay for this. I'm having dinner with someone," she said.

She settled up with the bartender, took her drink to one of the high tables and sat down to wait. She saw a few people she knew from town, but they glanced over her as if they didn't recognize her and she shook her head. She didn't think she looked so different with her hair up.

Finally, one of the parents of her horse-riding students recognized her and came over to chat with her for a few moments. It was nice to have someone to talk to while she was waiting for Will. She felt a little bit out of place here at the club. She didn't come from money. Her father made a good living and the ranch was worth a fair amount, but they weren't wealthy. They were ranchers.

Will walked in a few minutes later and scanned the room before spotting her. He smiled, buttoning his coat as he strode over to her. He looked good in his thin tie and his slim-fitting suit. His hair was slicked back, making him look like he'd just stepped out of one those television shows she loved to binge-watch.

She sighed.

Friends, she reminded herself.

"I didn't order you a drink," she said, wishing now she had.

"That's okay. I'll get one and join you," he said.

He was back in a moment, sitting across from her with a whiskey in one hand. "Sorry to keep you waiting."

"I don't mind. Did you get everything straightened out?"

"I did," he said. "How has it been for you?"

"Funny," she said. "I've seen a few people from town but most didn't recognize me."

"Really?"

"Yup. I'm a woman of mystery," she said. "I like it."

"Me, too. It's nice to be anonymous," he said.

"Are you usually recognized?" she asked. "I read a few articles about you online."

"Did you?" he asked. "That's interesting. But to answer your question, I'm only recognized at home. Mainly it's because I don't live that far from where I grew up. One subdivision over, actually, so I just know everyone when I go to the gym or the grocery store. And most people know about Lucy so it makes things awkward…"

She put her hand over his.

"Do you want to talk about her?" Amberley asked. "When my mom died everyone stopped mentioning her name. It was like she'd never existed and I wanted to talk about her. Finally, one night I lit into my daddy about it. And he said he missed her so much just hearing her name hurt and I told him for me, too, but ignoring her was making her disappear," Amberley said, feeling the sting of tears as she remembered her mom. She'd been gone for years now, but there were times like this when she still missed her and it felt fresh.

"I…I'm a little bit of both. I don't know if I want to talk about her," Will admitted. He took his hand from under hers and swallowed his drink in one long gulp.

"If you want to, I'm here for you," she said.

He nodded. "I'm going to go and check on our table."

She watched him walk away and she wondered if she'd said too much. But she knew that she couldn't have kept silent. He had admitted to her that he was stuck in a swamp and there was no clear path out of it. She suspected it was because he didn't know how to move on and still hold on to the past. And while Amberley knew she was no expert, she'd done her best to keep her mom alive while accepting the woman her dad had started dating when she'd turned eighteen.

So maybe she'd be able to help him.

Dinner started out a little stiff but soon they relaxed into a good conversation, mostly centering on music and books. They differed in that everything he owned was digital—both books and music—while Amberley had inherited her mother's record collection when she'd moved out and had a turntable in her house, where she listened to old country and rock from the '80s.

"What about scratches?"

"Well, that does make for some awkward moments when I'm singing along to a song that I've learned with all the skips in it. Records do that," she said with a wink. "And then I realize there's an entire phrase I've missed."

"You know I could show you how to download all the albums you already own on your phone so you could listen to them when you are riding," he said.

"I know how to do that, Will," she said. "I just prefer to listen to the albums at home. It reminds me of when I was growing up. Like Mom loved Michael Bolton and when I listen to his album I can remember Dad coming and the two of them dancing around. And I have a lot of CDs, too. Between the two of them I think they owned every album they loved on cassette, CD and vinyl. It's crazy," she said. "Dad stopped listening to it all after Mom died, but I wanted my brothers and sisters to have those memories, so Randy and I would put the albums on when Dad was out of the house."

"How many siblings do you have?"

"Four. Two brothers and two sisters. Randy is three years younger than me, then Janie, Michael and Tawny."

"Sounds like a houseful," he said. He'd always sort of wished for a bigger family but he'd been the only child and had gotten used to it.

"What about you?" she asked.

"Only child."

"Spoiled," she said, winking at him.

"Probably," he admitted. "Lucy and I had planned to have at least two kids. She said we should have an even number—she had two sisters and said one of them was always left out."

"It was that way at home a bit when Mom was still alive, but once she died and I became the boss when Dad wasn't home the dynamic changed."

"How old were you?" he asked.

"Thirteen," she said. "You know you could always have more kids if you remarry."

"Uh, I'm barely able to think about going on a date, I'm not sure more kids are in the cards for me," he said. "What about you? Do you hate the idea of being a mom since you kind of had to be one to your siblings?"

She sat back in her chair and tucked that tendril she'd spent so much time trying to curl behind her ear. She shook her head. "No. I sort of always wanted to have a family of my own."

There was something in the way she was talking that made him think she thought she wouldn't have a family of her own. "You're young. You can have a family someday."

She chewed her lower lip for a minute and then shook her head. "I can't. I physically can't have kids."

He was surprised and wanted to ask her more about it, but it seemed obvious to him that she didn't want to discuss it further. She started eating her dinner again and this time didn't look up.

He reached over and put his hand on top of hers, stopping her from taking another bite, and she looked up. There was pain in her eyes and it echoed the loss he felt in his soul when he thought about Lucy being gone.

"I'm sorry."

She nodded. "Thanks. Wow, I bet you're glad this isn't a real date."

"It is a real date," he said. Because he knew now that there was no way he could walk away from her. Yes, he had been hesitating, but when he'd bought the dress for her things had changed and he wasn't going to let it go back to where he'd been when he'd first come to Texas.

"No, we said friends."

"Friends can go on dates. How else do you think friends become lovers?"

She flushed. He loved her creamy complexion and the fact that her face easily broadcast her emotions. He guessed it went hand-in-hand with her bluntness. Amberley didn't hide any part of who she was.

"I can't deal if you are going to blow hot and cold again," she said. "I wasn't kidding around this afternoon. I mean, I understand where you are coming from—"

"Amberley? I told Chris that was you," Macy Richardson said, coming over to her. Macy's family had been members of the Texas Cattleman's Club forever. Chris had grown up here in Royal on the wrong sides of the tracks. But he'd gone away and made his fortune, only to come back to claim Macy and a membership at the club. Their daughter took riding lessons from Amberley.

"It is me," she said. "Probably didn't recognize me without my cowboy hat on. Macy and Chris, this is Will Brady. He's a guest of Chelsea Hunt's."

Will stood up and shook Macy's and Chris's hands. "I hear you're in town to help catch Maverick."

"I am," Will said.

"Good. I'm sure you're going to get the job done. Chelsea has a lot of good things to say about you," Macy said. "We will leave you to your dinner."

A few other members stopped by to chat with them, including Clay and Sophia, who seemed to be enjoying their night out.

When the interruptions were over, Will picked up the thread of their conversation. Amberley's accusations about his behavior were fair, and he owed her a response.

"You're right. I'm not going to do that to you again. I said friends to lovers. We can take this slow," he said.

But a part of him knew that slow was going to be hard with her. It almost felt like if it happened in a rush it would be easier for him to move past the memory of Lucy, but as he watched Amberley he knew that he was always moving forward. He was excited about the prospect of something fresh and new with her. He wasn't about to give up now that he had her. He could do slow, but he wouldn't do never.

"So books... Do you have a bunch of dog-eared paperbacks instead of ebooks?" he asked, changing the subject and trying to pretend like everything was normal.

"Dog-eared? I love my books—I don't treat them poorly. In fact, sometimes I buy the paperback and then read it on my tablet because I want to keep it in good shape," she admitted.

He had to laugh at the way she said it and then he noticed how she smiled when he laughed. Something shifted and settled inside of him and he realized that he wasn't going to let her ride out of his life until he knew her much better.

Will drove her home at the end of the night, playing a new track he'd downloaded of Childish Gambino. It had a funky sound that reminded her of some of the jazzy music her dad liked from the '80s.

"This is really interesting. I love it," she said.

"I thought you might like it," he said.

"Why?"

"Because I do and we seem to have similar taste in music," he said.

"You think so?"

He nodded. "Tonight I have learned we are more alike than either of us would have guessed."

She swallowed hard—he meant the loss. It was funny that grief should unite them, but then her grandmother always said her mom was up there watching out for her, so maybe that was the reason behind this.

"Were you surprised?" she asked.

"Yes, and shame on me for that. Because from

the moment you showed up on my front porch with Cara, I knew you weren't like any other woman I'd met before. A part of me put it down to you being a Texan, but I knew there was something about you that was just different from every other woman," he said.

"Well, not everyone can be born in the great state of Texas," she said with a wink. "You can't really hold that against other women."

He laughed, as she hoped he would. She noticed that he got her sometimes odd sense of humor and it made her feel good. As much as she'd sort of always crushed out city guys that she'd met, he was different. Maybe that was why she kept giving him a second chance.

"I wouldn't," he said solemnly.

"So do you have any country music on your device?"

"Big and Rich," he said.

"They're okay but I think you need to listen to some old-school country. I'll give you some of Dad's old cassettes," she said, again teasing him because she knew he would just download the songs. And he was right that some songs sounded better digitally remastered, but for the sake of not agreeing with him she was going to stick by her guns.

He groaned. "Just give me a list. Actually, give me a name and I'll put it on right now."

"How?"

"Verbal commands," he said.

"Does that work for you?" she asked.

"All the time. Why?"

"Well, Siri hates me. Whatever I say she changes

it to something crazy. I mean, it's not like I'm not speaking English," she said.

"Siri can't hate you, she's a computer program," Will said.

"Well, she does. One time I texted my cousin Eve and told her where to meet me and do you know what that phone sent her?"

"What?" he asked.

"'Meet me where we once flew the summer wind,'" Amberley said.

He burst out laughing. "You do have a bit of an accent."

"No crap," she said. "But that is crazy."

"When we get to your place I'll fix it so your phone can understand you," he said.

"You can do that?"

"Hell, yes," he said. "I might not be any good with people but I'm excellent with tech."

She looked over at him, his features illuminated whenever they passed under a streetlamp as they drove through Royal. "You're good with people."

"Some of them. I tend to lose my patience. But with tech I'm always good."

She hadn't seen that impatient side of him. She wondered if that was because he was only letting her see what he wanted. Maybe the grieving widower was all he wanted her to know about him. But then why would he be talking to her now? She was making herself a little crazy.

They had both been beat up by life and were doing their best to survive. And she didn't doubt that he liked her. She'd seen the way he watched her and she knew when a man wanted her.

The truth was she didn't want to be hurt again and her mind might have been saying that friends was enough for her, but she knew in her heart that she'd already started liking him.

She liked that he cared about Royal even though it wasn't his town. She liked the way he was with his daughter, even though raising her without his mother was obviously hurting him. She just plain liked him and that wasn't how she wanted to be feeling about him.

Friends.

That was easy. She was supposed to be keeping things friendly. Instead she was falling for him.

It would have been easier if she knew that he would stay, but he was a flight risk. She knew he was just tiptoeing through an emotional minefield, trying to figure out how to move on. And of course once Maverick was found there was no reason for Will to stay in Texas. And then she shifted things in her mind. What if he was a mustang stallion that just took a little longer to gentle to the saddle? What if she just approached him with stealth, could she win him that way?

And was she really going to try to win him over?

She twisted her head and looked out at the dark landscape as they left Royal and headed toward the Flying E. She saw the moon up there following her and then she spotted Venus and thought of her own special angel, and not for the first time in her adult life, she wished her mom was here to talk to. She needed some advice on what to do next. She wasn't someone to hedge her bets and she wanted to be all in with Will. But a part of her was afraid that it was just wishful thinking on her part.

He turned onto the Flying E property and slowed the car, as they were on the dirt road and not paved highway. When he stopped in front of her house she turned to face him.

He shut off the car and sat there for a long moment and she felt a tingle go through her entire body that wasn't unlike what she felt when she was sitting on the back of Montgomery waiting for a barrel run to start.

"So, you want to come in?"

Seven

The dinner hadn't gone as Will had expected and this end to the evening was no different. He'd told himself he wouldn't kiss her good-night. They'd said they'd go slow. Maybe if he repeated it enough times it would stick and he'd get the taste of her off his tongue.

Unfortunately, he was never going to get the vision of her wearing the gauzy, long-sleeved dress he'd bought for her out of his mind. And it didn't help matters that the hem of her dress had ridden up her legs. In the light of the moon and the illumination of the dashboard lights he could see the tops of her thighs.

He clenched his hands around the steering wheel to keep from reaching over and touching her. Lust was strong and sharp and it was burning out all the cells in his brain, making it impossible for him to think. He wanted to be suave and smooth, all the things he liked to think he usually was around a woman, but tonight he wasn't.

He'd told her things he'd never said to anyone else. Like making up stories under the stars and just talking about stuff. Not business or his baby, but stuff that he'd locked away when Lucy died. And all the sophistication he'd thought he'd cultivated over the years was gone. He wanted her and really there wasn't room for anything else. Maybe it was the way she'd watched him as he'd driven back to the ranch.

Hell, he didn't know.

Frankly, he didn't care.

"You really want me to come in?" he asked, his voice sounding rough. He cleared it but he knew short of burying himself hilt-deep between her legs there was nothing he could do about it.

"Do you want to come in?" she asked.

"Hell."

She turned in her seat and the fabric of the dress was pulled taut against the curves of her breasts and he could only stare at her body as she leaned in close. A wave of her perfume surrounded him and now he knew he wasn't leaving.

He reached across the gearbox in the middle of the two bucket seats and wrapped his hand around the back of her head. He slid his fingers along the back of her neck, and his hand brushed against the part where she'd twisted up her hair—he wanted it free and flowing around her shoulders but right now he wanted her mouth more.

He needed to feel her lips under his. To prove to himself that lust had addled his thinking. That there was no way she tasted as good as he remembered. She couldn't.

No woman could taste like sin and heaven at the same time.

He tried to justify this kiss just to prove to himself that it had been the absence of kissing in the past year that had made hers unforgettable.

But as he leaned in closer, watching as her lips parted and her tongue darted out to wet her lips, he knew that was a lie. There was a jolt of pure sexual need that went through him and his erection stirred, pressing tight against his pants. He wanted to shift to relieve some of the pressure but he needed the pain to keep him grounded. To remind himself this wasn't a fantasy but something that was truly happening.

Now.

He brushed his lips over hers and her hand came up to rest against his chest. Her fingers moved under his tie to the buttons of his shirt and slipped through. She brushed the tip of one finger over his skin just as he thrust his tongue deep into her mouth. She moaned, shifting on the seat to scoot closer to him. He felt her arms wrap around his neck and shoulders as she drew herself closer to him. He grabbed her waist, squeezing her as he caressed his way around to her back. She felt like a ball of fire in his arms. Like a mustang that was wild and would take him on the ride of his life if he could hold on long enough.

He had a feeling deep in his soul that he could never tame her.

Amberley was going to be the ride of his life, he knew that. And for a second the grief he'd shoved into a box before he'd gone out with her tonight tried to rear its ugly head, and in response he lifted his head and looked down into her face.

Her hair was starting to come loose from the chignon, thanks to his hands in her hair, and there was a flush on her face, her lips were parted. And her pretty brown eyes were watching him. A little bit with patience and a lot with need.

She needed this as much as he did.

Tonight had shown him that they were both broken in ways that the world would never see. He felt honored that she'd let him see the truth that was the real Amberley.

He put his forehead against hers, their breathing comingled as he wrapped both arms around her and lifted her from the seat. It took a little maneuvering and it wasn't comfortable at all, but he managed to move into the passenger seat and get her settled on his lap.

"That was…I didn't realize you were so strong," she said, softly.

"I'm not."

"You are. I'm not a lightweight," she said.

"Yes, you are. You are perfect," he said.

She put her fingers over his mouth. "Don't. I'm not perfect and you really don't think I am. No lies. This is…what we've both wanted since that moment in the field when you got off your horse. And I don't want to ruin it, but honesty…that has to be where this comes from."

He wanted that, too. Wanted this sweet Southern girl who was blunt and real and made him want things he wasn't sure he was ready for. But walking away wasn't going to happen.

He needed her.

But he didn't want to talk and if he was being honest with himself he didn't want to think at all.

Instead, he reached for the seat release and pushed it all the way back. She shifted around until she straddled him. He reached up and pulled the pins from her hair, then gently brought it forward until it hung in thick waves around her shoulders.

Carefully, slowly, he drew the fabric of the skirt part of her dress up to her waist until he could touch her thighs. They were smooth and soft but there was the underlying muscled hardness of her legs. She shifted against him, her hands framing his jaw as she tilted her head to the left. Her hair brushed against his neck as she lowered her mouth and sucked on his lower lip. She thrust her tongue deep into his mouth as she lowered her body against him.

And his pants were too tight. He reached between their bodies, his knuckles brushing against the crotch of her panties, and he felt the warmth of her there. But he focused on undoing his pants and sighed when he was free of the restriction of cloth.

He took her thigh in one hand and then squeezed, sliding his hand under the fabric of her panties and taking her butt in his hand. He drew her forward until she was rubbing over him.

He groaned and tore his mouth from hers.

He wanted to feel her naked against him.

"Shift up," he said.

"What?"

"I want to take your panties off."

She nodded, bracing herself on the seat behind him. She moved until he was able to draw her underwear down her legs and off. He tossed it on the driver's seat and then turned his attention to her breasts, which were in his face. He buried his head in her cleavage, turning his head to the left and dropping sweet kisses against her exposed flesh. She shivered and shifted her shoulders as she settled back on his lap, moving over him, and suddenly he didn't know how long he could last with her on top of him.

She was hot and wet and wanted him.

He found the zipper at the back of her dress and drew it down, and the bodice gaped enough for him to nudge the fabric aside until her breast was visible. She wore a demi bra that bared part of the full globe of her breast. He reached up and pulled the lacy fabric down until her nipple was visible and then leaned forward to suck it into his mouth. With his other hand, he caressed her back, drew his nail down the line of her spine to the small of her back, then cupped her butt and drew her forward again.

He encouraged her to move against him. She started to rock, rubbing her center over his shaft, and he felt a jolt at the base of his spine as his erection grew again.

He suckled harder on her nipple and she put her hands on his shoulders, rubbing against him with more urgency. He reached between their bodies, parting her until he could rub her clit with his finger. She groaned his name and put her hands in his hair, forcing his head back until her mouth fell on his. She thrust her tongue deep into his mouth, her tongue mimicking the movements of her hips.

He felt like he was about to explode and started dropping little nips all over the curves of both of her breasts and her neck. He tangled one hand in her hair as he traced the opening of her body, then pushed his finger slowly up into her.

She made a wild sound that just drove him higher and he thrust his finger up inside her, feeling her body tighten around it. Then he added a second finger and she shifted, until she had her hands braced on his shoulders. She rode him as fiercely as she'd ridden her horse as she chased the barrels in the ring.

He rubbed her with his thumb while continuing to thrust his fingers inside her and then she threw her head back and called his name in a loud voice as she shuddered in his arms before collapsing against him.

He kept his fingers in her body and wrapped his arm around her back, holding her to him. He was on the edge and wanted to come but a part of him wouldn't allow it. Giving her pleasure was one thing but taking it for himself was something he wasn't ready to do.

She shifted and he moved his fingers from her body. He was tempted to bring them to his mouth and lick them clean. Taste her in that intimate way. But he didn't. He felt her shift her hips and the tip of him was right there, poised at the entrance of her body.

He tightened his buttocks and shifted his hips without thinking, entering her without meaning to.

She felt so damn good. Her body wrapped tightly around his length. It was almost as if she was made for him.

She was tight and it was only as she shifted and he felt himself moving deeper into her that he realized what he was doing. He was in the front seat of his car, hooking up with Amberley.

Amberley.

He'd promised himself that he wasn't going to hurt her and he knew if he let this go any further…

He couldn't do it. He couldn't have sex with her and then lie in bed with her. He couldn't just take her on the front seat of his car. Their first time should be special.

He wanted to be better than he knew he was.

She tightened her inner muscles around him and he knew he was going to lose it right then. So he lifted her up and off him. Turned her on his lap so that she was seated facing to the side. Gingerly he reached for his underwear and tucked himself back into it. He was so on edge it would only take one or two strokes for him to come, but he wasn't going to do that.

Not now.

She deserved better than this. Bold and brash Amberley, who had always given him a kind of honesty that made him want to meet her more than halfway.

Now that his mind was back in the game and he wasn't being ruled by his hormones he realized that a part of him had chosen the front of the car because it wasn't the bedroom.

Like the bedroom was only for…

Lucy.

"Uh, what's going on here?" Amberley asked.

He couldn't talk right now. The only thing he was capable of saying would be a long string of her curse words. And she certainly didn't need to hear that.

"Will? It's okay. Whatever it is you're thinking, it's okay."

"It's not okay," he said.

She put her hands on his face and forced him to

look up at her. She leaned down and kissed him so softly and gently that he knew he didn't deserve to have her in his life.

"Yes, it is. Am I the first...since Lucy?"

He nodded. "It's not that I don't—"

"You don't have to explain," she said. "I am going to go into my house now."

He couldn't stop her even though a part of him wanted to. He wasn't ready to make love to a woman who wasn't his wife. It didn't matter that he knew Lucy was gone and that Amberley was sitting here looking more tempting that a woman had a right to.

He wasn't ready.

Damn.

He had a half-naked woman in his lap and he was about to let her walk away.

"I'm sorry," he said abruptly. There had been a lot of firsts since Lucy had died and he'd never thought about this situation. It had felt natural and right... and then it hadn't.

"Don't be. We're friends."

"Friends don't do what we just did," he said.

"Some of them do," she returned. "'Night, Will."

She opened the door and got out of the car, straightening the top of her dress. He reached out and caught her hand. Brought it to his lips and kissed the back of it. He wished he had words to tell her what this night meant to him. How she was changing him and the way he looked at life and himself, but he could only gaze up at her. She tugged her hand free and touched his lips before turning and walking away.

He watched her leave, knowing he should go after her. But he didn't. He just sat there for a few more minutes until he saw her door close and then he got out and walked around to the driver's side of the car and got in. He was breathing like he'd run a fifty-yard dash, then he put his head on the steering wheel, unable to move.

He was torn. His conscience said to go back home and sleep in his empty bed. Let the frustration he felt make sleep impossible because he deserved to suffer.

He was moving on when Lucy couldn't. But he knew that was survivor's guilt talking. He took a deep breath. But all he could smell was sex and Amberley, and he wanted her again. His mind might be preaching patience but his groin was saying to hell with that and to take what he needed. But he couldn't.

It wouldn't be right for Amberley.

He knew this was a first.

The therapist he'd seen after Lucy's death said each first was going to be like a milestone and everything would continue to get easier. Hell, it couldn't get any harder than this. But damn, when was that going to happen? He felt like Don Quixote tilting at windmills and not getting anywhere. He was chasing something that was always just out of reach. But for tonight— tonight he'd almost touched it.

He'd almost given himself permission to move on. But he wasn't ready. What if he never was? What if by the time he was, Amberley had given up on him? Was she the one?

She'd certainly felt like someone important as he'd held her in his arms. He wanted more from her. Wanted more for himself than he'd taken tonight. He just wasn't sure what kind of sign he was waiting for.

It wasn't like Lucy was going to tell him it was

okay to move on. She couldn't. He knew he was the only one who could decide when it was time.

Was it time?

Maybe it wasn't time that was the important thing, it was the person. And it had felt very right with Amberley.

He finally felt like he'd settled down enough to drive back to the guest house he was staying in. As he got out of the car, he fastened his pants and then looked down and saw her panties on his seat.

He lifted them up, tucked them into his pocket and walked into the house feeling like a man torn in two. A man with both the past and the future pulling at him.

He didn't know what he was going to have with Amberley, but as he walked into the house and locked up behind him, he realized that Erin had left a light on for him and he went down the hall to Faye's bedroom.

He looked down on his sleeping little girl and felt that punch in the heart, as he knew he had to make sure that she didn't lose both her mom and her dad that day that Lucy had died. He knew that she deserved to have a father who was participating in life, not one who was locked away in his office and spending his days and nights in the cyberworld because he was afraid to live in the real one.

He leaned over the side of the crib and kissed her forehead.

And he could only hope that Amberley had meant it when she said she forgave him for tonight because he wasn't done with that cowgirl yet.

Eight

Amberley didn't sleep well that night. She wasn't a heartless monster—she understood where Will was coming from. And when they were at dinner at the club she'd realized that he was going to take some extra time if they were going to be more than friends. And being friends…well, how could she not be his friend.

She was hurt. She didn't hook up and sleep around, not anymore. She had found a place for herself where she'd started to adjust to her life. She'd begun to feel like she'd found a peace that had always been just out of reach. Then Will Brady showed up, arousing feelings from her past and reawakening the passion she'd thought she'd buried a long time ago.

But as she stared down at her breakfast cereal she knew she had wanted some kind of romantic fantasy.

That was the problem with watching as much television as she did and reading as many books. There were times when she just wanted her life to have a little more romance than it did.

Last night in his car, Will had made her feel things that she hadn't ever felt before. It had been more intense than the other times she'd had sex.

She wasn't really eating her cereal so she carried the bowl to the sink, and even though she knew she should clean it out right now, she just dumped the bowl in the sink, rinsed the cereal down the drain and then left it.

She had told Clay that she'd break in one of the newer horses and she intended to use Sunday morning to do it. She had a lesson this afternoon and then she needed to keep practicing her barrel riding, as she was signed up for a rodeo at the beginning of November.

But this morning all she had to do was get Squire ready for riding and lessons. The hands mostly had their own horses or used some of the saddle horses that Clay kept on the ranch. And Amberley's job was to make sure they were all in good shape and exercised if they weren't being used.

She heard some sounds coming from the stall set away from the other animals at the end of the stables and turned in that direction. She saw Sophie, Clay's pregnant wife, standing outside the stall talking to the bull inside of it.

"Sophie? Everything okay?" Amberley asked as she walked down toward her.

The stall held Iron Heart…the very same bull that had ended Clay's bull-riding career. Clay had saved the animal from being euthanized and brought him to the Flying E ranch.

"Yeah, just talking about stubbornness with some-one who understands it."

Amberley had to laugh. "Clay."

Sophie nodded. "You'd think I was the first woman to ever be pregnant."

Babies again. It seemed that no matter how hard she tried she couldn't get away from pregnancy or babies. "I think it's sweet how protective he is."

"Well, that's probably because you're not the one being smothered," Sophie said with a small smile.

"I was once the one being ignored and told not to have a baby," Amberley said. She hadn't meant to. She was pretty sure that no one here knew about her past except her doctor in town.

"Oh, Amberley, I'm so sorry. Did you—"

"No. I had a miscarriage," Amberley said. "Gosh, I don't know why I'm telling you all this. I guess just to say that having Clay dote on you is a very good thing."

"I agree. Just wish he wasn't so stubborn all the time."

Amberley knew exactly how Sophie felt. "Aren't all men?"

"They are," Sophie said and then waved goodbye as she left the barn.

Amberley went back to Squire's stall, brushed and saddled the horse and then took him out for a ride. But she wasn't alone. Not in her mind. She remem-bered the way that Will had ridden when she'd taken him out here. She remembered how he'd looked when he'd gotten off his horse and looked up at her. Asked her for something she hadn't wanted to give him at the time.

Now she was wondering if that had been a mistake.

She was trying not to feel cheap and used. She'd meant it last night when she'd said she understood him calling things off. She had. She couldn't imagine the emotions he was going through as he tried to process his grief and move on from losing his wife. She only could funnel it through her experiences of losing her mom and of losing…

She shook her head to shove that thought away and focused on the ride. Squire wasn't really in the mood to run and when Amberley tried to force the issue he bucked and she hung on the first time, but when he did it again, she was knocked off and fell to the ground, landing hard on her shoulder.

Angry at herself for being distracted, she got up and took Squire's reins and started walking back to the stables. But the horse nudged her shoulder and she looked into those eyes and decided he was ready for another chance. She got back in the saddle and they took a leisurely gallop across the field, and she suddenly stopped thinking as she leaned low over Squire and whispered to him. Told him how he was born to run and that she was only here to guide him.

She had one of those moments where everything shifted inside her. Maybe it had been being bucked off the back of the horse that had shaken her and made her see things differently.

But she knew she couldn't keep doing everything in the exact same way. Squire liked being talked to. It had been a long time since she'd had a horse that needed to hear her voice. Mostly she communicated with clicks of her tongue and the movement of her thighs.

She realized that Will was like Squire and last night…well, last night he'd bucked her off, but if she was careful she could find a way to get him back into the stable. She shook her head.

Did she want to work that hard for a man whose life was somewhere else?

She drew in a sharp breath and realized that it didn't matter where his life was, he was going to be one big ol' regret if she didn't do everything she could to claim him. That she wasn't going to be able to just walk away. But she'd known that.

That was the reason why she'd said just to be friends even knowing there was no way she'd ever be satisfied with less than everything he had to give.

Last night he'd taken the first step in moving out of the past. She was willing to give him a little breathing room, but she wasn't going to let him retreat again.

She got back to the barn and stabled Squire and then went to her place to shower and change. She found that there was a note taped to her front door. She opened it.

Amberley,
     Thank you for an incredible evening. I'd like to take you out to dinner tonight. Please be ready at seven. Wear something glamorous.
Will

This was the romance she'd been wishing for. And as she opened her front door and went to her bedroom to try to find the right dress, she knew that he wasn't running this time. And her heart did that little fluttery thing when she thought about him.

Will had taken care of everything for his date with Amberley. In the meantime, he was busy at his computer. The program he'd loaded onto the server at the Texas Cattleman's Club was spitting out all kinds of data and Will focused on analyzing it.

Erin had gone to town to run an errand and Faye was sitting on his lap chewing on one of her teething toys and babbling to herself as she liked to do while he worked. He squeezed his little girl closer to him as he continued working. A few articles popped up that he hadn't read before.

One was about a recluse who seemed to have a beef with just about everyone in Royal. Adam Haskell.

The reason his name had come up in the database was that he had written several strongly worded letters to the members of the town commission as well as local business owners. He might not leave his house very often, but he was very active online using Yelp and other local forums to criticize most of Royal. Will used his smartpen to send the articles and the name to Max to get his feedback. Perhaps his friend would have more intel on Haskell.

Faye shifted around on his lap and he turned to set her on the floor. She crawled toward the big plastic keyboard he'd picked up for her in town recently and then shifted to her feet and took two wobbling steps.

She walked.

His baby girl...

She dropped back down and started crawling

again. Will forgot the computers and got down on the floor.

"Faye, come to Daddy," he said.

She looked at him and gave him that drooly grin of hers and then turned and crawled to him.

The doorbell rang and he scooped Faye into his arms and carried her with him as he went to answer it.

Amberley.

"Hi," she said. "I wasn't sure how I was supposed to let you know I was available for our date tonight."

"I thought you'd text."

"Oh, sorry," she said. "I was here so I thought I'd just stop by."

"It's okay. Want to come in?" he asked, stepping back so she could enter. Faye was already smiling and babbling at Amberley.

"If you're not busy," Amberley said.

"I'm not busy. But this one just took two wobbling steps. Want to see if you can help me get her to walk?" he asked.

"Did she?" Amberley asked. "I'd love to help."

He carried Faye into the living room and then he was kind of at a loss. He placed her on the ground and she crawled around and then sat up and looked at him.

"Let me help. You sit over there," Amberley said, scooping Faye up and moving a few feet from him. Then she set Faye down on her feet and held Faye's hands in each of hers.

Faye wobbled a bit and Will realized he wanted to get this on camera.

"Wait. Let me set up my camera. I don't want to miss this," he said.

"Go ahead. We are going to practice, aren't we?"

Amberley asked, squatting down next to Faye and talking to her.

She smiled at Faye and Will watched the two of them together. They were cute, his girls, but he didn't let himself dwell too much on that. Instead he got his camera set up so that he would be able to capture the entire walk from one side of the room to the other. Then he went back to sit down so his baby could walk to him.

"Okay, I'm ready," Will said.

"Are *you* ready?" Amberley asked Faye.

She wobbled and Amberley let Faye hold on to her fingers and she started moving slowly, taking one step and then another. Will hit the remote so that the camera would start recording. Amberley let go of one of Faye's hands, and then the other, and his daughter smiled at him as she started walking toward him.

He clapped his hands and called her and she came right to him. He felt tears stinging his eyes as he lifted her into his arms, hugging her and praising her for doing a good job.

"She's such a rock star," Amberley said.

"Sit down," Will said. "Let's see if she will walk back to you."

Amberley did. "Faye, come to me."

Will set her on her feet and steadied her, then she took off again in that unsteady gait, walking to Amberley, who kept talking to her the entire time.

She scooped Faye up when she got to her and kissed the top of her head and Will realized that he'd found someone special in Amberley. She had a big heart and she deserved a man who would cherish that heart and give her the family she'd always craved. He wanted to believe he could be that man but he still had his doubts.

They spent another half hour letting Faye walk back and forth between them until Erin got back home.

"Look what Faye has mastered," Will said. "Amberley, go over there."

She did and they got Faye set up to walk over to her and Will noticed a look on Erin's face that he'd never seen before. It was almost as if she was disappointed that she hadn't been here for Faye's first steps. And suddenly he realized this was the first milestone in Faye's life that he hadn't shared with Erin.

"Sorry you missed her first steps," Will said. "I recorded it, though. She's so eager to go."

"She is. She's growing up so fast," Erin said.

"Yes, she is," Will agreed.

"Well, I'll leave you two alone," Erin said. "Are you still going out tonight?"

"Yes, I'm going out with Amberley."

"Oh, that's nice," Erin said.

Amberley left a few minutes later because she still had a lot to do, but Will felt deep inside that something had changed between them and he couldn't help getting his hopes up.

Amberley wasn't sure what she'd expected but the limousine Will pulled up in wasn't it. Will wore a dinner jacket and formal shirt and bow tie. He had his hair spiked and there was excitement and anticipation in those forest green eyes of his. She'd twisted her hair up and tonight the style and her hair seemed to be on the same page.

The dress she'd picked was a fitted dress in a deep purple color with sheer sleeves and a tiny gold belt. She'd paired it with some strappy gold heels that matched the belt. She put on the amber pendant he'd given her and some pearl drop earrings that her dad had given her when she'd turned eighteen. She felt further from her cowgirl self than she ever had before, yet perfectly at home in her skin.

"Damn, you look good," he said.

"Ditto," she said with a wink. "Why do we have a limo?"

"In case things get heated in the car again," he said.

"I assumed when you said you were spending the night that you meant at my place," she said.

"I did," he said. "I just really wanted to shower you with luxury and a limo seemed the right choice. Are you ready to go?"

She nodded. She didn't bother locking her door since the only way on or off the ranch was through the main drive. Will put his hand on the small of her back as they walked to the car. The driver was waiting by the door and he held it open for her. She wasn't sure how to get into the car and still look ladylike.

"Well, you can dress the girl up but that's about it," she said. "How the heck am I supposed to get into the car?"

"You sit down, ma'am, then swing your legs inside," the driver said.

"Thanks," she said. She wasn't embarrassed at having to ask. The truth was if she didn't know how to do something, unless she asked about it, she was never going to learn. She sat down and looked up at

Will as she swung her legs into the car and then she scooted over on the seat and he just smiled at her and then climbed in the way she would have.

"Next time we rent one of these I'm going to insist you wear a kilt so you have to do the same crazy maneuver I had to do," she said.

"Deal," he said.

The driver closed the door and she realized the back of the limo was very intimate. The lighting was low and Will put his arm along the back of the seat and drew her into the curve of his body.

"Thank you for coming out with me tonight," he said.

"Thanks for asking me out. You are spoiling me."

"Figured I had to make up for it since you already know I'm spoiled," he said with a grin that was both cocky and sweet.

"I was just being a bit jealous because I'm one of five and we always had to share everything. You haven't ever really acted spoiled around me," she said.

"Thanks," he said sardonically. The car started moving.

"Where are we going?"

"It's a surprise," he said, taking a silk blindfold from his pocket. "In fact, I'm going to have to insist you put this on."

"Uh, I'm not into any of that kinky *Fifty Shades* stuff," she said. She'd read the books, and while it had been exciting on the page, it wasn't really her thing.

"Understood. This is just to preserve the surprise I have in store for you."

"Okay," she said, turning to allow him to put the blindfold on her.

As soon as he did it, she felt more vulnerable than she would have expected. She reached out to touch him, her hand falling to his thigh. She felt the brush of his breath against her neck and then the warmth of his lips against her skin. She turned her head and felt the line of his jaw against her lips and followed it until their lips met.

Will let her set the pace, which she liked. But then he sucked her lip into his mouth as he rubbed his thumb over the pulse beating at the spot where her neck met her collarbone. She closed her eyes.

The scent of his aftershave and the heat of his body surrounded her.

The limo stopped and Will stopped kissing her.

Damn. He had distracted her. She hadn't been paying attention to anything. Not even how long they'd been in the car.

She reached up to take off the blindfold. "Leave it," he said.

"Will."

"It's part of the surprise," he said. "Trust me?"

Trust him.

She wasn't sure…which was a complete lie. She did trust him or she wouldn't be here. Or maybe it didn't matter if she trusted him or not. She wanted to be here and she was going to do whatever he asked.

Except for the kinky stuff…maybe.

She nodded.

"Good. Now scoot this way," he said, drawing her across the seat. She felt a blast of cold air as the door of the limo was opened and then Will kept his hand on hers, drawing her forward until she was on the edge of the seat.

"Swing your legs around," he said.

She did.

The ground beneath her sandals felt like dirt, not pavement.

"Where are we?"

He didn't answer her question. Instead he lifted her into his arms. "Please come back for us in two hours."

"Yes, sir," the driver said, and Amberley wrapped her arms around Will's shoulders, listening to the sound of the limo driving away.

Then Will started walking and the breeze blew around them a bit chilly until she felt a blast of heat, but they hadn't gone inside. He set her on her feet and took off the blindfold and she saw that they were on a wooden platform with those large infrared heating things positioned around a table. There were twinkle lights strung over the top of the table set for two and covered chafing dishes on a buffet next to it.

The ranch land spread out as far as the eye could see. The sky had started to darken and as she glanced up she saw her angel star.

"Surprised?"

More than he would ever know. It was as if he'd glimpsed into her soul and saw every romantic notion she'd ever had and then amped it up to provide this evening for her. Which meant her heart was in for a whole heap of trouble.

Nine

After almost losing her life at eighteen, Amber had promised herself she was going to live in the moment. And it was something that she'd always strived to do. On the back of a horse it was easy—there was no time to worry about if she was behaving the right way or if someone could see her imperfections. She just hadn't always felt comfortable in her own skin. But tonight she did. In town running errands it was a struggle, which was why she usually had to brace herself before she left her truck and walked among everyone else.

It was easier in Royal because no one knew her history the way folks back in Tyler did. But tonight was one of the few times where she felt totally present and like nothing else mattered.

She faltered a little when she saw the dishes he'd

had made for them. Some of them looked so fancy she was tempted just to stare at them instead of eat them. But Will put her at ease. He was snapping photos and then telling her that he was posting the photos of them online. She figured it was something like the photo story app that Cara had shown her but she wasn't interested.

She didn't want to connect with a world that was bigger than the ranch or Royal and maybe a few folks back in Tyler. That was good enough for her.

Will looked like she imagined a prince would look. He was polished and he talked easily and kept the conversation moving along from topic to topic. He knew horses and led her onto the topic of polo ponies and where she saw the breeding changes leading that field. And it didn't matter that she was dressed like a woman and not a cowgirl—she felt at ease talking about the animals.

"I did read an article last month that talked about a breeding program that a Saudi prince was spearheading. I think it's interesting in that he is working on increasing agility while maintaining stamina."

"That makes sense. I knew a guy in college who had gone to Europe to learn a centuries-old custom of Spanish horse dancing. It is basically training the horse to do very practiced moves, not unlike the Olympic horse events but even more controlled. He used some of those practices when we were playing polo and they worked," Will said.

"There really is room for crossover in all types of training. I was recently trying a technique with Montgomery that I saw used in the Olympics. Barrel racing is speed and mastery not only over the horse, but also over yourself."

"How often do you practice?" he asked.

"I try to get a couple of hours in every day. I am only really participating now when I can get away from the ranch," she said.

"And I couldn't tell the pattern you were using, but is there one? Or do you just have to circle all of the barrels in the least amount of time."

She took a bite of her dinner. "You have to go in a cloverleaf pattern and the one who does it the quickest is named the winner. They use an electric eye to do the timing. The key is to get as close to the barrels as you can so that you are taking the shortest route around them all."

"I'd love to watch you compete sometime," he said.

"Sure. I'll let you know the next time I'm going to a rodeo. I try to stay local here in Texas."

"Cool," he said and she wondered what that meant. Was he going to be in Texas for a while?

It wasn't really a response but she was living in the now. So that meant not pointing out that he could be back in Seattle before her next rodeo. Or would he?

She didn't ask the question because, to be honest, that would make things more complicated. Give her another thing to worry about it and that wasn't what she wanted right now.

"I've never had a guy buy me clothes before. Not even my dad. He used to have my grandma buy us stuff or take us shopping," Amberley said.

"Was it odd? It just reminded me of you," he said.

"Well, you were right. I would never have picked it out. I was surprised when I put it on," she said.

"I'm not surprised, I could picture you in it as soon as I saw it."

"Well, aren't you clever?" she said, winking at him. He was too charming for his own good. She suspected he knew it, as well, because he kept moving through life like nothing could touch him.

She wondered if that was how he had dealt with losing his wife all along or if it was just with her that he ran. Because some of the time he'd seemed to be okay. But then she remembered the other night, when he'd stopped himself from making love to her.

And she wondered if he was pretending like she was. She had gotten pretty damn good at believing the lie she told herself that she was okay. She wanted it to stop being a lie. And she knew she wanted to help Will get to a place where he was okay, too.

She suspected that it would happen in its own time and she knew she had to be patient, but a big part of her was afraid that time was going to take him back to Seattle before she could witness him getting there.

"So there I was standing in the middle of the river in Montana with a client that Dad wanted to impress, and he's asking me where I learned my fly-fishing technique, and all I could think of was if I say the Wii, Dad's never going to forgive me," Will said to Amberley as they finished up their meal. They had been having the most carefree conversation, and Amberley loved how he was telling all these personal stories from his childhood.

"What'd you do? I would have straight up said a video game," she said.

"I said natural instinct," Will said as he took a

sip of his wine. "Then my dad came over and said, 'Yup, that boy has a natural instinct for bull.' The client started laughing and I did, too, and honestly it was one of the first times my dad and I connected."

"That's funny. So did the client do what your dad wanted?" Amberley asked.

"Yes. Dad offered me a job after that, but as much fun as the trip to Montana was I knew that I didn't want to have to work that hard to charm people. Computers are easier," he said. "So I turned down the job and that pissed the old man off but I already had the job offer from Max so he got it."

"What does Max do?" Amberley asked.

"He's an ex-hacker-turned-billionaire tech genius. He owns St. Cloud Security Solutions. I'm the CTO for the company…the Chief Technology Officer."

"Dad would have been happy for me to stay on our ranch," Amberley said. "But I knew if I did then I'd spend the rest of my life there. It would have been easy to hide out there and just keep doing what I'd been doing."

"You wanted more," he said.

"I did. I still do. I like working for Clay and Sophie now that they are a couple, but I really would like to have my own stables someday," she said. If she had one dream it was that. She'd let horses take over the parts that she'd thought she'd fill with kids and a husband.

"Why would you have been hiding out if you had stayed at home?" he asked. "You seem like you grab life by the—I mean, you're pretty gutsy."

She smiled at the way he said that. She had tried grabbing life by the balls, but it had grabbed back, and her father said that actions had consequences, which she'd never gotten until that summer.

She took a deep breath. She'd thought telling Will about the hysterectomy would be the hard part, but this was a big part of who she was and why she was here in Royal.

"Um, well, I… This is sort of a downer, maybe we should save it for another night," she said.

Will nodded. "If that's what you want. But I want to know more about you, Amberley. Not the stuff that everyone can find out. The real you. And I think whatever made you want to hide is probably important."

She pushed her plate forward and folded her arms over each other on the table as she leaned forward. It was cozy and intimate at the table. Will had created an oasis for them in the middle of the Texas night.

"I took a job working at a dude ranch the summer I graduated from high school. I was thinking about what I'd do next and I knew I wasn't going to college. It just wasn't for me."

"Makes sense. You have a lot of natural ability with horses and I read about your rodeo wins online."

"You did?" she asked. "I didn't realize you'd looked me up."

"Yeah. I wanted to know more about you even as I was running from you and pretending that you didn't fascinate me."

"That's corny and sweet," she said.

"Thanks, I think."

Will made her feel like she mattered. It was kind, and it wasn't that others hadn't done that but he made her feel like she mattered to him. That it was personal and intimate and she hadn't had that before.

"So, you're on a dude ranch…"

She sat back in the chair and the words were there in her mind and she practiced them before saying them. It was easy in her head to remember what had happened. The cheap wine they'd bought at the convenience store. The way he'd never driven a pickup truck, so he had convinced her to let him drive. And then when he'd parked it and moved over to make out with her in the front seat until it had gone much farther.

Then of course she'd gotten pregnant and had expected Sam to be, well, a better man than he was. Of course, he'd said he was back to his real life and he'd help her financially but wanted nothing to do with her or the baby. It had hurt and there were times when his rejection haunted her. It made it easier for her to isolate herself on the ranch. But she wasn't going to say any of that to Will.

"There had been a group of guys from back east staying as guests at the ranch. They'd decked themselves out in Western clothes and they were flirty and fun and I ended up hooking with one of them. It was my first time and not his, and I'm afraid that freaked him a little bit and then…" She paused. She wasn't sure she could say the next part.

She looked at Will. He'd stopped eating and was watching her carefully.

She took a deep breath and the words spilled out quickly. Like tearing off a bandage, she did it as fast as she could. "I got pregnant. But there were complications, I started hemorrhaging and I almost died. I did lose the baby, and the only way to save me was for me to have a hysterectomy."

She stopped talking and it felt too quiet. Like even the animals and insects that had been in the background before were surprised by her words. She blinked and realized how much she hated telling this story. She never wanted to do it again.

Will didn't say anything and she started to regret telling him, and then he got up and walked around the table. He pulled her to her feet and into his arms and hugged her close. He didn't say anything to her, just wrapped her in his body, and the panic and the pain that had always been buried with that story started to fade a little bit as he held her and made her feel like she was okay.

That she wasn't damaged and broken.

Will didn't know the words to make everything all right and he could tell by the rusty way the story had come out that she was still a little broken from everything that had happened. He knew because no matter how many firsts he had after Lucy's death there were still things that bothered him. And there was no way that he was ever going to be completely washed clean of the past.

And now he knew that Amberley wasn't going to be, either. She was deeply scarred, as he was.

Hell, he wanted to do something to fix this thing that he couldn't fix.

He thought about how caring about someone could suck sometimes. He'd loved Lucy but had been unable to save her and he was starting to care more deeply for Amberley than he wanted to admit and there was no way in hell he could ever fix what had happened to her. No matter how much he wanted to.

"Siri, play Amberley playlist."

The playlist started and it was Jack Johnson's "Better Together." It was the perfect song for how he felt at this moment. He pulled her into the curve of his body and took one hand in his and kept his other wrapped around her waist as he danced her around the table, singing underneath his breath in that off-key way of his.

"You have a playlist for me?" she asked, tipping her head to the side and resting her cheek against his shoulder.

"I do. It's a bunch of songs that you might not have on vinyl," he said, hoping for a smile. He'd made the playlist this afternoon after she'd left his house. He'd wanted to give her something.

She rewarded him with a little half smile. And then he kept dancing and singing to her. He knew there were some pains that words couldn't heal and that time could only scab over. He had been debating his own pain for a year, trying to figure out if he was going to scar or just have a scab that he kept scratching and refreshing the hurt.

"I like this one," she said.

"I do, too," he said.

He wanted them to be better together. They could bring out the best in each other. Tonight he felt they'd jumped over that first hurdle. But he knew each of them was going to have more obstacles that they would bring to the relationship.

"I think we are going to be more than friends," he said.

"Me, too. I want more than that from you," she said. "But I don't want to make another mistake. I picked a guy who had nothing in common with me before. A man who didn't look at the world the same way I do."

"I care about you, cowgirl," he admitted.

"Me, too, city boy," she said with a grin.

The song changed to "SexyBack" and she just arched one eyebrow at him.

"Oops. Not sure how this got on there," he said.

"Maybe you were thinking about the way our last date ended," she said with a sassy grin.

Music had done what he couldn't as there were sweet and fun songs in the playlist, and after about five songs he noticed she wasn't tense and the tightness around her mouth had faded. She was laughing and smiling and while he still ached for her and the pain she'd gone through, he felt better for having cheered her up.

"So what do you think? Is there a place for the twenty-first-century technology in your music life?" he asked.

"You're a complete goofball, Will. I told you I use the music app on my phone," she said.

"You did but you said it was just for stuff you already loved."

"Not all the songs you selected are newer," she pointed out. "I think you like my kind of music."

"I do like it. And I was trying to ease you into it. Keep the shock value low," he said, aware that they were both talking about something inconsequential to keep from talking about the real emotions that were lying there between them. The truth that was there in the silence under the music that just kept playing on.

"Thank you."

"You're welcome," he said. "How does dessert sound?"

"Sweet?"

Some of her spunk was coming back and that was exactly what he'd been hoping for. "Good, because I asked for pineapple upside-down cheesecake with a salted caramel sauce."

"That sounds interesting," she said.

"Exactly what I was aiming for." He held her chair out for her and she sat back down.

He cleared away the dinner dishes and then brought back dessert. Everything had been set up by a private chef he'd hired in Royal. The dishes had been labeled and set up so that he could easily find them.

"Coffee or an after-dinner drink?" he asked.

"Coffee would be nice," she said.

"Decaf?" he asked.

"God, no," she said.

Another thing they had in common. He poured them each a cup of coffee from the carafe that had been prepared and then took his seat across from her again. He ignored the questions that still rattled around in his head. Instead he looked around at the night sky.

"My app still isn't doing what I want it to, so I'm not sure we are going to see anything fabulous in the sky tonight," Will said. He was unsure how to get the conversation back on track now.

"That's okay. I'm pretty happy sitting here staring at you," she said.

"Yeah?"

"Yup," she said. "Did that thing you did at the club last night work?" she asked.

"I think it might have. Do you know Adam Haskell?"

"Know him personally? No," she said. "But I do know his reputation. He seems to have a gripe about everyone and everything in town. Do you know he gave my riding lessons a low score on Yelp even though he's never taken a class from me?"

"I'm not surprised. He showed up in a relay link that I was chasing and then when I searched on his name it seemed to make sense that he might be the one releasing everyone's secrets. Do you know if he has any computer knowledge?" Will asked. Being able to post a bad review on Yelp and trolling people on social networks didn't take any real knowledge of computers or hacking. And a part of him had thought that Maverick was more skilled than Haskell seemed to be.

Ten

Will was just about to ask Amberley more questions about Haskell when his phone pinged. He ignored it, after making sure it wasn't Erin. Then it pinged again and started ringing.

"Sorry about this but I think I need to take this," Will said.

"Go ahead," Amberley said.

"Brady," he said, answering his phone.

"St. Cloud," Max said. "Where the hell are you? It looks like Haskell might be our man. I need you to come to Royal now. He's leading the cops on a high-speed car chase and I'm with a judge, the sheriff and a lawyer right now getting a warrant to search his property. I need you to analyze what we find and tell me if he's our man."

Will wasn't ready to end his evening with Amber-

ley but business had to come first. This business, anyway. Once Maverick was caught he would be free to
focus on Amberley and see where this was leading.

"I'll be there as quickly as I can," he said.

"Good. I'm texting you Haskell's address. Meet
me there."

He ended the call and then looked over at Amberley, who was watching him carefully. "Haskell is
on the run and Max is getting permission for me to
go through his computer. I'm sorry to cut our date
short—"

"No, don't be. I want that bastard Maverick caught
as much as everyone else in Royal does. What can
I do?"

"I could probably use your help going through
things at Haskell's if you want to come with me."

"Will the cops let me help?"

"I don't know," he said. "But I didn't want our
night to end."

"Me, either. I think I would. I don't really want to
go home yet."

"Okay. Let me get the limo and we will head out."

The limo driver was quick to retrieve them and
Will had him take them to his car, tipped the driver
to move a box from the trunk over to his car while
he and Amberley went inside and then sent the driver
home. He checked in on Faye and updated Erin on
what was happening before he and Amberley drove
into town.

"I never imagined your life would be like this. I
figured you just did things on your computer and
that was it."

Will laughed. "Usually it's not this exciting. In

a big city Haskell could have slipped away anony-
mously. And if he was smarter he'd be driving sen-
sibly instead of leading the cops on a high-speed
chase."

"I know. He's not the brightest bulb according to
the gossip I've heard at the diner."

"Really?"

"Yes, why?" she asked.

"It's nothing," he said. But in his mind there was
a new wrinkle to Haskell being Maverick. It would
take someone really smart to set up the kind of cover
that Will had encountered while trolling the web for
Maverick's true identity. It seemed a bit far-fetched
that someone people considered not so bright would
be able to do something like this on his own.

Was he working with someone?

Will was confident he'd be able to find the answers
on Haskell's computer.

"Catching cyber criminals isn't usually like this.
Though one time I did have to chase a guy down an
alleyway. He'd had a program running on the police
scanner to alert him if cops were dispatched to his
property. It was a clever bit of code," Will said. He'd
tried to convince the hacker to give up breaking into
secure systems and bring him over to work for him
but the guy wasn't interested.

"That must have been… Was it scary? I mean, are
hackers and cyber criminals usually armed?"

"Some of them are. But usually I find the evidence
and I don't go with the cops to arrest a criminal unless they are on some sort of mobile relay, where I
have to track them while the cops move in. One time
I had to wear a bulletproof vest and was stationed in

a SWAT truck. There were all these guys with guns and riot gear on and there I was with my laptop…I felt like the biggest nerd."

"You could never be a nerd," she said.

"Thanks. But I can be. I'm sorry our date has taken a crazy turn."

"I'm not. Honestly this is the most exciting thing I've ever done," Amberley said.

He shook his head. There was pure joy in her voice and he realized again how young she was. True, there were only four years between them and she'd had a very harrowing experience when she was eighteen, but the way she was almost clapping her hands together at the thought of being part of the investigation enchanted him. And turned him on.

"Why are you looking at me like that?" she asked.

"Like what?" he countered, trying to sound innocent, not like he'd been imagining her wrapped around him while he kissed her senseless.

"You know," she said.

"Uh, this is the place," Will said as he turned into the driveway of a run-down ranch-style house. The yard was overgrown and there was a big sign that said Keep Off the Grass and No Solicitors.

As they got out of the car, Will noticed there was also a sign in the front window that read Protected by Smith & Wesson.

"Not the friendliest of men," Amberley said. "So what do we do now?"

Max was waiting outside for them and a patrol car was parked at the curb with the lights flashing. Some of the neighbors poked their heads out of the front door but most weren't interested.

"Thanks for coming. The sheriff wants us to help go over the house with his team just to be an extra set of computer expert eyes. He thinks we might see something relevant that his officers would overlook since it's not the kind of crime they are used to dealing with," Max said. "Did I interrupt a date?"

"Yes."

"I'm sorry," Max said. "Dang, I wish this had happened another night."

"Me, too. But it didn't. So let's get this taken care of," Will said.

Max knew that this was the first real date that Will had been on since Lucy's death.

"Do you want to take his computer back to your place?" Max asked.

"Let me see the setup first," Will said. "Do you know Amberley Holbrook? She's the horse master at Clay's ranch."

"Nice to meet you Amberley," Max said.

"Same."

They went into Haskell's house and the cops were gathering other evidence while Max, Will and Amberley found his computer. "This doesn't look very sophisticated."

"No," Will agreed. "It looks like it's about ten years old."

Not that you needed a new or sophisticated machine to hack. Most of the time if he ran from a DOS prompt he could get into over-the-counter software and some social media sites.

Will hit the mouse to see if there had been a program running or if there was a security login.

And then he sat down in the dirty chair to get

to work. He lost himself in the computer programming…or tried to. But the smell of Amberley's perfume lingered in the room and he couldn't help but think this was one time when he didn't want work distracting him from his real life.

Tonight he'd come closer than ever to finding something with Amberley that he hadn't wanted to admit had been missing in his life.

Max and Will talked quietly while the computer ran some program. Everyone had something to do and she was just standing in the corner trying not to get in anyone's way.

She hadn't seen Will work before. She stood there watching him when she thought no one was looking. He was intense as his fingers moved over the keyboard. He took a small dongle from his key ring and plugged it into the USB drive and first lines of text started scrolling on the screen, which meant nothing to her, but Will nodded and then started typing on the keyboard.

"He's one of the best in the world."

She glanced over her shoulder at Max St. Cloud, who stood next to her. She didn't know much about the man except he was Will's partner at St. Cloud Security Systems. She also knew he was engaged to Natalie Valentine, a local wedding dress designer.

"He's awesome," she said, then realized how lame that sounded. "Sorry, I'm really better with horses than people."

Max laughed in a kind way. "It's okay. I should probably leave you alone but I was curious about you."

That didn't sound very reassuring.

"Why?"

"Will hasn't done anything but work since... Faye's birth. I think you're the first woman he's been out with," Max said.

"I know," she said. She was the first. That's why she should be cautious about falling for Will. He was a city guy who'd lost his spouse, so in her mind there were danger signs all around him. But he was also the guy who'd made her a special playlist and could ride like he'd been born in the saddle.

"Good," Max said. "Want to help me look for USB drives, other storage devices, a tablet, maybe an external hard drive?"

"Sure," Amberley said. "I know what some of those things are but what's an external hard drive?"

Max smiled. "Should be a rectangle shape and thin. Follow me, the lead detective needs to give us some gloves and tell us how to search."

Amberley followed him into the other room and after a brief explanation of what they were to do and orders to track down an officer and let him know if they found anything, they were both sent to look.

"If you take the living room and I take the bedroom we might be able to finish this search quickly and get you back on your date," Max said.

"Sounds good," she said.

She followed Max out of the room where Will was working and went into the living room. It was dusty and cluttered, but as Amberley walked around the room she noticed a system. There was a pile of *Royal Gazettes* next to his recliner. The weekly newspaper was stacked up almost to the arm of the chair. She glanced down at the paper on top. It was the one from two weeks ago that had run the story of Will coming to town to help find and stop Maverick.

He'd underlined the word *Maverick*. That was interesting. It could be a clue or maybe Haskell was just ticked off that someone else was ruining the lives of Royal's citizens and taking over his role.

Amberley sorted through the top papers and noticed that he'd used his black pen to mark every story relating to the cyber menace. Was it a kind of trophy for him? Seeing the stories about himself in the paper? She set them in a neat stack on the seat of the chair to show to the officers who were in the house and then started looking through the mess on the side table. There were prescription pill bottles and a community college book on computer software that looked to be about three years old. She stuck that on her pile of stuff and kept moving.

She found some other things that were personal and she realized how odd it was to be going through someone else's house. Haskell always seemed like an old curmudgeon to her when she'd seen him in town but she found a picture of him on one of the bookshelves with a girl from when he'd been in his twenties. He'd been smiling at the camera and he had his arms wrapped around the woman. Amberley didn't recognize her but she wondered what had happened to her.

Was she the reason why Haskell hated the residents of Royal so much now?

"Find anything?" Max asked as he entered the room.

"Not the hard drive, but I did find these papers,

where he has underlined every mention of Maverick. Not really hard evidence but I saw on a crime show that serial criminals like to keep references to their crime as a sort of trophy. So this might mean something. And I found this old computer book on his table. Maybe he was brushing up his skills?" Amberley said. "There's a lot of junk and dust in this room."

"In this house," Max said. "I think the papers might be a lead. And the computer book, let me see that, please."

She handed it to Max. He opened the book and read some of Haskell's handwritten notes. "Let me see if Will can make anything of this."

She followed Max back into the area where Will was. Will turned when they entered.

"He was definitely using an external source," Will told them. "I think if we find that we might find the evidence we need. Did you two find anything?"

"We found this," Max said, handing it over to Will. "It was an MS training class. So not anything in here that would help him mask his online presence. So we're done here?"

"I think so," Will said.

"I'll let everyone know," Max said, leaving the room.

Will went back to the small home office and Amberley followed him, watching from the doorway as he pounded his fists on the desk.

Going in to check on Will hadn't seemed like a bad idea until she put her hands on his shoulders and he pulled her closer to him. He was frustrated—she could see that. He stood up and she looked into his eyes and she wanted to say something or do something to help him not feel so hampered by this investigation.

"Let's finish this up so we can get back to our date," Will said. "I'm not close to being finished with you."

She hoped she looked calmer than she felt because every part of her was on fire and she knew that she'd changed. That sharing the past with Will had freed her in a way she hadn't expected it to.

The secret that she'd always hid from the men she'd hooked up with had been a weight she hadn't even been aware of until now. Until she was free of it. She heard the cops talking and Max went in to talk to Will and she just stood there in the cluttered, dusty living room, knowing that her entire world had changed.

A new hope sprang to life inside her and she wondered if she'd found a man she could trust.

Eleven

"I should get you back home," Will told her as they walked out of Haskell's house.

"Okay," Amberley said, glancing at her watch. "I have to be up early for the horses."

"Wait a second," he said, turning and leaving her by his car to go over to where Max stood.

She watched as he spoke to Max, his business partner and friend, and remembered how Max had talked to her. She wasn't sure if he'd been warning her to be careful with his friend, or just warning her that Will might not be ready for whatever was happening between them.

She rubbed her hand along the back of her neck and shivered a bit. The night was chilly and she was outside without a coat on. But it wasn't too cold. She just suddenly felt very unsure.

And she didn't like it. It wasn't as if Max had said anything that she hadn't been aware of, she knew that Will hadn't dated since Lucy's death. She knew that she might be someone he cared for but she might also be the woman he was using to help him get over losing his wife. But hearing it from someone else's mouth was making her think that maybe she wasn't being smart.

Her heart didn't care and neither did her body. In fact, maybe her being his temporary woman was exactly the right thing for her. He was her first in many ways, too. The first guy she'd told about losing the baby. The first guy she'd really cared about since she was eighteen.

She'd thought she loved Sam. Well…at least cared about him. But this thing she felt for Will was so much stronger. She didn't know if it was real, either. And it was harder than she had anticipated to keep her cool. Not to let her emotions overwhelm her. But when Will came back over, shrugged out of his jacket and draped it over her shoulders, she felt like she was fighting a losing battle inside of herself.

"Max is going to text me if he hears anything," Will said. "Let's go home."

Home.

An image of her, Will and Faye popped into her mind and she didn't want to shove it out. She wanted it to be true. Watching Faye take her first steps today and feeling that punch of joy in her stomach had made her realize that she could have a family. She didn't have to give birth to love a child. And while a part of her realized that it was dangerous to think that way about Will and Faye, another part of her was already putting herself in the picture.

"Okay."

He held open the door for her and she slid into the passenger seat. She slipped her arms into the sleeves of Will's jacket. It smelled like his aftershave and after she fastened her seat belt she put her hands in the pockets and felt something…

She pulled it out. It was a photo. She glanced down at it and saw Lucy. He was carrying around a picture of his wife. The door opened and she shoved the photo back in her pocket, but it caught on the fabric and he noticed her hand as he slid behind the wheel.

"What's that?" he asked.

She felt like there was a weight in the pit of her stomach… "This."

She handed it to him.

He took it and as he did she noticed there was typed information on the back of the photo. And she realized what it was. She had a card like that with her mom's picture on it that she'd gotten at her funeral. It was Lucy's funeral card.

"I—I haven't worn that jacket since the day we buried her," Will said. "I didn't even realize it was in there."

He looked down at the picture and ran his thumb over her features and Amberley felt like she'd interrupted a very private moment. She shouldn't be in the car with him. Or wearing his jacket or even falling for him. She didn't know where Will was in his head but he wasn't with her. Would he ever fully be able to be with her?

That thought hurt more than she'd expected it to.

"She would have liked you," Will said.

"Would she?" Amberley asked.

Watching Will gently caress his late wife's picture gave Amberley an odd feeling. Like when she had cut herself with a knife cooking dinner and she knew she'd cut herself, but it didn't start bleeding right away or hurt for a few seconds. The wound was there. She was just in denial about how deep it went.

"Yes. It's not…I'm not holding on to the past," Will said. "This isn't like the other night."

"Please, you don't have to explain."

"But I want to. Lucy is gone and she's a part of my past," Will said. "She'll always be a part of my life because of Faye."

"I know that. Really I do. I'm not upset," she said. She was trying to make the words true by saying them with conviction but in her heart, she was sad. And she felt just a little bit sorry for herself.

"Amberley."

She looked over at him and she'd never seen him so intense before.

"I want you to know that I'm not dating you just to try to move on from Lucy's death. And I know that we haven't had much time together but I'm not fooling around with you and using you."

She wanted to believe him. He had said the words that she could have asked him to say but she wasn't too sure they were the truth.

Will dropped off Amberley at her place, where she shrugged out of his jacket and gave it back to him. "Thanks for a very interesting date."

"You're welcome," he said. He wanted to come in.

His gut said that he shouldn't just let her walk away, but he didn't know if pushing her now was the right thing to do. So he waited until she was safely inside her house and then drove back to his place.

But when he got there he just sat in the car holding Lucy's picture. Life with Lucy had been uncomplicated. They'd met in college and both of them had come from similar backgrounds. Everyone had said they were a match made in heaven. And while he loved her and cared for her, he knew they'd been growing apart in the months before Faye's birth.

Sometimes he suspected his guilt stemmed from that. That he'd been drifting out of their marriage when she'd died. He went home and the house was quiet with everyone sleeping. He checked in on Faye.

He had the funeral card that Amberley had found earlier and brought it into Faye's room with him. When he looked down at his sleeping daughter's face he could see the resemblance to Lucy. It was growing stronger every day and it made him miss his wife.

He felt a pang in his heart when he thought about raising their daughter alone. And there was a part of him that wondered if he'd ever really be able to bring another woman into their lives. He liked Amberley. He wanted her fiercely but he didn't know if he was right for her.

If she was just a good-time girl, then he wouldn't hesitate to get involved, but everything had changed tonight when she'd told him about the child she'd lost. There was a hidden vulnerability to her that he couldn't ignore now that he'd glimpsed it. And no matter how hot they might burn together he sensed

that she was going to want more from him. And he
knew she deserved more from him. He couldn't do it.

After a restless night he woke up early and went
into the kitchen, where Erin was feeding Faye breakfast. He poured himself a cup of coffee and then sat
down.

"How was your date?" Erin asked.

"It was okay. We did get a break in the Maverick
case last night."

"That's good," Erin said. "So does that mean we
won't be here much longer?"

"I'm not sure yet," Will said. "Why?"

"Just wondering if I should start packing up our
stuff. I've got to run a few errands in town this morning," Erin said.

"We'll probably be here at least until the end of
the month," he said.

"Okay," she said.

"I'll watch Faye while you go to town," Will said.

"Are you sure?" she asked.

"Yes. I missed spending time with her last night
and you had to work overtime."

"You know I don't mind."

Will nodded at her. "I do know that. But I also
know errands go quicker without Faye."

"True. Thanks, Will."

"No problem," he said. He moved around to take
the spoon from Faye. "Go on. I've got breakfast."

Erin quickly left the room. He touched his daughter's face and she cooed and blinked up at him.

"Hello, angel," he said. "You're hungry this morning."

She kicked her legs and arms and smiled at him. "Dadada."

"That's right. Daddy's here," he said as he scooped her up into his arms.

He held her close and buried his face in the soft curls at the top of her head. He changed her diaper and then carried her into his office. "Ready to help Daddy work?"

"Dadadada," Faye said.

"I'll take that as a yes," he said, then grabbed his laptop and Faye's little toy computer and sat down in the big double chair in the corner. He put his laptop on his lap after he'd set down Faye and she reached for her toy and mimicked his motions.

Then she looked over at him and smiled.

He smiled back at her as she started pounding on the keys with her fingers. His little computer whiz.

He knew he should be looking up some of the information he had found on Haskell's computer, but Amberley was on his mind and he typed her name into the search bar instead. He saw the pictures of her in the rodeo and then did a deeper search and found an old newspaper article from when she was a junior in high school. It was a profile of her as the junior barrel-racing champ with her horse. She looked so young and innocent.

Only seeing that photo of her and comparing it with the woman he knew now showed how much life had changed her. He leaned back and Faye crawled over to him and climbed on his lap the way she did. He lifted her with one hand and shifted his computer out of her way with the other.

She looked at the picture on the screen.

He looked down at her.

"Dadada," she said. Then babbled a string of words that made no sense to him.

Had she recognized Amberley? They'd played together for an entire afternoon but would that be enough for her to recognize her?

And was he doing Faye a disservice by allowing her to get attached to Amberley when Will wasn't sure what was going to happen between them. Sure he'd told her he saw a future with her, but now he was having second thoughts. How could he promise her something like a future when he wasn't even sure where he was going to be in a month's time. He was pretty sure he wasn't going to stay in Royal. His entire family was in Bellevue. His parents and Faye's maternal grandparents. But Lucy's sisters didn't live in Bellevue; one of them was in Oregon and the other in San Francisco.

And after she'd seen that picture of Lucy in his pocket was she going to want to be with him? Did she think he was still hung up on his wife?

Hell.

There were no answers, only more confusion and a little bit of sadness because if there was ever a woman he wanted in his life it was Amberley. She suited him. She wasn't his twin, which was probably why he enjoyed her so much. She was blunt and funny and unafraid to admit when something confused her. She was sassy and spunky and he wanted her to have all the happiness that he saw on her face in that picture when she'd been sixteen.

He didn't want to be the man who'd completed

what the jerk from the dude ranch had started. The man who showed her that she couldn't trust.

But how could he do that for Amberley and not risk hurting himself. He'd promised himself that he would never fall in love again when he'd held Lucy's hand as she lay dying. He'd never felt that abandoned and alone before and he'd promised himself that he'd never feel that way again.

Amberley went about her business all morning, ignoring Will and anyone who wasn't four-legged. Cara arrived on Monday afternoon with the latest news about Adam Haskell. After he'd crashed his car and been captured, an ambulance had transported him to the hospital. Apparently his condition was still critical.

"Sheriff Battle impounded the car. I heard they had to medevac Mr. Haskell to the hospital after he crashed on the highway," Cara said.

"Sounds like it was nuts," Amberley said.

That meant that Will was probably going to be done here in Royal. Everyone seemed to agree that Haskell was Maverick and she was afraid that Will was going to leave now. It hardly mattered that she was still upset with him for the way their date had ended and angry at herself for letting pride make her send him away. But she was tired of trying to compete against a ghost for him.

But she couldn't change the past. She knew that better than anyone.

"Why do you think they were after Haskell? Maybe they finally got tired of his crappy online reviews."

Amberley glanced over at Cara, who was smiling and texting while she was talking to her. "What do you know about Haskell?" Amberley asked. Cara's family had lived in Royal for generations.

Cara looked up from her phone at Amberley. "Not much. He really didn't like high school kids. One time I tried to sell him a magazine subscription and he was a jerk."

"Why did you even bother?"

"Someone dared me," Cara said.

They worked in silence for twenty minutes until they were done with the horses, and Amberley wanted to pretend she'd found some inner peace about Will, but she hadn't.

"Amberley?"

"Yes."

"Will you watch me run the barrels? I need to gain a second or two and I can't figure out where," Cara said.

"Sure. The barrels are set up. I'll go and walk the path while you saddle up." Amberley walked out of the barn and over to the ring to double-check that everything was where it should be.

She noticed that Erin was walking toward the stables with Faye in her arms. The little girl was wearing a pair of denim overalls and a rust-colored long-sleeved shirt underneath it.

"Hi, Erin," Amberley said as the other woman came over to her. Faye held her hands out toward Amberley and she reached over to let her grab on to her finger as the baby babbled at her.

"Hiya," Erin said. "We were out for our afternoon

walk and I thought she might like to see some of the horses."

"Perfect. Cara is going to be out in a minute with her horse to practice. That will be fun to watch."

Amberley couldn't help thinking that Erin was here for something other than to watch the horses. And when Cara came out and noticed they had company, she gave Amberley a look.

"Warm up, Cara. Then let me know when you're ready to take your run," she said. She had a stopwatch on her phone that she'd use to time Cara after she warmed up.

"I didn't realize you were working," Erin said.

"It's okay. You haven't been over to the stables to ride. Do you like horses?" Amberley asked.

"I don't know. I mean, I read books with horses in them growing up but I've never been on one," Erin said.

"We can fix that. Do you want to go for a ride?" she asked.

"Yeah. Sort of. I'm not sure when, though," Erin said.

"Well, the best way to get to know horses is grooming them. And I think even little Miss Faye would like to be in the stables. When Cara is done with her run we could go and meet the horses," Amberley said.

"I'd like that," Erin said.

Faye squirmed around and reached for Amberley. Erin arched an eyebrow at her and held Faye out toward her. Amberley took the little girl in her arms and hugged her. She was going to miss Faye when she and Will left. And though she hadn't spent that much time with the baby she knew she'd become attached to her.

Not her smartest move.

But then everything about Will Brady rattled her.

Cara rode over to the fence and smiled down at Faye.

"Who is this little cutie?"

"Faye Brady. Will's daughter," Amberley said.

"She's adorable," Cara said.

Amberley agreed and she realized that she wanted this little girl to be hers. She wanted that image of the family that had popped into her head last night to be real and she knew it couldn't be. Finding Haskell meant Will would be leaving. Maverick was done terrorizing Royal and Will Brady was going to be leaving Texas and taking a piece of her heart with him.

She handed Faye back to Erin as Cara started doing her run. And Amberley tried to settle up with the fact that this was her life.

Twelve

Sheriff Battle, Will was told, had found a hard drive and some other incriminating evidence in Haskell's car. The police had brought it over to him this afternoon and Will was trying to break the security code to access the info within. The coding was different from anything he'd found on Haskell's home computer. It was more complex and nuanced than what he'd seen before.

Will was on the fence as to whether the same programmer could be responsible for both codes. Haskell had used a complex passcode on his computer, but the security on the hard drive was different. Will used all the skills he'd developed as a hacker back in his teenage days, before he'd settled down to working on the right side of the law.

He kept Max and the sheriff up-to-date on his

progress and after spending six hours working at a cramped desk, he got into the hard drive and found all of the files that Maverick had used to blackmail and scandalize Royal.

"This is it," Will said, calling over the sheriff. "All the files and the paths he used to upload the information are on here. This is pretty much your smoking gun."

"Just what I wanted to hear," Sheriff Battle said. He pulled his cell phone from his pocket. "I'm going to call the hospital and see if he's awake for questioning. Wonder if he has asked for a lawyer yet? Thanks for your help, Will."

"No problem, Sheriff," Will said.

The sheriff turned away and Will heard him ask for Dr. Lucas Wakefield. Will's own phone pinged and he saw that he had a text from Max, who was coming into the building. He went to meet him in the hallway.

"The hard drive had all the evidence the sheriff needs to charge Haskell. He's on the phone to the hospital right now to see if Haskell can be questioned. I'm a little concerned that the coding and some of the scripts on the hard drive were way too sophisticated compared to the home computer, but maybe he was just trying to cover his trail," Will said. "I'll put together some questions about that for the sheriff to ask when they interrogate Haskell."

"There won't be an interrogation," Sheriff Battle said as he came into the hallway. Will and Max turned to face him. "Haskell is dead."

The crash had involved Haskell's car flipping over when he hit a guard rail on the highway. They'd had to use the jaws of life to get him out of the car and then he'd been medevaced to the hospital.

"Well, hell," Will said. He didn't like the lack of closure on this case. He was used to catching hackers and seeing them brought to justice. The entire thing with Haskell was making the back of his neck itch. Something wasn't right. It had been too easy to find the hard drive in his vehicle. Though to be fair, Haskell probably hadn't expected to crash his car and die.

Max had some stronger expletives and the sheriff looked none too happy, either. Will didn't know about the other two but he was beyond ticked off. Hacking was one thing and unmasking cyberbullies was something that he was known for. It frustrated him that he was having such a difficult time unmasking Maverick. And it ticked him off even more to think that the man who'd had the messy house and seemed to have only taken a computer class at the community college had outsmarted everyone in Royal for months before he was fatally injured in a car crash.

Things weren't adding up as far as Will was concerned.

"What were you saying about maybe there being more than one person involved?" Sheriff Battle asked Will.

"It was just a theory. I can't confirm it without information from Haskell. He might have been smarter than everyone thought and used the town's perception of him as cover," Will said.

"Do you feel confident that I can tell the townspeople that Haskell was Maverick?" the sheriff asked him.

No. He didn't. And that wasn't like him. Had he let Amberley distract him from his job? Had he missed something obvious that he shouldn't have? He couldn't say and both men were looking at him for an answer. "The hard drive belonged to Maverick," Will said. "That is definite. But there is no real proof that it was Haskell's or that he programmed it."

"That's not good enough," the sheriff said.

"You could announce that Maverick's been caught and see what happens," Max suggested.

"I'm still running that program from the club's server and I can use the code on the hard drive to start a trace back…to see if I can tie the code to any known hackers on the dark web," Will said.

"Okay. Let's do it. I'm going to hold a press conference and say that we believe Haskell was Maverick. If there are no more attacks then… Hell, this isn't the way I like to do a job. It's half guesswork," Sheriff Battle said.

"I wish we had more to go on but without talking to Haskell there's just not enough on the drive or his personal computer to tie the two together," Will said.

He didn't like it. It felt to him like there was something more going on here.

"Well, I guess we're going to have to play the cards we've been dealt," the sheriff said.

"It could be a group effort," Will said. "In which case exposing Haskell might convince the other members or his partner to go underground."

The sheriff went out to make his announcement and Max took one look at Will and said, "Let's go get a drink."

The two of them went over to the Texas Cattleman's Club, and about thirty-five minutes later the television over the bar was carrying the press conference announcing that Maverick had been identified. A lot of people in the club were surprised but not overly so.

"He always had a beef with the townsfolk of Royal," someone remarked.

"Guess it was his way of getting back at all those supposed slights."

Max took a swallow of his scotch and Will did the same. He couldn't shake the feeling that something wasn't right. Chelsea Hunt joined them a few minutes later.

Will only had to glance at her to know she didn't believe that the trouble with Maverick was over, either. "Scotch?"

"Yes," Chelsea said as she sat down next to Max. "The sheriff brought me up to speed before he started his press conference."

"This isn't the way I expected this to end," Max said.

"Something tells me this isn't over," Will said. "It just doesn't feel like it."

And he was right.

He got a text three hours later when he was halfway back to the ranch that nude pictures of Chelsea Hunt had shown up on the website Skinterest.

The release of the photos seemed to be timed to embarrass the sheriff's department. Will pulled the car over to call Max; he didn't know Chelsea well enough to call her.

"St. Cloud," Max said.

"It's Will. I'm not back at my computer yet but I wanted to let you know that I can run a trace to see if the posting of the nude photos was time delayed or if they were put up after the sheriff's news conference."

"Good. This has gotten out of hand," Max said. "Chels is beyond ticked off. We need to know if it was Haskell."

"I'll do what I can. I'll be in touch soon," he said, hanging up.

The culprit had identified himself as Maverick and there was no doubt in anyone's mind that he was to blame since the way the photos were released was similar to the other scandals Maverick had caused. And after all, Chelsea was the one who'd been spearheading the effort to stop Maverick and she and Max were old buddies, which was how Will and Max had ended up in Royal.

Will remotely started the trace from the Skinterest site and then texted Max back that he should have something in a few hours. He was pissed. It felt like Maverick was thumbing his nose at them. He'd waited until after Sheriff Battle's press conference and, of course, the news that Adam Haskell had died in the hospital. It wasn't that the track was cold; they still had a few leads, but it was damn sure not as hot as it once had been.

Max told him to take the afternoon and evening off and they'd regroup tomorrow to figure out what to do next.

Next?

Will didn't bother to text Max back after that, he just got back on the road. He knew where he needed to be now and it wasn't the guest house he'd called home these last few weeks.

It didn't even matter to him that the way he'd left things with Amberley was less than ideal. He needed her. Needed to see her.

She was another loose end here in Royal and he was tired of running. Tired of feeling like he was losing. He needed to talk to her and…well, more. But he didn't dwell on these things as he pulled up in front of her house.

He sat in the car for a good ten minutes, debating between going up to her door and going somewhere else.

Maybe he would be better suited going to town and finding a rowdy bar and drinking and maybe getting into a fight to work out his frustration. But then her front door opened and she leaned there against the doorjamb wearing a pair of faded jeans and a top that hugged her curves. Her hair was pulled back in its customary braid.

She chewed her lower lip as their eyes met.

He turned off his car, shutting off the sound of screaming death metal that he'd put on because it suited his mood, and got out.

"We lost Maverick. It wasn't Haskell."

"I heard the news," she said. "Cara was texting with one of her friends in town when the Skinterest link popped up."

"I'm so…I don't know why I came here. I'm frustrated and edgy and I just couldn't go home and the only place I want to be is with you."

She nodded. "Then come on in."

He crossed her yard in angry steps and climbed

up the stairs. She stepped back to give him room to walk past her. But as soon as he stepped inside and smelled the fragrance of apples and cinnamon, his temper started to calm.

"I've got whiskey or beer, if you want to drink. I've got a deck of cards if you want to play poker. I would say we could go for a ride but I'm not a big fan of riding when you're upset. I think it puts the horse in danger," she said.

"I don't want to ride horses," he said.

"Good. So what's it going to be? Did I list anything that sounds good to you?" she asked.

"No," he said. "I want you. I can't think of anything except your mouth under mine and my body inside yours."

She flushed but didn't move from where she stood with her back against the cream-colored wall. Then, with a nudge of her toe, she pushed the front door. It closed with a thud and she stepped away from the wall.

"Where do you want me?" she asked.

"Are you sure?" he asked. Because even as he was walking toward her, his blood running heavy in his veins, he wanted to give her a chance to say no.

"Yes. Make that a 'hell, yes.' I have been aching for you, Will. Every night when I go to bed I'm flooded with fantasies of you and me together. That orgasm you gave me was nice but it only whetted my appetite and left me hungry for more."

"I'm hungry, too," he said.

Will walked forward until not even an inch of space separated them. He pulled her into his arms, kissing her slowly, thoroughly and very deeply. He caught her earlobe between his teeth and breathed into her ear, then said, "I'm not sure how long I can last."

She shivered delicately, her hands clutching his shoulders, before she stepped back half an inch.

"That's okay," she said, and it was. She had been dreaming of this moment—when he would forget about everything except her, when he needed her more than anything else. She wasn't about to let him slip away again without knowing what it was like to make love to him.

She tugged the hem of her thermal shirt higher, drawing it up her body, and he touched her stomach. His hands were big and warm, rubbing over her as she pulled the shirt up and over her head. She tossed it on the floor and he put his hands on her waist, turning her to face the mirror in the hallway.

He undid the button of her jeans and then slowly lowered the zipper. She stared at them in the hall mirror, concentrating on his hands moving over her body. Then, she glanced up to see he was watching her in the mirror, as well.

Their eyes met and he brought his mouth to her ear, and whispered directly into it, "I love the way you look in my arms."

He stepped back, tugged at her jeans and then slid them down her legs. She shimmied out of them, leaving her clad in only a pair of whisper-thin white cotton panties. Delicately she stepped out of the jeans pooled at her ankles, balancing herself by putting one hand on the table in front of her.

The movement thrust her breasts forward. He unclasped her bra, her breasts falling free into his waiting hands. She looked in the mirror as a pulse of pure desire went through her. He stood behind her, his erection nestled into the small of her back. His hands cupped her breasts, and his eyes never left her body as his fingers swirled around her nipples.

She turned in his arms, reaching up to pull his head down to hers. Her mouth opened under his and she wanted to take it slow but she couldn't. She was on fire for him. He was everything she ever wanted in a man and he was here in her arms.

He slid his hands down her back and grasped her buttocks, pulling her forward until he could rub the crown of his erection against her center. She felt the thick ridge of his shaft against her through the fabric of his pants. He reached between them to caress her between her legs.

He lowered his head, using his teeth to delicately hold her nipple while he flicked it with his tongue, and she moaned his name. She brought her hands up to his hair and held his head to her. He lifted his head and blew against her skin. Her nipples stood out. He ran the tip of one finger around her aroused flesh. She trembled in his arms.

Lowering his head, he took the other nipple in his mouth and suckled her. She held him to her with a strength that surprised her. She never wanted to let him go.

Her fingers drifted down his back and then slid around front to work on the buttons of his shirt. She pushed his shirt open. He growled deep in his throat when she leaned forward to brush kisses against his chest.

He pulled her to him and lifted her slightly so that her nipples brushed his chest. Holding her carefully, he rotated his shoulders and rubbed against her. Blood roared in her ears. She reached for his erection as he shoved her panties down her legs. He was so hard as she stroked him. She needed him inside her body.

He caressed her thighs. She moaned as he neared her center and then sighed when he brushed his fingertips across the entrance to her body.

He slipped one finger into her and hesitated for a second, looking down into her eyes. She didn't want his fingers in her, she wanted him. She bit down on her lower lip and with minute movements of her hips tried to move his touch where she needed it. But then she realized what she was doing and reached between them, tugging on his wrist.

"What?"

"I want you inside me," she said. Her words were raw and blunt and she felt the shudder that went through him.

He plunged two fingers into her humid body. She squirmed against him. "I will be."

"I need you now."

He set her on her feet and turned her to face the mirror.

"What are you doing?" she asked, looking over her shoulder at him.

"I want you to watch us as I make love to you. Bend forward slightly."

She did as he asked. Her eyes watched his in the mirror. "Take your shirt off, please. I want to see your chest."

He smiled at her as he finished taking off the shirt

she'd unbuttoned. His tie was tangled in the collar but he managed to get them both off. He leaned over her, covering her body with his larger one.

He bent his legs and rubbed himself at the entrance of her body. She pushed back against him but he didn't enter her. He was teasing her and she was about to burn up in his arms.

"Will."

"Just a second," he said. "Keep your eyes on mine in the mirror."

"Yes," she said, meeting his forest green gaze with her own.

He bit down on her shoulder and then he cupped both of her breasts in his hands, plucking at her aroused nipples. He slipped one hand down her body, parting her intimate flesh before he adjusted his stance. Bending his knees and positioning himself, he entered her with one long, hard stroke.

She moaned his name and her head fell forward, leaving the curve of her neck open and vulnerable to him. He bit softly at her neck and she felt the reaction all the way to her toes when she squirmed in his arms and thrust her hips back toward him, wanting to take him deeper.

He caressed her stomach and her breasts. Whispered erotic words of praise in her ears.

She moved more frantically in his arms, her climax so close and getting closer each time he drove deep. His breath brushed over her neck and shoulder as he started to move faster, more frantically, pounding deep into her.

He slid one hand down her abdomen, through the slick folds of her sex. Finding her center. He stroked the aroused flesh with an up-and-down movement that felt exquisite and drove her closer and closer to her climax.

He circled that aroused bit of flesh between her legs with his forefinger then scraped it very carefully with his nail. She screamed his name and tightened around his shaft. Will pulled one hand from her body and locked his fingers on hers on the hall table. Then penetrated her as deeply as he could. Biting down on the back of her neck, he came long and hard.

Their eyes met in the mirror and she knew that she wasn't falling for him. She'd fallen. She wanted this man with more than her body. She wanted him with her heart and with her soul.

Thirteen

Will lifted Amberley into his arms and carried her into the living room. She had deserved romance and a night to remember and he'd given her sex. He wanted it to be more. Because she was more than a hookup to him.

"Are you feeling relaxed now?" she asked with a grin.

"I'm definitely calmer than I was when I arrived," he said, pulling her onto his lap and holding her closer. "I'm sorry if I was too—"

"You were fine. We both needed that. For the first time I feel like you let your guard down around me," she said.

He had.

He shouldn't have because that meant he was letting her in and he wasn't sure there was room in the gray and gloomy parts of his soul. He had been too good at keeping everyone at arm's length. And now he was unsure what would come next.

"Want to talk about it?" she asked.

"No."

"Sorry. I thought maybe if you talked about what Maverick was doing I could help. Offer some insights."

Of course.

Maverick.

She hadn't read his mind and seen the tortured way he was trying to figure out how to hold on to her and not let go of Lucy. He had to get past that. This was the first time he'd made love to a woman since his wife's death. Maybe the second time like their second date would help him move forward.

"I hadn't thought of it that way," he said.

"I'm not sure why I offered to talk except that I'm nervous. I don't know what to do now."

"What do you usually do?" he asked.

She flushed. "I don't have a habit. I'm still new to this."

"Oh…" That was telling. She'd never trusted a man enough to have him in her house.

And here he was.

"Okay, well, do you want me to leave?" he asked.

"No. Will, you are the one guy that I really want to stay. I need you here."

She needed him.

Those words warmed his heart and made him feel invincible. Like he would do anything for her.

He knew that feeling.

He was falling in love with her.

His heart, which he'd thought was down for the count, was beating again and beating for this woman.

"How about if you go get a shower while I set up a little surprise for you in the bedroom."

"What kind of surprise? I thought you came here without thinking about it?"

"Enough with the questions, cowgirl, it's a yes or no, that's it."

"Yes."

"Stay in the bathroom until I come and get you," he said.

"I will."

She walked away and he watched her leave. He wanted to make sure he committed as much of Amberley to memory as he could. He stayed there on the couch for another minute then stood, fastened his jeans and put on his shirt.

He saw her jeans, shirt and underwear strewn in the hallway and remembered the animalistic passion that had taken over him.

Maybe that was what it had taken to break through the icy wall he'd put around his heart. But there was no going back now.

He folded her clothes and set them on the table by the door and then went out to his car and opened the trunk, where he had placed the box from their romantic dinner. The box he was supposed to have put to good use then. Well, now was definitely the right time.

He opened the box and took out the CD he'd made for her. She liked old-school stuff and he thought the music mix he'd burned onto it would be a nice surprise for her the next time she got in her truck.

He opened the door to the cab, which she never kept locked, pulled down the visor and grabbed the keys. He turned the key to the accessory position and ejected the CD she had in there. Garth Brooks.

He wasn't surprised. He pushed in the CD he'd made for her and then shut off the truck and got out after putting the keys back up in the visor.

He reentered the house and heard her singing in the shower and smiled to himself.

He wanted this night to be perfect. He wanted to give her a gift that was equal to what she'd given him when she'd welcomed him into her life and her body.

Luckily the flowers he'd had in the box were still somewhat preserved and he took his time placing rose petals in a path from the bathroom door leading to the bed. Then he strewed them on the bed. Next he took the candles out of the box and put them on different surfaces. They were fragrant lavender and he lit them before stepping back to admire his handiwork.

He heard the shower shut off. But he wasn't ready yet. He took one of the low wattage Wi-Fi stereo bulbs that he'd placed in the box and installed it in the lamp next to her bed.

Then he cued up his "Amberley" playlist and connected his iPhone wirelessly to the lightbulb. He hit Play and went to the bathroom door, realizing he was overdressed for this. He took off his clothes, neatly folding them on the comfy chair in the corner of the room.

"Will? Are you out there?"

"I am. Stay there," he ordered.

He walked over to the bathroom and opened the

door, quickly stepping inside so he wouldn't ruin the surprise that waited for her.

He washed up quickly at the sink while she combed her hair. "I need you to close your eyes."

"I'm still not—"

"Into the kinky stuff. I know," he said with a laugh.

She made him happy. And he hadn't realized what a gift joy was until he'd spent so long without it in his life.

"Can I open my eyes now?" she asked.

"Yes."

She wasn't sure what she'd been expecting but this was the perfect romantic fantasy. There were rose petals under her feet, candles burning around the room and soft, sensual music playing.

Will put his hands on her shoulders and guided her to the bed.

"Surprised?"

"Yes!"

She turned in his arms and he took her mouth in his, letting his hands wander over her body, still amazed that she was here in his arms.

She buried her red face against his chest. "I wasn't sure if I would see you again or if you were going to leave and go back to Bellevue without saying goodbye."

Her words hurt him but he couldn't argue with them. He hated that he'd done this to her. That his own grief and doubts had been transferred to her.

"I promise I would never leave without saying goodbye," he said. Then to distract her, he picked up a handful of the rose petals that littered the bed and, turning her onto her back, he dropped them over her breasts.

She shivered and her nipples tightened. He arranged the petals on each of her breasts so that her nipples were surrounded by the soft rose petals. "I'm not surprised. You're a noticing kind of guy."

He leaned down to lick each nipple until it tightened. Then he blew gently on the tips. She raked her nails down his back.

"Are you listening to me?" she demanded.

He made a murmuring sound, unable to tear his gaze from her body. He'd never get enough of looking at her or touching her—he was starting to fall for her and that felt like a betrayal. Something he wouldn't let himself think about tonight.

"I'm listening to your body," he said, gathering more rose petals. He shifted farther down her body and dropped some on her stomach.

Her hand covered his. She leaned up, displacing the petals on her breasts. She took the petals on her stomach and moved them around until they formed a circle around her belly button.

He did just that, taking his time to fix the petals and draw her nipples out by suckling them. He moved the petals on her stomach, nibbling at each inch of skin underneath before replacing the rose petals. Then he kneeled between her thighs and looked down at her.

He picked up another handful of petals and dropped them over the red hair between her legs. She swallowed, her hands shifting on the bed next to her hips.

"Open yourself for me," he said.

Her legs moved but he took her hands in his, bringing them to her mound. She hesitated but then she pulled those lower lips apart. The pink of her flesh looked so delicate and soft with the red rose petals around it.

"Hold still," he said.

He arranged the petals so that her delicate feminine flesh was the center. He leaned down, blowing lightly on her before tonguing that soft flesh. She lifted her hips toward his mouth.

He drew her flesh into his mouth, sucking carefully on her. He crushed more petals in both of his fists and drew them up her thighs, rubbing the petals into her skin, pushing her legs farther apart until he could reach her dewy core. He pushed his finger into her body and drew out some of her moisture, then lifted his head and looked up her body.

Her eyes were closed, her head tipped back, her shoulders arched, throwing her breasts forward with their berry hard tips, begging for more attention. Her entire body was a creamy delight accented by the bloodred petals.

He lowered his head again, hungry for more of her. He feasted on her body the way a starving man would. He brought her to the brink of climax but held her there, wanting to draw out the moment of completion until she was begging him for it.

Her hands left her body, grasped his head as she thrust her hips up toward his face. But he pulled back so that she didn't get the contact she craved.

"Will, please."

He scraped his teeth over her clitoris and she screamed as her orgasm rocked through her body.

He kept his mouth on her until her body stopped shuddering and then slid up her.

"Your turn," she said, pushing him over onto his back.

She took his erection in her hand and he felt a drop of pre-cum at the head. She leaned down to lick it off him. Then took a handful of the rose petals and rubbed them up and down his penis.

She followed her hand with her tongue, teasing him with quick licks and light touches. She massaged the petals against his sac and then pressed a few more even lower. Her mouth encircled the tip of him and she began to suck.

He arched on the bed, thrusting up into her before he realized what he was doing. He pulled her from his body, wanting to be inside her when he came. Not in her mouth.

He pulled her up his body until she straddled his hips. Then using his grip on her hips, he pulled her down while he pushed his erection into her body.

He thrust harder and harder, trying to get deeper. He pulled her legs forward, forcing them farther apart until she settled even closer to him.

He slid deeper into her. She arched her back, reaching up to entwine her arms around his shoulders. He thrust harder and felt every nerve in his body tensing. Reaching between their bodies, he touched her between her legs until he felt her body start to tighten around him.

He came in a rush, continuing to thrust into her until his body was drained. He then collapsed on the bed, laying his head between her breasts. He didn't want to let her go. But he wasn't sure he deserved to keep her.

* * *

I would never leave without saying goodbye.

The words suddenly popped into her head as Will got up to grab them both some water from the kitchen.

He'd said he wouldn't leave without saying goodbye.

But that meant he was still planning to leave.

She sat up, pulling the blanket with her to cover her nakedness.

He came back in with two bottles of water and a tray of cheese and crackers. "Thought you might want a snack."

"Thanks," she said.

He sat on the edge of the bed and she crossed her legs underneath her. Why had he done all of this? Created the kind of romantic fantasy that made her think…well, that he could love her. And he was only going to leave?

He handed her a bottle of water and she took it, putting it on the nightstand beside her bed.

"Will, can I ask you something?"

"Sure," he said.

"Did you say you won't leave without saying goodbye?"

"Yes. I wouldn't want you to wonder if I'd gone," he said.

"So you are still planning to leave?" she asked.

He twisted to face her.

"Yes. You know my life is back in Bellevue," he said. "I'm just here to do a job."

He was here to do a job.

She'd known that. From the beginning there had

been no-trespassing signs all over him and she'd tried to convince herself that she knew better.

But now she knew she hadn't.

"Then what the hell is all of this?"

He stood up and paced away from the bed over to the chair where his clothes were and pulled on his pants.

"It was romance. The proper ending to our date last night. I wanted to show you how much you mean to me."

She wasn't following the logic of that. "If I mean something to you then why are you planning to leave? Or did you think we'd try long-distance dating?"

"No, I didn't think that. Your life is here, Amberley, I know that. My world… Faye's world is in Bellevue."

"Don't you mean Lucy's world?" she asked. "Faye seems to like Royal pretty well and as she's not even a year old I think that she'd adjust. You said yourself Lucy's parents travel and your folks seem to have the funds to visit you wherever you are."

"It's my world, too," he said. "I care about you, Amberley, more than I expected to care about another woman again, but this…isn't what I expected. I made a promise to myself that I'd never let another woman into my life the way I did with Lucy. Losing her broke me. It was only Faye and friends like Max that kept me from disappearing. And I can't do that again."

She wasn't sure why not. "I'm willing to risk everything for you."

She watched his face. It was a kaleidoscope of emotions and, for a brief moment, as his mouth softened into that gentle smile of his, she thought she'd gotten through to him.

"I'm not. It's not just myself I have to think of. It's Faye, as well," he said. "And it's not fair to you to put you through that. You've lost enough."

"Lost enough? Will, I think…I think I love you. I don't want to lose you," she said. "If you asked me to go with you to Bellevue, I would." She knew she was leaving herself completely open but she had lost a lot in her young life. First her mom, then her innocence and then her baby. And she'd thought she'd stay locked away for the rest of her life but Will had brought her back to the land of the living.

If she didn't ride all out trying to win him over, then she would be living with regret for the rest of her life.

"You would?" he asked.

"Yes. That's what you do when you love someone."

Saying she loved him was getting easier. She got up from the bed and walked over to him. She put her hand on his chest and looked up into his eyes.

"I know your heart was broken and battered when Lucy died. I know that you are afraid to risk it again. But I think we can have a wonderful life together. I just need to know that you're the kind of man who will stand by my side and not turn tail and run."

He put his hand over hers and didn't say a word. He lowered his head and kissed her, slowly, deeply, and she felt like she'd gotten through to him. Like she'd finally broken the wall around his heart.

He lifted her in his arms and carried her back to the bed. "Will?"

Instead of answering he kissed her. The kiss was

long and deep and she felt like it was never going to end. And it didn't end until he'd made love to her again.

She wanted to talk. It felt like they needed to but he pulled her closer to him and she started to drift off to sleep in his arms. His hand was so soothing, rubbing up and down her back, and she wondered if words were really needed. She'd finally found the life she'd always wanted in the arms of the man she loved.

When she woke in the morning she sat up and realized she was alone in bed.

"Will?"

She got up and walked through the house but it was almost silent. She had always liked this time of the morning. She wondered if Will would like to take a morning ride. She wanted to show him the south pasture.

The clock echoed through the house and she realized it was very quiet.

Too quiet.

It was empty except for her.

He hadn't made love to her last night. It hadn't been the joining of two hearts that she'd thought it was. That had been his way of saying goodbye.

Tears burned her eyes and she sank down on the floor, pulling her knees to her chest and pressing her head against them. Why was she so unlovable? What was it about her that made men leave? And why couldn't she find a man who was as honorable as she believed him to be?

Fourteen

Amberley had thought she was ready for whatever happened with Will, but waking up alone… She should have expected it, but she hadn't and she was tired. She called Clay's house and asked for some time off. He wasn't too pleased to be down a person right around the big Halloween festival they were hosting this coming weekend and she promised she was just taking a quick trip home and she'd be back for that.

But there were times when a girl needed to be home. She wanted to see her brothers and sisters and just be Amberley, not the complicated mess she'd become since that city slicker had come into her life with his spiked hair and tight jeans. He'd looked at her with those hungry eyes and then left her wanting more.

Enough.

She wasn't going to find answers in her own head. She needed space and she needed to stop focusing on Will Brady. He had left. He'd said goodbye in a way she'd never really expected him to.

She got Montgomery into his horse trailer and then hit the road. She wasn't going to even glance at the guest house where Will and Faye were staying, but she couldn't help her eyes drifting that way as she pulled by his place. His car was in the drive, like that mattered. He wasn't in the right frame of mind to be her man. In a way she guessed he was still Lucy's.

She tried to tell herself she hadn't been a fool again but the truth was she felt like an idiot. What a way to be starting a long drive. She hit a button on the radio and the CD she had cued up wasn't one she'd put in there. She ejected it and read the Sharpie-written label.

Old-School Mix Tape For My Cowgirl.

She felt tears sting the backs of her eyes.

God, why did he do this? Something so sweet and simple that could make her believe that there was more between the two of them than she knew there was. She'd given him three chances and each time he'd wormed his way even deeper into her heart. And yet she was still sitting here by herself.

She couldn't resist it and finally put the CD back into the player and the first song that came on was "SexyBack."

She started to laugh and then it turned to tears.

He'd set the bar pretty high and it left both of them

room to fall. He'd made her expect things from him that she'd never thought she'd find with anyone else.

She hit the forward button and it jumped to the next track. That Jack Johnson song that he'd danced with her to. The one that had cured her broken heart and her battered inner woman who'd felt broken because she couldn't have her own child. He'd danced with her and made that all okay.

And maybe…

Maybe what?

"Hell, you're an idiot, Amberley. You used to be smart but now you are one big fat dummy. He's messed up."

But she knew that wasn't true or fair. He was broken, too. And she'd thought they were falling in love, that they would be able to cure each other, but instead…they were both even more battered than before. She should have known better.

Her and city guys didn't mix. Did she need some big-ass neon sign to spell it out?

She had no idea as the miles passed but the flat Texas landscape dotted with old oil derricks changed to the greener pastures of the hill country and she just kept driving. She'd expected the pain of leaving to lessen the farther she got from the Flying E ranch but it didn't. So when she stopped to let Montgomery out of the trailer and give him some water, she couldn't help herself. She wrapped her arms around her horse's neck and allowed herself to cry. Montgomery just neighed and rubbed his head against hers.

She put him back in the trailer, wiped her eyes and got back on the road again, pulling onto the dirt road that led to her family ranch just after sunset. She pulled over before she got to the house, putting her head on the steering wheel.

"God, please let me fall out of love with him," she said.

She put the truck back in gear and drove up to the old ranch house where she'd grown up, and the comfort she'd wanted to find there was waiting.

Her siblings all ran out to meet her. Her brothers took Montgomery to the stables while her sisters dragged her into the kitchen to help them finish baking cookies. They chatted around her and the ache in her heart grew. She knew she'd wanted this kind of family for herself and while it was true Will wasn't the last man on the planet, he'd touched her deep in her soul.

She'd started dreaming again about her future, had allowed herself to hope that she could have a family like this of her own, and now it was gone.

It was going to take a lot for her to trust a man enough to want to dream about sharing her life with him. And she was pretty damn sure she wasn't going to be able to love again.

He dad came in and didn't seem surprised to see her.

"Clay called and said you were heading this way. Everything okay?" he asked.

"Yes. Just missed seeing you all and we always carve pumpkins together," Amberley said.

"Yay. Dad said you might not make it home this year," her sister said. "But we knew you wouldn't disappoint us."

"That's right. Dad just knows how busy life is on

the ranch. I was lucky to get a few days off before the Halloween rodeo we're having on the Flying E."

Her dad nodded but she could tell that he knew she was here for more than a seasonal activity. Her siblings brought out the pumpkins and they all gathered around the table and worked on their masterpieces. She sang along to her dad's old "Monster Mash" album from K-Tel that he'd had as a boy growing up.

Tawny slipped her arms around Amberley as they were each picking a pumpkin to carve. "I'm glad you're home. I missed you."

"I missed you, too," Amberley said. "Daddy sent me a video of your barrel run last weekend. Looking good, little missy."

"Thank you. Randy said one day I might be as fast as you," Tawny said.

Amberley ruffled her fifteen-year-old sister's hair. "I'm guessing you're going to be faster than me one day soon."

"She might," Daddy said. "Randy's got himself a girl."

"Dad."

"Do you?" Amberley asked. "How come that's never come up when you call me?"

"A man's allowed to have some secrets."

"Unless Daddy knows them," Michael said.

"How did Daddy find out?" Randy asked.

"I might have told him that you were sweet on someone in town," Michael said.

Randy lunged toward Michael and the two of them started to scuffle the way they did and Amberley laughed as she went over and pulled Randy off his younger brother. "Want to talk about her?"

"No. Let's carve pumpkins," Randy said.

And they did. Each of them worked on their own gourd, talking and teasing each other. Amberley just absorbed it all. As much as she loved the quiet of her cottage she had missed the noise of family. She felt her heart break just a little bit more. When she was in Will's arms it was easy to tell herself that she could have had this with him. Could have had the family of her own that she'd always craved.

After everyone was done carving they took their jack-o'-lanterns to the front porch and put candles inside them. They then stood back to admire their handiwork. Her dad came over and draped his arm around Amberley's shoulder.

"You okay, girl?" he asked.

"I will be," she said.

"You need to talk?"

"Not yet, Daddy. I just needed some hugs and to remember what family felt like," she said.

Her father didn't say anything else, just drew her close for a big bear hug that made her acknowledge that she was going to be okay. She was a Holbrook and they didn't break…well, not for good.

Her heart was still bruised but being back with her family made her realize that the problem wasn't with her. It was with Will. He'd told her that he was in a world of firsts and she should have given him space, or at the very least tried to protect her heart a little more because he wasn't ready for love. And a part of her realized he might never be.

* * *

Will locked himself away in his office, telling Erin that he couldn't be disturbed. There were no leads on Maverick and that was fine with him. He wasn't in any state of mind to track down a kid who'd hacked his parents' Facebook accounts, much less a cyberbully who was too clever for his own good.

His door opened just as he was reaching for the bottle of scotch he kept in his desk. He was going to get drunk and then in a few days he was going to pack up and go back to Bellevue. But he didn't want to leave Amberley. He wished there was a way to talk to Lucy. To tell her he was sorry for their fighting and that he had never thought he'd find someone to love again. But that he had.

He loved Amberley. He knew that deep in his soul. But he had been too afraid to stay. He realized that losing her the way he'd lost Lucy would break him completely. That he'd never survive that. So instead of staying, he left.

"I said I'm busy."

Will saw his partner standing in the doorway with Chelsea. She looked tougher than the last time he'd seen her and he couldn't say he blamed her. "Come in. Sorry for being so rude a moment ago."

"That's fine," Chelsea said. "I've been biting everyone's heads off, as well. Did you find anything on the remote trace you did?"

Max followed her into his office and they both sat down on the couch against the wall. Will turned back to his computer.

"Yes. The coding was the same as what we recovered on the hard drive and I can tell you that it wasn't a time-delayed post. The person who put the photos up definitely has a Skinterest profile so I have been working on getting into that," Will said. "I should have an answer for you in a few days."

"Thank you," Chelsea said. "I am not above hacking the site if I have to. I'm done playing games with Maverick."

"I think we all are," Will said.

Chelsea's phone went off and she shook her head. "I have to get back to town. Thanks for your help on this project, Will."

"I wish I could have gotten to Haskell before he ran," Will said.

"Me, too," Max said. "Go on without me, Chels. I need to talk to my partner."

She nodded and then left. Max reached over, pushing the door shut.

"Give me everything you have so far," Max said.

"Why?"

"Because I think you have been working this too hard. You need a break."

"Uh, we're partners. I don't work for you," Will said.

"We are also friends. And you need a break," Max said. "I think you've been too busy. I think you should take a break."

Will turned in his chair to look at Max. He didn't want to do this. He needed time before he was going to be anything other than a douche to anyone who spoke to him.

"I can't."

"You can," Max said. "This isn't about Maverick."

"How do you know?"

"Because I saw the way the two of you were the other night," Max said.

"I don't know what you saw," Will said.

"Lying to me is one thing, I just hope you aren't lying to yourself," Max said.

His friend had always had a pretty good bullshit detector. "Hell."

Max laughed and then walked over to Will's desk, looked in the bottom drawer and took out the scotch. "Got any glasses?"

Will opened another drawer and took out two glasses. Max poured them both a generous amount and then went to sit on the chair in the corner where Will and Faye usually sat.

He took a swallow and Will did as well, realizing that Max was waiting for him to talk.

"I—I think I'm in love with her. And I don't know if I should be. What if I let her down? What if I can't be the man she needs me to be."

"Good. It's about time. Lucy wouldn't have wanted you to die when she did."

"But I did, Max. I lost some part of myself when she died that day. It was so unexpected."

"I know. I remember. But time has passed and she'd forgive you for moving on."

"I don't want to forget her," he said after a few minutes had passed. That was his fear along with the one that something would happen to Amberley now that he had let her into his heart, as well.

"You won't. Faye looks like Lucy and as she grows up, she'll remind you of her, I'm sure of that," Max said. "But if you are still punishing yourself you won't see it. All you will ever see is your grief."

Will knew Max was right. "I think I feel guilty that I have this new love in my life. You know Lucy and I were having some problems before...well, before everything. Just fighting about how to raise Faye and if Lucy should quit her job."

"You aren't responsible for her death," Max said. "You were fighting—all couples do that. It had nothing to do with what happened to Lucy."

"Logically I know that. But..." Will looked down in his drink. "It's hard to forgive myself."

"You're the only one who can do that," Max said, finishing his drink. "But I do know that you have to move forward. So that's why I'm going to do you a favor."

"You are?"

"Yup. You are on official leave from St. Cloud."

He leaned forward in his chair. "Are you serious?"

"Sort of. I'm not firing you but I think you need to take some time off. Don't worry about the investigation, we got this without you. You've been working nonstop and grieving and I think it's time you started living again."

"What if she won't take me back?" Will asked his friend.

"If she loves you, she will," Max said.

Max got up to leave a few minutes later and Will said goodbye to his friend, then walked him out. He realized that he'd been stuck in the past because of guilt, but also because of fear. And he wasn't afraid anymore. Amberley had said she loved him, and he'd made love to her and walked away rather than let her see how vulnerable that made him.

And he did love her.

He wanted to make his life with her. He scooped Faye up off the floor where she was playing and swung her around in his arms. His baby girl laughed and Will kissed her on the top of her head.

"Are you okay?" Erin asked.

"I'm better than okay," he said.

In fact he needed to get making plans. He needed to show a certain cowgirl that he wanted to be in her life and that he could fit into it.

He asked Erin to keep an eye on Faye while he went to find Clay Everett. He was going to need some serious lessons in being a Texas man if he was going to win over Amberley. He knew he'd hurt her and he hoped she could forgive him. Because he was determined to spend the rest of his life showing her how wrong he'd been and how much he loved her.

Amberley felt refreshed from her time with her family but she was glad to be back on the Flying E. The time away had given her some perspective. Will was in a tough spot and maybe he'd get past it and come back to her. But if he didn't...well, she knew that she wasn't the kind of woman to give her heart lightly. And she also wasn't the kind of woman to wallow in self-pity. She loved him and though living without him wasn't what she wanted, she'd give him time to realize what he was missing out on.

"Hi, Amberley," Clay called as she walked over to the area where the rodeo was set up on the Flying E. She saw Emily and Tom Knox, who had recently announced they were expecting a baby boy. Brandee Lawless was there taking a break from all the wedding planning she'd been doing and Natalie and Max were hanging together near the bleachers.

They had two rings set up and some bleachers for townsfolk. All of the kids from town were dressed up in their Halloween costumes.

"Hey, Clay. I just finished my shift at the dummy steer booth. The kids love roping those horns mounted in the hay bales. Where do you need me now?" she asked. She might have decided that she could give Will time, but she had discovered that it was easier to do that if she stayed busy.

"I'm glad to hear it," Clay said. "Why don't you take a break?"

She sighed. "I'd rather keep busy."

"I think you might want to check out the next contestant in the steer-roping competition," Clay said. "A certain city slicker is determined to prove he's got what it takes to be a cowboy."

"Will?"

Clay just shrugged.

"Are you crazy? He can ride. But roping a steer? That's dangerous," Amberley said.

"The man has something to prove," Clay said.

"Yeah, that he's lost his mind," Amberley said, taking off at a run toward the steer-roping ring. She pushed her way to the front of the crowd and saw Erin and Faye standing there. Erin just shook her head when Amberley walked up to her.

"Can you believe this? I always thought he was a smart guy," Erin said. "I'm afraid to watch this."

"Me, too. What is he thinking?"

"That he must prove something," Erin said. "Or

maybe he isn't. You know how guys and testosterone are."

She did. But Will had always seemed different. She leaned on the railing and looked across the way at the bay where the steer was waiting to be released and then saw Will waiting, as well.

"Will Brady!" she yelled.

He looked over to her.

"You're going to get yourself killed."

"Well, I love you, cowgirl and I need to prove that I'm worthy to be your man. So if I die at least I'll die happy."

What?

He loved her.

She didn't have a chance to respond as the steer was released and Will went into action. He roped the steer on his second try and in a few seconds he had it subdued. He'd had a good teacher and she suspected it had been Clay Everett. She ran around the ring to where Will was as he entered and threw herself into his arms.

He caught her.

"Did you mean it?" she asked.

"Yes. I love you."

"I love you, too."

He kissed her long and hard, and cheers and applause broke out. When he set her on her feet Erin brought Faye over to them. Will wrapped the two of them in his arms.

"Now my world is right. I have both of my girls back here in my arms."

He led them away from the crowd.

"I'm sorry I left the way I did. I was afraid of

letting you down and of not being the man you needed."

"It's okay. I kept forgetting that you were going through firsts and that I promised you time."

"I've had all the time I need."

"I'm glad."

Later that evening, after Faye had been bathed and put to bed, Will carried Amberley down the hall to the bedroom.

He put her on her feet next to the bed. "I can't believe you're really here, cowgirl."

"I can't believe you participated in a steer-roping competition for me," she said. He was everything she had always wanted in a man and never thought she'd find.

He was perfect for her.

He leaned down and kissed her so tenderly.

"Believe it, Amberley. There is nothing I won't do for you."

He undressed her slowly, caressing her skin and then following the path of his hands with his mouth. She couldn't think as he stood back up and lifted her onto the bed. He bent down to capture the tip of her breast in his mouth. He sucked her deep in his mouth, his teeth lightly scraping against her sensitive flesh. His other hand played at her other breast, arousing her, making her arch against him in need.

She reached between them and took his erection in her hand, bringing him closer to her. She spread her legs wider so that she was totally open to him. "I need you now."

He lifted his head; the tips of her breasts were

damp from his mouth and very tight. He rubbed his chest over them before sliding deep into her body.

She slid her hands down his back, cupping his butt as he thrust deeper into her. Their eyes met—staring deep into his eyes made her feel like their souls were meeting. She'd never believed in finding Mr. Right. Everything that had happened to her at eighteen had made it seem as if that wasn't in the cards for her. Everything that was until she met Will.

She felt her body start to tighten around him, catching her by surprise. She climaxed before him. He gripped her hips, holding her down and thrusting into her two more times before he came with a loud grunt of her name.

She slid her hands up his back and kissed him deeply. "You are so much wilder than that steer I tried to tame earlier."

His deep laughter washed over her and she felt like she'd found her place here in his arms. The family she'd always craved and never thought she'd have.

He held her afterward, pulling her into his arms and tucking her up against his side. She wrapped her arm around him and listened to the solid beating of his heart. She understood that Will was going to need her by his side, not because he didn't respect her need to be independent, but because of the way Lucy had been taken from him.

She understood him so much better now than she ever could have before. And because she had her own weaknesses, she didn't want him to feel that way with her. Will had given her back something she wasn't sure she could have found on her own.

"Are you sleeping?" he asked.

She felt the vibration of his words through his chest under her ear. She shifted in his embrace, tipping her head so she could see the underside of his jaw.

"No. Too much to think about." This had been at once the most terrifying and exciting day of her life. She felt like if she went to sleep she might wake up and find none of it had happened. "I'm not sure I can live in Bellevue. I mean, my life—"

"We're not going to live in Bellevue. I'm going to buy a ranch right here in Royal. Someplace where you can have as many horses as you want and we can raise Faye and maybe adopt some brothers and sisters for her."

"You'd do that?"

"Yes. Frankly, the thought of you being pregnant would have scared the crap out of me. I wouldn't have wanted to risk losing you and there are plenty of kids in the world who need parents," he said, rubbing his hand down her back. "Does a big family sound good to you?"

"It does," she said.

He rubbed his hand up and down her arm. "Perfect. So I guess you're going to have to marry me."

She propped herself up on his chest, looking down at him in the shadowy night. "Are you asking me?"

He laughed at that. "No. I'm telling you. You want to, but you might come up with a reason why we should wait and I'm not going to."

"Are you sure?"

He rolled over so that she was under him. Her legs parted and he settled against her. His arms braced on either side of her body, he caught her head in his hands and brought his mouth down hard on hers. When he came up for air, long minutes later, he said, "I promise I most definitely am."

She believed him. Will wasn't the kind of man to make promises lightly. When he gave his word, he kept it.

"Will?"

"Right here," he said, sinking back down next to her on the bed.

"I love you, city slicker."

"And I love you, cowgirl."

* * * * *

NANNY MAKES THREE

CAT SCHIELD

For Jeff and Roxanne Schall
of Shada Arabians

One

Shortly after the 6:00 a.m. feeding, Liam Wade strode through the barn housing the yearling colts and fillies, enjoying the peaceful crunching of hay and the occasional equine snort. It was January 1, and because of the way horses were classified for racing and showing purposes, regardless of their calendar age, every horse in every stall on the ranch was now officially a year older.

Dawn of New Year's Day had never been a time of reflection for Liam. Usually he was facedown in a beautiful woman's bed, sleeping like the dead after an evening of partying and great sex. Last year that had changed. He'd left the New Year's Eve party alone.

His cell phone buzzed in his back pocket, and he pulled it out. The message from his housekeeper made him frown.

There's a woman at the house who needs to speak to you.

Liam couldn't imagine what sort of trouble had come knocking on his door this morning. He texted back that he was on his way and retraced his steps to his Range Rover.

As he drove up, he saw an unfamiliar gray Ford Fusion in the driveway near the large Victorian house Liam's great-great-grandfather had built during the last days of the nineteenth century. Liam and his twin brother, Kyle, had grown up in this seven-bedroom home, raised by their grandfather after their mother headed to Dallas to create her real estate empire.

Liam parked and turned off the engine. A sense of foreboding raised the hair on his arms, and he wondered at his reluctance to get out of the truck. He'd enjoyed how peaceful the last year had been. A strange woman showing up at the crack of dawn could only mean trouble.

Slipping from behind the wheel, Liam trotted across the drought-dry lawn and up the five steps that led to the wraparound porch. The stained glass windows set into the double doors allowed light to filter into the wide entry hall, but prevented him from seeing inside. Thus, it wasn't until Liam pushed open the door that he saw the infant car seat off to one side of the hall. As that was registering, a baby began to wail from the direction of the living room.

The tableau awaiting him in the high-ceilinged room was definitely the last thing he'd expected. Candace, his housekeeper, held a squalling infant and was obviously trying to block the departure of a stylish woman in her late fifties.

"Liam will be here any second," Candace was saying. With her focus split between the child and the blonde woman in the plum wool coat, his housekeeper hadn't noticed his arrival.

"What's going on?" Liam questioned, raising his voice slightly to be heard above the unhappy baby.

The relief on Candace's face was clear. "This is Diane Garner. She's here about her granddaughter."

"You're Liam Wade?" the woman demanded, her tone an accusation.

"Yes." Liam was completely bewildered by her hostility. He didn't recognize her name or her face.

"My daughter is dead."

"I'm very sorry to hear that."

"She was on her way to see you when she went into

labor and lost control of her car. The doctors were unable to save her."

"That's very tragic." Liam wasn't sure what else to say. The name Garner rang no bells. "Did she and I have an appointment about something?"

Diane stiffened. "An appointment?"

"What was your daughter's name?"

"Margaret Garner. You met her in San Antonio." Diane grew more agitated with each word she uttered. "You can't expect me to believe you don't remember."

"I'm sorry," Liam said, pitching his voice to calm the woman. She reminded him of a high-strung mare. "It's been a while since I've been there."

"It's been eight months," Diane said. "Surely you couldn't have forgotten my daughter in such a short period of time."

Liam opened his mouth to explain that he wasn't anywhere near San Antonio eight months ago when it hit him what the woman was implying. He turned and stared at the baby Candace held.

"You think the baby's mine?"

"Her name is Maggie and I know she's yours."

Liam almost laughed. This was one child he knew without question wasn't his. He'd been celibate since last New Year's Eve. "I assure you that's not true."

Diane pursed her lips. "I came here thinking you'd do the right thing by Maggie. She's your child. There's no question that you had an affair with my daughter."

He wasn't proud of the fact that during his twenties, he'd probably slept with a few women without knowing their last name or much more about them other than that they were sexy and willing. But he'd been careful, and not one of them had shown up on his doorstep pregnant.

"If I had an affair with your daughter, it was a long time ago, and this child is not mine."

"I have pictures that prove otherwise." Diane pulled a

phone out of her purse and swiped at the screen. "These are you and my daughter. The date stamp puts them at eight months ago in San Antonio. Are you going to deny that's you?"

The screen showed a very pretty woman with blond hair and bright blue eyes, laughing as she kissed the cheek of a very familiar-looking face. Kyle's. A baseball cap hid his short hair, but the lack of a scar on his chin left no doubt it was Kyle and not Liam in the picture.

"I realize that looks like me, but I have a twin brother." Liam was still grappling with seeing his brother looking so happy when Diane Garner slipped past him and headed toward the entry. "But even so, that doesn't mean the baby is a Wade."

Diane paused with her hand on the front doorknob. Her eyes blazed. "Margaret dated very infrequently, and she certainly didn't sleep around. I can tell from the pictures that she really fell for you."

Either Diane hadn't heard Liam when he explained that he had a twin or she saw this as an excuse. While he grappled for a way to get through to the woman, she yanked the door open and exited the house.

Stunned, Liam stared after her. He was ready to concede that the child might be a Wade. A DNA test would confirm that quickly enough, but then what? Kyle was on active duty in the military and not in a position to take on the responsibility of an infant.

The baby's cries escalated, interrupting his train of thought. He turned to where Candace rocked the baby in an effort to calm her and realized Diane Garner intended to leave her granddaughter behind. Liam chased after the older woman and caught her car door before she could close it.

"Are you leaving the baby?"

"Margaret was on her way to see you. I think she meant

to either give you Maggie or get your permission to give her up. There were blank forms to that effect in her car."

"Why?"

"She never wanted to have children of her own." Diane's voice shook. "And I know she wouldn't have been able to raise one by herself."

"What happens if I refuse?"

"I'll turn her over to child services."

"But you're the child's grandmother. Couldn't you just take care of her until we can get a DNA test performed and…"

"Because of health issues, I'm not in a position to take care of her. You're Maggie's father," Diane insisted. "She belongs with you."

She belonged with her father. Unfortunately, with Kyle on active duty, could he care for a baby? Did he even want to? Liam had no idea—it had been two years since he'd last spoken with Kyle. But if the child was a Wade—and Liam wasn't going to turn the child out until he knew one way or another—that meant she belonged here.

"How do I get in contact with you?" Liam asked. Surely the woman would want some news of her grandchild?

"I gave my contact info to your housekeeper." The older woman looked both shaken and determined. "Take good care of Maggie. She's all I have left." And with more haste than grace, Diane pulled her car door shut and started the engine.

As the gray car backed down the driveway, Liam considered the decision his own mother had made, leaving him and Kyle with her father to raise while she went off to the life she wanted in Dallas. He'd never really felt a hole in his life at her absence. Their grandfather had been an ideal blend of tough and affectionate. No reason to think that Maggie wouldn't do just as well without her mother.

He returned to the house. Candace was in the kitchen

warming a bottle of formula. The baby continued to show-case an impressive set of lungs. His housekeeper shot him a concerned glance.

"You let her go?" Candace rocked the baby.

"What was I supposed to do?"

"Convince her to take the baby with her?" She didn't sound all that certain. "You and I both know she isn't yours."

"You sound pretty sure about that."

Liam gave her a crooked smile. Candace had started working for him seven years ago when the former house-keeper retired. Diane Garner wasn't the first woman to show up unexpected and uninvited on his doorstep, al-though she was the first one to arrive with a baby.

"You've been different this last year." Candace eyed him. "More settled."

She'd never asked what had prompted his overnight transformation from carefree playboy to responsible busi-nessman. Maybe she figured with his thirtieth birthday he'd decided to leave his freewheeling days behind him. That was part of the truth, but not all.

"I've been living like a monk."

She grinned. "That, too."

"What am I supposed to do with a baby?" He eyed the red-faced infant with her wispy blond hair and unfocused blue eyes. "Why won't she stop crying?"

"She's not wet so I'm assuming she's hungry." Or maybe she just wants her mother. Candace didn't say the words, but the thought was written all over her face. "Can you hold her while I get her bottle ready?"

"I'd rather not."

"She won't break."

The child looked impossibly small in Candace's arms. Liam shook his head. "Tell me what to do to get a bottle ready."

The noise in the kitchen abated while the baby sucked greedily at her bottle. Liam made the most of this respite and contacted a local company that specialized in placing nannies. Since it wasn't quite seven in the morning, he was forced to leave a message and could only hope that he'd impressed the owners with the urgency of his need. That done, he set about creating a list of things that baby Maggie would need.

Hadley Stratton took her foot off the accelerator and let her SUV coast down the last thirty feet of driveway. An enormous Victorian mansion loomed before her, white siding and navy trim giving it the look of a graceful dowager in the rugged West Texas landscape.

The drive from her apartment in Royal had taken her fifteen minutes. Although a much shorter commute than her last job in Pine Valley, Hadley had reservations about taking the nanny position. Liam Wade had a playboy reputation, which made this the exact sort of situation she avoided. If he hadn't offered a salary at the top of her range and promised a sizable bonus if she started immediately, she would have refused when the agency called. But with student loans hanging over her head and the completion of her master's degree six short months away, Hadley knew she'd be a fool to turn down the money.

Besides, she'd learned her lesson when it came to attractive, eligible bosses. There would be no repeat of the mistake she'd made with Noah Heston, the divorced father of three who'd gone back to his ex-wife after enticing Hadley to fall in love with him.

Parking her SUV, Hadley headed for the front door and rang the bell. Inside a baby cried, and Hadley's agitation rose. She knew very little about the situation she was walking into. Only that Liam Wade had a sudden and urgent need for someone to care for an infant.

A shadow darkened the stained glass inset in the double door. When Hadley's pulse quickened, she suspected this was a mistake. For the last hour she'd been telling herself that Liam Wade was just like any other employer. Sure, the man was a world-class horseman and sexy as hell. Yes, she'd had a crush on him ten years ago, but so had most of the other teenage girls who barrel raced.

A decade had gone by. She was no longer a silly fangirl, but a mature, intelligent, *professional* nanny who knew the risks of getting emotionally wrapped up in her charges or their handsome fathers.

"Good morning, Mr. Wade." She spoke crisply as the door began to open. "Royal Nannies sent me. My name is—"

"Hadley..." His bottle-green eyes scanned her face.

"Hadley Stratton." Had he remembered her? No, of course not. "Stratton." She cleared her throat and tried not to sound as if her heart was racing. Of course he knew who she was; obviously the agency had let him know who they were sending. "I'm Hadley Stratton." She clamped her lips together and stopped repeating her name.

"You're a nanny?" He executed a quick but thorough assessment of her and frowned.

"Well, yes." Maybe he expected someone older. "I have my résumé and references if you'd like to look them over." She reached into her tote and pulled out a file.

"No need." He stepped back and gestured her inside. "Maggie's in the living room." He shut the door behind her and grimaced. "Just follow the noise."

Hadley didn't realize that she'd expected the baby's mother to be ridiculously young, beautiful and disinterested in motherhood until she spied the woman holding the child. In her late forties, she was wearing jeans, a flannel shirt and sneakers, her disheveled dark hair in a messy bun.

"Hadley Stratton. Candace Tolliver, my housekeeper."

Liam cast a fond grin at the older woman. "Who is very glad you've come so quickly."

Candace had the worn look of a first-time mother with a fussy baby. Even before the introductions were completed, she extended the baby toward Hadley. "I've fed her and changed her. She won't stop crying."

"What is her normal routine?" Hadley rocked and studied the tiny infant, wondering what had become of the child's mother. Smaller than the average newborn by a few pounds. Was that due to her mother's unhealthy nutritional habits while pregnant or something more serious?

"We don't know." Candace glanced toward Liam. "She only just arrived. Excuse me." She exited the room as if there were something burning in the kitchen.

"These are her medical records." Liam gestured toward a file on the coffee table. "Although she was premature, she checked out fine."

"How premature?" She slipped her pinkie between the infant's lips, hoping the little girl would try sucking and calm down. "Does she have a pacifier?"

Liam spoke up. "No."

Hadley glanced at him. He'd set one hand on his hip. The other was buried in his thick hair. He needed a haircut, she noted absently before sweeping her gaze around the room in search of the normal clutter that came with a child. Other than a car seat and a plastic bag from the local drugstore, the elegant but comfortable room looked like it belonged in a decorating magazine. Pale gray walls, woodwork painted a clean white. The furniture had accents of dusty blue, lime green and cranberry, relieving the monochrome palette.

"Where are her things?"

"Things?" The rugged horseman looked completely lost.

"Diapers, a blanket, clothes? Are they in her room?"

"She doesn't have a room."

"Then where does she sleep?"

"We have yet to figure that out."

Hadley marshaled her patience. Obviously there was a story here. "Perhaps you could tell me what's going on? Starting with where her mother is."

"She died a few days ago in a traffic accident."

"Oh, I'm sorry for your loss." Hadley's heart clenched as she gazed down at the infant who had grown calmer as she sucked on Hadley's finger. "The poor child never to know her mother."

Liam cleared his throat. "Actually, I didn't know her."

"You had to have…" Hadley trailed off. Chances were Liam Wade just didn't remember which one-night stand had produced his daughter. "What's your name, sweetheart?" she crooned, glad to see the infant's eyes closing.

"Maggie. Her mother was Margaret."

"Hello, little Maggie."

Humming a random tune, Hadley rocked Maggie. The combination of soothing noise and swaying motion put the baby to sleep, and Hadley placed her in the car seat.

"You are incredibly good at that."

Hadley looked up from tucking in the baby and found Liam Wade standing too close and peering over her shoulder at Maggie. The man smelled like pure temptation. If pure temptation smelled like soap and mouthwash. He wore jeans and a beige henley beneath his brown-and-cream plaid shirt. His boots were scuffed and well worn. He might be worth a pile of money, but he'd never acted as though it made him better than anyone else. He'd fit in at the horse shows he'd attended, ambling around with the rest of the guys, showing off his reining skills by snagging the flirts who stalked him and talking horses with men who'd been in the business longer than he'd been alive. His cockiness came from what he achieved on the back of a horse.

"This is the first time she's been quiet since she got here." His strained expression melted into a smile of devastating charm. "You've worked a miracle."

"Obviously not. She was just stressed. I suspect your tension communicated itself to her. How long has she been here?"

"Since about seven." Liam gestured her toward the black leather couch, but Hadley positioned herself in a black-and-white armchair not far from the sleeping child. "Her grandmother dropped her off and left."

"And you weren't expecting her?"

Liam shook his head and began to pace. "Perhaps I should start at the beginning."

"That might be best."

Before he could begin, his housekeeper arrived with a pot of coffee and two cups. After pouring for both, she glanced at the now-sleeping child, gave Hadley a thumbs-up and exited the room once more. Liam added sugar to his coffee and resumed his march around the room, mug in hand.

"Here's what I know. A woman arrived this morning with Maggie, said her name was Diane Garner and that her daughter had died after being in a car accident. Apparently she went into labor and lost control of the vehicle."

Hadley glanced at the sleeping baby and again sorrow overtook her. "That's just tragic. So where is her grandmother now?"

"On her way back to Houston, I'm sure."

"She left you with the baby?"

"I got the impression she couldn't handle the child or didn't want the responsibility."

"I imagine she thought the child was better off with her father."

"Maggie isn't mine." Liam's firm tone and resolute

expression encouraged no rebuttal. "She's my brother's child."

At first Hadley didn't know how to respond. Why would he have taken the child in if she wasn't his?

"I see. So I'll be working for your brother?" She knew little of the second Wade brother. Unlike Liam, he hadn't been active in reining or showing quarter horses.

"No, you'll be working for me. Kyle is in the military and lives on the East Coast."

"He's giving you guardianship of the child?"

Liam stared out the large picture window that overlooked the front lawn. "He's unreachable at the moment so I haven't been able to talk to him about what's going on. I'm not even sure Maggie is his."

This whole thing sounded too convoluted for Hadley's comfort. Was Liam Maggie's father and blaming his absent brother because he couldn't face the consequences of his actions? He wouldn't be the first man who struggled against facing up to his responsibilities. Her opinion of Liam Wade the professional horseman had always been high. But he was a charming scoundrel who was capable of seducing a woman without ever catching her name or collecting her phone number.

"I'm not sure I'm the right nanny for you," she began, her protest trailing off as Liam whirled from the window and advanced toward her.

"You are exactly what Maggie needs. Look at how peaceful she is. Candace spent two hours trying to calm her down, and you weren't here more than ten minutes and she fell asleep. Please stay. She lost her mother and obviously has taken to you."

"What you need is someone who can be with Maggie full-time. The clients I work with only need daytime help."

"The agency said you go to school."

"I'm finishing up my master's in child development."

"But you're off until the beginning of February when classes resume."

"Yes." She felt a trap closing in around her.

"That's four weeks away. I imagine we can get our situation sorted out by then, so we'd only need you during the day while I'm at the barn."

"And until then?"

"Would you be willing to move in here? We have more than enough room."

Hadley shook her head. She'd feel safer sleeping in her own bed. The thought popped into her mind unbidden. What made her think that she was in danger from Liam Wade? From what she knew of him, she was hardly his type.

"I won't move in, but I'll come early and stay late to give you as much time as you need during the month of January. In the meantime, you may want to consider hiring someone permanent."

Despite what Liam had said about Maggie being his brother's child, Hadley suspected the baby wasn't going anywhere once the DNA tests came back. With the child's mother dead and her grandmother unwilling to be responsible for her, Liam should just accept that he was going to need a full-time caregiver.

"That's fair."

Liam put out his hand, and Hadley automatically accepted the handshake. Tingles sped up her arm and raised the hair on the back of her neck as his firm grip lingered a few seconds longer than was professionally acceptable.

"Perhaps we could talk about the things that Maggie will need," Hadley said, hoping Liam didn't notice the odd squeak in her voice.

"Candace started a list. She said she'd get what we needed as soon as you arrived." His lips curved in a wry grin. "She didn't want to leave me alone with the baby."

"Why not?"

"It might seem strange to you, but I've never actually held a baby before."

Hadley tore her gaze away from the likable sparkle in Liam's arresting eyes. She absolutely could not find the man attractive. Hadley clasped her hands in her lap.

"Once you've held her for the first time, you'll see how easy it is." Seeing how deeply the baby was sleeping, Hadley decided this might be a great opportunity for him to begin. "And there's no time like the present."

Liam started to protest, but whatever he'd been about to say died beneath her steady gaze. "Very well." His jaw muscles bunched and released. "What do I do?"

Two

Going balls-out on a twelve-hundred-pound horse to chase down a fleeing cow required steady hands and a calm mind in the midst of a massive adrenaline rush. As a world-class trainer and exhibitor of reining and cutting horses, Liam prided himself on being the eye of the storm. But today, he was the rookie at his first rodeo and Hadley the seasoned competitor.

"It's important that you support her head." Hadley picked up the sleeping baby, demonstrating as she narrated. "Some babies don't like to be held on their backs, so if she gets fussy you could try holding her on her stomach or on her side."

Hadley came toward him and held out Maggie. He was assailed by the dual fragrances of the two females, baby powder and lavender. The scents filled his lungs and slowed his heartbeat. Feeling moderately calmer, Liam stood very still while Hadley settled Maggie into his arms.

"There." She peered at the sleeping child for a moment before lifting her eyes to meet Liam's gaze. Flecks of gold floated in her lapis-blue eyes, mesmerizing him with their sparkle. "See, that wasn't hard."

"You smell like lavender." The words passed his lips without conscious thought.

"Lavender and chamomile." She stepped back until her path was blocked by an end table. "It's a calming fragrance."

"It's working."

As he adjusted to the feel of Maggie's tiny body in his arms, he cast surreptitious glances Hadley's way. Did she remember him from her days of barrel racing? He hadn't seen her in ten years and often looked for her at the events he attended, half expecting her name to pop up among the winners. At eighteen she'd been poised to break out as a star in the barrel-racing circuit. And then she'd sold her mare and disappeared. Much to the delight of many of her competitors, chief among them Liam's on-again, off-again girlfriend.

"I almost didn't recognize you this morning," he said, shifting Maggie so he could free his right arm.

Hadley looked up at him warily. "You recognized me?"

How could she think otherwise? She'd been the one who'd gotten away. "Sure. You took my advice and won that sweepstakes class. You and I were supposed to have dinner afterward." He could tell she remembered that, even though she was shaking her head. "Only I never saw you again."

"I vaguely remember you trying to tell me what I was doing wrong."

"You had a nice mare. Lolita Slide. When you put her up for sale I told Shannon Tinger to buy her. She went on to make over a hundred thousand riding barrels with her."

"She was a terrific horse," Hadley said with a polite smile. "I'm glad Shannon did so well with her."

Liam remembered Hadley as a lanky girl in battered jeans and a worn cowboy hat, her blond hair streaming like a victory banner as her chestnut mare raced for the finish line. This tranquil woman before him, while lovely in gray dress pants and a black turtleneck sweater, pale hair pulled back in a neat ponytail, lacked the fire that had snagged his interest ten years earlier.

"We have a three-year-old son of Lolita's out in the barn.

You should come see him. I think he's going to make a first-class reining horse."

"I don't think there will be time. Infants require a lot of attention."

Her refusal surprised him. He'd expected her to jump at the chance to see what her former mount had produced. The Hadley he remembered had been crazy about horses.

"Why'd you quit?"

Hadley stared at the landscape painting over the fireplace while she answered Liam's blunt question. "My parents wanted me to go to college, and there wasn't money to do that and keep my horse. What I got for Lolita paid for my first year's tuition."

Liam considered her words. When was the last time he'd been faced with an either-or situation? Usually he got everything he wanted. Once in a while a deal didn't go his way, but more often than not, that left him open for something better.

Maggie began to stir, and Liam refocused his attention on the baby. Her lips parted in a broad yawn that accompanied a fluttering of her long lashes.

"I think she's waking up." He took a step toward Hadley, baby extended.

"You did very well for your first time."

Unsure if her tiny smile meant she was patronizing him, Liam decided he'd try harder to get comfortable with his niece. Strange as it was to admit it, he wanted Hadley's approval.

"Would you like a tour of the house?" Liam gestured toward the hallway. "I'd like your opinion on where to put the baby's room."

"Sure."

He led the way across the hall to the dining room. A long mahogany table, capable of seating twelve, sat on a black-and-gold Oriental rug. When he'd overhauled the house six years ago, bringing the plumbing and wiring up to code, this was the one room he'd left in its original state.

"It's just me living here these days, and I haven't entertained much in the last year." The reason remained a sore spot, but Liam brushed it aside. "When my grandfather was alive, he loved to host dinner parties. Several members of Congress as well as a couple governors have eaten here."

"When did you lose him?"

"A year and a half ago. He had a heart condition and died peacefully in his sleep." Grandfather had been the only parent he and Kyle had ever known, and his death had shaken Liam. How the loss had hit Kyle, Liam didn't know. Despite inheriting half the ranch when their grandfather died, his brother never came home and Liam dealt with him only once or twice a year on business matters.

"I remember your grandfather at the shows," Hadley said. "He always seemed larger than life."

Liam ushered her into the large modern kitchen. Her words lightened Liam's mood somewhat. "He loved the horse business. His father had been a cattleman. Our herd of Black Angus descends from the 1880s rush to bring Angus from Scotland."

"So you have both cattle and horses?"

"We have a Black Angus breeding program. Last year we sold two hundred two-year-olds."

"Sounds like you're doing very well."

After a quick peek in the den, they finished their tour of the first floor and climbed the stairs.

"Business has been growing steadily." So much so that Liam wasn't able to do what he really loved: train horses.

"You don't sound all that excited about your success."

He'd thought the abrupt cessation of his personal life would provide more time to focus on the ranch, but he'd discovered the more he was around, the more his staff came to him with ideas for expanding.

"I didn't realize how focused my grandfather had been on the horse side of the business until after his heart problems forced him into semiretirement. Apparently he'd been keeping things going out of respect for his father, but his heart wasn't really in it."

"And once he semiretired?"

"I hired someone who knew what he was doing and gave him a little capital. In three years he'd increased our profits by fifty percent." Liam led Hadley on a tour of three different bedrooms. "This one is mine."

"I think it would be best if Maggie is across the hall from you." Hadley had chosen a cheerful room with large windows overlooking the backyard and soft green paint on the walls. "That way when she wakes up at night you'll be close by."

While Liam wasn't worried about being up and down all night with the infant, he preferred not to be left alone in case something went wrong. "Are you sure I can't convince you to live in?"

"You'll do fine. I promise not to leave until I'm sure Maggie is well settled."

That was something, Liam thought. "If you have things under control for the moment, I need to get back to the barn. I have several calls to make and an owner stopping by to look at his crop of yearlings."

"Maggie and I will be fine."

"Candace should be back with supplies soon, and hopefully we'll have some baby furniture delivered later today. I'll have a couple of the grooms empty this room so it can be readied for Maggie."

Hadley nodded her approval. In her arms, the baby began to fuss. "I think it's time for a change and a little something to eat."

"Here's my cell and office numbers." Liam handed her his business card. "Let me know if you need anything."

"Thank you, I will."

The short drive back to the barn gave Liam a couple minutes to get his equilibrium back. Kyle was a father. That was going to shock the hell out of his brother.

And Liam had received a shock of his own today in the form of Hadley Stratton. Was it crazy that she was the one who stuck out in his mind when he contemplated past regrets? Granted, they'd been kids. He'd been twenty. She'd barely graduated high school the first time she'd made an impression on him. And it had been her riding that had caught his attention. On horseback she'd been a dynamo. Out of the saddle, she'd been quiet and gawky in a way he found very appealing.

He'd often regretted never getting the chance to know anything about her beyond her love of horses, and now fate had put her back in his life. Second chances didn't come often, and Liam intended to make the most of this one.

The grandfather clock in the entry hall chimed once as Hadley slipped through the front door into the cold night air. Shivering at the abrupt change in temperature, she trotted toward her SUV and slid behind the wheel. An enormous yawn cracked her jaw as she started the car and navigated the circular drive.

In order for Hadley to leave Liam in charge of Maggie, she'd had to fight her instincts. The baby was fussier than most, probably because she was premature, and only just went to sleep a little while ago. Although Liam had gained confidence as he'd taken his turn soothing the frazzled infant, Hadley had already grown too attached to the motherless baby and felt compelled to hover. But he needed to learn to cope by himself.

Weariness pulled at her as she turned the SUV on to the deserted highway and headed for Royal. Her last few assignments had involved school-age children, and she'd forgotten how exhausting a newborn could be. No doubt Liam would be weary beyond words by the time she returned at seven o'clock tomorrow morning.

This child, his daughter, was going to turn his world upside down. Already the house had a more lived-in feeling, less like a decorator's showplace and more like a family home. She wondered how it had been when Liam and his brother were young. No doubt the old Victorian had quaked with the noisy jubilance of two active boys.

Twenty minutes after leaving the Wade house, Hadley let herself into her one-bedroom apartment. Waldo sat on the front entry rug, appearing as if he'd been patiently awaiting her arrival for hours when in fact, the cat had probably been snoozing on her bed seconds earlier. As she shut the front door, the big gray tabby stretched grandly before trotting ahead of her toward the kitchen and his half-empty food bowl. Once it was filled to his satisfaction, Waldo sat down and began cleaning his face.

The drive had revived her somewhat. Hadley fixed herself a cup of Sleepytime tea and sipped at it as she checked the contents of the bags a good friend of hers had dropped off this afternoon. After seeing what Candace had bought for the baby, Hadley had contacted Kori to purchase additional supplies. She would owe her friend lunch once Maggie was settled in. Kori had shown horses when she was young and would get a kick out of hearing that Liam Wade was Hadley's new employer.

Hadley had a hard time falling asleep and barely felt as if she'd dozed for half an hour when her alarm went off at five. Usually she liked to work out in the morning and eat a healthy breakfast while watching morning news, but today she was anxious about how things had gone with Liam and Maggie.

Grabbing a granola bar and her to-go mug filled with coffee, Maggie retraced the drive she'd made a mere five hours earlier. The Victorian's second-floor windows blazed with light, and Hadley gave a huge sigh before shifting the SUV into Park and shutting off the engine.

The wail of a very unhappy baby greeted Hadley as she let herself in the front door. From the harried expression on Liam's face, the infant had been crying for some time.

"It doesn't sound as if things are going too well," she commented, striding into the room and holding out her arms for the baby. "Did you get any sleep?"

"A couple hours."

Liam was still dressed for bed in a pair of pajama bottoms that clung to his narrow hips and a snug T-shirt that highlighted a torso sculpted by physical labor. Hadley was glad to have the fussy baby to concentrate on. Liam's helplessness made him approachable, and that was dangerous. Even without his usual swagger, his raw masculinity was no less potent.

"Why don't you go back to bed and see if you can get a little more sleep?"

The instant she made the suggestion, Hadley wished the words back. She never told an employer what to do. Or she hadn't made that mistake since her first nanny job. She'd felt comfortable enough with Noah to step across the line that separated boss and friend. For a couple months that hadn't been a problem, but then she'd been pulled in too deep and had her heart broken.

"It's time I headed to the barn," Liam said, his voice muffled by the large hands he rubbed over his face. "There are a dozen things I didn't get to yesterday."

His cheeks and jaw were softened by a day's growth of beard, enhancing his sexy, just-got-out-of-bed look. Despite the distraction of a squirming, protesting child in her arms, Hadley registered a significant spike in her hormone levels. She wanted to run her palms over his broad shoulders and feel for herself the ripple of ab muscles that flexed as he scrubbed his fingers through his hair before settling his hands on his hips.

Light-headed, she sat down in the newly purchased rocking chair. Liam's effect on her didn't come as a surprise. She'd had plenty of giddy moments around him as a teenager. Once, after she'd had a particularly fantastic run, he'd even looked straight at her and smiled.

Hadley tightened her attention on Maggie and wrestled her foolishness into submission. Even if Liam was still that cocky boy every girl wanted to be with, she was no longer a susceptible innocent prone to bouts of hero worship. More important, he'd hired her to care for this baby, a child who was probably his daughter.

"Do you think she's okay?" Liam squatted down by the rocker. He gripped the arm of the chair to steady himself, his fingers brushing Hadley's elbow and sending ripples of sensation up her arm.

"You mean because she's been crying so much?" Hadley shot a glance at him and felt her resolve melting beneath the concern he showered on the baby. "I think she's just fussy. We haven't figured out exactly what she likes yet. It might take swaddling her tight or a certain sound that calms her. I used to take care of a baby boy who liked to fall asleep listening to the dishwasher."

"I know we talked about this yesterday," Liam began, his gaze capturing hers. "But can you make an exception for a few weeks and move in here?"

"I can't." The thought filled her with a mixture of excitement and panic. "I have a cat—"

"There's always plenty of mice in the barn."

Hadley's lips twitched as she imagined Waldo's horror at being cut off from the comforts of her bed and his favorite sunny spot where he watched the birds. "He's not that sort of cat."

"Oh." Liam gazed down at Maggie, who'd calmed

enough to accept a pacifier. "Then he can move in here with you."

Hadley sensed this was quite a compromise for Liam, but she still wasn't comfortable agreeing to stay in the house. "I think Maggie is going to be fine once she settles in a bit. She's been through a lot in the last few days."

"Look at her. She's been crying for three hours and you calm her down within five minutes. I can't go through another night like this one. You have to help me out. Ten days."

"A week." Hadley couldn't believe it when she heard herself bargaining.

Triumph blazed in Liam's eyes, igniting a broad smile. "Done." He got to his feet, showing more energy now that he'd gotten his way.

After a quick shower and a cup of coffee, Liam felt a little more coherent as he entered his bookkeeper/office manager's office. Ivy had been with Wade Ranch for nine years. She was a first cousin twice removed, and Grandfather had hired her as his assistant, and in a few short years her organizational skills had made her invaluable to the smooth running of the ranch.

"Tough night?" Ivy smirked at him over the rim of her coffee cup. She looked disgustingly chipper for seven in the morning. "Used to be a time when you could charm a female into doing your bidding."

Liam poured himself a cup of her wickedly strong brew and slumped onto her couch. "I'm rusty." Although he'd persuaded Hadley to move in for a week. Maybe it was just babies that were immune.

"Have you considered what you're going to do if the baby isn't Kyle's?"

As Ivy voiced what had filtered through Liam's mind several times during the last twenty-four hours, he knew he'd better contact a lawyer today. Technically, unless he claimed the child as his, he had no legal rights to her.

"I really believe Kyle is her father," Liam said. "I'm heading to a clinic Hadley recommended to have a DNA test run. I figured since Kyle and I are identical twins, the results should come back looking like Maggie is my daughter."

And then what? Margaret was dead. With Kyle estranged from his family, it wasn't likely he or Maggie would spend much time at Wade Ranch. And if Liam was wrong about his brother being Maggie's father, Diane Garner might give her up to strangers.

Liam was surprised how fast he'd grown attached to the precious infant; the idea of not being in her life bothered him. But was he ready to take on the challenge of fatherhood? Sure, he and Kyle had done okay raised by their grandfather, but could a little girl be raised by a man alone? Wouldn't she miss a mother snuggling her, brushing her hair and teaching her all the intricacies of being a woman? And yet it wasn't as if Liam would stay single forever.

An image of Hadley flashed through his thoughts. Beautiful, nurturing and just stubborn enough to be interesting. A year ago he might not have given her a second thought. Hadley was built for steady, long-term relationships, not the sort of fun and games that defined Liam's private life. She'd probably be good for him, but would he be good for her? After a year of celibacy, his libido was like an overwound spring, ready to explode at the least provocation.

"Liam, are you listening to me?" Ivy's sharp tone shattered his thoughts.

"No. Sorry. I was thinking about Maggie and the future."

Her expression shifted to understanding. "Why don't we

talk later this afternoon. You have a fund-raising meeting at the club today, don't you?"

He'd forgotten all about it. Liam had been involved with the Texas Cattleman's Club fund-raising efforts for Royal Memorial's west wing ever since it had been damaged by a tornado more than a year ago. The grand reopening was three weeks away, but there remained several unfinished projects to discuss.

"I'll be back around three."

"See you then."

Fearing if he sat down in his large office, he might doze off, Liam headed into the attached barn where twelve champion American quarter horse stallions stood at stud. Three of them belonged to Wade Ranch; the other nine belonged to clients.

Liam was proud of all they'd accomplished and wished that his grandfather had lived to see their annual auction reach a record million dollars for 145 horses. Each fall they joined with three other ranches to offer aged geldings, sought after for their proven ranch performance, as well as some promising young colts and fillies with top bloodlines.

At the far end of the barn, double doors opened into a medium-sized indoor arena used primarily for showing clients' horses. One wall held twenty feet of glass windows. On the other side was a spacious, comfortable lounge used for entertaining the frequent visitors to the ranch. A large television played videos of his stallions in action as well as highlights from the current show and racing seasons.

Liam went through the arena and entered the show barn. Here is where he spent the majority of his time away from ranch business. He'd grown up riding and training reining horses and had won dozens of national titles as well as over a million dollars in prize money before he'd turned twenty-five.

Not realizing his destination until he stood in front of

the colt's stall, Liam slid open the door and regarded WR Electric Slide, son of Hadley's former mount, Lolita. The three-year-old chestnut shifted in the stall and pushed his nose against Liam's chest. Chuckling, he scratched the colt's cheek, and his mind returned to Hadley.

While he understood that college and grad school hadn't left her the time or the money to own a horse any longer, it didn't make sense the way she'd shot down his suggestion that she visit this son of her former mount. And he didn't believe that she'd lost interest in horses. Something more was going on, and he wasn't going to let it go.

Three

Hadley sat in the nursery's comfortable rocking chair with Maggie on her lap, lightly tapping her back to encourage the release of whatever air she'd swallowed while feeding. It was 3:00 a.m., and Hadley fended off the house's heavy silence by quietly humming. The noise soothed the baby and gave Hadley's happiness a voice.

She'd been living in the Wade house for three days, and each morning dawned a little brighter than the last. The baby fussed less. Liam smiled more. And Hadley got to enjoy Candace's terrific cooking as well as a sense of accomplishment.

Often the agency sent her to handle the most difficult situations, knowing that she had a knack for creating cooperation in the most tumultuous of households. She attributed her success to patience, techniques she'd learned in her child development classes and determination. Preaching boundaries and cooperation, she'd teach new habits to the children and demonstrate to the parents how consistency made their lives easier.

Feeling more than hearing Maggie burp, Hadley resettled the baby on her back and picked up the bottle once more. Her appetite had increased after her pediatrician diagnosed acid reflux, probably due to her immature digestive system, and prescribed medication to neutralize her stomach acids. Now a week old, Maggie had stopped losing weight and was almost back to where she'd started.

In addition to the reflux problem, Maggie had symptoms of jaundice. Dr. Stringer had taken blood samples to run for DNA, and the bilirubinometer that tested jaundice levels had shown a higher-than-average reading. To Liam's dismay, the doctor had suggested they wait a couple weeks to see if the jaundice went away on its own. He'd only relaxed after the pediatrician suggested they'd look at conventional phototherapy when the blood tests came back.

By the time Hadley settled Maggie back into her crib, it was almost four in the morning. With the late-night feedings taking longer than average because of Maggie's reflux problem, Hadley had gotten in the habit of napping during the day when the baby slept. The abbreviated sleep patterns were beginning to wear on her, but in four short days she would be back spending the night in her tiny apartment once more.

Yawning into her pajama sleeve, Hadley shuffled down the hall to her room. Seeing that her door was open brought her back to wakefulness. In her haste to reach Maggie before she awakened Liam, Hadley hadn't pulled her door fully shut, and after a quick check under the bed and behind the chair, she conceded that the cat was missing. Damn. She didn't want to tiptoe around the quiet house in search of a feline who enjoyed playing hide-and-seek. Given the size of the place, she could be at it for hours.

Silently cursing, Hadley picked up a pouch of kitty treats and slipped out of her room. The floorboards squeaked beneath her. Moving with as much stealth as possible, she stole past Liam's room and headed toward the stairs.

Once on the first floor, Hadley began shaking the treat bag and calling Waldo's name in a stage whisper. She began in the living room, peering under furniture and trying not to sound as frustrated as she felt. No cat. Next, she moved on to the den. That, too, was feline free. After a quick and fruitless sweep of the dining room, she headed into the kitchen, praying Waldo had found himself a perch on top of the refrigerator or made a nest in the basket of dirty clothes in the laundry room. She found no sign of the gray tabby anywhere.

Hadley returned to the second floor, resigned to let the cat find his own way back, hoping he did before Liam woke up. But as she retraced her steps down the dim corridor, she noticed something that had eluded her earlier. Liam's door was open just wide enough for a cat to slip inside. She paused in the hall and stared at the gap. Had it been like that when she'd passed by earlier? It would be just like Waldo to gravitate toward the one person in the house who didn't like him.

She gave the pouch of cat treats a little shake. The sound was barely above a whisper, but Waldo had fantastic hearing, and while he might disregard her calls, he never ignored his stomach. Hadley held her breath for a few tense, silent seconds and listened for the patter of cat paws on the wood floor, but heard nothing but Liam's deep, rhythmic breathing. Confident that he was sound asleep, she eased open his door until she could slip inside.

Her first step into Liam's bedroom sent alarm bells shrilling in her head. Had she lost her mind? She was sneaking into her employer's room in the middle of the night while he slept. How would she explain herself if he woke? Would he believe that she was in search of her missing cat or would he assume she was just another opportunistic female? As the absurdity of the situation hit her, Hadley pressed her face into the crook of her arm and smothered a giggle. Several deep breaths later she had herself mostly back under control and advanced another careful step into Liam's room.

Her eyes had long ago grown accustomed to the darkness, and the light of a three-quarter moon spilled through the large window, so it was easy for her to make out the modern-looking king-size bed and the large man sprawled beneath the pale comforter. And there was Waldo, lying on top of Liam's stomach looking for all the world as if he'd found the most comfortable place on earth. He stared at Hadley, the tip of his tail sweeping across Liam's chin in a subtle taunt.

This could not be happening.

Hadley shook the pouch gently and Waldo's gold eyes narrowed, but he showed no intention of moving. Afraid that Liam would wake if she called the cat, Hadley risked approaching the bed. He simply had to move on his own. In order to pick him up, she'd have to slide her hand between Waldo's belly and Liam's stomach. Surely that would wake the sleeping man.

Pulling out a treat, she waved it in front of the cat's nose. Waldo's nose twitched with interest, but he displayed typical catlike disdain for doing anything expected of him. He merely blinked and glanced away. Could she snatch up the cat and make it to the door before Liam knew what had happened? Her mind ran through the possibilities and saw nothing but disaster.

Maybe she could nudge the cat off Liam. She poked the cat's shoulder. Waldo might have been glued where he lay. Working carefully, she slid her finger into his armpit and prodded upward, hoping to annoy him into a sitting position. He resisted by turning his body to stone.

Crossing her fingers that Liam was as sound a sleeper as he appeared, Hadley tried one last gambit. She scratched Waldo's head and was rewarded by a soft purr. Now that he was relaxed, she slid her nails down his spine and was rewarded when he pushed to his feet, the better to enjoy the caress. Leaning farther over the mattress, she slid one hand behind his front legs and cupped his butt in her other palm when she felt the air stir the fabric of her pajama top against her skin.

Hadley almost yelped as a large hand skimmed beneath the hem of her top and traced upward over her rib cage to the lower curve of her breast. Awkwardly looming over Liam's bed, her hands wrapped around an increasingly unhappy feline, she glanced at Liam's face and noticed that while his eyes remained closed, one corner of his lips had lifted into a half smile.

Liam was having an amazing dream. He lay on a couch in front of a roaring fire with a woman draped across him. Her long hair tickled his chin as his hands swept under her shirt, fingers tracing her ribs. Her bare skin was warm and soft beneath his caress and smelled like lavender and vanilla.

It was then he realized whom he held. He whispered her name as his palm discovered the swell of her breast. His fingertips grazed across her tight nipple and her body quivered in reaction, He smiled. A temptress lurked beneath her professional reserve and he was eager to draw her out. Before he could caress further, however, something landed on his chest with a thump.

The dream didn't so much dissolve as shatter. One second he was inches away from heaven, the next he was sputtering after having his breath knocked out. His eyes shot open. Darkness greeted him. His senses adjusted as wakefulness returned.

The silken skin from his dream was oh so real against his fingers. As was the disturbed breathing that disrupted the room's silence.

"Hadley?"

She was looming over his bed, frozen in place, her arms extended several inches above his body. "Waldo got out of my room and came in here. I was trying to lift him off you when you…" Her voice trailed off. She gathered the large gray cat against her chest and buried her face in his fur.

Liam realized his hand was still up her pajama top, palm resting against her side, thumb just below the swell of her breast. The willpower it took to disengage from the compromising position surprised him.

"I was dreaming…" He sat up in bed and rubbed his face to clear the lingering fog of sleep. "Somehow you got tangled up in it."

"You were dreaming of me?" She sounded more dismayed than annoyed.

He reached for the fading dream and confirmed that she had been the object of his passion. "No." She'd already pegged him as a womanizer; no need to add fuel to the fire. "The woman in my dream wasn't anyone I knew."

"Perhaps it was Margaret Garner."

It frustrated him that she continued to believe Maggie was his daughter. "That's possible, since I never met her." His tone must have reflected his frustration because Hadley stepped away from his bed.

"I should get back to my room. Sorry we woke you."

"No problem." Liam waited until the door closed behind her before he toppled backward onto the mattress.

The sheer insanity of the past few moments made him grin. Had she really sneaked into his room to fetch the cat? Picturing what must have happened while he slept made him chuckle. He wished he could have seen her face. He'd bet she'd blushed from her hairline to her toes. Hadley didn't have the brazen sensuality of the women who usually caught his interest. She'd never show up half dressed in his hotel room and pout because he'd rather watch a football game than fool around. Nor would she stir up gossip in an attempt to capture his attention. She was such a straight arrow. Her honesty both captivated and alarmed him.

Rather than stare sleepless at the ceiling, Liam laid his

forearm over his eyes and tried to put Hadley out of his mind. However, vivid emotions had been stirred while he'd been unconscious. Plus, he was having a hard time forgetting the oh-so-memorable feel of her soft skin. With his body in such a heightened state of awareness, there was no way Liam was going to just fall back asleep. Cursing, he rolled out of bed and headed for the shower. Might as well head to the barn and catch up on paperwork.

Three hours later he'd completed the most pressing items and headed out to the barn to watch the trainers work the two-year-olds. At any time, there were between twenty and thirty horses in various stages of training.

They held classes and hosted clinics. For the last few years, Liam had taught a group of kids under ten years old who wanted to learn the ins and outs of competitive reining. They were a steely-eyed bunch of enthusiasts who were more serious about the sport than many adults. At the end of every class, he thanked heaven it would be a decade before he had to compete against them.

"Hey, boss. How're the colts looking?" Jacob Stevens, Liam's head trainer, had joined him near the railing.

"Promising." Liam had been watching for about an hour. "That bay colt by Blue is looking better all the time."

"His full brother earned over a quarter of a million. No reason to think Cielo can't do just as well." Jacob shot his boss a wry grin. "Think you're going to hold on to him?"

Liam laughed. "I don't know. I've been trying to limit myself to keeping only five in my name. At the moment, I own eight."

Until Hadley had shown up, he'd been seriously contemplating selling Electric Slide. The colt was going to be a champion, but Liam had more horses than he had time for. If only he could convince Hadley to get back in the saddle. He knew she'd balk at being given the horse, but maybe she'd be willing to work him as much as time permitted.

"Thing is," Jacob began, "you've got a good eye, and the ranch keeps producing winners."

Liam nodded. "It's definitely a quality problem. I've had a couple of good offers recently. Maybe I need to stop turning people down."

"Or just wait for the right owner."

"Speaking of that. Can you get one of the guys to put Electric Slide through his paces? I want to get some video for a friend of mine."

"Sure."

As he recorded the chestnut colt, Liam wasn't sure if he'd have any luck persuading Hadley to come check out the horse, but he really wanted to get to the bottom of her resistance.

Lunchtime rolled around, and Liam headed back to the house. He hadn't realized how eager he was to spend some time with Maggie and Hadley until he stopped his truck on the empty driveway and realized Hadley's SUV was absent.

Candace was pulling a pie out of the oven as he entered the kitchen. Her broad smile faded as she read the expression on his face. "What's wrong?"

"Where's Hadley?"

"Shopping for clothes and things for Maggie." Candace set a roast beef sandwich on the center island and went to the refrigerator for a soda. "The poor girl hasn't been out of here in days."

"She took Maggie with her?"

"I offered to watch her while she was gone, but the weather is warm, and Hadley thought the outing would do her some good."

"How long have they been gone?"

"About fifteen minutes." Candace set her hands on her hips and regarded him squarely. "Is there some reason for all the questions?"

"No."

Liam wondered at his edginess. He trusted Maggie was in good hands with Hadley, but for some reason, the thought of both of them leaving the ranch had sparked his anxiety. What was wrong with him? It wasn't as if they weren't ever coming back.

The thought caught him by surprise. Is that what was in the back of his mind? The notion that people he cared about left the ranch and didn't come back? Ridiculous. Sure, his mother had left him and Kyle. And then Kyle had gone off to join the navy, but people needed to live their lives. It had nothing to do with him or the ranch. Still, the sense of uneasiness lingered.

Royal Diner was humming with lunchtime activity when Hadley pushed through the glass door in search of a tuna melt and a chance to catch up with Kori. To her relief, her best friend had already snagged one of the booths. Hadley crossed the black-and-white checkerboard floor and slid onto the red faux-leather seat with a grateful sigh.

"I'm so glad you were able to meet me last-minute," Hadley said, settling Maggie's carrier beside her and checking on the sleeping infant.

She'd already fed and changed the baby at Priceless, Raina Patterson's antiques store and craft studio. Hadley had taken a candle-making class there last month and wanted to see what else Raina might be offering.

"Thanks for calling. This time of year is both a blessing and a curse." Kori was a CPA who did a lot of tax work, making January one of her slower months. "I love Scott, but his obsessive need to be busy at all times gets on my nerves." Kori and her husband had started their accounting company two years ago, and despite what she'd just said, the decision had been perfect for them.

"You're the one doing me a favor. I really need your

advice." Hadley trailed off as the waitress brought two Diet Cokes.

They put in their lunch order and when the waitress departed, Kori leaned her forearms on the table and fixed Hadley with an eager stare.

"This is fantastic. You never need my help with anything."

Her friend's statement caught Hadley off guard. "That's not true. I'm always asking for favors."

"Little things, sure, like when you asked me to pick up baby stuff for Miss Maggie or help with your taxes, but when it comes to life stuff you're so self-sufficient." Kori paused. "And I'm always boring you with the stuff that I'm going through."

Hadley considered. "I guess I've been focused on finishing my degree and haven't thought much beyond that. Plus, it's not like I have a social life to speak of."

Kori waved her hands. "Forget all that. Tell me what's going on."

Embarrassment over her early-morning encounter with Liam hadn't faded one bit. Her skin continued to tingle in the aftermath of his touch while other parts of her pulsed with insistent urgency. The only thing that kept her from quitting on the spot was that he'd been asleep when he'd slid his hand beneath her clothes.

"Oh my goodness," Kori exclaimed in awe. "You're blushing."

Hadley clapped her hands over her cheeks. "Am I?"

"What happened?"

"Waldo got out of my room last night when I got up for Maggie's feeding, and when I tracked him down, he was in Liam's room, curled up right here." Hadley indicated where her cat had been on Liam's anatomy.

"You said he isn't a cat person. Was he mad?"

"He was asleep."

Kori began to laugh. "So what happened?"

"I tried to lure him off with a treat, but Waldo being Waldo wouldn't budge. As I was picking him up…" Swept by mortification, Hadley closed her eyes for a span of two heartbeats.

"Yes?" Kori's voice vibrated with anticipation. "You picked him up and what?"

"I was leaning over the bed and Liam was sleeping. And dreaming." Hadley shuddered. "About having sex with some woman, I think."

"And?" Kori's delighted tone prompted Hadley to spill the next part of her tale.

"The next thing I knew, his hand was up my shirt and he—" she mimed a gesture "—my breast." Her voice trailed off in dismay.

"No way. And you're sure he was asleep?"

"Positive. Unfortunately, I was so shocked that I didn't keep a good hold of Waldo and he jumped onto Liam's chest, waking him. I don't think he knew what hit him."

"What did he say?"

"I honestly don't remember. I think I mumbled an apology for waking him. He retrieved his hand from beneath my pajama top and I bolted with Waldo."

"Did you talk to him later?"

"He was gone before Maggie woke up again, and then I took off before he came home for lunch." Hadley glanced at her charge to make sure the baby was sleeping soundly. "What am I supposed to say or do the next time I see him?"

"You could thank him for giving you the best sex you've had in years."

"We didn't have sex." Hadley lowered her voice and hissed the last word, scowling at her friend.

"It's the closest thing you've had to a physical encounter in way too long." Kori fluffed her red hair and gazed in disgust at her friend. "I don't know how you've gone so long without going crazy. If Scott and I go three days without sex we become vile, miserable people."

Hadley rolled her eyes at her friend. "I'm not in a committed, monogamous relationship. You and Scott have been together for seven years. You've forgotten how challenging being single is. And if you recall, the last time I fell in love it didn't work out so well."

"Noah was an ass. He led you on while he was still working through things with his ex-wife."

"She wanted him back," Hadley reminded her friend. "He'd never stopped loving her even after finding out she'd cheated on him. And he was thinking about his kids."

"He still hedged his bets with you. At the very least, he should have told you where things stood between them."

On that, Hadley agreed. Five years earlier, she'd been a blind fool to fall in love with Noah. Not only had he been her employer, but also things had moved too fast between them. Almost immediately he'd made her feel like a part of the family. Because it was her first time being a nanny, she hadn't understood that his behavior had crossed a line. She'd merely felt accepted and loved.

"That was a long time ago." Thinking about Noah made her sad and angry. He'd damaged her ability to trust and opened a hole in her heart that had never healed. "Can we get back to my more immediate problem? Do I quit?"

"Because your boss sleep–felt you up?" Kori shook her head. "Chalk it up to an embarrassing mistake and forget about it."

"You're right." Only she was having a hard time forgetting how much she enjoyed his hands on her skin. In fact, she wanted him to run his hands all over her body and make her come for him over and over.

Kori broke into her thoughts. "You're thinking about him right now, aren't you?"

"What?" Hadley sipped at her cold drink, feeling overly warm. "No. Why would you think that?"

"You've got the hots for him. Good for you."

"No. Not good for me. He's my boss, for one thing. For another, he's a major player. I knew him when I used to race barrels. He had girls chasing after him all the time, and he enjoyed every second of it."

"So he's a playboy. You don't need to fall in love with him, just scratch an itch."

"I can't." Hadley gave her head a vehement shake to dispel the temptation of Kori's matter-of-fact advice. "Besides, I'm not his type. He was asleep during most of what happened this morning."

"Wait. Most?"

Hadley waved to dismiss her friend's query. "It might have taken him a couple extra seconds to move his hand."

Kori began to laugh again. "Oh, he must have really been thrown for a loop. You in his bedroom in the middle of the night with the cat."

The picture Kori painted was funny, and Hadley let herself laugh. "Thank you for putting the whole thing in perspective. I don't know why I was so stressed about it."

"Maybe because despite your best intentions, you like the guy more than you think you should."

Hadley didn't even bother to deny it. "Maybe I do," she said. "But it doesn't matter, because no matter how attractive I may find him, he's my boss, and you know I'm never going there again."

Four

After missing Maggie and Hadley at lunchtime, Liam made sure he was home, showered and changed early enough to spend some time with his niece before dinner. She was in her crib and just beginning to wake up when he entered her room. Hadley wasn't there, but he noticed the red light on the baby monitor and suspected she was in her room or downstairs, keeping one ear tuned to the receiver.

Before Maggie could start to fuss, Liam scooped her out of the crib and settled her on the changing table. Already he was becoming an expert with the snaps and Velcro fastenings of Maggie's Onesies and diapers. Before the baby came fully awake, he had her changed and nestled in his arm on the way downstairs.

The domestic life suited him, he decided, entering the kitchen to see what Candace had made for dinner. The large room smelled amazing, and his mouth began to water as soon as he crossed the threshold. He sneaked up behind Candace and gave her a quick hug.

"What's on the menu tonight?"

"I made a roast. There's garlic mashed potatoes, green beans and apple pie for dessert."

"And your wonderful gravy."

"Of course."

"Is Jacob joining us?"

"Actually, we're going to have dinner in town. It's the seventh anniversary of our first date."

Candace and Jacob had been married for the last six years. They'd met when Candace had come to work at Wade Ranch and fell in love almost at first sight. They had the sort of solid relationship that Liam had never had the chance to see as he was growing up.

"You keep track of that sort of thing?" Liam teased, watching as Candace began fixing Maggie's bottle.

"It's keeping track of that sort of thing that keeps our relationship healthy."

Liam accepted the bottle Candace handed him, his thoughts wrapped around what she'd said. "What else keeps your relationship healthy?"

If the seriousness of his tone surprised her, the housekeeper didn't let on. "Trust and honesty. Jacob and I agreed not to let things fester. It's not always easy to talk about what bugs us, especially big issues like his sister's negative attitude toward me and the fact that I hate holding hands in public. Thank goodness we're both morning people and like the same television shows, or we'd never have made it this far."

As Liam watched Maggie suck down the formula, he let Candace's words wash over him. He'd never actually been in a relationship, healthy or otherwise. Oh, he dated a lot of women, some of them for long periods of time, but as he'd realized a year ago, not one of them wanted more than to have a good time.

At first he'd been shocked to discover that he'd let his personal life remain so shallow. Surely a thirty-year-old man should have had at least one serious relationship he could look back on. Liam hadn't been able to point to a single woman who'd impacted his life in any way.

He didn't even have mommy issues, because he'd never gotten to know her. She was a distracted, preoccupied guest at Christmas or when she showed up for his birthday. When she couldn't make it, expensive presents arrived and were dutifully opened. The most up-to-date electronics, gift cards, eventually big checks. For Liam, their mother had been the beautiful young woman in the photo framed by silver that sat on Grandfather's desk. According to him, she'd loved her career more than anything else and wasn't cut out to live on a ranch.

"…and of course, great sex."

The last word caught his attention. Liam grinned. "Of course."

Candace laughed. "I wondered if you were listening to me. Turns out you weren't."

"I was thinking about my past relationships or lack thereof."

"You just haven't found the right girl." Candace patted him on the arm, adopting the persona of wise old aunt. "Once she shows up, you'll have all the relationship you can handle. Just remember to think about her happiness before your own and you'll be all right."

Liam thought about his past girlfriends and knew that advice would have bankrupted him. His former lovers wanted the best things money could buy. Expensive clothes, exotic trips, to be pampered and spoiled. Living such an affluent lifestyle had been fine for short periods of time, but at heart, Liam loved the ranch and his horses. None of his lady friends wanted to live in Royal permanently. It was too far from the rapid pace of city life.

"I'm out of here," Candace said, slipping her coat off the hook near the kitchen door. "You and Hadley should be able to handle things from here. See you tomorrow." She winked. "Probably for lunch. You'll have your choice of cereal or Pop-Tarts for breakfast."

Grimacing, Liam wished her a good night and returned his attention to Maggie. The greedy child had consumed almost the entire bottle while he'd been talking to Candace. Knowing he should have burped her halfway through, he slung a towel over his shoulder and settled her atop it. Hadley's simple ways of handling Maggie's reflux issues had made a huge difference in the baby's manner. She was much less fussy.

Liam walked around the kitchen, swaying with each stride to soothe the infant. He'd been at this for ten minutes when Hadley entered the room. She'd left her hair down tonight, and the pale gold waves cascaded over the shoulders of her earth-tone blanket coat. The weather had turned chilly and wet in the early evening, and Hadley had dressed accordingly in jeans and a dark brown turtleneck sweater.

"Have you already fed her?" Hadley approached and held her hands out for the baby. She avoided meeting his gaze as she said, "I can take her while you eat."

"Maggie and I are doing fine." The baby gave a little burp as if in agreement. "Why don't you fix yourself a plate while I give her the rest of her bottle? I can eat after you're done."

Hadley looked as if she wanted to argue with him, but at last gave a little nod. "Sure."

While he pretended to be absorbed in feeding Maggie, Liam watched Hadley, thinking about their early-morning encounter and wondering if that accounted for her skittishness. Had he done more while asleep than she'd let on? The thought brought with it a rush of heat. He bit back a smile. Obviously his subconscious had been working overtime.

"Look, about this morning—" he began, compelled to clear the air.

"You were sleeping." Hadley's shoulders drooped. "I intruded. I swear I won't let Waldo get out again."

"Maybe it's not good for him to be cooped up all the time."

"My apartment is pretty small. Besides, you don't like cats."

"What makes you say that?" Liam had no real opinion either way.

Hadley crossed her arms over her chest and gave him the sort of stern look he imagined she'd give a disobedient child. "You suggested I put him in the barn."

"My grandfather never wanted animals in the house, so that's what I'm used to."

"The only time Waldo has been outside was after the house where he lived was destroyed by the tornado. He spent a month on his own before someone brought him to Royal Haven, where I adopted him. He gets upset if I leave him alone too long. That's why I couldn't stay here without bringing him."

Talking about her cat had relaxed Hadley. She'd let down her guard as professional caretaker, and Liam found himself charmed by her fond smile and soft eyes. No wonder she had such a magical effect on Maggie. She manifested a serenity that made him long to nestle her body against his and...

Desire flowed through him, brought on by a year of celibacy and Hadley's beauty. But was that all there was to it? Over the last year, he hadn't been a hermit. Promoting the ranch meant he'd attended several horse shows, toured numerous farms. Every public appearance provided opportunities to test his resolve, but not one of the women he'd met had tempted him like Hadley.

Liam cleared his throat, but the tightness remained. "Why don't you bring him down after dinner so he and I can meet properly and then let him have the run of the house?"

"Are you sure?"

He'd made the suggestion impulsively, distracted by

the direction his thoughts had taken, but it was too late to change his mind now. "Absolutely."

The exchange seemed to banish the last of her uneasiness. Unfortunately, his discomfort had only just begun. Maggie had gone still in his arms, and Liam realized she was on the verge of sleep. Knowing her reflux required her to remain upright for half an hour, he shifted her onto his shoulder and followed Hadley to the kitchen table where he ate most of his meals since his grandfather had died.

"Is something the matter?" Hadley asked. She'd carried both their plates to the table.

"No, why?"

"You're frowning." She sat down across from him. "Do you want me to take Maggie?"

"No, she's fine." In less than a week he'd mastered the ability to hold the baby and do other things at the same time. He picked up his fork. "I was just thinking that I haven't used the dining room much since my grandfather died. Every meal he ate in this house was in there. I find it too big and lonely to use by myself."

"You could eat there with Maggie."

"*We* could eat there with Maggie."

Her eyes widened briefly before she gave a reluctant nod. "Of course, I would be there to take care of Maggie."

Liam didn't think they were on the same page. He'd been thinking of her in terms of companionship. She'd obviously assumed he'd want her as Maggie's caretaker. Or was she deliberately reminding him of their different roles in the household?

"I promised I'd bring Maggie down to the barn tomorrow for a visit. I'd like you to come with us." Now that the DNA results had come back indicating that Maggie was Kyle's daughter, he was eager to introduce her to everyone.

"Of course." Hadley didn't sound overly enthusiastic.

"She's a Wade, which means she's going to be spending a lot of time there."

"Or she may take after…my mother. She left the ranch to pursue a career in real estate and rarely visits." He had no idea what had prompted him to share this about his mother.

"Not everyone is cut out for this life, I suppose."

Or for motherhood. She'd left her sons in the care of their grandfather and hadn't returned more than a handful of times during their childhood. Liam knew it had bothered Grandfather that his only child didn't want anything to do with her family's legacy. As for how Kyle felt, Liam and his brother rarely discussed her.

"You mentioned that you're finishing up your degree. What are your plans for after graduation?"

Hadley smiled. "I've submitted my résumé to several school districts in Houston. That's where my parents live."

"You're not planning on staying in Royal then?"

"I like it here. My best friend and her husband run an accounting firm in town. I'm just not sure there are enough job opportunities in the area for someone just starting out in my field. And I'm an only child. My parents hate that I live so far away."

"What sort of a job are you looking for?" Liam found himself wanting to talk her into remaining in the area.

"School counseling. My undergraduate degree is in teaching, but after a couple years, I decided it wasn't my cup of tea and went back for my master's."

"You're certainly good with children," Liam said. "Any school would be lucky to have you."

While they spoke, Hadley had finished eating. She took charge of Maggie, settling her into the nearby infant seat while Liam finished his dinner. He made short work of Candace's excellent cooking and set both of their plates in the sink.

"Can I interest you in a piece of caramel apple pie? Candace makes the best around."

"Sure." Hadley laughed. "I have a weakness for dessert."

Liam heated both pieces in the microwave and added a scoop of ice cream to each. With Maggie sound asleep, she no longer provided any sort of distraction, and Liam was able to focus his full attention on Hadley.

"I took some video of Electric Slide being worked today. Thought you might be interested in seeing him in action." He pulled up the footage he'd taken with his phone and extended it her way. "Even though he's young, I can already tell he has his mother's work ethic and athleticism. I'd love your opinion on him."

"You're the expert," she reminded him, cupping the phone in her hands.

"Yes, but as I was discussing with my head trainer today, I have too many horses, and I need to figure out which ones I should let go."

"You're thinking of selling him?" She looked up from the phone's screen, her expression concerned.

And with that, Liam knew he'd struck the right chord at last.

Knowing she shouldn't care one way or another what Liam did with his horses, Hadley let her gaze be drawn back to the video of the big chestnut colt racing across the arena only to drop his hindquarters and execute a somewhat sloppy sliding stop. His inexperience showed, but she liked his balance and his willingness.

Lolita had been a dream horse. For two years she and Hadley had dominated as barrel racers and scored several championships in the show ring. During that time she'd had several offers to purchase the mare but couldn't imagine being parted from her.

Until Anna's accident, when everything changed.

"He's a nice colt," she said, making an effort to keep her reply noncommittal. She replayed the video, paying close attention to the horse's action. He looked so much like his mother. Same three white socks. Same shoulder and hip. Same nose-out gesture when he moved from a lope into a gallop. How many classes had she lost before that little quirk had been addressed?

"Maybe you can give him a try when you come to the barn tomorrow."

Her stomach tightened as she contemplated how much fun it would be to ride Lolita's son. But Hadley hadn't been on a horse in ten years, not since Anna had ended up in a wheelchair. Remorse over her role in what happened to her friend had burdened Hadley for a decade. The only thing that kept her from being overwhelmed by guilt was her vow never to ride again. And that was a small sacrifice compared with what Anna was living with.

"I'm afraid I don't ride anymore."

"I'm sure you haven't lost any of your skills."

Hadley found dark amusement in his confidence. She was pretty sure any attempt to swing into a saddle would demonstrate just how rusty she was.

"The truth is I don't want to ride." She didn't think Liam would understand her real reason for turning him down.

"But you might enjoy it if only you got back in the saddle."

The man was as stubborn as he was persuasive, and Hadley wasn't sure how to discourage him without being rude. "I assure you I wouldn't. I was pretty crazy about horses when I was young, but it no longer interests me."

"That's a shame. You were a really talented rider."

Her heart gave a little jump. "I really loved it."

"And it showed. Shannon used to complain about you all the time." Liam's intent gaze intensified his allure. "That's when I started watching you ride, and I figured out why all the other girls lost to you."

"Lolita."

"She was a big part of it, but you rode the hell out of her."

Hadley shook her head. "You said it yourself. Shannon won a lot on Lolita."

"Yeah, but her times never matched yours."

The temptation to bask in Liam's warm regard almost derailed Hadley's professionalism. The man had such a knack for making a woman feel attractive and desirable. But was he sincere? She'd labeled him a player, but maybe she'd done that to keep from being sucked in by his charm. The way he cared about Maggie made Hadley want to give him the benefit of the doubt. And yet he hadn't known he'd gotten her mother pregnant. That didn't exactly illustrate his accountability.

"Does Shannon still own her?" Parting with the mare had been one of the hardest things Hadley had ever done.

"No. She sold her after a couple years."

"How did you end up with one of her foals?"

"A client of mine in California had him."

"And Lolita?" For someone who claimed she was no longer interested in anything horse-related, Hadley was asking a lot of questions. But Lolita had been special, and she wanted to hear that the mare had ended up in a good home.

"I don't know." Her disappointment must have shown because Liam offered, "I can find out."

Hadley waved off his concern. "Oh, please don't bother. I was just…curious."

"It's no problem. Jack is a good friend."

"Really, don't trouble yourself. I'm sure she's doing great." A wave of nostalgia swept over Hadley. She wished she could say she hadn't thought about Lolita for years, but that wasn't at all the case.

Hadley didn't realize she was still holding Liam's phone until it began to ring. The image of a stunning brunette appeared on the screen. The name attached to the beautiful face: Andi. She handed Liam back his phone and rose.

"I'll take Maggie upstairs."

Andi looked like the sort of woman he'd want privacy to talk to. Hadley was halfway up the back stairs before she heard him say hello. She didn't notice the disappointment dampening her mood until she reached the nursery and settled into the rocking chair that overlooked the enormous backyard. What did she have to be down about? Of course Liam had a girlfriend. He'd always had a girlfriend, or probably several girls that he kept on ice for when he found himself with a free night.

And yet he hadn't gone out once since she'd moved into the house. He spent his evenings watching sports in the large den, laptop open, pedigrees scattered on the sofa beside him. Back when she'd been a teenager, she'd spent a fair amount of time poring over horse magazines and evaluating one stallion over another. Although it was a hobby, she liked to think her hours of study had been instrumental in how well she'd done in selecting Lolita.

Until coming to Wade Ranch, Hadley hadn't realized how much she missed everything having to do with horses. The familiar scents of the barn that clung to the jacket that Liam hung up in the entry roused emotions she'd suppressed for a long time. She missed riding. Barrel racing was in turns exhilarating and terrifying. Competing in a Western pleasure class might not be an adrenaline rush, but it presented different challenges. And no matter the outcome, a clean ride was its own reward.

Tomorrow when she took Maggie to the barn to visit Liam, she needed to keep a handle on her emotions. Liam was a persuasive salesman. He would have her butt in a saddle before she knew what was happening. Hadley shook her head, bemused and unable to comprehend why he was so determined to revive her interest in horses.

Could it be that his own passion was so strong that he wanted everyone to share in what he enjoyed? Hadley made a mental note to feel Candace out on the subject tomorrow. That settled, she picked up the book she'd been reading and settled back into the story.

A half hour later, Liam appeared in the doorway. He'd donned a warm jacket and was holding his hat.

"I have to head back to the barn. One of the yearlings got cut up in the paddock today and I need to go check on him." Liam's bright green gaze swept over her before settling on Maggie snuggled in her arms. "You two going to be okay in the house by yourselves?"

Hadley had to smile at his earnest concern. "I think we'll be fine."

"It occurs to me that I've been taking advantage of you." His words recalled their early morning encounter, and Hadley's pulse accelerated.

"How so?" she replied, as calmly as her jittery nerves allowed.

"You haven't had any time off since that first night, and I don't think you were gone more than five hours today."

"I don't mind. Maggie isn't a lot of trouble when she's sleeping, and she does a lot of that. I've been catching up on my reading. I don't have a lot of time for that when I'm in school. Although, I do have my last candle-making class at Priceless tomorrow. We're working with molds. I'd like to make it to that."

"Of course."

Almost as soon as Liam left the old Victorian, Hadley wished him back. Swaddled tight in a blanket, Maggie slept contentedly while Hadley paced from parlor to den to library to kitchen and listened to the wind howl outside. The mournful wail made her shiver, but she was too restless to snuggle on the couch in the den and let the television drown out the forlorn sounds.

Although she hadn't shared an apartment in five years, she never thought of herself as lonely. Something about living in town and knowing there was a coffee shop, library or restaurant within walking distance of her apartment was reassuring. Out here, half an hour from town, being on her own in this big old house wasn't the least bit comfortable.

Or maybe she just wanted Liam to come back.

Five

Promptly at ten o'clock the next morning, Hadley parked her SUV in front of the barn's grand entrance and shut off the engine. She'd presumed the Wade Ranch setup would be impressive, but she'd underestimated the cleverness of whoever had designed the entry. During warmer months, the grass on either side of the flagstone walkway would be a welcoming green. Large pots filled with Christmas boughs flanked the glass double doors. If Hadley hadn't been told she was about to enter a barn, she would have mistaken her destination for a showcase mansion.

Icy wind probed beneath the hem of Hadley's warm coat and pinched her cheeks when she emerged from the vehicle's warmth and fetched Maggie from the backseat. Secure in her carrier, a blanket over the retractable hood to protect her from the elements, the infant wouldn't feel the effects of the chilly air, but Hadley rushed to the barn anyway.

Slipping through the door, Hadley found herself in a forty-foot-long rectangular room with windows running the length of the space on both sides. To her right she glimpsed an indoor arena, empty at the moment. On her left, the windows overlooked a stretch of grass broken up into three paddock areas where a half-dozen horses grazed. That side of the room held a wet bar, a refrigerator and a few bar stools.

On the far end of the lounge, a brown leather couch

flanked by two matching chairs formed a seating area in front of the floor-to-ceiling fieldstone fireplace. Beside it was a doorway that Hadley guessed led to the ranch offices.

Her rubber-soled shoes made no sound on the dark wood floor, and she was glad. The room's peaked ceiling magnified even the slightest noise. She imagined when a group gathered here the volume could rattle the windows.

A woman in her early fifties appeared while Hadley was gawking at the wrought iron chandeliers. They had a Western feel without being cliché. In fact, the whole room was masculine, rugged, but at the same time had an expensive vibe that Hadley knew would appeal to a clientele accustomed to the finer things.

"Hello. You must be Hadley." The woman extended her hand and Hadley grasped it. "I'm Ivy. Liam told me you'd be coming today."

"Nice to meet you." Hadley set the baby carrier on the table in the center of the room and swept the blanket away. "And this is Maggie."

"She's beautiful." Ivy peered at the baby, who yawned expansively. "Liam talks about her nonstop."

"I imagine he does. Having her around has been a huge change for him." Hadley unfastened the straps holding the baby in the carrier and lifted her out. Maggie screwed up her face and made the cranky sounds that were a warm-up for all-out wailing. "She didn't eat very well this morning, so she's probably hungry. Would you hold her for me while I get her bottle ready?"

"I'd be happy to." Ivy didn't hesitate to snuggle Maggie despite the infant's increasing distress. "Liam has been worthless since this little one appeared on his doorstep."

Hadley had filled a bottle with premeasured powdered formula and now added warm water from the thermos she carried. "I think discovering he's a father has thrown him for a loop, but he's doing a fantastic job with Maggie."

"You think he's Maggie's father?"

Something about Ivy's neutral voice and the way she asked her question caught Hadley's attention. "Of course. Why else would Maggie's grandmother have brought her here?" She shook Maggie's bottle to mix the formula and water.

"It's not like Liam to be so careless. May I?" Ivy indicated the bottle Hadley held. "With someone as good-looking and wealthy as Liam, if he wasn't careful, a girl would have figured out how to trap him before this."

"You think Kyle is Maggie's father?"

"That would be my guess."

"But I thought he was based on the East Coast and never came home. Candace told me Maggie's mom was from San Antonio."

Hadley was uncomfortable gossiping about her employer, but reminded herself that Ivy was his family and she'd asked a direct question.

Ivy smiled down at the baby. "She's Kyle's daughter. I'm sure of it."

Any further comment Hadley might have made was forestalled by Liam's arrival. His cheeks were reddened by cold, and he carried a chill on his clothes. Hadley's pulse tripped as his penetrating gaze slid over her. The brief look was far from sexual, yet her body awakened as if he'd caressed her.

"Here are my girls," he said, stopping between Ivy and Hadley. After greeting Maggie with a knuckle to her soft cheek, he shifted his attention to Hadley. "Sorry I wasn't here to greet you, but I was delayed on a call. What do you think of the place so far?"

"Impressive." Warmth poured through her at the inconsequential brush of his arm against hers. "I never expected a ranch to have a barn like this." She indicated the stone fireplace and the windows that overlooked the arena. Staring around the large lounge kept her gaze from lingering on Liam's infectious grin and admiring the breadth of his shoulders encased in a rugged brown work jacket.

"It's been a work in progress for a while." He winked at Ivy, who rolled her eyes at him.

The obvious affection between the cousins didn't surprise Hadley. Liam had an easy charisma that tranquilized those around him. She'd wager that Liam had never once had to enforce an order he'd given. Why bully when charm got the job done faster and easier?

"I imagine a setup like this takes years to build."

"And a lot of convincing the old man," Ivy put in. "Calvin was old-school when it came to horses. He bred and sold quality horses for ranch work. And then this one came along with his love of reining and his big ideas about turning Wade Ranch into a breeding farm."

Liam tossed one of Maggie's burp rags on his shoulder and eased the infant out of Ivy's arms. "And it worked out pretty well," he said, setting the baby on his shoulder. "Come on, let's go introduce this little lady around."

With Liam leading the way through the offices, his smile broad, every inch the proud parent, he introduced Hadley to two sales associates, the breeding coordinator, the barn manager and a girl who helped Ivy three mornings a week.

Hadley expected that her role as Maggie's nanny would relegate her to the background, but Liam made her an active part of the conversation. He further startled her by bringing up her former successes at barrel racing and in the show ring. She'd forgotten how small the horse business could be when one of the salespeople, Poppy Gertz, confessed to rejoicing when Hadley had retired.

"Do you still compete?" Hadley questioned, already anticipating what the answer would be.

"Every chance I get." The brunette was in her midthirties with the steady eye and swagger of a winner. "Thinking about getting back into the game?"

At Hadley's head shake, Poppy's posture relaxed.

"We're going to get her into reining," Liam said, shifting Maggie so she faced forward.

Hadley shook her head. "I'm going to finish getting my masters and find a job as a guidance counselor." She reached out for the infant, but Liam turned away.

"Maggie and I are going to check out some horses." His easy smile was meant to lure her after them. "Why don't you join us." It was a command pitched as a suggestion.

Dutifully she did as he wanted. And in truth, it wasn't a hardship. In fact, her heartbeat increased at the opportunity to see what Wade Ranch had to offer. She'd done a little reading up about Liam and the ranch on the internet and wasn't surprised at the quality of the horses coming out of Liam's program.

They started with the stallions, since their barn was right outside the barn lounge. While Liam spoke in depth about each horse, Hadley let her thoughts drift. She'd already done her research and was far more interested in the way her body resonated with the deep, rich tone of Liam's voice. He paused in front of one stall and opened the door.

"This is WR Dakota Blue." Pride shone in Liam's voice and body language.

"He's beautiful," Hadley murmured.

The stallion stepped up to the door and nuzzled Liam's arm, nostrils flaring as he caught Maggie's scent. An infant her age couldn't clearly see objects more than eight to ten inches away, so Hadley had to wonder what Maggie made of the stallion.

"She isn't crying," Liam said as the horse lipped at Maggie's blanket. "I guess that's a good sign."

"I don't think she knows what to make of him."

"He likes her."

The stallion's gentleness and curiosity reminded her a lot of how Liam had first approached Maggie. Watching horse and owner interact with the infant, something unlocked inside Hadley. The abrupt release of the constriction left her reeling. How long had she been binding her emotions? Probably since she'd shouldered a portion of responsibility for Anna's accident.

"Hadley?" Liam's low voice brought her back to the present. He'd closed the door to the stallion's stall and stood regarding her with concern. "Is everything okay?"

"Yes. I was just thinking how lucky Maggie is to grow up in this world of horses." And she meant that with all her heart. As a kid Hadley had been such a nut about horses. She would have moved into the barn if her parents let her.

"I hope she agrees with you. My brother doesn't share my love of horses." Liam turned from the stall, and they continued down the aisle. "You miss it, don't you?"

What was the point in denying it? "I didn't think I did until I came to Wade Ranch. Horses were everything until I went off to college. I was remembering how much I missed riding and what I did to cope."

"What did you do?"

"I focused on the future, on the career I would have once I finished school."

"I'm not sure I could give up what I do."

Hadley shrugged. "You've never had to." She considered his expression as he guided her through the doors that led into the arena and wondered what it would be like to be him, to never give up something because of circumstances. "Have you ever considered what would happen if you lost Wade Ranch?"

His grin was a cocky masterpiece. "I'd start over somewhere else."

And that summed up the differences between them. Hadley let life's disappointments batter her. Liam shrugged off the hits and lived to fight another day. Which is exactly what drew her to him. She admired his confidence. His swagger. What if she hadn't let guilt overwhelm her after Anna's accident? What if she'd stood up to her parents about selling Lolita and changed her major when she realized teaching wasn't her cup of tea?

"I wish I'd gotten to know you better back when I was racing barrels," she said, letting him guide her toward a narrow wooden observation deck that ran the length of the arena.

He handed over Maggie. "You could have if you hadn't disappeared after my advice helped you win the sweepstakes. You were supposed to thank me by taking me to dinner."

"I thought you were kidding about that." Only she hadn't. She'd been thrilled that he'd wanted to go out with her. But Anna's accident had happened before she had the chance to find out if his interest in her was real. "Besides, I wasn't your type."

"What sort of type was that?"

She fussed with Maggie's sweater and didn't look at him. "Experienced."

Liam took the hit without an outward flinch. Inside he raged with frustration. "I'm not sure any woman has a worse opinion of me than you do." It was an effort to keep his voice neutral.

"My opinion isn't bad. It's realistic. And I don't know why you'd care."

Women didn't usually judge him. He was the fun guy to have around. Uncomplicated. Charming. With expensive taste and a willing attitude. But Hadley wanted more than an amiable companion who took her to spendy restaurants and exclusive clubs. Glib phrases and seduction wouldn't work on her. He'd have to demonstrate substance, and Liam wasn't sure how to go about that.

"I care because I like you." He paused a beat before adding, "And I want you to like me."

Without waiting to see her reaction, he strode across the arena toward the horse being led in by one of the grooms. He'd selected four young horses to show Hadley in the hopes of enticing her to get back in the saddle. Why it was so important to see her ride again eluded him. As always he was just going with his gut.

Liam swung up into the saddle and walked the gelding toward the raised viewing deck. "This is a Blue son. Cielo is three. I think he has a great future in reining. At the moment I personally own eight horses and I need to pare that down to five. I'm going to put him and three others through their paces, and I want you to tell me which you think I should keep and which should go."

Hadley looked appalled. "You can't ask me to do that. I'm no judge."

"When I'm done riding all four you will tell me what you think of each." He bared his teeth at her in a challenging smile. "I value your opinion."

He then spent ten minutes working Cielo through his paces all the while staying aware of Hadley's body language and expression. With Maggie asleep in her arms, Hadley had never looked so beautiful, and Liam had a hard time concentrating on his mounts. After he rode all four horses, he had a special one brought out.

"You might recognize Electric Slide from his video."

Hadley's color was high and her eyes were dancing with delight, but her smile dimmed as he approached with the colt her former mare had produced. "I can't get over how much he looks like his mother."

"Want to give him a try?"

She shook her head. "It's been too long since I've ridden, and I'm not dressed for it."

He recognized a lame excuse when he heard one. She'd worn jeans and boots to the barn and didn't want to admit the real reason for her reluctance.

"Next time." Liam swung into the saddle and pivoted the colt away.

Disappointment roared through him, unfamiliar and unpleasant. He couldn't recall the last time he'd invested so much in a project only to have it fall flat. Was that because he didn't throw himself wholly into anything, or because he rarely failed at things he did? His grandfather would say that if he was consistently successful, he wasn't challenging himself.

Isn't that why he'd quit dating a year ago and refocused on Wade Ranch? He'd grown complacent. The horse business was growing at a steady pace. He enjoyed the companionship of several beautiful women. And he was bored.

Liam's mind was only half on what he was doing as he rode Electric Slide. The pleasure had gone out of the exhibition after Hadley turned down a chance to ride. After a little while, he handed the colt off and strode across the arena toward her.

"It's almost noon," he said. "Let's go back to the house and you can tell me which horses I should keep over lunch."

"Sure."

As they ate bowls of beef stew and crusty French bread, Hadley spelled out her take on each of the horses he'd shown her.

"Cielo is a keeper. But I don't think you'd part with him no matter what anyone said to you."

"You're probably right." He missed talking horses with someone. Since his grandfather died, Liam hadn't had anyone to share his passion with. "What did you think of the bay filly?"

"Nice, but the roan mare is better, and bred to Blue you'd get a really nice foal." Hadley's gaze turned thoughtful as she stirred the stew with her spoon. "I also think you'd be fine letting the buckskin go. He's terrific, but Cielo will be a better reining horse." Her lips curved. "But I'm not telling you anything you hadn't already decided."

"I appreciate your feedback. And you're right. Of the four I showed you, I'd selected three to sell. But your suggestion that I breed Tilda to Blue was something I hadn't considered."

Her smile warmed up the already-cozy kitchen. "Glad I could help. It was fun talking horses. It was something my friends and I did all the time when I was younger. I always imagined myself living on a ranch after I finished school, breeding and training horses."

Liam's chest tightened. Hadley possessed the qualities he'd spent the last year deciding his perfect woman must have. Beautiful, loving, maternal and passionate about horses.

"Of course, that wasn't a practical dream," Hadley continued. "My parents were right to insist I put my education first. I figured that out not long after I started college."

"But what if you could have figured out a way to make it work? Start small, build something."

"Maybe ten years ago I could have." Her voice held a hint of wistfulness. A moment later, all nostalgia vanished. "These days it's no longer what I want."

Her declaration put an end to the topic. Liam held his gaze steady on her for a moment longer, wondering if he'd imagined her overselling her point. Or was he simply wishing she'd consider giving up her future plans and sticking around Royal? He'd grown attached to her in a very short period of time and wanted to see more of her. And not as his niece's nanny.

Liam pushed back from the table. "I have a meeting late this afternoon at the Texas Cattleman's Club, but I'll be back in time for you to make your class at seven."

"Thank you. I really enjoy the class as much for the company as the candle making." She carried their bowls to the sink and began rinsing them. "When I'm in school, I don't have a lot of free time."

"Sounds like you don't make enough time for fun," he said.

"I keep telling myself that I'll have plenty of time to enjoy myself once I'm done with school. In the meantime, I make the most of the free hours I have."

Liam was mulling Hadley's attitude as he strode into the Texas Cattleman's Club later that day. Originally built as a men's club around 1910, the club opened its doors to women members as well a few years ago. Liam and his grandfather had been all for the change and had even supported the addition of a child care center. For the most part, though, the decor of the original building had been left intact. The wood floors, paneled walls and hunting trophies created a decidedly masculine atmosphere.

As Liam entered the lounge and approached the bar, he overheard one table discussing the Samson Oil land purchases. This had been going on for months. Several ranchers had gone bankrupt on the heels of the destructive tornado that had swept through Royal and the surrounding ranches. Many of those who'd survived near financial ruin had then had to face the challenge of the drought that reduced lakes and creeks and made sustaining even limited herds difficult. Some without established systems of watering tanks and pumps had been forced to sell early on. Others were holding out for a miracle that wouldn't come.

"I guess I know what's on the agenda for the meeting

today," Liam mentioned as he slid into the space between his best friend, David "Mac" McCallum, and Case Baxter, current president of the Texas Cattleman's Club. "Has anybody heard what's up with all the purchases?"

Mac shook his head. "Maybe they think there are shale deposits."

"Fracking?" The man on the other side of Mac growled. "As if this damned drought isn't bad enough. What sort of poison is that process going to spill into our groundwater? I've got two thousand heads relying on well water."

Liam had heard similar complaints every time he set foot in the clubhouse. The drought was wearing on everyone. Wade Ranch relied on both wells and a spring-fed lake to keep its livestock watered. He couldn't imagine the stress of a situation where he only had one ever-dwindling source to count on.

"Mellie tells me the property lawyer who's been buying up all the land for Samson Oil quit," Case said. His fiancée's family owned several properties the oil company had tried to buy. "She's gotten friendly with one of her tenants, the woman who owns the antiques store in the Courtyard. Apparently she and Nolan Dane are involved."

"Howard Dane's son?"

"Yes, and Nolan's going back to work with him doing family law."

Liam missed who asked the question, but Case's answer got him thinking about Kyle. That his brother was still out of touch reinforced Liam's growing conviction that Maggie deserved a parent who was there for her 24/7. Obviously as long as he was on active duty, Kyle couldn't be counted on. Perhaps Liam should reach out to an attorney familiar with family law and see what his options might be for taking over custody of his niece. He made a mental note to give the man a call the next morning and set up an appointment.

"Maybe we should invite him to join the club," Liam suggested, thinking how their numbers had dwindled over the last year as more and more ranchers sold off their land.

"I think we could use some powerful allies against Samson Oil," Case said. "Nolan might not be able to give us any information on his former client, but he still has a background in property law that could be useful."

The men gathered in the bar began to move toward the boardroom where that night's meeting was to be held.

"How are things going for you at home?" Mac asked. "Is fatherhood all it's cracked up to be?"

"Maggie is not my daughter," Liam replied, wearying of everyone assuming he'd been foolhardy. "But I'm enjoying having her around. She's really quite sweet when she's not crying."

Mac laughed. "I never thought I'd see you settling down."

"A year ago I decided I wanted one good relationship rather than a dozen mediocre ones." Liam was rather impressed with how enlightened he sounded.

"And yet you've buried yourself at the ranch. How are you any closer to a good relationship when you don't get out and meet women?"

"I've heard that when you're ready, the right one comes along." An image of Hadley flashed through his mind.

Mac's hand settled forcefully on Liam's shoulder. "You're talking like an idiot. Is it sleep deprivation?"

"I have a newborn living with me. What do you think?"

But Liam knew that what was keeping him awake at night wasn't Maggie, but her nanny and the persistent hope that Waldo might sneak into Liam's bedroom and Hadley would be forced to rescue him a second time. Because if that happened, Liam had prepared a very different end to that encounter.

Six

Ivy entered Liam's office with her tablet in hand and sat down. The back of the chair thumped against the wall, and her knees bumped his desk. She growled in annoyance and rubbed her legs. Unbefitting his status as half owner of the ranch, Liam had one of the tiniest offices in the complex. He preferred to spend his days out and about and left paperwork for evenings. When he met with clients, he had an informal way of handling the meetings and usually entertained in the large lounge area or brought them into the barns.

"I'm finalizing your plans for Colorado this weekend," she said, her finger moving across the tablet screen. "The caterer is confirmed. A Suburban will be waiting for you at the airport. Give Hannah Lake a call when you land, and she will meet you at the house."

Ivy kept talking, but Liam had stopped listening. He'd forgotten all about the skiing weekend he was hosting for five of his clients. The tradition had begun several years ago. They looked forward to the event for months, and it was far too late to cancel.

"Liam?" Ivy regarded him with a steady gaze. "You seem worried. I assure you everything is ready."

"It's not that. I forgot that I was supposed to be heading to Colorado in a couple days. What am I going to do about Maggie?"

"Take her along." She jotted a note on the tablet with a stylus. "I'll see if they can set up a crib in one of the rooms."

"Have you forgotten this is supposed to be a guys' weekend? A chance for everyone to get away from their wives and families so they can smoke cigars, drink too much scotch, ski and play poker?"

"Sounds lovely." Ivy rolled her eyes.

Liam pointed at Ivy's expression. "And that is exactly what they want to get away from."

"I don't know what you're worrying about. Bring Hadley along to take care of Maggie. The house is big enough for a dozen people. No one will even know they're there."

Ivy's suggestion made sense, but Liam's instincts rebelled at her assumption that no one would realize they were present. He would know. Just like every other night when she slept down the hall.

"That's true enough, and Maggie is doing better at night. She barely fusses at all before going back to sleep." Liam wondered how much of a fight Hadley would make about flying to Colorado. He got to his feet. It was late enough in the afternoon for him to knock off. He'd been looking forward to spending a little time with Maggie before dinner. "I'd better give Hadley a heads-up."

"Let me know if she has anything special to arrange for Maggie." With that, Ivy exited the office.

Liam scooped his hat off the desk and settled it on his head. As he drove the ten minutes between barns and house, Liam considered the arguments for and against taking Maggie with him to Colorado. In the ten days since his niece had become a part of his life, he'd grown very attached to her. When his brother contacted him, Liam intended to convince him to give the baby up. With the dangerous line of work his brother was in, Maggie would be better off with the sort of stable home environment found here on Wade Ranch.

Liam entered the house and followed the scent of wood smoke to the den. Hadley looked up from her book as Liam entered. "You're home early."

"I came home to spend some time with Maggie." And with her. Had he imagined the way her eyes had lit up upon seeing him? They'd spent a great deal of time together in the last few days. All under the guise of caring for Maggie, but Liam knew his own motives weren't as pure as he'd let on.

"She had a rough afternoon."

She glanced down at the sleeping infant nestled in her arms. Hadley's fond expression hit Liam in the gut.

"She looks peaceful now."

"I only got her to sleep half an hour ago." Hadley began shifting the baby in her arms. "Do you want to hold her?"

"Not yet. I spent most of the day in the saddle. I'm going to grab a shower first."

He rushed through his cleanup and ran a comb through his damp hair. Dressed in brown corduroy pants and a denim shirt, he headed back to the den. The afternoon light had faded until it was too dark for Hadley to read, but instead of turning on the lamps, she was relying on the flickering glow of the fire. Outside, the wind howled, and she shivered.

"Is it as chilly as it sounds?"

"I suspect the windchill will be below freezing tonight."

He eased down on the couch beside her and took the baby. Their bodies pressed against each other hip to knee during the exchange, and Liam smiled as her scent tickled his nose. They'd become a well-oiled machine in the last few days, trading off Maggie's care like a couple in sync with each other and their child's needs. It had given him a glimpse of what life would be like with a family. Liam enjoyed Hadley's undemanding company. She'd demonstrated an impish sense of humor when sharing stories of her fellow nannies' adventures in caretaking, and he was wearing down her resistance to talking about horses by sharing tales of people she used to compete against.

"I have a business trip scheduled in a couple days," Liam began, eyeing Hadley as he spoke. Her gaze was on the baby in his arms.

"How long will you be gone?"

"I rented a house in Colorado for a week, but usually I'm only gone for four days." He paused, thinking how he'd prefer to stay in this cozy triangle with Hadley and Maggie rather than flying off to entertain a group of men. "It's a ski weekend for five of my best clients."

"Are you worried about leaving Maggie here?"

"Yes. I want to bring her along." He paused a beat before adding, "I want you to come, as well." He saw the arguments building in her blue eyes. He already had the answer to her first one. "Candace has offered to take Waldo, so you don't have to worry about him."

"I've never traveled with a client before." She wasn't demonstrating the resistance he'd expected. "Are you sure there will be room for us?"

"The house is quite large. There are seven bedrooms. Ivy is coordinating the trip and said you should let her know about anything you think Maggie might need. She is already making arrangements for a crib."

"When would we leave?"

"We'll fly up in two days. I like to get in a day early to make sure everything is in place. Is that enough time for you to get what you'll need?"

"Sure." But she was frowning as she said it.

"Is something wrong?"

She laughed self-consciously. "I've never seen snow before. What will I need to buy besides a warm coat?"

"You've never seen snow?" Liam was excited at the

thought of being there when Hadley experienced the beauty of a winter day in the mountains.

"For someone as well traveled as you are, that must seem pretty unsophisticated."

Liam considered her comment. "You said you'd never traveled with your clients. Is that because you didn't want to?"

"It's mostly been due to school and timing. I always figured there'd be plenty of time to travel after I graduated and settled into a job with regular hours and paid vacation time."

Her wistful smile gave him some notion of how long and arduous a journey it had been toward finishing her master's degree.

He felt a little hesitant to ask his next question. "Have you flown in a small plane before?"

"No." She drew the word out, her gaze finding and holding his. Anxiety and eagerness pulled at the corners of her mouth. "How small is small?"

Small turned out to be forty feet in length with a forty-three-foot wingspan. Hadley's heart gave a little bump as she approached the elegant six-seat jet with three tiny oval windows. She didn't know what she'd been expecting, maybe a single-prop plane with fixed wheels like the ones used by desperate movie heroes to escape or chase bad guys.

"This doesn't look so scary, does it?" She whispered the question to a sleepy Maggie.

Hadley stopped at the steps leading up to the plane. Liam had gone ahead with her luggage and overnight bag carrying all of Maggie's things. Now he emerged from the plane and reached down to take Maggie's carrier.

"Come on in." Liam's irresistible grin pulled Hadley forward.

She almost floated up the stairs. His charm banished her nervousness, allowing her to focus only on the excitement of visiting Colorado for the first time. Not that she'd see much of it. Her job was to take care of Maggie. But even to glimpse the town of Vail covered in snow as they drove past would be thrill enough.

The plane's interior was luxurious, with room enough for a pilot and five passengers. There were six beige leather seats, two facing forward and two backward as well as the two in the cockpit. She knew nothing about aviation equipment, but the instrument panel placed in front of the pilot and copilot seats had three large screens filled with data as well as an abundance of switches and buttons and looked very sophisticated.

"I set up Maggie's car seat here because I thought you'd prefer to face forward. You'll find bottles of water and ice over there." He pointed to the narrow cabinet behind the cockpit. "There's also a thermos of hot water to make Maggie's bottle."

"Thank you. I made one before we left because it helps babies to adjust to altitudes if they're sucking on something."

"Great. We should be set then."

Hadley settled into her seat and buckled herself in. She looked up in time to see Liam closing the airplane's door.

"Wait," she called. "What about the pilot?"

The grin he turned on her was wolfish. "I am the pilot." With a wink, he slid into the left cockpit seat and began going through a preflight check.

Surprise held her immobile for several minutes before her skin heated and her breath rushed out. For almost two weeks now his actions and the things he'd revealed about himself kept knocking askew her preconceived notions about him. It was distracting. And dangerous.

To avoid fretting over her deepening attraction to Liam,

Hadley pulled out Maggie's bottle and a bib. As the plane taxied she had a hard time ignoring the man at the controls, and surrendered to the anxiety rising in her.

What was she doing? Falling for Liam was a stupid thing to do. The man charmed everyone without even trying.

As the plane lifted off, her stomach dipped and her adrenaline surged. Hadley offered Maggie the bottle and the infant sucked greedily at it. Out the window, land fell away, and the small craft bounced a little on the air currents. To keep her nervousness at bay, Hadley focused all her attention on Maggie. The baby was not the least bit disturbed by the plane's movements. In fact, her eyes were wide and staring as if it was one big adventure.

After what felt like an endless climb, the plane leveled off. Hadley freed Maggie from her car seat so she could burp her. Peering out the window, she saw nothing but clouds below them. With Liam occupied in the cockpit and Maggie falling asleep in her arms, Hadley let her thoughts roam free.

Several hours later, after Liam landed the plane at a small airport outside Vail, their rental car sped toward their destination. When she'd stepped off the plane, Hadley had been disappointed to discover that very little snow covered the ground. She'd imagined that in the middle of January there would be piles and piles of the white stuff everywhere she looked. But now, as they neared the mountains, her excitement began to build once more.

Framed against an ice-blue sky, the snow-covered peaks surrounding the town of Vail seemed impossibly high. But she could see the ski runs that started near the summit and carved through the pine-covered face of each mountain. Liam drove the winding roads without checking the navigation, obviously knowing where he was headed.

"What do you think?"

"It's beautiful."

"Wait until you see the views from the house. They're incredible."

"Do you rent this house every year?"

"A longtime friend of my grandfather owns it."

"I didn't realize you like to ski."

"I had a lot more free time when I was younger, but these days I try to get out a couple times a year. I go to New Mexico when I can get away for a weekend because it's close."

"It must be nice having your own plane so you can take off whenever you want."

"I'm afraid it's been pretty idle lately. I've spent almost ninety percent of my time at the ranch this year."

And the other ten percent meeting Maggie's mother and spending the night with her. Hadley glanced into the backseat where the baby was batting at one of the toys clipped to her car seat.

"You said that's been good for your business," Hadley said, "but don't you miss showing?"

"All the time."

"So why'd you give it up?" From the way Liam's expression turned to stone, she could tell her question had touched on something distasteful. "I'm sorry. I didn't mean to pry. Forget I said anything."

"No, it's okay. A lot of people have asked me that question. I'll tell you what I tell them. After my grandfather died, I discovered how much time it takes to run Wade Ranch."

She suspected that was only half of the reason, but she didn't pry anymore. "Any chance your brother, Kyle, will come back to Texas to help you?"

"No." Liam's answer was a clipped single syllable and discouraged further questions. "I'm finding a balance between ranch business as a whole and the horse side that I love. Last summer I hired a sales manager for the cattle division. I think you met Emma Jane. She's been a terrific asset."

She *had* terrific assets, Hadley thought wryly. The beautiful blonde was memorable for many reasons, not the least of which was the way her eyes and her body language communicated her interest in Liam. That he'd seemed oblivious had surprised Hadley. Since when did a man who enjoyed having beautiful women around not notice one right beneath his nose?

Maybe becoming a father had affected him more than Hadley had given him credit for.

Liam continued, "But it's not like having someone I could put in charge of the entire operation."

Obviously Liam was stretched thin. Maybe that's why he'd been looking so lighthearted these last few days. The break from responsibility would do him good.

Forty minutes after they'd left the airport, Liam drove up a steep driveway and approached a sprawling home right at the base of the mountain.

"We're staying here?" Hadley gawked at the enormous house.

"I told you there was enough room for you and Maggie." He stopped the SUV beside a truck and shot her a broad smile. "Let's get settled in and then head into town for dinner. It's a quarter mile walk if you think Maggie would be okay."

"We can bundle her up. The fresh air sounds lovely." The temperature hovered just above freezing, but it was sunny and there wasn't any wind, so Hadley was comfortable in her brand-new ski jacket and winter boots.

A tall man in his midsixties with an athletic bounce to his stride emerged from the house and headed straight for Liam. "Mr. Wade, how good to have you with us again."

"Hello, Ben." The two men shook hands, and Liam turned to gesture to Hadley, who'd unfastened Maggie from her car seat and now walked around to the driver's side. "This is Ms. Stratton and Maggie."

"Ivy mentioned you were bringing family with you this year. How nice."

The vague reference to family disturbed Hadley. Why couldn't Liam just admit that he had a daughter? He obviously loved Maggie. What blocked him from acknowledging her as his? This flaw in his character bothered Hadley more than it should. But it was none of her business. And it wasn't fair that she expected more of him. Liam was her employer. She had no right to judge.

"Nice to meet you, Ben," she said.

While Liam and Ben emptied the SUV of luggage and ski equipment, Hadley carried Maggie inside and passed through the two-story foyer to the large living room. The whole front of the house that faced the mountain was made up of tall windows.

"There's a nice room upstairs for you and Maggie." Liam came over to where she stood staring at the mountain range. "Ben said he was able to get a crib set up in there."

Hadley followed Liam up a broad staircase. At the top he turned right. The home sprawled across the hillside, providing each bedroom with a fantastic view. The room Hadley and Maggie were to share was at the back of the house and looked west, offering views of both mountains and the town. At four in the afternoon, the sun was sliding toward the horizon, gilding the snow.

"Is this okay?"

"It's amazing." The room was large by Hadley's standards, but she guessed it was probably the smallest house offered. Still, it boasted a queen-size bed, plush seating for two before the enormous picture window and a stone fireplace that took up most of the wall the bed faced. The crib had been set up in the corner nearest to the door that led to the hall.

"I'm next door in case you need me."

Her nerves trumpeted a warning at his proximity. Not that there was any cause for alarm. She and Liam had been sleeping down the hall from each other for almost two weeks.

Plus, it wasn't as though they would be alone. Tomorrow, five others would be joining them, and from the way Liam described past years, the men would be occupied with cards, drinking and conversation late into the night.

"What time should I be ready to leave for dinner?"

"I think we won't want to have Maggie out late. What if we leave here in an hour?"

"I'll have both of us ready."

With Maggie snug in her new winter clothes and Hadley dressed for the cold night air in a turtleneck sweater and black cords, they came downstairs to find Liam waiting in the entry. He held Hadley's insulated jacket while she slid her feet into warm boots and then helped her into the coat. The brush of his knuckles against her shoulders caused butterflies to dance in her stomach. The longing to lean backward against his strong chest was so poignant, Hadley stopped breathing.

Because she'd had her back to him, Liam had no idea how the simple act of chivalry had rocked her equilibrium. Thank goodness she'd learned to master her facial expressions during her last five years of being a nanny. By the time Liam picked up Maggie's carrier, set his hand on the front door latch and turned an expectant gaze upon her, she was ready to offer him a polite smile.

Liam closed and locked the door behind them and then offered his arm to help Hadley negotiate the driveway's steep slope.

"You have Maggie," she told him, considering how lovely it would be to snuggle against his side during the half-mile walk. "Don't worry about me." She might have convinced him if her boots hadn't picked that second to skid on an icy patch.

"I think I can handle a girl on each arm," he said, his voice rich with laughter.

Hadley slipped her arm through Liam's and let him draw her close. The supporting strength of his muscular arm was supposed to steady her, not weaken her knees, but Hadley couldn't prevent her body from reveling in her escort's irresistible masculinity.

At the bottom of the driveway, Hadley expected Liam to release her, but he showed no inclination to set her free. Their boots crunched against the snow-covered pavement as they headed toward town. Sunset was still a little ways off, but clouds had moved in to blanket the sky and speed up the shift to evening. With her heart hammering a distracting tattoo against Hadley's breastbone, she was at a loss for conversation. Liam seemed okay with the silence as he walked beside her.

The restaurant Liam chose was a cute bistro in the heart of Vail Village. "It's my favorite place to eat when I come here," he explained, holding open the door and gesturing her inside.

The early hour meant the tables were only a third full. The hostess led them to a cozy corner table beside the windows that ran along the street front and offered a wonderful view of the trees adorned with white lights. Above their heads, small halogen lights hung from a rustic beam ceiling. A double-sided stone fireplace split the large room into two cozy spaces. White table linens, candlelight and crystal goblets etched with the restaurant's logo added to the romantic ambience.

"I hope the food is half as good as the decor," Hadley commented, bending over Maggie's carrier to remove the infant from her warm nest before she overheated.

"I assure you it's much better. Chef Mongillo is a culinary genius."

Since becoming Maggie's nanny, Hadley had grown accustomed to the rugged rancher Liam was at home and forgot that his alter ego was sophisticated and well traveled. And by extension, his preferred choice of female companionship was worldly and stylish. This abrupt return to reality jarred her out of her dreamy mood, and she chastised herself for forgetting her role in Liam's life.

Taking refuge behind the tall menu, she scanned the delicious selection of entrees and settled on an ahi tuna dish with artichoke, black radish and egg confit potato. The description made her mouth water. Liam suggested the blue crab appetizer and ordered a bottle of sauvignon blanc to accompany it.

She considered the wisdom of drinking while on duty, but deliberated only a few seconds before her first sip. The crisp white burst on her taste buds and her gaze sought Liam. The glint lighting his eyes was a cross between amusement and appreciation. Heat collected in her cheeks and spread downward.

She spoke to distract herself from the longing his scrutiny awakened. "This is delicious."

"Glad you like it." His deep voice pierced her chest and spurred her heart to race. "I'm really glad you were willing to come along this weekend."

This is not a date.

"Are you kidding? You had me at snow." She tried to sound lighthearted and casual, but ended up coming across breathless and silly. Embarrassed, she glanced away. The view out the window seemed the best place for her attention. What she saw made her catch her breath. "And speaking of snow…"

Enormous white flakes drifted past the window. It was

so thick that it was almost impossible to see the storefronts across the cobblestoned street.

"It's really beautiful. I can see why you come here."

"I arranged the weather just for you." As lines went, it wasn't original, but it made her laugh.

Hadley slanted a wry glance his way. "That was very nice of you."

"And I'm sure the guys will be happy to have fresh powder to ski."

When the waiter brought their appetizer, Liam asked about the weather. "How many inches are you expecting?"

"I've heard anywhere from eight to twelve inches here. More elsewhere. It's a pretty huge system moving across the Midwest."

"That's not going to be good for people trying to get in or out of here."

"No. From what I've heard, the Denver airport is expecting to cancel most if not all of their flights tomorrow. I don't know about Eagle County." Which was where they'd landed a few hours earlier.

"Sounds like we're going to be snowed in," Liam said, not appearing particularly concerned.

Hadley didn't share his nonchalance. "What does that mean for your guests?"

"I'll have to check in with them tonight. They might be delayed for a couple days or decide to cancel altogether depending on how long the storm persists."

"But…" What did she plan to say? If the storm moving in made inbound travel impossible, they certainly couldn't fly out. Which meant she, Maggie and Liam were going to be stuck in Vail for the foreseeable future. Alone.

Hadley focused on the food in front of her, annoyed by her heart's irregular beat. What did she think was going to happen in the next few days? Obviously her hormones

thought she and Liam would engage in some sort of passionate affair.

The idiocy of the notion made her smile.

Seven

Liam knew he'd concealed his delight at being snowed in with Hadley, so why was she so distracted all of a sudden? And what was with the smile that curved her luscious lips?

He cleared his throat to alleviate the sudden tightness. "I take it you like blue crab?"

Hadley glanced up, and her eyes widened as she met his gaze. "Yes. It's delicious." Her attention strayed toward the window and the swiftly falling flakes. "It's really magical."

Her dreamy expression startled him. He'd become accustomed to her practicality and was excited that her professional mask might be slipping.

With the snow piling up outside, they didn't linger over dinner. As much as Liam would have enjoyed several more hours of gazing into her eyes and telling stories that made her laugh, they needed to get Maggie home and tucked in for the night. His disappointment faded as he considered that they could continue the conversation side by side on the living room sofa. Without the barrier of a table between them, things could get interesting.

"Ready?" he asked, as he settled the check and stood. "Sure."

Helping her into her coat gave him the excuse to move close enough to inhale her scent and give her shoulders a friendly squeeze. He hoped he hadn't imagined the slight hitch of her breath as he touched her.

Liam gestured for Hadley to go ahead of him out of the restaurant. They retraced their steps through town, navigating the slippery sidewalk past trees strung with white lights and shop windows displaying their wares. Liam insisted Hadley take his arm. He'd enjoyed the feel of her snuggled against him during the walk into town.

Once the commercial center of the town was behind them, the mountain once again dominated the view. As they strolled along, boots sinking into an inch of fresh snow, Liam was convinced he couldn't have planned a more romantic walk home. The gently falling snow captured them in a world all their own, isolating them from obligations and interruptions.

Hadley laughed in delight as fat flakes melted on her cheeks and eyelashes. He wanted to kiss each one away and had a hard time resisting the urge to take her in his arms to do just that. If not for the weight of Maggie's carrier in his hand, he doubted if he could have resisted.

The strength of his desire for Hadley gave him pause. It wasn't just sexual attraction, although heaven knew his lust flared every time she came within arm's reach. No, it was something more profound that made him want her. The way she took care of Maggie, not as if she was being paid to look after her but with affection and genuine concern for her welfare.

He could picture them as partners in the ranch. She had a great eye when it came to seeing the potential in horses, and he had no doubt if she would just remember how much she enjoyed her days of showing that she would relish being involved with the ranch's future.

Yet she'd demonstrated complete disinterest in the horses, and he had yet to figure out why, when it was obviously something she'd been passionate about ten years earlier. Maybe he should accept that she was planning to leave Royal after she graduated. Plus, she'd invested five years getting a graduate degree in guidance counseling. Would she be willing to put that aside?

"You're awfully quiet all of a sudden," Hadley commented. "Cat got your tongue?"

He snorted at her. "I was just thinking about the girl I met ten years ago."

"Which one? There must have been hundreds." An undercurrent of insecurity ran beneath her teasing.

Liam decided to play it straight. "The only one that got away."

His declaration was met with silence, and for a moment the companionable mood between them grew taut with anticipation. He walked on, curious how she'd respond.

"You can't really mean me," she said at last. "You must have met dozens of girls who interested you where the circumstances or the timing weren't right."

"Probably. But only one sticks out in my mind. You. I truly regret never getting a chance to know you better."

While she absorbed this, they reached the driveway of the house where they were staying and began to climb. In minutes he was going to lose her to Maggie's bedtime ritual.

"Why did you sell Lolita and disappear?"

She tensed at his question. "You asked me before why I was no longer interested in horses. It's the same reason I stopped showing. At that sweepstakes show, my best friend fell during her run. She wanted really badly to beat me, so she pushed too hard and her horse lost his footing. He went down with her under him. She broke her back and was paralyzed."

"I remember hearing that someone had been hurt, but I didn't realize how serious it was."

"After that I just couldn't race anymore. It was my fault that she rode the way she did. If I hadn't... She really wanted to beat me." Hadley let out a shaky sigh. "After it happened she refused to talk to me or see me."

Liam sensed there was more to the story he wasn't getting, but didn't want to push deeper into a sensitive issue. "I don't want to downplay your guilt over what was obviously a tragedy, but don't you think it's time you forgave yourself for what happened?"

Hadley gave a bitter laugh. "My best friend is constantly getting on my case for not letting go of mistakes I've made in the past. She's more of a learn-something-and-move-on sort of a girl."

"Maybe if you start riding again you could put it behind you?"

"I'll think about it."

Which sounded like a big fat *no* to Liam's ears. As soon as they entered the front door, Hadley took Maggie's carrier.

"Thank you for dinner."

"You're welcome."

"I'd better get this one into bed." She paused as if having more to say.

"It's still early. I'm going to bet there's some seriously decadent desserts in the kitchen. Ivy knows my guest John Barr has quite a sweet tooth, and she always makes sure it's satisfied."

"It's been a long day, and I'm dying to finish the mystery I started on the plane. I'll see you in the morning."

Liam watched her ascend the stairs and considered following, but decided if she refused to have dessert with him, she was probably not in the mood for his company. He'd ruined what had been a promising evening by asking about matters that were still painful to her. Well, he'd wanted to get to know her better, and he'd succeeded in that.

Pouring himself a scotch, Liam sat down in front of the enormous television and turned on a hockey game. As he watched the players move about the rink, his thoughts ran to the woman upstairs. Getting to know her was not going to be without its ups and downs. She was complicated and enigmatic.

But Liam hadn't won all his reining titles because he lacked finesse and patience. He thrived on the challenge of figuring out what each horse needed to excel. No reason he couldn't put those same talents to use with Hadley.

He intended to figure out what this filly was all about, and if he was lucky—the news reports were already talking about airport shutdowns all over the Midwest—it looked as though he'd have four uninterrupted days and nights to do so.

After a restless night pondering how some inexplicable thing had changed in her interaction with Liam, Hadley got up early and went to explore the gourmet kitchen. Up until last night she'd characterized her relationship with him as boss and employee. Maybe it had grown to friendship of a sort. They enjoyed each other's company, but except for that time she'd gone to retrieve Waldo from his bedroom—which didn't count—he'd never given her any indication that the physical desire she felt for him was reciprocal.

Because of that, Hadley had been confident she could come on this trip and keep Liam from seeing her growing attraction for him. That was before they'd had a romantic dinner together and then walked home in the snow. Now a major storm system had stalled over the Midwest, stranding them alone in this snowy paradise, and she was in trouble.

"I'm sorry your clients won't make the skiing weekend," she said, her gaze glued to the pan of bacon she was fixing. Nearby a carton of eggs sat on the granite counter; she was making omelets.

"I'm not." Liam's deep voice sounded far too close behind her for comfort. "I'm actually looking forward to spending the time with you."

She should ignore the lure of his words and the invitation she'd glimpsed in his eyes the night before. Hadn't she learned her lesson with Noah? Getting emotionally involved with clients was never smart. She couldn't lie to herself and pretend the only thing she felt for Liam was sexual attraction. Granted, there was a great deal of lust interfering with her clear thinking, but she wasn't the type to lose her mind over a hot guy.

What Liam inspired in her was a complicated mixture of physical desire, admiration and wariness. The last was due to how she wanted to trust his word when he claimed he wasn't Maggie's father. Obviously the man had a knack for making women come around to his point of view. She was back to pondering his apparent sincerity and her susceptibility. What other outrageous lie could he tell her that she would believe?

Liam had propped his hip against the counter beside her and was watching her through narrowed eyes. "What can I help you with?"

"You never offer to help Candace." The statement came out sounding like an accusation.

"I've given up trying. Haven't you noticed she doesn't like anyone interfering in her kitchen?" He reached across her to snag a piece of cooked bacon off the plate where it cooled. His gaze snagged hers as he broke the piece in half and offered part to her. "I'm completely at your disposal. What would you like me to do?"

Hadley told herself there was no subtext beneath his question, but her body had a completely different interpretation. She wanted to turn off the stove and find a use for the kitchen that had nothing to do with cooking.

"I'm going to make omelets. Can you get the ingredients you want in yours from the fridge?"

Liam's lazy smile suggested that he'd heard the uneven-
ness of her tone and had an idea he'd put it there. But he
didn't push his advantage. Instead, he did as she asked, and
Hadley was left with space to breathe and a moment to cool
off. Almost immediately she discovered how this had backfired. The gap between them didn't bring relief from her
cravings, but increased her longing for him. She was in a
great deal of trouble.

Without asking, he pulled out a cutting board and began
chopping onion and tomatoes. Engrossed in the task, he
didn't notice her stare. Or that's what she thought until
he spoke.

"Candace doesn't work 24/7," he commented, setting a
second pan on the six-burner stove and adding olive oil. "I
have been known to cook for myself from time to time."

"Sorry for misjudging you."

"You do that a lot."

"Apologize?"

"Jump to negative conclusions about me."

"That's not true."

"Isn't it?" He dumped the diced onions into the pan
and stirred them. "From the moment you walked into my
house you pegged me as a womanizing jerk who slept
with some random woman, got her pregnant and never
contacted her again."

She couldn't deny his statement. "I don't think you're
a jerk."

"But you think I treat women like playthings."

"It's none of my business what you do."

Liam's breath gusted out. "For the rest of this trip I give
you a pass to speak your mind with me. I'm not going to
dance around topics while you keep the truth bottled up."

"Fine." Hadley couldn't understand why she was so annoyed all of a sudden. "Back when I used to show, you had
a reputation for going through girls like chewing gum."

"Sure, I dated a lot, and I know that not every girl was happy when I broke things off, but I never treated any of them like they were disposable."

"What do you call sleeping with them once and then never calling again?"

"I never did that. Who said I did?"

"A friend of mine knew someone..." Hadley trailed off. Why hadn't she ever questioned whether what Anna had said about him was true?

Anger faded from Liam's green eyes. "And because she was your friend, you believed her."

Liam shook his head and went back to stirring the onions. While Hadley searched for answers in his expression, he added raw spinach to the pan and set a lid on it.

"We have cheddar and Cojack cheese," Liam said. "Which would you prefer?"

"Cojack." Hadley had finished with the bacon while they'd been talking and began cracking eggs for their omelets. She moved mechanically, burdened by the notion that she'd done Liam a great injustice. "I'll pour some orange juice. Do you want toast? There's some honey wheat that looks good."

"That's fine. I'll finish up the omelets." His neutral tone gave away none of his thoughts, but Hadley moved around the large kitchen with the sense that she was in the wrong.

Instead of eating in the formal dining room, Hadley set the small kitchen table. She paused to stare out the window at the new blanket of snow covering the mountains and gave a small thank-you to the weather gods for giving her and Liam this weekend alone. He was a far more complicated man than she'd given him credit for, and she welcomed the opportunity to get inside his head between now and when they returned to Royal.

A few minutes later, Hadley carried Maggie's carrier to the table and Liam followed her with plates of omelets and the bacon. Awkward silence had replaced their companionable chatter from the previous evening. It was her fault. She'd wounded him with Anna's tale. But whom was she supposed to believe? Her best friend at the time or a man who admitted to *dating* a lot of women?

The delicious omelet was like a mouthful of sand. Hadley washed the bite down with orange juice and wondered what she was supposed to believe. For ten years she'd lived with guilt over the pain her actions had caused Anna. What if none of it had been as her friend said?

"I know you haven't had any reason to believe I've left my playboy ways behind me," Liam began, his own food untouched. "And perhaps I deserve your skepticism, but I'd like to point out that nothing has happened between you and me, despite my strong attraction to you."

"Strong…attraction?" Hadley fumbled out the words, her heart hammering hard against her ribs.

His gaze was direct and intense as he regarded her. "Very. Strong."

What could she say to that? She looked to Maggie for help, but the baby had her attention locked on the string of stuffed bugs strapped to the handle of her carrier and was too content to provide a convenient distraction.

"I wish you weren't," she said at last, the statement allowing her to retreat from a very dangerous precipice.

"That makes two of us. And I have no intention of worsening your opinion of me by doing anything that makes you uncomfortable. I wouldn't bring it up at all except that I wanted to illustrate that I'm done with casual relationships." He picked up his fork and began breaking up his omelet.

"When you say casual relationships…"

"Ones that are primarily sexual in nature." His head bobbed in a decisive nod.

"So you're not…"

"Having sex? No." He gave her a rueful grin. "I haven't been with anyone in a year."

That wasn't possible. "But Maggie…"

"Isn't mine. She's my brother's daughter."

Hadley stared at him, saw that this wasn't a come-on or a ploy. He was completely serious. And she wanted to believe him. Because if he hadn't been with anyone in a year, that meant he might not be the player she'd taken him for. Suddenly, the speed at which she was falling for him was a little less scary than it had been five minutes ago.

"Why haven't you…?"

He took pity on her and answered her half-asked question. "When Grandfather died and I inherited half of Wade Ranch, it suddenly became apparent that the women I'd been involved with saw me as a good time and nothing more."

"And you wanted to be more?" She couldn't imagine Liam being anything less than completely satisfied with who he was, and this glimpse into his doubts made him more interesting than ever.

"Not to be taken seriously bothered me a great deal."

Hadley was starting to see his problem. "Maybe it was just the women in your sphere who felt that way. If you found some serious women, maybe then you'd be taken seriously."

"You're a serious woman." His green eyes hardened. "And you've been giving me back-off vibes from the moment we met."

"But that's because I work for you and what sort of professional would I be if I let myself get involved with my employer?" *Again.* She clung to the final thought. This conversation had strayed too deep into personal territory.

"You won't be working for me forever. What happens then? Does a serious girl like you give me a chance?"

* * *

Liam watched Hadley's face for some sign of her thoughts. Sharing the details of his recent personal crisis had been a risk. She could decide he was playing her. Building up sympathy to wear down her defenses. Or she might write him off as a sentimental fool in desperate need of a strong woman. The thought of that amused him.

"I...don't know."

He refused to be disappointed by her answer. "Then obviously I have my work cut out for me."

"What does that mean?"

"You need to be convinced I'm sincere. I'm up for the challenge."

"Is that what you think? That I need to be convinced I'm wrong about you?" She shook her head in disgust. "I can make up my own mind, thank you."

Torn between admiration and frustration, Liam debated his next words. "I seem to be saying everything wrong today." To his amazement, she smiled.

"I might be harder on you than you deserve. It's really not for me to offer an opinion on your past behavior or judge the decisions you've made." She glanced at Maggie and then fastened serious blue eyes on him. "You're wonderful with Maggie, and that's the man I'd like to get to know better."

In business and horses, this would be the sort of breakthrough he'd capitalize on. But her next words deflated his optimism.

"Unfortunately, you are also my boss, and that's a line I can't cross."

But she wanted to. He recognized regret in her downcast eyes and the tight line of her lips. With the snow still falling, he would have plenty of time to turn her to his way of thinking. The chemistry between them was worth exploring. As were the emotions she roused in him. She wouldn't react well to being rushed, but it appeared he'd have several days with which to nudge her along.

"Any idea how you'd like to spend the day?" he asked. "It's unlikely we'll be dug out any time soon,"

She gestured to the mountain. "I thought you'd be dying to go skiing. Isn't all this new powder a skier's dream?"

How to explain his reluctance to leave her behind? "It's not as much fun alone."

"That makes sense." But her expression didn't match her words.

"You don't look convinced."

"You've never struck me as a man who sits still for long. I can't imagine you'll be happier here than out on the slopes."

"Are you trying to get rid of me for some reason?"

"No. Nothing like that."

"I don't want to leave you and Maggie alone."

"We'd have been alone if your guests showed up. No reason anything has to be different."

Except that it was. This was no longer a business trip. It had morphed into a vacation. And Liam had very different expectations for how he'd like to spend his time.

That night's dinner had been arranged for six, but since it was beef medallions in a red wine sauce with mushrooms, herb-roasted potatoes and creamed spinach, it had been a simple matter for the chef to make only two portions.

With the chandelier lights dimmed and flickering candlelight setting a romantic scene, the tension kept rising between them. Liam had dated enough women to recognize when a woman was attracted to him, but he'd never known one as miserable about it as Hadley.

"You are obviously uncomfortable about something," he commented, breaking the silence that had grown heavier since the chef had presented them with dessert and left for the night.

"Why would you say that?"

"Because you are as jumpy as a filly being stalked by a mountain lion."

Her brows drew together. "That's ridiculous."

"What's on your mind?" he persisted, ignoring her protest. When she pressed her lips together and shook her head, he decided to talk for her. "Let me guess. Since you started acting all skittish shortly after learning we were going to be snowed in alone together, you think I'm going to seduce you." Liam sipped his wine and observed her reaction.

"I don't think that."

He could see that was true. So what gave her cause for concern? "Oh," he drew the word out, "then you're worried you're going to try to seduce me."

One corner of her mouth lifted in a self-deprecating grin. "As if I could do that." She had visibly relaxed thanks to his bluntness.

"You aren't giving yourself enough credit."

She rolled her eyes, but refrained from arguing. "I thought you'd given up casual sex."

"I have. Which should make you feel more relaxed about our circumstances." He set his elbows on the table and leaned forward.

"Okay, maybe I'm a little on edge."

"What can I do to put you at ease?"

"Nothing. It's my problem."

"But I don't want there to be a problem."

"You really aren't going to let this go, are you?"

He shook his head. "What if I promise that whatever you say will not be held against you after we leave here?" He spread his arms wide. "Go ahead, give me your best shot."

"It's awkward and embarrassing."

She paused as if hoping he'd jump in and reassure her again. Liam held his tongue and tapped his chest to remind her he could take whatever she had to dish out.

"I'm attracted to you, and that's making me uncomfortable, because you're my boss and I shouldn't be having those sorts of feelings for you."

He'd been expecting something along those lines and wished she wasn't so damned miserable about feeling that way. "See, that wasn't so hard. I like you. You like me."

"And nothing can happen between us."

"If that's what you really want." If that was the case, he would respect her decision. But nothing would convince him to like it.

"It is." Her expression closed down. "I made a mistake once, and I promised myself I'd never do anything like that ever again."

"You are too hard on yourself. Everyone screws up. You shouldn't beat yourself up about it."

"That's what my best friend tells me."

"Sounds like a smart friend." Liam dropped the subject. Asking her to confide in him would only cause her to shut down, and he didn't want that to happen. "What should we do after dinner? We could watch a movie. Or there's board games stored in the front closet if you think you can best me at Monopoly or backgammon."

"You don't really want to play either of those, do you?"

"Not really."

"I suppose if you were entertaining clients, you'd go out to a bar, or if you didn't have the energy for that after a full day of skiing, you'd sit around drinking scotch and smoking cigars."

"Something like that." Neither of those activities sounded like much fun while his thoughts were filled with Hadley's soft lips yielding beneath his and the wonders of her generous curves pressed against his body. Gripped by a fit of restlessness, Liam pushed back from the table. "You know, I think I'll head into town and grab a drink. Don't wait up. It'll probably be a late night. I'll see you tomorrow."

Eight

Hadley sat in miserable silence for several minutes after the front door closed behind Liam, cursing her decision to push him away. Was it fair that doing the right thing made her unhappy? Shouldn't she be feeling wretched only after acting against her principles?

With a disgusted snort, Hadley cleared the dessert dishes from the table and set them in the sink. With a lonely evening stretched out before her, she puttered in the kitchen, washing the plates and wineglasses, wiping down the already-immaculate counters and unloading the dishwasher.

None of these tasks kept her thoughts occupied, and she ran her conversation with Liam over and over in her head, wishing she'd explained about Noah so Liam would understand why it was so important that she maintain a professional distance.

After half an hour she'd run out of tasks to occupy her in the kitchen and carried Maggie upstairs. The baby was almost half-asleep and showed no signs of rousing as Hadley settled her into the crib. For a long time she stared down at the motherless child, her heart aching as she contemplated how fond she'd become of the baby and realized that the end of January was fast approaching.

Soon she wouldn't have to worry over Maggie's welfare. Liam would find another nanny. It shouldn't make her heart ache, and yet it did. Hadley began to pace the comfortable guest room. Once again she'd let her heart lead instead of her head. Nor was it only her charge who had slipped beneath her skin. Liam had skirted her defenses as well. Earlier that day she'd accepted that Liam wasn't Maggie's father, but yet he'd demonstrated a willingness to step up and raise his niece, and that said a lot about his character.

Hadley stopped to peer out the window but could see nothing but fat white flakes falling past the glass. The day she'd driven up the driveway to the ranch house, she'd never dreamed that the crush she'd developed on him a decade earlier might have been lying dormant all these years. Born of hero worship and adolescent fantasies, it shouldn't have survived all the life lessons Hadley had learned. Her guilt over the role she'd played in Anna's accident, her poor judgment with Noah, the financial consequences of choosing the wrong career. All of these should have made her incapable of acting foolishly.

So far they had.

But that was before Liam Wade reentered her life. Before, she couldn't think about the man without longing to fall into bed with him, ignoring all consequences for the chance to be wildly happy for a few hours.

The baby made a sound, and Hadley went to make sure she was still asleep. Over the past week, Maggie had grown more vocal as she slept.

Hadley settled a light blanket over the baby, knowing she was fussing for no good reason. She still couldn't calm the agitation that zinged along her nerves in the aftermath of turning aside Liam's advances during dinner.

"I should have just slept with him," she murmured, the declaration sounding unbearably loud in the silent house. Then at least she'd have a good reason to regret her actions.

"It's not too late to change your mind," a low male voice said from the doorway.

Startled, Hadley whirled in Liam's direction. Heat seared her cheeks as she spotted him lounging against the door jam, an intense gleam in his half-lidded eyes. "I thought you went out."

"I did, but it wasn't any fun without you." He advanced toward her, his intent all too clear.

When his arms went around her, pulling her tight against his strong body, Hadley stopped resisting. This is what she wanted. Why fight against something that felt this right?

"Kiss me quick before I change my mind," she told him, her head falling back so she could meet his gaze. "And don't stop."

She laced her fingers through his hair as his mouth seized hers. Nerve endings writhing like live electric wires, she lost all concept of gravity. Up. Down. Left. Right. Without Liam's arms anchoring her to him, she would have shot into space like an overheated bottle rocket.

After the first hard press of his lips to hers, Liam's kiss gentled and slowed. He took his time ravishing her mouth with a bit of pressure here and a flick of his tongue there. Hadley panted in a mix of excitement and frustration. He'd been so greedy for that first kiss. She'd expected what followed would be equally fast and demanding.

"Your lips are amazing," he murmured, nipping at her lower lip. "Soft. Pliant. I could spend all night just kissing you."

Pleasure speared downward as his tongue dipped into the shallow indents left behind by his tender bite. "Other parts of me are just as interesting." She arched her back and rubbed her breasts against his chest, hoping he'd take the hint and relieve their ache.

"I imagine you will provide an unlimited source of fascination." He nuzzled his lips against her neck and bracketed her hips with his long fingers, pulling her against his erection. "Shall we go to my room and see?"

"Oh yes."

He surprised her by scooping her into his arms and carrying her next door. He set her on her feet in the middle of the dark room and pushed her to arm's length.

"I'm going to turn on the fireplace so we have some light. Then I'm going to take off your clothes and spend the rest of the night pleasuring every inch of your body."

His words left her breathless and giddy. "That sounds great," she replied, reaching out to the footboard for balance. "But I demand equal time to get to know you."

White teeth flashed in the darkness as he shot her a wolfish smile. "I love a woman who knows what she wants."

While he crossed to the enormous stone fireplace, Hadley took advantage of his back being turned to strip off her sweater and shimmy out of her black stretch pants. Clad only in a pale blue camisole and bikini briefs, she shivered in anticipation. The gas fireplace lit with a *whoosh*, and Liam turned back to her as flames began to cast flickering shadows around the room. In the dimness, his eyes seemed impossibly bright as his gaze traveled over her.

"You are gorgeous."

Although his tone gave the words a sincerity she appreciated, Hadley doubted she measured up to the women he'd been with in the past. "So are you." A sudden rush of shyness made her sound flip, but Liam didn't seem to notice.

He held out his hand. "Come here."

She couldn't have resisted his command even if her feet had been glued to the floor. More than anything she wanted his hands on her.

Together they stripped off his sweater and the longsleeve shirt beneath. Firelight highlighted the perfection of his arms, shoulders and abs as her fingers trailed along his hot, silky skin.

"You have such an amazing body," she murmured, marveling at the perfection of every hard muscle. "I'm a little worried that you'll be disappointed in me."

He chuckled. "You have nothing to fear. You are beautiful in every way."

As if to demonstrate that, his hands began to slide upward, catching the hem of her camisole and riding it from her hips to her ribs. Hadley closed her eyes to better savor the magic of his palms gliding over her skin and threw her head back as he reached her breasts, cupping them briefly before sweeping the camisole over her head.

"I was right," he murmured, dropping to his knees to press a kiss to her abdomen.

Hadley quaked as his mouth opened and he laved her skin from belly button to hip. With his head cupped in her hands, she fought to maintain her balance as his fingers hooked in her panties and rode them down her legs. With one knee he nudged her feet apart, and she shut her eyes as his fingers trailed upward, skimming the sensitive inside of her thighs until he reached the spot where she burned.

As his fingers brushed against her pubic hair, she cried out in surprise. He'd barely touched her, and her insides were tense and primed to explode.

"You like that." He wasn't asking a question. "What about this?"

With one finger he opened her and slipped into her wetness. Hadley gasped as pleasure hammered her. Her knees began to shake, threatening to topple her.

"I can't...stand."

He cupped her butt in his hands and steadied her. "I've got you, baby. Just let go."

Her knees buckled, and Liam guided her downward and just a little forward so she ended up straddling his thighs, her breasts flattened against his hard chest. He cupped her head in his hand and brought their lips together once more. This kiss, deep and hungry, held none of the gentle restraint he'd shown earlier. It was a demonstration of his passion for her, and she was enthralled by his need.

"You need to get naked," she gasped as he rolled her beneath him on the thick, fluffy throw rug.

"Soon."

His mouth trailed moisture down her neck and over the upper curve of her breast. As delicious as it was to be slowly devoured by him, the desire clawing at her was building to a painful crescendo. She writhed beneath him, her sensitive inner thighs rasping against his soft corduroy pants as she lifted her knees to shift him deeper into the cradle of her hips.

"Oh, Liam. That's so good."

He'd taken one nipple into his mouth, and the erotic tug sharpened her longing. She ached to feel him buried inside her. Her nails bit into his sides, breath coming in shallow pants as he rocked his hips and drove his erection against her.

When she slipped her hands between them and went for the button that held his trousers closed, he caught her wrists and raised her arms over her head.

"Patience," he murmured before turning his attention to her other breast.

She thrashed her head from side to side as sensation overwhelmed her. Trapped as she was beneath him, Hadley was still able to rotate her hips and grind herself against his hard length. Liam groaned and his lips trailed down her body.

It had never been this good before. Fire consumed her at Liam's every kiss. His hot breath skated across her sensitive flesh. Suddenly her hands were free. Liam continued to slide lower; his shoulders shifted between her thighs, spreading her wide. He grazed his fingertips across her nipples, ripping a moan from her.

Before she'd even registered the pleasure of his large hands cupping her breasts, he dipped his tongue into her hot wet core and sent her spiraling into orbit. Anticipation had been gnawing on her all day, and Liam's expert loving drove her fast and hard into her first orgasm. As it ripped through her, Hadley panted his name. His fingers dug into her backside, holding her tight against his mouth as she shuddered and came in what felt like endless waves of pleasure.

"Nice," she murmured. "Very, very, very nice."

Once her body lay lifeless in the aftermath of her climax, Liam dropped a light kiss on her abdomen and left her to strip off the rest of his clothes. Despite the lack of strength in her limbs, Hadley struggled up onto her elbows to better watch his gorgeous body emerge.

She was awed by his broad shoulders, bulging biceps, washboard abs, but when he stripped off his trousers and she got a glimpse of his strong thighs and the spectacular chiseling of his firm butt, she forgot how to breathe. His erection sprang out as he peeled off his underwear, and her gaze locked on its rigid length.

She licked her lips.

"Do that again and this won't last long," Liam growled as he withdrew a condom from his wallet and made quick work of sliding it on.

She raised an eyebrow. "You're prepared?"

"I've been prepared since the day you walked into my house."

His impassioned declaration made her smile. She held out her arms to him and he lowered himself onto her. Almost immediately the tip of him found where she needed him most, but he held back and framed her face with his hands.

"I don't take this next step lightly," he told her, showing way more restraint than Hadley could manage at the moment.

As much as she appreciated what he was trying to communicate about the depth of his desire for her, she shied away from letting his affirmation into her heart. If this wasn't about two people enjoying an enormous amount of sexual chemistry, she might lose herself to the fantasy that they had a future. Where Liam was concerned, she had to maintain her head.

But all perspective was lost as he kissed her. Not waiting for him to take charge, she drove her tongue into his mouth and let him taste her passion and longing. Something in her soul clicked into place as she fisted her hands in his hair and felt him slide into her in one smooth stroke.

They moaned together and broke off the kiss to pant in agitated gasps.

"Like that," she murmured, losing herself in Liam's intense gaze. She tipped her hips and urged him deeper. "Just like that."

"There's more," he promised, beginning to move, sliding out of her with delicious deliberation before thrusting home.

"That's…" She lost the words as he found the perfect rhythm.

And then it was all heat and friction and a rapidly building pressure in her loins that demanded every bit of her attention. Being crushed beneath Liam's powerful body as he surged inside her was perhaps the most amazing experience of Hadley's life. She'd never known such delirious joy. He was passionate, yet sensitive to her body in a way no one had ever been before.

The beginnings of a second orgasm caught her in its grip. Liam continued his movements, driving her further and further toward fulfillment without taking his own. In a blurry part of her mind, she recognized that and dug her fingers into his back.

"Come with me," she urged, closer now.

"Yes."

At his growl she began to break apart. "Now."

His thrusts grew more frantic. She clung to him as wave after wave of pleasure broke over her. Liam began to shudder as he reached his own climax. She thought she heard her name on his lips as a thousand pinpoints of light exploded inside her. He was everything to her, and for a long, satisfying moment, nothing else mattered.

The weather cleared after thirty-six hours, but neither Liam nor Hadley looked forward to heading back to Texas when the airports reopened. What had happened between them was too new, its metamorphosis incomplete. Liam dreaded the return to reality. The demands of the ranch were sure to overwhelm him, and he wanted more time alone with Hadley.

The wheels of the Cessna Mustang touched down on the Royal airport runway and a sense of melancholy overwhelmed Liam. He sighed as he came in sight of his hangar. The last four days had been perfect. The solitude was exactly what he'd needed to break through Hadley's shell and reach the warm, wonderful woman beneath.

She was funny and sensual. He'd loved introducing her to new foods and wines. She'd matched his ardor in bed and demonstrated a curiosity that amused him. Once she'd let loose, she'd completely mesmerized him. He hadn't been able to get enough of her. And when they were too exhausted to move, he'd held her in his arms and enjoyed the peaceful sounds of her breathing.

He'd never felt in tune with a woman like this. Part of it was likely due to the year off he'd taken to reevaluate his priorities. Hadley was the package. She captivated him both in and out of bed and let him know pretty fast that his past practices in dealing with women weren't going to work on her. He had to be original. She deserved nothing but his best.

Maggie fussed as he locked up the plane. She hadn't slept much on the way home and was probably overtired. He watched Hadley settle the baby into the car seat and sensed the change in the air. Hadley's expression had grown serious, and her eyes lost their infectious sparkle. Playtime was over. She was back on the job.

"She's going to be fine as soon as she gets home and settled into her crib," Hadley said, coaxing the baby to take her pacifier.

"Maybe you should spend the night in case she doesn't settle down."

Hadley shook her head. "I'll stay until you get back from checking in at the ranch, but I can't stay all night."

"Not even if I need you?"

"You'll do just fine without me."

He wasn't sure if she had missed his meaning or if she was pretending not to understand that he wanted her to spend the night with him. Either way, she'd put enough determination behind her declaration to let him know no amount of persuasion was going to change her mind.

"I'm going to miss you," he said, trying a different approach.

"And I'm going to miss you," she replied, her voice brisk and not the least bit romantic. "But that was Colorado and this is Texas. We had a nice time, but it's over."

To Liam's shock, he realized he was back to square one. "I think it takes two people to decide it's over."

"You're my boss. We just need to get things back to normal."

"Or we need to change what normal is."

She didn't look happy. "I'm not sure what you mean."

"We made a great start getting to know each other these last few days. I'd like to continue."

"I don't feel comfortable in that sort of arrangement."

"Then why don't you quit?" He would not fire her. She needed to choose to be with him. "If it's about the money, I'll pay you until the end of the month."

Her mouth popped open, but before she could speak, Maggie let loose a piercing wail. "Why don't we talk about this later? I really think Maggie needs to get home."

Liam agreed, but hated the idea of postponing the conversation. He wanted to batter her with arguments until she came around to his point of view. Giving her space to think would only give her space to fortify her defenses.

"Fine. But we will talk later."

Only they didn't. By the time Liam returned from the ranch offices, it was close to midnight. Hadley was half-dead on her feet, only just having gotten Maggie to sleep after a rough evening. She was in no condition to listen to his arguments for continuing what they'd begun in Colorado, and he had to watch in frustrated silence as she put Waldo in his carrier and drove away.

With disappointment buzzing in his thoughts like a pesky fly, he expected sleep to elude him. But he'd underestimated his own weariness and shortly after his head hit the pillow, he fell asleep.

When the dream came, it didn't feature Hadley, but his mother. They stood in the ranch house's entry hall and he was desperately afraid. She was leaving. He clung to her hand and begged her not to go. She tugged hard against his grip, her face a mask of disgust.

"Mommy, don't go."

"Why would I want to stay with you? I left because I couldn't bear to be trapped in this prison of a ranch in the middle of nowhere."

"But I need you."

"I never wanted to be a mother. You and your brother were a mistake."

She ripped free and strode through the front door without ever looking back. Liam followed her, but it was as if he moved through mud. His short legs couldn't propel him fast enough, and he reached the broad wraparound porch just in time to see her taillights disappear down the driveway.

Liam woke in a sweat. His throat ached and heart pounded as he recalled his mother's words. As realistic as the exchange had felt, he recalled no such event from his childhood. His subconscious had merely been reacting to Hadley's evasiveness. So why hadn't his dream featured her?

Lingering pain carved up his chest. He felt weak and unsteady. A child's fear pummeled him. Buried deep in his mind was the horror of being rejected by his mother. She was supposed to love him and care for him. Instead, she'd demonstrated no remorse when she'd abandoned her sons to pursue her real estate career.

And it was this defining fact that had caused him to never fully invest himself in romantic relationships. He couldn't bear the idea of giving his heart to a woman only to have her choose something else over him. Deep down, what he craved was lasting love.

His heart had led him to Hadley. And given the timing of his dream, his subconscious was worried that he'd made a huge mistake.

Hadley was in the nursery folding a freshly laundered basket of Maggie's clothes when Liam appeared. He'd been subdued and circumspect around her the last couple days, and she suspected she'd done too good a job convincing him that what had happened between them in Vail had been a singular event never to be repeated.

But that wasn't at all what she wanted. She was pretty

sure she'd fallen in love with him during those four days. And that left her in a quandary.

"I know it's short notice," he said. "But will you be my date for the grand reopening of Royal Memorial's west wing tomorrow night?"

The word *date* caused a spike in Hadley's heartbeat. She told herself to stop being stupid.

"Sure. What time should I have Maggie ready?"

"Not Maggie." His green eyes pierced her facade of professionalism. "You. It's a cocktail party complete with adult beverages, finger food and fancy duds." He kept his voice light, but his expression was stony.

"Of course I'll go with you." She matched his tone, kept her glee hidden. "I've heard wonderful things about the new wing. You and the other members of the Texas Cattleman's Club were instrumental in raising the funds that enabled the restoration to move forward, weren't you?"

"We felt it was important for the community to get the hospital back to one hundred percent as soon as possible." He took her hand, threaded his fingers through hers. "How about I pick you up at seven?"

Her brain short-circuited at the way he was staring at their joined hands. As if the simple contact was at once comforting and a puzzle he couldn't figure out.

"Sure." Before she recognized what she planned to do, Hadley stepped into Liam's space and lifted onto her toes to plant a kiss on his lips.

All day long she'd been thinking about how much she wanted to be in his arms. Not to feel the stirring passion of his lovemaking, but the heart-wrenching bliss of their connection, which consisted of both sexual and spiritual components. The blend was different from anything she'd ever known, and she'd begun to neglect her defenses.

Liam brought their clasped hands to his chest and slid his free hand beneath her hair to cup her head. He explored her lips with tantalizing pressure, giving her the merest taste of passion. Although she'd initiated the kiss, she was happy to let him set the pace.

When at last his lips lifted from hers, they were both breathing unsteadily.

"I've been thinking about kissing you all day," he murmured, lips trailing over her ear, making her shudder. "I can't concentrate anymore. The entire ranch staff thinks I've lost my mind."

His words excited a flurry of goose bumps. "It's that way for me, too. I forgot to put a diaper back on Maggie before I put her back in her Onesie this morning. And then I made her bottle and put it into the cupboard instead of the container of formula."

"Will you stay at the ranch tomorrow night after the party?"

She wanted to very much, but would this interfere with her determination not to get emotionally involved? "If you wish."

"I very much wish."

"Then that's what I'll do."

Nine

Liam wasn't sure how he was going to make it through the grand opening, when all he could think about was what he had to look forward to afterward. He pulled his truck into a visitor space at Hadley's apartment building and stepped out. For tonight's event he'd exchanged denim and plaid in favor of a custom-tailored charcoal suit.

Anticipation zipped along his nerve endings as he pushed the button in the entry vestibule that would let Hadley know he'd arrived. Her voice sounded distorted as she told him to come up. Her apartment was on the second floor. He stepped into the elevator, feeling the give of the cables as it adjusted to his weight. The building had obviously seen a lot of tenants, because it showed wear and tear in the carpets, layers of paint and light fixtures.

Standing before Hadley's door, Liam paused to assess his state of agitation. Had he ever been nervous going to pick up a woman for a date? Yet here he stood, palms sweating, heart thundering, mouth dry.

The door opened before he lifted his hand to knock. Hadley looked surprised to see him standing in the hallway. Waldo rushed forward to wind himself around Liam's legs.

"Hi." She gestured him in. "I thought maybe the elevator had decided to be fussy again."

He picked up the cat without taking his eyes from Hadley and stepped into her apartment. "You look beautiful."

She wore a figure-skimming sleeveless black dress with a round neckline and a half-circle cutout that bared her cleavage. Despite there being nothing overtly provocative about the style, Liam thought she looked incredibly sexy. She'd pinned her blond waves up in a complicated hairstyle that looked as if it could tumble onto her shoulders at any second. And he badly wanted to make that happen. Body alive with cravings better reserved for later that evening, he shifted his gaze to her only jewelry, a pair of long crystal earrings that swung in sassy rhythm as she tipped her head and regarded him curiously.

"Thank you." Her half smile captivated him. "You look nice, as well. I'll grab my purse and we can get going." She picked up a small black clutch and a sheer red scarf sparkling with clusters of sequins that she draped over her shoulders. It added a flamboyant touch to her otherwise monochrome black ensemble.

Realizing he was staring at her like a smitten teenager, Liam cleared his throat. His brain was having trouble summoning words. "All set?"

"Are you expecting a large crowd tonight?" she asked as she fit her key into the lock and set the dead bolt.

"About a hundred. Those responsible for coordinating the fund-raising efforts and the largest contributors."

"What a wonderful thing you've done."

Her glowing praise lightened his step. He laced his fingers through hers and lifted her hand to brush a kiss across her knuckles. "It was a group effort," he said, feeling unusually humble. "But thank you."

In truth, he was proud of the work he and the other members of the Texas Cattleman's Club had done in the aftermath of the tornado. As leaders in the community, they'd banded together during the time of crisis and although progress had been slow, they'd restored the town to its former state.

The drive from Hadley's apartment to the hospital took ten minutes. Liam filled the time with a description about an outfit his cousin Ivy had bought for Maggie that featured a chambray Onesie with three tiers of ruffles and a crocheted cowboy hat and boots.

"Complete with yarn spurs." Liam shook his head in mock dismay.

"How adorable." Hadley regarded his expression with a wry smile. "You are just going to have to get used to the fact that girls love to dress up and look pretty."

"I know," he grumbled, knowing she loved to scold him. "But is it really going to be all frilly stuff and hair bows?"

"Yes."

Liam pulled to a stop in front of the hospital's new west wing entrance, and the look he gave Hadley made her laugh. A year ago he never would have imagined himself discussing an infant's wardrobe, much less with a beautiful woman.

A valet opened the passenger door and helped Hadley out of the truck. Liam was grinning as he accepted the ticket from the uniformed attendant and caught up with Hadley, sliding his hand over her hip in a not-so-subtle show of ownership. She sent him an unguarded smile of such delight, his chest hurt. If this was heartache, bring it on.

"This is amazing," Hadley murmured as they entered the spacious lobby of the redesigned west wing, taking in the patterned marble floors and triangular glass ceiling over the entrance. In the center of the room, a bronze statue of a cowboy roping a running cow had the names of all those who'd lost their lives during the tornado etched around the base. "A wonderful tribute."

Spying Case Baxter, Liam drew Hadley toward the rancher, who had eyes only for the redhead beside him.

"Case," Liam called to gain his attention.

The president of the Cattleman's Club looked away from his fiancée and blinked as if to reorient himself. At last his gaze focused on Liam.

"Hey, Liam." His teeth flashed as he extended his hand to meet Liam's. "Mellie, you've met Liam Wade."

"Of course." A friendly smile curved her lips. Her green eyes darted toward Hadley before settling back on Liam. "At the reception when Case was elected president."

"And this is Hadley Stratton." Liam didn't explain how they knew each other. Why introduce her as Maggie's nanny when she'd become so much more? "Mellie Winslow and Case Baxter, our club president."

The two couples finished exchanging greetings and Case spoke. "Gotta hand it to you, Liam." He gestured around, his grin wide, posture relaxed. "This is one hell of a facility."

"Have you toured the neonatal unit?" Mellie asked.

"We just arrived," Hadley admitted, completely at ease tucked into the half circle of Liam's left arm. After their conversation in Vail, he'd half expected her to balk at going public with their developing relationship.

"The whole wing is really terrific," Mellie was saying, "but that unit in particular is very impressive."

Liam agreed. He'd seen the neonatal facility during his many trips to the hospital in his role as chairman of the fund-raising committee, but he was looking forward to showing it to Hadley.

"Why don't we head up now," he suggested, seeing Hadley's interest. There would be plenty of time later to catch up with Mac, Jeff Hartley and other members of the Texas Cattleman's Club. "We'll catch up with you later," he told Case.

"They seem like a nice couple," Hadley commented as they waited for the elevator that would take them to the maternity ward on the fourth floor.

"I don't know Mellie all that well, but Case is a great guy and they appear happy."

The elevator doors opened, and Liam gestured Hadley ahead of him.

Despite the crowd gathered to party in the lobby, they had the elevator to themselves. As soon as the car began to move, Liam tugged Hadley into his arms and dropped his lips to hers.

The instant Liam kissed her, Hadley wrapped her arms around his neck and yielded to his demand. Frantic to enjoy the few seconds of isolation, they feasted on each other. But all too soon, a *ding* announced that they'd reached their floor, cutting short their impassioned embrace.

"Damn these modern elevators," Liam muttered, his hands sliding off her body.

Hadley, her cheeks hot in the aftermath of the kiss, smiled foolishly. She surveyed his chiseled lips, searching for any sign that her red lipstick had rubbed off. Taking the hand Liam offered her, she stepped past a tour group that was waiting to head downstairs.

"Let's see if we can catch that tour," he said, tugging her down the hallway toward a group of well-dressed guests listening to a tall, handsome man in his late thirties.

"Next is our neonatal unit," the man said, gesturing down the hall as he started forward.

"That's Dr. Parker Reese," Liam explained, tucking Hadley's hand into the crook of his arm. "He's a neonatal specialist. Brilliant guy. We're lucky to have him."

It was hard to focus on Dr. Reese's description of the neonatal unit's state-of-the-art equipment and dedicated staff while her senses were filled with the scent, sight and feel of Liam so close beside her.

He stiffened, dragging Hadley out of her musings. She returned her attention to the speaker only to discover Dr.

Reese had passed off the tour to a slender nurse with blond hair pulled back into a bun and a brisk way of speaking.

"We call her Janey Doe," the nurse said, a hint of sadness clouding her direct green gaze. "She is holding her own, but each day is a struggle. However, thanks to Dr. Reese…" The nurse glanced up at the tall doctor, and Hadley got the impression that equal parts personal and professional admiration curved her lips.

The crowd began to follow Dr. Reese toward the birthing suites, but Liam showed no interest in continuing on. He made a beeline straight for the nurse and introduced himself.

"Hello, I'm Liam Ward. And this is Hadley Stratton."

"Clare Connelly." The nurse shook their hands. "Thank you for all your hard work on the restoration of this wing. It's such an amazing facility to work in."

"It was an important project for our town." Although his words were courteous, his tone was strained. "I was wondering if you could tell me a little bit more about Janey Doe."

Knowing that she had missed a big chunk of the story, Hadley scanned Liam's expression, noticed his tight lips, the muscle jumping in his jaw and wondered at his interest.

"She was found on the floor of a truck stop thirty miles from here…"

"No sign of her mother?" Liam's question reverberated with disgust.

Clare shook her head slowly. "None, I'm afraid."

"You mean she just left her there?" Hadley's chest tightened. "How could she do something like that?"

"She was probably young and scared. Janey was very small and obviously premature. It's possible the mother thought she was dead and freaked out."

Hadley appreciated how Clare stuck up for Baby Janey's mother but could see that none of her assumptions had eased Liam's displeasure. He was staring into the neonatal unit, his attention laser focused on the middle incubator. Was Maggie on his mind? Without knowing for certain that Maggie was related to Liam, Diane Garner had left her granddaughter in his care. Or was he thinking how his own mother had left him to be raised by his grandfather?

"What will happen to her?" Hadley asked, her own gaze drawn toward the incubator and the precious bundle. The baby was hooked up to a feeding tube, oxygen and monitors, making it impossible to get a clear look at her face.

"She'll go into foster care and eventually be adopted." Although the words were hopeful, the nurse's smile was strained.

Hadley recognized that look. She'd seen it on the faces of plenty of her fellow nannies who'd grown too attached to their charges.

"Thank you for your time." Liam glanced down at Hadley, his expression unreadable. "Shall we rejoin the party?"

All warmth had been leeched from his manner by the story of Baby Janey. Hadley nodded and strolled back toward the elevator at Liam's side. Although her hand remained tucked in his arm, the emotional distance between them was as wide as an ocean. She recognized that this had nothing to do with her. Liam had retreated behind walls she couldn't penetrate, defenses a young boy had erected to deal with his mother's abandonment.

"Why don't we get out of here," Hadley suggested as they descended in the elevator. "I don't think you're in the mood for a party anymore."

"You're right." One side of his lips kicked up. His gaze warmed as he bent down to brush a kiss across her lips. "But I should at least spend an hour here. If for no other reason than to show off my gorgeous date."

Hadley blushed at the compliment. It didn't matter what

anyone else thought of her looks; as long as she could bask in Liam's sizzling admiration, she felt flawless.

By the time the elevator doors opened, Liam seemed to have gotten past whatever had affected him in the neonatal unit. Once again the charming rascal she adored, he worked his way around the room, collecting smiles and promises of funds for several pieces of equipment the hospital still needed.

Watching him work, Hadley reveled in his charisma and marveled at his ability to strike just the right chord with everyone he met. This is what made him an astute businessman and a masterful horseman. He didn't approach every situation with the same tactic.

"I'm ready to get out of here if you are," he murmured in her ear an hour later.

"Absolutely," she replied, anticipating what awaited them back at the ranch house.

On the ride home, Liam lapsed back into silence, his public persona put aside once more. Hadley stared at his profile in concern. Her hopes for a romantic evening fled. Liam's troubled thoughts preoccupied him.

As Liam unlocked the front door, Hadley set aside her disappointment and decided to see if she could get him to open up. "How about I make some coffee and we talk about what's bothering you?"

Liam's chin dipped in ascent. "I'll get a fire started in the den."

Once she got the coffee brewing, Hadley ran upstairs to check on Maggie. She found the baby sleeping and Candace in the rocking chair, reading on her tablet. The housekeeper looked up in surprise as Hadley crossed to the crib.

"You're home early. Did you have fun?"

"It was a nice party. The facilities are wonderful." Hadley knew she hadn't directly answered Candace's question. While she'd enjoyed the company and the conversation,

Liam's mood after learning about Janey Doe had unsettled her. "Thanks for watching Maggie. Any problems?"

Candace got to her feet. "She went to sleep at eight and hasn't made a peep since."

"Good." Maggie's hair was soft beneath Hadley's fingers as she brushed a strand off the baby's forehead. "I made some coffee if you're interested in joining us for a cup."

"No, thanks. I'm almost done with this book. I'm going to head back to the carriage house and finish it."

The two women headed downstairs. Liam was in the kitchen and gave Candace a cheerful thank-you as she left. By the time the housekeeper pulled the back door shut behind her, icy air filled the space. Hadley shivered and filled the mugs Liam had fetched from the cupboard. Cradling the warm ceramic in her hands, she led the way into the den and settled on the sofa.

Liam set his mug on the mantel and chose to stand, staring into the fire. "I'm sorry I was such bad company tonight."

"You weren't bad company." Hadley was careful not to let her disappointment show. "Obviously something is bothering you. Do you feel like talking about it?"

"It was hearing about Janey Doe."

"That was a very upsetting story." She refrained from adding her own opinion on the subject, wanting Liam to share his thoughts.

"Her mother just leaving her like that. On the floor of a public bathroom. She could have died."

Hadley kept her voice neutral. "She was fortunate that someone found her."

"I thought it was bad that Maggie's grandmother left her with us. This is so much worse. How could any mother abandon her child like that?"

"Not every woman is cut out for motherhood." Hadley

thought about all the families she'd worked for in the last five years and all the stories shared by her fellow nannies. "Sometimes the responsibility is more than they can handle."

"You mean they wish they'd never given birth."

Trying her best to hide a wince, Hadley responded, "I mean that parenting can be challenging, and sometimes if a woman has to do it alone, she might not feel capable."

"Perhaps if she's young and without financial means, I could understand, but what can you say about a woman who has family and fortune and turns her back on her children so she can pursue her career?"

Not wanting to sound as if she were picking sides, Hadley chose her next words carefully. "That she acted in her best interest and not in the best interest of her children."

Liam crossed to the sofa and joined Hadley. A huge gust of air escaped his lungs as he picked up her hand and squeezed her fingers. "Maggie must never know that her grandmother left her with us the way she did. I won't have her wondering why she didn't want to keep her."

This was the true source of Liam's disquiet, Hadley realized. Whether he acknowledged it or not, being abandoned by his mother had sabotaged his ability to trust women. And where did that leave Hadley?

Liam could feel the concern rolling off Hadley as he spoke. He'd grown attuned to her moods since their days in Vail and didn't have to see her expression to know her thoughts.

Hadley covered their clasped hands with her free one and squeezed. "It's okay to be angry with your mother for not being there for you."

The knot of emotions in his chest tightened at her words. Not once as a child had he seen his grandfather demonstrate anything but understanding toward the daughter who'd run out on her children. Liam had grown up thinking that what his mother had done was acceptable, while inside him was a howling banshee of anger and hurt that was never given a voice.

"You might feel better if you talked through how it made you feel."

"I don't know how to begin." The words, long bottled up inside him, were poised to explode. "I grew up thinking it was okay that she chose to leave us with Grandfather."

"Why?"

"She had a career that she loved, and like you said earlier, she really wasn't cut out to be a mom. She got pregnant when she was seventeen. Our father was on the rodeo circuit and had no interest in settling down to raise a family. Mother felt the same way. Grandfather always said she had big dreams." Liam offered up a bitter laugh. "I guess Kyle and I are lucky she decided to have us at all."

Hadley's shocked intake of breath left Liam regretting the venomous statement.

"You don't mean that."

"No," he agreed. "Although I've thought it a hundred times, I don't think she ever considered terminating her pregnancy. In that respect, she didn't take the easy way out."

"Getting back to what you said earlier, growing up did you really think that it was okay she left you with your grandfather, or was that just a coping mechanism?"

"In my mind, I understood her decision. I can't explain to you why that made sense. Maybe because it happened when we were babies and I never knew any different. But recently I started realizing that deep down inside, I hated her for leaving us."

He'd coped by becoming a champion rider. Throwing himself into competition had preoccupied him in his teenage years. The closer he'd gotten to manhood, the less he thought about his mother's absence. The day he'd kissed a girl for the first time, he'd stopped caring.

"Grandfather wasn't exactly the most affectionate guy in the world, but he loved us in his tough-guy way. It might have been different if we were girls, but growing up on the ranch, we had more father figures than anyone could ever want."

"You sound very well adjusted." Her tone said otherwise. "Do you think not having a mother affected your relationships with women?"

"You mean because I never got married?"

"You have a well-earned reputation for being a playboy. I can't imagine you trusted your heart after what your mother did."

"I'll admit to having a wandering eye when it came to women, but that's changed."

"Just because you think you're ready to settle down doesn't mean you've learned to trust." She smiled to take the sting out of the words, but her eyes reflected wariness.

"You're the first woman I've been with in a year," he reminded her, voice rasping as frustration overcame him. "I think that proves I'm already settled down. And I trust you."

Doubt continued to shadow her eyes. He shifted on the couch, angling his body toward her. Gripped by the urgent need to kiss her, Liam dipped his head, shortening the distance between them. He would demonstrate that he was serious about her.

Before he could kiss her, Hadley set her fingertips on his lips. "Thank you for sharing how you felt about your mother not being around. I know that couldn't have been easy."

"It wasn't." And yet it had been a relief to share his anger and sense of betrayal with her. "Thank you for listening."

A moment earlier he'd had something to prove, but the mood was no longer right for seduction. Instead, he planted a friendly kiss on her cheek and held her in a tight hug.

"Let's go upstairs," she murmured, her hands sliding beneath his suit coat, fingers splaying over his back. "I want to make love to you."

At her declaration Liam took a massive hit to his solar plexus. Pulse quickening, he caught her by the hand and drew her toward the stairs. They climbed together in a breathless rush. By the time they reached his bedroom, he was light-headed and more than a little frantic to get them both naked.

Once they crossed the threshold, Hadley plucked the pins from her hair, and it tumbled around her shoulders. Liam came to stand behind her, pushing the thick mass of blond hair away from her neck so he could kiss the slender column and make her shiver. He stripped off his jacket and shirt before turning his attention to the zipper of her dress. With more urgency than finesse, he stroked the dress down her body. When it pooled at her feet, he skimmed his palms back upward, hesitating over the ticklish spot beside her hip bones and investigating each bump of her ribs. The rise and fall of her chest grew less rhythmic as he unfastened her strapless bra and tossed the scrap of fabric on to a nearby chair.

Her hand came up to the back of his head as he cupped her breasts in his palms, thumbs flicking over her tight nipples. She shuddered, her head falling back against his chest, eyes closed as she surrendered to his touch. Although the tightness in his groin demanded that he stop all the foreplay and get down to business, Liam had no intention of rushing. He'd rather savor the silken heat of her skin and bring her body as much pleasure as it could take before seeking his own release.

She turned in his arms, her soft breasts flattening

against his chest as she lifted on tiptoe and sought his mouth with hers. She cupped his face in her hands to hold him still while her tongue darted forward to toy with his. Liam crushed her to him, his fingers dipping below her black lace panties to swallow one butt cheek and lift her against his erection.

They both groaned as he rocked against her. She lifted her foot and wrapped her leg around his hips, angling the bulge behind his zipper into the warm, wet cleft between her thighs. The move unraveled all of Liam's good intentions. He plucked her off her feet and moved toward the bed. She set the soles of her feet against his calves to keep him anchored between her thighs and impatiently removed his belt. It was torture to let her undress him. Every time her fingers glanced off his erection, he ground his teeth and bit back a groan. Only by watching the play of emotions race across her beautiful features was he able to maintain his control. By the time she'd slid open his zipper and pushed the pants down his thighs, his nerves screamed with impatience.

Liam stripped off pants, shoes, socks and underwear without ever taking his eyes off Hadley. With a sensual smile she moved backward, making room for him on the mattress. He stalked onto the bed, fitting between her spread thighs, covering her torso with his before claiming her lips in a hard kiss and her body with a single deep thrust.

He loved the way her hips lifted to meet his. How she arched her back and took him all the way in. Her chest vibrated with a moan. A matching sound gathered in his lungs. For a long moment they lay without moving, lips and tongues engaged.

Framing her face in his hands, Liam lifted his lips from hers and stared into her eyes. "Thank you for being my date tonight." It wasn't what he'd intended to say, but nevertheless his words pleased her.

"Thank you for asking. I had a lovely time."

"Lovely?" He grinned. "Let's see if we can't upgrade that to fantastic."

Her eyebrows lifted, daring him to try, while her fingers stroked down his sides. "We're off to a wonderful start."

Liam nuzzled his face into her throat and began to move inside her. "We certainly are."

Ten

The night after the party at the hospital, Hadley was back on the neonatal floor she and Liam had toured. After receiving Maggie's blood work back, Dr. Stringer had determined she should undergo phototherapy treatments for her jaundice. Despite being overwhelmed with ranch business, Liam had accompanied them, wearing his concern openly, but once he discerned how straightforward the process was, he'd relaxed.

Maggie had been stripped down to her diaper and placed in an incubator equipped with a light box that directed blue fluorescent light onto her skin. The light was meant to change the bilirubin into a form that Maggie could more easily expel through her urine. While the procedure was simple, it also took time to work. Maggie would be in the hospital for a couple days while undergoing the treatment. Hadley had agreed to stay with her to let Liam focus on the ranch.

Hadley caught herself humming as she fed Maggie her late-afternoon bottle. After the party at the hospital and the night spent in Liam's arms, she'd stopped resisting what her heart wanted and let herself enjoy every moment of her time with Liam. Why fight against the inevitable? She'd fallen deeply in love with the man.

While a part of her couldn't help but compare what was between her and Liam to what she'd had with Noah, deep down, Hadley recognized the vast difference between the two relationships. With Noah she'd never enjoyed any sort of emotional security. As much as he'd gone on and on about how much he wanted her, how his kids adored her, she always got the sense that he was looking over her shoulder for someone else. It turned out that someone else had been his ex-wife.

Liam never once let her think she was second best. His focus was always completely on her, and Hadley found that both comforting and wildly exciting. For the first time in a long time, she'd stopped focusing on the future and lived quite happily in the moment. School would start when it started. Her time with Maggie would grow shorter. Already arrangements had been made for the new nanny to start at the end of the month. This freed Hadley from her professional responsibilities, and she was eager to see where her relationship with Liam led.

Maggie's eyelids started to droop before the bottle was finished. Hadley set it aside, lifted the infant onto her shoulder and patted her back to encourage a burp. A nurse stood by to test Maggie's bilirubin levels. The staff members were monitoring her every hour or so. Hadley was calling Liam with the results.

His concern for Maggie's welfare had warmed her when she thought the baby was his daughter. Now that she knew Maggie was his brother's child, Liam's commitment was just another reason Hadley found him so attractive.

She was tired of restraining her emotions. Liam made her happy, and she thought he felt the same way about her. When Maggie left the hospital, Hadley promised herself she would stop holding back.

Several days after the hospital party, Liam had an appointment with former Samson Oil lawyer Nolan Dane, who'd joined his father's family law practice. Recently,

Nolan had been accepted for membership in the Texas Cattleman's Club, and the more Liam got to know the man, the more he liked him. The idea that had begun percolating in his mind took on a whole new urgency on the trip back from Colorado. With Maggie in the hospital and Hadley staying with her, the notion had solidified into a plan that required a savvy lawyer.

Liam stepped into Nolan's office. "Looks like you're all settled in."

Nolan grinned. "It's taken longer than I figured on. I didn't expect to be so busy this early in my start-up."

"That must mean you're good. Looks like I've come to the right place."

"Can I offer you coffee or water before we get started?" Nolan gestured Liam into a chair at the round conference table.

"Thanks, but I'm good." While Nolan took a seat, Liam pulled out the paternity test as well as Maggie's birth certificate and her mother's death certificate that Diane Garner had sent at his request.

Nolan found a blank page on his yellow legal pad and met Liam's gaze. "What can I help you with?"

"I have a situation with my twin brother's baby." Liam explained how Maggie had come to Wade Ranch and showed Nolan the DNA results. "Maggie is definitely Kyle's daughter. As soon as I received the test back, I left messages for him on his cell and with the navy."

"How long ago was this?"

"About two weeks."

"And you haven't heard back?"

"Only that the message was delivered. He's a SEAL, which probably means he's on a mission overseas." Liam leaned forward. "And that's where my concerns lie. I don't know a lot about Kyle's domestic situation, but based on his past track record, I'm guessing he's not in a long-term relationship and certainly isn't in a position to take care of a baby."

"You're not in regular contact?"

"Not since he left Royal and joined the navy." Liam wasn't proud of the way he and Kyle had drifted apart, but growing up they'd been uniquely dissimilar in temperament and interests for identical twins.

"And it sounds like the child's grandmother, Diane Garner, is reluctant to be responsible for Maggie."

"She has serious medical issues that prevent her from taking care of Maggie. Which leaves Kyle." Liam paused to give his next words weight. "Or me."

"You want custody?"

While Liam's first instinct was to say yes, he intended to do what was best for Maggie. "I'd like to evaluate all the options."

One corner of Nolan's lips twitched. "You don't have to be diplomatic with me, Liam. I'm here to help you out. Now, what do you want?"

"I'd like custody, but what is most important is to do right by Maggie." Liam gathered his thoughts for a long moment. "I have concerns that while Kyle is off on missions, he'll have to rely on others to take care of her for extended periods of time. And what happens if he's hurt…" Or killed. But Liam couldn't go there. Most days he didn't give Kyle a thought, but sometimes a news report would catch his attention and Liam would wonder what his brother was up to.

"Do you know if Kyle and Margaret were in touch before she drove to Wade Ranch?" Nolan continued to jot down items on his legal pad. "I'm trying to get a sense of their relationship."

"I don't know, but I have to think if Kyle had any idea he was going to be a father that he would have let me know." Liam wanted to believe his brother would step up and do the right thing by his daughter. Yet the fact that Kyle hadn't been in contact disturbed Liam. "That leads me to believe that he didn't know. Either because she hadn't told him or she had the same trouble getting a hold of him I'm having."

Liam didn't add that it was possible Margaret had been nothing more than a weeklong fling for Kyle and he'd had no intention of keeping in touch.

"Because Margaret died in childbirth and she and Kyle weren't married, only her name appears on Maggie's birth certificate. Normally what would happen in this sort of case is that both parties would fill out an AOP. That's an Acknowledgment of Paternity. This form would normally be filled out and signed at the hospital. Or through a certified entity that would then file it with the Vital Statistics Unit. Unfortunately, without Margaret alive to concede that your brother is the child's father, this case will have to go to court. Of course, DNA evidence will prove Kyle's the father. But with you two being identical twins and no way of proving which one of you is the father..." After a long silence, broken only by the scratch of his pen across the legal pad, Nolan glanced up. His eyes gleamed. "I can see why you came to me. This situation is by no means clear-cut."

"No, it's not." But at least Liam had a clearer picture of what he wanted. Tension he didn't realize he'd been holding unwound from his shoulder muscles. "How do you suggest we proceed?"

"Let's find out what we can about Margaret and her time with Kyle in San Antonio. I have an investigator I've worked with there. If you give me the go-ahead, I'll contact him."

"Do you think I have a case for retaining custody of Maggie?" Before he let Kyle take Maggie away, Liam intended to make sure his brother was willing to fight for her. And fight hard.

"A lot will depend on how determined your brother is

to be a father. You and your brother aren't in contact. We should probably check on Kyle's current financial status and personal life as well and see what sort of environment Maggie would be going into. I think you're right that between the two situations, Wade Ranch promises the most stability for a baby. But a judge might reason that you're both single men and that Maggie should be with her father."

Her *single* father who might be activated at a moment's notice and be out of the country who knew how long.

"What if I were engaged?" Liam suggested, voicing what had been running through his head since his trip to Colorado. "Or married?"

Nolan nodded. "Might sway a judge. Are you?"

"Not yet." For a year Liam had pondered the benefits of settling down. All he'd been waiting for was the right woman. Hadley fit the bill in every way. She was smart, beautiful and great with Maggie. After Colorado he'd decided he'd be a complete idiot not to lock her down as soon as possible before she finished school and headed off to pursue a career elsewhere. "But I plan to pop the question to a special lady in the very near future."

Hadley rocked a sleepy Maggie as she checked out the photos of Liam's family on the walls of the ranch office.

"Thanks for bringing lunch," Liam said. "The day has been crazy."

With calving time a couple weeks away and a whole host of unexpected issues popping up, Liam and Ivy had decided to work through lunch. The weather had turned warmer and Hadley was feeling restless, so she'd offered to bring their meal to the barn.

As if Liam's words had the power to summon trouble, one of the hands appeared in the doorway. "Dean told me to stop by and see if you had an hour or so free. Sam is out sick," the hand said. "Barry is off visiting his kid in Tulsa. We could use some help cutting the cows who aren't pregnant."

"Sure." Liam shifted his weight in the direction of the door, but glanced at Hadley before taking a step. "Ever cut cattle?"

She shook her head, sensing what was coming and wondering why Liam, knowing what he did, would ask her to ride with him.

"Like to try?"

Hadley was surprised by her strong desire to say yes. "What about Maggie?"

"I'd be happy to watch her until you get back," Ivy offered, cooing at the infant. "You'd like to hang out with Cousin Ivy until they get back, wouldn't you?" Maggie waved her arms as if in agreement. "Or I can drive her back to the house if it gets too late."

"See?" Liam's eyes held a hard glint of challenge. "All settled. Let's go find you a mount."

While her gut clenched in happy anticipation of getting on a horse again, Hadley rationalized her agreement by telling herself it was work, not pleasure. She was doing something her employer requested. Never mind that he'd been trying to figure out a way to get her back in the saddle since she'd stepped into his home two and a half weeks ago.

Excitement built as he led her outside to the paddocks where they turned out the horses during the day. Twelve horses occupied four enclosures.

Liam nodded toward a palomino mare in the farthest right paddock. The only horse in the fenced-in area, she stood in the middle, tearing at the winter grass with strong white teeth. "Daisy could use some exercise. I don't think she's been ridden much in the last year. I'll get one of the guys to saddle her for you."

"I can saddle my own horse," Hadley retorted, insulted. "Besides, I'd like to get to know her a little before I get on."

"Okay. She's a nice mare. You shouldn't have any trouble with her on the ground."

As Liam's last three words registered, she glanced over at him, but discovered nothing in his expression to arouse her suspicions. Surely he wouldn't put her on a green horse after such a long absence from the saddle. Once upon a time her skills might have been first-rate, but a decade had passed since she'd used those particular muscles. Riding a horse wasn't the same as riding a bike.

"You said she hasn't been ridden much in the last year?" Hadley decided a little clarification might be in order. "But she has been ridden, right?"

"Oh, sure." Liam walked over to the fence and picked up the halter and lead rope hung on the gate. "We were going to breed her last year, but that didn't work out. So she's just been hanging around, waiting to become a mother." He opened the gate and handed Hadley the halter. "She's easy to catch. I'll meet you in that barn over there." He indicated the building that housed the horses in training. "You might want to do a couple circles in the indoor ring before we head out."

Sensing something was up despite Liam's neutral expression and bland tone, Hadley slipped the halter onto the mare and led her to the building Liam had indicated. He hadn't yet arrived, so Hadley got busy with currycomb and brush. She smiled as the mare leaned into the grooming. Obviously Daisy appreciated Hadley's efforts.

She would have preferred to take more time with the mare, but Liam showed up, leading a gorgeous bay stallion that was already saddled and ready to go. Hadley returned his nod before tossing the saddle onto Daisy's back, settling it in just the right spot and tightening the cinch as if she'd done it last week instead of ten years earlier. Working just as efficiently, she slipped the bit into the mare's mouth and fitted the headstall into place.

"Ready?"

All at once she became aware of Liam's attention and grew self-conscious. "I think so."

"Come on. I'll work the kinks out of Buzzard while you try out Daisy."

Leading Daisy, Hadley followed Liam and the bay into the arena. What if she made a complete hash of it and ended up getting dumped? While Hadley fussed with Daisy's girth and grappled with her nerves, Liam swung up onto the stallion's back. Buzzard took several steps sideways as Liam settled his weight, but quickly relaxed beneath the pressure of his rider's legs and the steadiness of Liam's hands on the reins.

The guy was an amazing rider, and Hadley felt a fangirl moment coming on. Embarrassed at her gawking, she set her foot in the stirrup. Daisy was a little shorter than Lolita, but she felt her muscles protest as she threw her leg up and over the mare's back. Before she'd completely found her balance, Daisy's muscles bunched beneath her and the mare crow-hopped a half dozen times while Hadley clung to the saddle horn, laughter puffing out of her with each jolt of Daisy's four hoofs hitting the ground.

At last the mare got her silliness out of her system and stood still while Hadley retrieved her breath.

"You okay?"

"Fine." Hadley could feel the broad smile on her face. "Is she going to be like this the whole time?"

"No. She just wanted to make sure you were going to stay on. You passed."

"She was testing me?" The notion struck Hadley as ludicrous. What sort of horse had Liam put her on?

"She's a smart horse." His lips kicked up. "Needs a smart rider."

Apparently Daisy wasn't the only one doing the testing. Hadley keyed the mare into a walk and then took five minutes to work through all her gaits. Whoever had trained the palomino had done a fabulous job. She was a dream to ride.

"Let's go cut some cattle," Hadley said, all too aware how closely Liam had been observing her.

Liam didn't think a woman's pleasure had ever been as important to him as Hadley's. Between their lovemaking in Vail and the joy she'd demonstrated cutting cattle today, especially when Daisy had kept a heifer from returning to the herd, he was convinced he would know true happiness only if he continued delighting Hadley.

Would he have felt the same a year ago? Remaining celibate for twelve months had given him a greater appreciation of companionship. Being with Hadley had enabled him to understand the difference between what he'd had with his former girlfriends and true intimacy. Granted, he'd only barely scratched the surface with her. Instinct told him she was rich with complex layers she didn't yet trust him to see. Moving past her defenses wasn't anything he wanted to rush. Or force.

He had a good thing going. Why make a mistake and risk losing her?

"That was amazing," Hadley crowed. Cheeks flushed, eyes dancing with excitement, she was as vibrant as he'd ever seen her. "You knew I'd love this when you suggested I ride her."

"She's a natural, boss," one of the ranch hands commented, his gaze lingering on Hadley longer than Liam liked.

"I figured she would be."

The urge to growl at the cowboy was nearly impossible to repress. Obviously, Liam wasn't the only one dazzled by the attractive Ms. Hadley Stratton. And since he hadn't yet staked a public claim, the rest of the male population assumed she was fair game. That situation was not to his liking. Time he did something to change it.

Liam nudged his stallion forward and cut Hadley off from the admiring cowboys with the ease of someone accustomed to working cattle. "It's late. We should be getting back to Maggie."

Her eyes lost none of their sparkle as she nodded. "I've probably strained enough muscles for one day." She laughed. "I can tell I'm going to be in pain tomorrow, but it was worth it."

"I'm glad you like Daisy." Liam decided to push his luck. "She could probably stand a little work if you felt inclined."

Hadley hesitated but shook her head. He was making progress since the last time he'd tried to persuade her to ride. He wanted her to talk to him, to share how she was feeling. They'd discussed her friend's accident, and Hadley had mulled his suggestion that she move past the guilt that she'd carried for years. Had something about that changed?

"I'm due to go back to school in a week. I don't know how I'd make time."

He'd found a permanent nanny for Maggie. Liam and Hadley had agreed that being together would not work if she was still his employee. But he was realizing that she would no longer be an everyday fixture in his life, and that was a situation he needed to fix.

"I don't mind sharing you with the horses," he said, keeping his voice casual. He'd never had to work so hard to keep from spooking a woman.

"Oh, you don't?" She gave him a wry smile. "What if I don't have enough time for either of you?"

Liam's grip on the reins tightened and Buzzard began trotting in place. If he thought she was flirting, he'd have shot back a provocative retort, but Liam had gotten to know Hadley well enough in the last few weeks to know she had serious concerns.

"Move in with me."

The offer was sudden, but he didn't surprise himself when he made it.

"You already have a full-time nanny moving in."

"Not as a nanny."

Her eyes widened. "Then as what?"

"The woman I'm crazy about." He'd never been in love and had no idea if that's what he felt for Hadley. But he'd been doing a lot of soul-searching these last few days.

"You're crazy about me?" The doubt in her voice wasn't unexpected.

He'd known she wouldn't accept his declaration without some vigorous convincing. Hadley wasn't one to forgive herself easily for past mistakes. She'd fallen for her first employer, only to have her heart torn up when the jerk got back together with his ex-wife. That wasn't a judgment error she would make a second time. And she was already skeptical of Liam's past romantic history.

"If we weren't on these damned horses I'd demonstrate just how crazy."

Liam ground his teeth at her surprise. What kept her from accepting how strong his feelings had become? The mildest of her saucy smiles provoked a befuddling rush of lust. He pondered what her opinion would be on a dozen decisions before lunch. Waking up alone in his big bed had become the most painful part of his day.

"This is happening too fast."

"I'm not going to bail on you."

"I know."

"You don't sound convinced." He was determined to change her mind. "What can I say to reassure you?"

"You don't need to say anything."

After regarding her for a long moment, he shook his head. "I've dated a lot of women."

"This is your way of convincing me to take a chance on you?"

He ignored her interruption. "Enough to recognize that how I feel about you is completely foreign to me." He saw he'd hit the wrong note with the word *foreign*. "And terrific. Scary. Fascinating. I've never been so twisted up by a woman before."

"And somehow you think this is a good thing?"

"You make me better. I feel more alive when I'm with you. Like anything is possible."

She blinked several times. "I think that's the most amazing thing anyone has ever said to me."

"I don't believe that. I do, however, believe that it might be one of the first times you've let yourself hear and trust one of my compliments." He was making progress if she'd stopped perceiving everything he said as a ploy.

"You might be right."

They'd drawn within sight of the ranch buildings, and Liam regretted how fast the ride had gone. He hadn't received an answer from Hadley, and the time to pursue the matter was fast coming to an end.

"I hope that means you're beginning to believe me when I tell you how important you've become to me."

"It's starting to sink in." She watched him from beneath her eyelashes. "But are you ready to have me move in?"

"Absolutely." His conviction rang in his answer. "But it's not the only thing I want."

This was something else he'd thought long and hard about. It wasn't just his feelings for Hadley that were driving him, but also his need to give Maggie a loving home and create for her the sort of stable family denied him and Kyle.

"No?"

"What I really want is for us to get married."

Eleven

While Hadley wondered if she'd heard him correctly, Liam pulled a ring box out of his coat pocket and extended it her way. She stared at it, her heart thundering in her ears. It wasn't the most romantic of proposals, but she had to bite her lower lip to keep from blurting out her acceptance. It took half a minute for her to think rationally.

"I haven't said yes or no to moving in," she reminded him, pleased that she sounded like a sensible adult instead of a giddy teenager.

"I'm afraid I've gone about this in a clumsy fashion." His confident manner belied his words. "I've never asked a woman to marry me before. Especially not one I've known less than a month."

Hadley's brain scrambled to think logically. "And the reason you're rushing into marriage?"

"I'm not rushing into marriage," he corrected her with a wily grin. "I'm rushing into an engagement."

"Semantics." She waved away his explanation. "Are you sure you don't want to live together for a while and see how it goes?"

"I've already lived with you for a while and it's been terrific. I want to keep on living with you. I need you in my life. That's not going to change if we wait to get engaged. Right now your plan is to finish school and move to Houston. I want you to make a life with me in Royal instead."

Hadley clutched her reins in a white-knuckled grip and made no move toward the tempting ring box. "Are you sure this is what you want?"

From the way the light in his eyes dimmed, it wasn't the answer he'd hoped for, but he had to know her well enough to realize she wouldn't jump aboard his runaway freight train without thinking things through. After all, her career goals were designed to carry her far from Royal. And that was something she'd have to reconsider if she married him.

"Are you questioning whether I know my mind?" He lifted the enormous diamond ring from its nest of black velvet and caught her left hand. His eyes mesmerized her as he slid the ring on her finger. "I took a year off dating and spent the time thinking through what I wanted in a woman. I wouldn't have slept with you in Vail if I hadn't already made up my mind that you were special." Liam dismounted and handed off Buzzard's reins to one of the grooms.

"But marriage?" She stared at the ring, mesmerized by the diamond's sparkle.

Here was proof that Liam's proposal wasn't something impulsive and reckless. He'd come prepared to ask her to marry him. And yet he hadn't said anything about love.

"It's been on my mind constantly since we came back from Colorado."

Hearing she hadn't been the only one who'd felt the connection they'd established that snowy weekend eased her mind somewhat. She dismounted and surrendered Daisy to the groom as well. Her feet barely touched the dirt as she walked the short distance to Liam and took the hand he held outstretched.

He tugged her to him and lifted her chin with gentle fingers until their gazes met. "You fill my thoughts when we're apart and make me mad with longing to take you in my arms when we're together."

Liam's assertion awakened a deep, profound thrumming in her heart. "I know the feeling," she said, lifting onto her toes to offer him a single kiss. "I'd better get back to Maggie."

He wrapped a strong arm around her waist and held her snug against his muscular chest. "Will you stay tonight?"

"I can't. I'm having dinner with Kori."

"Afterward?"

She laughed and danced beyond his reach. "I've been neglecting the other guy in my life so I'm going to sleep with him."

"That guy better be Waldo," he growled, but his eyes sparkled with amusement below lowered brows.

"I don't have time for anyone else."

"Bring him with you when you come back. It's time you both settled permanently at the ranch house."

Engagement. Moving in. It was all happening so fast. Her heart hammered against her ribs in a panicked rhythm. All too aware she hadn't actually agreed to marry Liam, despite accepting his ring, she opened her mouth, but her thoughts were too scattered to summon words. He might have been considering this move for a while, but for her this development was brand-new and she needed to think things through.

One of Liam's ranch hands approached, citing a problem with a mare, and Hadley took the opportunity to slip away. As she wove through the connected barns on her way back to the ranch offices, her mood shifted from giddy to concerned. She might not have said yes to marriage, but she'd accepted his ring and kept her doubts to herself.

What had happened to being practical? Falling in love with Liam for starters. How was she supposed to think straight when the man made her feel like it was the Fourth of July, Thanksgiving and Christmas all rolled into one perfect holiday?

Thank goodness she was having dinner with Kori. Talking to her best friend would help sort things out.

Kori held Hadley's engagement ring mere inches from her nose and scrutinized the diamond. "You're not seriously thinking about marrying him, are you?"

"Well, I haven't said no." Hadley wasn't sure why her friend had done such a complete turnaround. "What's changed since last week when you told me to go for it?"

"Sex, yes." Kori regarded her friend as if she'd sprouted a second head as she opened the oven and removed her famous shepherd's pie. The succulent aroma of meat and savory gravy filled the kitchen. "Marriage, no."

Hadley held the plates while Kori filled them. Her friend's unexpected reaction to Liam's proposal was disheartening. "You're right. It's moving too fast."

"For you, yes." Kori and Scott had taken about a month to decide they wanted to be together forever. But they'd spent four years planning and saving money for their wedding.

"What if it feels right?" Hadley set the plates on the table while Kori followed with the salad.

"Did Noah feel right?"

Noah had been about safety. She'd been second-guessing her decision to change careers and had been worried about money. The notion of marrying a stable man had taken that burden off her shoulders.

"At the time." Hadley had no trouble admitting the truth of her failing. In the last five years she'd done a lot of soul-searching to understand why she'd failed to see that Noah was more interested in a mother for his children than a partner for life.

Kori nodded. "You are the most practical person I know until a single guy comes along needing help with his kids and you get all wrapped up in the idea of being a family."

It was her Achilles' heel, and she was wise enough to avoid putting herself in situations like the one with Noah. Like the one with Liam. As much as Hadley needed to hear Kori's blunt summary of her shortcomings, she wanted to protest that things with Liam were different. But were they?

Kori regarded her with a sympathetic expression while she topped off their wineglasses. "I know this isn't what you want to hear."

"You aren't saying anything I haven't thought a hundred times in the last month. I don't know why I do this. It's not like I didn't have a perfectly normal childhood. My parents are happily married, rarely fight and support me in everything I do."

"Don't be so hard on yourself. You are a born caretaker and one of the most nurturing people I know. It's in your nature to get overly invested, which is why you hated teaching a class of thirty kids. You might make a difference with one or two, but it's hard to give each child the sort of attention they need." Kori hit the problem squarely on the head. "Being a guidance counselor suits you so much better."

"I know." Hadley sighed. "But none of this helps me with what to do about Liam's marriage proposal. I really do love him."

"You haven't known him very long."

Hadley couldn't believe Kori of all people would use that argument. "Not directly, but I saw a lot of him ten years ago when I was barrel racing. I had a crush on him then. He was always nice to me. Never made me feel like I was going to be his next conquest." And for Liam, that was saying something.

"Because you weren't that sort of girl," Kori reminded her. "You told me while your friends dated extensively you weren't interested in boys, only horses."

"I was interested in Liam."

"Let me guess. He didn't know you existed?"

"At first, but toward the end of my last show season, that changed. I used to compete with his on-and-off girlfriend, and he'd sometimes show up to watch her. Most of the time I beat her, and he started congratulating me on my rides. At first I thought he was doing it to make her mad, but then I realized he meant it. One thing about Liam, he was always a horseman first and everything else came after."

"So things were warming up between you. What happened?"

"Anna was my best friend at the time, and she had a huge thing for him."

"But he liked you?"

Hadley shrugged. "He was way out of my league."

"What would you have done if he'd made a play for you?"

"Freaked out in true teenage fashion." Hadley trailed off as she recalled how much more intense her emotions had been in those days. Every problem had seemed crippling. Her success had sent her straight into orbit. "I'd never had a crush on anyone before, and Liam was older by a couple years and had a lot of experience. I told myself he couldn't possibly be interested in me that way."

"But you hoped he might be?"

"Sure, but it was complicated."

"Because of Anna?"

"Yes." Hadley hadn't told anyone the story behind Anna's accident. Ashamed that her friend was paralyzed as a result of something Hadley had said in a moment of anger, she'd punished herself all these years by avoiding something she loved: horses. "It bugged her that he'd go out of his way to comment on my rides but didn't notice her at all."

"What did she expect? That you'd tell him to stop being nice to you?" At Hadley's shrug, her friend sighed. "You should've told her to go to hell."

"I did something so much worse, and as a consequence my best friend lost the use of her legs."

Kori's eyes widened. "You need to tell me the whole story."

Haley killed the last of the wine in her glass and refilled from the bottle. "It was July and Wade Ranch was throwing a huge party at their stalls in the show barn to promote one of their stallions. Anna had been flirting with Liam for a month and was convinced he was finally showing interest when he invited her to the celebration. She dragged me along because she didn't want to go alone and then promptly ditched me to go hang with Liam. I lost track of her and spent the night hanging out with some of the other barrel racers.

"It was getting late and Anna didn't want to leave, so I arranged to get a lift with someone else. A little before we took off, I went to check on Lolita for the last time to make sure she had water and because being with her calmed me down. I was mad at Anna for chasing a guy who didn't act like he was into her."

"Because if he had been into her she wouldn't have had to chase him."

"Right." Several girls at the party had poked fun at Anna for thinking Liam could possibly be interested in her. "So, there I was in the stall with Lolita and guess who appears."

"Liam?" Kori said his name with such relish that Hadley had to smile.

"Liam. At first I thought maybe Anna was looking for me and got Liam to help her, but turns out he'd just followed me."

"Where was Anna?"

"I don't know. And really, for a little while, I didn't care. Liam and I talked about my upcoming ride the next day and he offered me advice for how to take a little time off my turns. I was grateful for the feedback and when I told him that, he said that if I won, I could take him out to dinner with my prize money."

"He asked you out?"

"I guess." Even now doubt clouded Hadley's tone. Even with Liam's engagement ring on her finger, she had a hard time believing that he'd been the slightest bit interested in her. She'd been so plain and uninteresting compared with his other girlfriends.

"You guess?" Kori regarded her in bemusement. "Of course he did."

Hadley shrugged. "Like I said, he was nice to a lot of people."

"But you had to suspect he wouldn't have tracked you to Lolita's stall if he wasn't interested in you."

"I could barely hope he liked me. I was excited and terrified. His reputation was something I wasn't sure I could deal with. He dated extensively." She put air quotes around *dated*. "I was eighteen and I'd never really been kissed."

"So did you win and go to dinner with him?"

"I won, but we never went out. Anna rode after I did the next day and had her accident."

"You haven't explained how that was your fault."

"Anna overheard Liam and I talking about dinner and me agreeing to his terms. She interrupted us and told me she was leaving and if I wanted a ride I'd better come with her. Considering I'd been ready to go an hour earlier, her demand seemed pretty unreasonable. I was tempted to tell her I'd already made other arrangements, but she was obviously upset so I agreed to head out."

"She was jealous that Liam had asked you out."

"That's what I figured, but on the way to the car I tried to explain to her that he was just helping me out with my riding."

"And she didn't believe you."

"No. She'd figured out I liked him and accused me of going behind her back. When I denied it, she went ballistic. Said that the only reason he noticed me was because I beat his girlfriend and that I wasn't his type. She insisted I would be the laughingstock of the barn if I kept believing he would ever want to date me."

"Sounds like things she should have been telling herself."

While Hadley agreed with Kori, at the time, each word had struck like a fist. "I wish I hadn't been so surprised by her attack. If I'd been able to stay calm, I might have been able to reason with her. But what she was saying were the same things that had been running through my head. To hear them from my best friend... I was devastated."

"So you didn't tell her she was the one who was acting like an idiot?"

"No." And now they'd arrived at the part of the story Hadley was most ashamed of. "I told her that if Liam only noticed me because of my riding she was out of luck. The way she rode, no wonder he had no idea who she was."

"Ouch."

Hadley winced. "Not my finest moment. And for the last ten years I've regretted those words."

"But it sounds like she was asking to have the truth served up to her."

"Maybe, but she was my best friend. I should have been more understanding. And because of what I said, the next day she pushed too hard and fell badly. So, now you see. If I'd not let my temper get the best of me, Anna never would have tried to prove she was the better rider and wouldn't have fallen and broken her back."

"And you haven't ridden since."

"No." It was a small sacrifice to make for being a bad

friend. "Until today. And now I'm engaged to the guy who came between Anna and me with tragic results."

"And I can tell you still aren't guilt free over moving on. So, as your best friend of seven years, I give you permission to get on with your life and stop beating yourself up over something you said to your friend who was acting like a greedy bitch a decade ago." Kori lifted her wineglass and held it out to Hadley.

Pushing aside all reluctance, Hadley picked up her glass and gently clinked it with Kori's. The crystalline note rang in the dining nook, the sound proclaiming an end to living in the past and the beginning of her bright future.

She'd given enough time and energy to her mistakes. She deserved to be happy, and being Liam's wife, becoming a family with him and Maggie, was the perfect way to spend the rest of her life.

Liam sat on the couch in the den, using one hand to scroll through the report Nolan's investigator had sent him regarding Margaret Garner while cradling a snugly swaddled Maggie in his other arm. She'd been fussy and agitated all day, and her appetite had waned. Hadley had noticed Maggie's temperature was slightly elevated and Liam was glad she was scheduled for a follow-up visit with her pediatrician tomorrow. Maggie continued to show signs of jaundice, and this had both Liam and Hadley concerned.

As a counterpoint to Liam's agitation over Maggie's health issues, Waldo lay on the sofa back directly behind Liam's head, purring. Although he'd grown up believing that cats belonged in barns, keeping the mouse population under control, he'd grown fond of Hadley's fur ball and had to concede that the feline had a knack for reading moods and providing just the right companionship. Just yesterday Liam had been irritated by a particularly demanding client, and Waldo had spent a hilarious ten minutes playing with one of Hadley's ponytail holders, cheering him up.

The only member of his family not sitting on the den's sofa was Hadley. After dinner she'd gone upstairs to call her parents and tell them about the engagement. They'd been on a cruise several days ago when Liam had popped the question and hadn't been immediately available to receive their daughter's news. Hadley was concerned that they'd view the engagement as moving too fast, and Liam had suggested that they take Maggie to Houston this weekend so everyone could meet.

With an effort, Liam brought his attention back to the report. Despite only spending four days on the job, the investigator had built a pretty clear picture of Maggie's mom. Margaret Garner had worked at home as a freelance illustrator and had a pretty limited social life. She'd dated rarely, and her friends had husbands and children who kept them busy. So busy, in fact, that none of them had had a clue that Margaret was pregnant. Nor had there been any contact between her and Kyle after their weeklong affair. The investigator hadn't been able to determine how the two had met, but after digging into Margaret's financials, he'd figured out when the fling had happened.

Margaret's perfectionism and heavy workload explained why she hadn't gone out much, but a couple of her friends had known Margaret since college and confided that they thought Margaret might have had some depression issues. From what the investigator could determine, she'd never sought medical help for that or gone to see a doctor when she'd discovered she was pregnant.

"Well, that's done," Hadley announced, her voice heavy as she crossed the room and settled onto the couch beside him.

"How did it go with your parents?"

"They were surprised." Her head dropped onto his shoulder. She'd been anxious about how the conversation would go all through dinner. Hadley was an only child and from her description of them, Liam got the impression they didn't exactly approve of some of the choices she'd made in the last few years. Especially when she'd quit teaching and moved to Royal in order to get her master's degree.

"What are you working on?"

"I had an investigator look into Margaret Garner's background."

"You hired an investigator? Why?" She peered more closely at the report on his computer screen.

"Nolan suggested it."

"Who is Nolan?"

"Nolan Dane is a family law attorney I hired."

"You hired a lawyer?"

Liam realized he probably should have shared his plans with her regarding Maggie before this, but hadn't anticipated that she'd be surprised. "Because I'm seeking custody of Maggie."

"Have you told your brother?"

"Kyle hasn't responded to my messages about Maggie yet."

Hadley sat up and turned on the cushions to face him. "Don't you think you should talk to him before you make such a big decision regarding his daughter?"

"I think it's obvious from the fact that it's been three weeks and I haven't heard from him that he's not in a place where he can be a father. Either he's overseas and unavailable or he's choosing not to call me back. Whichever it is, Maggie deserves parents who can always be there for her." He studied her expression with a hint of concern. "I thought you'd be on board with this. After all, you love Maggie as much as I do and have to admit we make terrific parents."

Her brows came together. "I guess I thought we'd be great with kids someday. As soon as I accepted that Maggie was your brother's daughter, I guess I thought she'd end up with him."

"Are you trying to tell me you can't see yourself as Maggie's mother?"

"Not at all. I love her..." But it was obvious that Hadley was grappling with something.

"Then what's going on?"

"I was just wondering how long you'd been thinking about this." Her tone had an accusatory edge he didn't understand.

"I've been considering what's best for Maggie since Diane Garner left her on my doorstep."

"And have you thought about what's best for your brother?"

Liam struggled for patience in the face of her growing hostility. "I'm thinking about the fact that he's a navy SEAL and likely to be called to duty at any time. He's not married and lives on the East Coast, far from family. Who is going to take care of Maggie while he's gone for weeks, maybe months at a time?" Liam met Hadley's gaze and didn't care for the indictment he glimpsed in her beautiful blue eyes. "I think Maggie would be better off here with us."

"He's not married." She spoke deliberately as if determined to make a point. "So he's not the best person to raise Maggie."

"He's a career military man with no family support," Liam corrected her, unsure why she wasn't agreeing with him. "How often will he miss a school event? How likely is it he'll be around for her first steps, first words, first... everything."

"You're not married, either," Hadley pointed out, her voice barely audible.

"But I'm engaged."

"Is that why you proposed?"

"What do you mean?"

"Obviously a married couple would be a stronger candidate in a custody battle."

"Sure." Why deny it? She wasn't a fool, and she knew him well enough to suspect he'd want to put forth the strongest case for Maggie.

However, the instant the admission was out, Hadley's whole demeanor transformed. All trace of antagonism vanished. She sagged in defeat.

Liam rushed to defend his rationale. "I'd like to point out that I've never asked any woman to marry me before you," he continued, more determined than ever to convince Hadley how much he needed her. "I want us to spend the rest of our lives together. With Maggie. As a family."

"I am such an idiot."

"I don't understand." He'd missed her jump in logic. "Why do you think you're an idiot?"

"Because it's just like Noah all over again."

"Noah?" The guy who'd broken her heart? "That's absurd. I asked you to marry me. He didn't."

"He said he wanted us to be together, too." Hadley shot to her feet and backed away, but her eyes never left Liam. "Only what he wanted was someone to take care of his kids and his house. Someone to be there when he got home at the end of the day and in his bed at night."

"You don't seriously think I proposed to you simply because I wanted you to fill a role." In order to keep Maggie slumbering peacefully, Liam kept his volume low, but made sure his outrage came through loud and clear.

"Everyone is right. It happened too fast." Hadley covered her mouth with her fingertips as a single tear slid down her cheek.

The sight of it disturbed him. He was fast losing control

of this situation and had no idea how to fix it. "Everyone? You mean your parents?"

"And my best friend, Kori. Not to mention the look on Candace's face when she found out."

"So what if our engagement happened fast?" Marrying Hadley meant both she and Maggie would stay with him at Wade Ranch. "That doesn't mean my motives are anything like you're painting them to be."

She pulled off her engagement ring and extended it to him. "So if I give this back to you and say I want to wait until I'm done with school to discuss our future, you'd be okay with it."

Liam made no move to take the ring back. Gripped by dismay, he stared at her, unable to believe that she was comparing him to some loser who'd used her shamelessly and broken her heart five years earlier.

"You're overreacting."

"Am I?" She crossed her arms over her chest. "When you proposed, you never told me you loved me."

No, he hadn't. He'd known he couldn't live without her, but he'd been consumed with winning custody of Maggie and afraid that Hadley would receive a job offer in Houston that would cement her plans for the future. He hadn't been thinking about romance or love when he'd proposed.

"That was wrong of me and I'm sorry. But I did tell you that I couldn't imagine life without you."

She shook her head. "You said you needed me in your life. That should've warned me that there was more motivating you than love."

"What does it matter what motivated me when it all comes down to how much we want to be together and how committed we are to being a family?"

"I really want that," she said, coming forward to set the engagement ring on the end table. "But I can't be in a relationship with you and know that your reasons for being in it are based on something besides love."

A lifetime of suppressed heartache at his mother's abandonment kept Liam from speaking as Hadley reached past him and disengaged her cat from his snug nest. Waldo's purring hadn't ceased during their argument, and Liam felt a chill race across his skin at the loss of the cat's warmth. It wasn't until she began to leave the room that he realized his mistake.

"Don't leave." He pushed aside his laptop and pursued Hadley into the hallway. "Hadley, wait."

She'd reached the entryway and slipped her coat off the hook. "I think it will be better if Waldo and I move back to my apartment. I'll be back in the morning to take care of Maggie." She didn't point out that the new nanny was set to start work in four days, but Liam was all too aware that he was on the verge of losing her forever.

"Maybe you're right and we moved too fast," he said. "But don't think for one second that I've changed my mind about wanting to spend the rest of my life with you." He extended his hand to catch her arm and stop her from leaving, but she sidestepped him, the unresisting cat clutched to her chest.

"I think it would be better for both of us if we focused on our individual futures. I have to finish school. You have a custody case to win. Once things settle down we can reconnect and see how we feel."

"If you think I'm going to agree to not see you for the next few months you've got it wrong."

"Of course we'll see each other." But her words weren't convincing. She set down the cat. Waldo stretched and wrapped himself around her legs while she donned her coat. Then, picking up her purse and the cat, Hadley opened the front door. "But I'm going to be crazy once classes start again, and you've got a couple hundred cattle set to give birth. Let's give ourselves a couple weeks to see where we're at."

"You're not going to be able to brush me off that easily," he growled as she slipped through the front door and pulled it closed behind her, leaving him and Maggie alone in the enormous, echoing Victorian mansion.

Twelve

Hadley was still reeling from déjà vu as she let herself into her apartment and set Waldo on the floor. The silver tabby's warmth had been a comfort as she'd sped through the early-evening darkness toward her tiny apartment.

How could she have been so stupid as to let herself get blinded by love a second time? So much for being five years older and wiser. She was obviously no less desperate; otherwise she wouldn't have become Liam's convenient solution the way she'd been Noah's. Honestly, what had happened to her common sense?

With her emotions a chaotic mess, Hadley looked for something in her apartment to occupy her, but after straightening a few pillows, dusting and running the vacuum, she ran out of tasks. While water boiled for a cup of tea, she wished her classes had resumed. At least then she'd have a paper to write or a test to study for. Something to occupy her thoughts and keep her mind off Liam.

She could call Kori and pour her heart out. Hadley rejected the idea as soon as it occurred to her. She wasn't ready to tell anyone that she'd screwed up again. The injury to her pride was still too fresh. Not to mention the damage to her confidence. As for the pain in her heart, Hadley could scarcely breathe as she considered all she'd lost tonight. Not just Liam, but Maggie as well.

Would it have been so bad to marry Liam and become

Maggie's mom? The whole time she'd been falling in love with Liam, she'd thought he and Maggie were a package deal. And then came their trip to Colorado. When she'd decided to believe him about his brother being Maggie's dad, letting her heart lead for a change hadn't felt one bit scary. She'd assumed Kyle would eventually come to Wade Ranch and take responsibility for Maggie. It never occurred to her that Liam intended to fight his brother for custody and that he might propose in order to appear to be the better candidate.

Desperate for a distraction from her turbulent thoughts, Hadley carried the hot tea to her small desk and turned on the computer. Before she'd considered her actions, she cued up the internet and impulsively ventured on to a popular social media site. Her fingers tapped out Noah's name and she pushed Enter before she could change her mind.

In seconds his page appeared and her heart gave a little jump as she stared at the photo of him and his kids that he used as his profile picture. Five years had gone by. Peter and Nikki were eight and seven now. They looked happy in their father's arms. Noah's wife wasn't in the shot, and Hadley searched through some of his other photos to see if she showed up anywhere. There were pictures of her with both kids, but none of her with Noah. Were they still married? Nothing in his profile information gave her a clue.

Feeling more than a little stalkerish, Hadley searched for Anna, but found no sign of her onetime friend. She almost left the website, inclined to switch to something with less potential for heartache, when she decided to search for Anna's sister, Char. And there she found Anna. Only she wasn't Anna Johnson any more. She was Anna Bradley now. A happily married woman with two beautiful girls.

Hadley stared at the photos in numb disbelief. This is the woman she'd been feeling guilty about for ten years? Anna hadn't wallowed in her misfortune. She hadn't sat around letting life pass her by. She'd gone to college in Dallas, become an engineer, gotten married and was busy raising a two- and a four-year-old.

It was as if the universe had reached out a hand and smacked Hadley on the back of the head and yelled, *snap out of it*. Noah had moved forward with his life. He had his kids and seemed to be in a good place with his wife or ex-wife. Anna was thriving with a career and family. Apparently Hadley was the only one stuck in limbo.

With revelations pouring over her like ice water, Hadley shut down the computer and picked up a notebook and a pen. It was time for her to stop dwelling on what had happened in the past and to consider how she envisioned her future. What was her idea of a perfect career? Where did she want to live? Was the love in her heart strong enough to overcome her doubts and fears?

Liam entered the pediatrician's office and spotted Hadley seated by the wall, Maggie's carrier on the chair beside her. Overnight the baby's temperature had risen, and the concern radiating from Hadley caused a spike in his anxiety.

"How is she?" he asked as he sat beside Maggie and peered in her carrier.

"A little bit worse than she was when I arrived this morning. She wouldn't eat and seems listless. I'm glad we had this appointment scheduled today."

Hadley was obviously distraught, and Liam badly wanted to offer her the comfort of his embrace, but yesterday she hadn't believed him when he'd told her there was more to his proposal than his determination to seek custody of Maggie. What made him think that a miracle had occurred overnight to change her mind?

"Do you think the jaundice is causing this?"

"More likely the jaundice is a symptom of something more serious."

"Damn it." The curse vibrated in his chest as anxiety flared. He stared down at the sleeping baby. "I can't lose her."

"Liam, you're not going to lose her." Hadley reached across Maggie's carrier and set her fingers on his upper arm.

The light contact burned through him like a wildfire, igniting his hope for a future with her. She loved him. The proof was in her supportive tone and her desire to reassure him. But as he reached to cover her hand with his, she withdrew. When she spoke again, her voice had a professional crispness.

"She's going to be fine."

He hated the distance between them. He'd been wrong to propose to her as part of a scheme to win custody of Maggie. Even though it hadn't been his only reason for asking her to marry him, she'd been right to feel as if he'd treated her no better than Noah.

But how could he convince her to give him another chance when she'd rejected everything he'd already said and done? As with the subject of Maggie's paternity, she was either going to believe him or she wasn't. She'd been burned before, and her lack of trust demonstrated that she hadn't yet moved on. He'd have to be patient and persistent. Two things he was known for when it came to horses, but not in his personal life.

"Hadley, about what happened last night—"

A nurse appeared in the waiting room and called Maggie's name before Hadley could respond. Liam ground his teeth as he and Hadley followed the nurse into an exam room. He refocused his attention on Maggie as the nurse weighed and measured her. After it was determined that her temperature had climbed to 102, the nurse left to fetch Dr. Stringer.

Liam's tension ratcheted upward during the wait. Hadley sat beside him with Maggie cradled in her arms. She'd fixed her gaze on the door to the hall as if she could summon the doctor by sheer will.

After a wait that felt like hours but was less than ten minutes, Maggie's doctor appeared. Dr. Stringer made a quick but thorough examination of his patient, returned her to Hadley's arms and sat down, his expression solemn.

"I'm concerned that she's running a temperature and that the jaundice hasn't gone away after the phototherapy treatments," Dr. Stringer said. "I'd like to draw blood and recheck her bilirubin levels. If they continue to remain high we may want to look at the possibility of doing a blood transfusion."

Liam felt rather than heard Hadley's sharp intake of breath. She had leaned her shoulder against his as the doctor had spoken. The seriousness of Maggie's medical condition was a weight Liam was glad not to have to bear alone.

"Maggie is a rare blood type," Liam said. "AB negative. Is that going to pose a problem finding donors?"

The doctor shook his head. "Not at all. In fact, where O is the universal donor blood type, AB is the universal recipient. But let's not get ahead of ourselves. I'm going to have the nurse draw some blood and then we'll see where we're at."

Maggie's reaction to the blood draw was not as vigorous as Liam expected it to be, and he took that as a sign that she was even sicker than she appeared. This time as they sat alone in the exam room, Liam reached for Hadley's hand. Her fingers were ice cold, but they curved to hold fast to his.

Their second wait was longer, but no less silent. Liam's

heart thumped impatiently, spreading unease through every vein. Beside him, Hadley, locked in her own battle with worry, gripped his hand and stared down at Maggie. Both of them had run out of reassuring things to say.

The door opened again and Dr. Stringer entered. "Looks like it's not her bilirubin levels that are causing the problem," he said, nothing about his manner suggesting this was good news.

"Then what's going on?" Liam asked.

"We're seeing a high level of white blood cells that points to infection. Because of the jaundice and the fact that she's a preemie, I'd like you to take Maggie to the hospital for further testing. I've already contacted my partner, Dr. Davison. He's on call at the hospital today and will be waiting for you."

"The hospital?" Hadley sounded stunned. "It's that serious?"

"At this point we don't know, but I would rather err on the side of caution."

Liam nodded. "Then we'll head right over."

Hadley sat in the passenger side of Liam's Range Rover as he drove to the hospital and silently berated herself for being a terrible caregiver.

"This isn't your fault," Liam said, demonstrating an uncanny knack for knowing what she was thinking.

"You don't know that."

"She only just recently started showing signs of an infection."

"But we don't know how long this has been brewing. You heard the doctor. He said it could have been coming on slowly for a long time. What if she was sick before we went to Colorado and then we walked to town and back? Maybe that's when things started."

"We can't know for sure and you'll make yourself crazy if you keep guessing."

"I should never have…" She trailed off, biting her lip to stifle the rest of the sentence.

"Should never have what?" Liam demanded, taking his eyes off the road to glance her way.

She answered in a rush. "Slept with you."

"Why? Because by doing that you stopped being a good nanny?" He snorted derisively.

Hadley shifted away from his irritation and leaned her head against the cool window. "Maggie was my responsibility. I got distracted."

"She's my responsibility, too," he reminded her. "I'm just as much at fault if something happens to her. You know, one of these days you should stop blaming yourself for every little thing that goes wrong."

With a shock, Hadley realized that Liam was right. She'd taken responsibility for other people's decisions, believing if she'd been a better friend, Anna wouldn't have gotten hurt, and if she'd been more affectionate with Noah or acted more like a parent to his children instead of their nanny, he might not have gone back to his ex-wife.

"It's a habit I should break," she said, her annoyance diminished. "It's really not anyone's fault she's sick. Like the doctor said, her birth wasn't routine. The infection could have been caused by any number of things."

Neither spoke again, but the silence was no longer charged by antagonism. Hadley cast several glances in Liam's direction, wishing she hadn't overreacted last night after finding out Liam intended to seek custody of Maggie. But she'd gone home and filled two sheets of paper with a list of everything that made her happy. It had taken her half a page before she'd begun to break free of the mental patterns she'd fallen into. But it was the last two items that told the real story.

Horses.

Liam.

That it had taken her so long to admit what she needed in her life to be truly happy was telling.

Liam dropped her and Maggie off at the emergency entrance and went to park. Hadley checked in at reception and was directed to the waiting room. She was told someone would come down from pediatrics to get them soon.

To Hadley's relief they only had to wait ten minutes. Liam never even had a chance to sit down before they were on their way to a private room in Royal Memorial's brand-new west wing.

A nurse entered the room while Hadley lifted Maggie from her carrier. "Hello, my name is Agnes and I'll be taking care of Maggie while she's here."

"It's nice to meet you." Hadley followed Agnes's directions and placed Maggie in the bassinet. It was hard to step away from the baby and let the nurse take over, but Hadley forced herself to join Liam by the window.

Liam gave her a tight smile. "She's in good hands."

"I know." Hadley was consumed by the need for Liam's arms around her. But she'd relinquished all rights to his reassurances last night when she'd given back his engagement ring.

The nurse took Maggie's vitals and hooked her up to an IV.

"Because she's not yet four weeks," Agnes began, "we're going to start her on antibiotics right away. It may take twenty-four to forty-eight hours to get the lab results back, so we'd like to take this precaution. The good news is that it hasn't seemed to affect her lungs. That's always a concern with a premature baby." Agnes offered a reassuring smile before continuing. "Dr. Davison will be by in a little while to talk to you."

"Thank you," Liam said while Hadley crossed to Maggie.

"She looks even tinier hooked up to the IV."

Liam came to stand beside her and stared down at Maggie. A muscle jumped in his jaw. His eyes had developed a haunted look. Suddenly it was Hadley's turn to offer comfort.

"She's going to be fine."

"Thank you for being here," he said. "It's…"

She'd never know what he intended to say because a man in a white lab coat entered the room with Agnes at his heels.

"Good morning, I'm Dr. Davison. I've spoken with Dr. Stringer and he filled me in on what's been going on. I'm sure you're anxious to hear about the tests we ran on Maggie," The doctor met each of their gazes in turn before shifting his attention to the infant. "What we're looking at is a blood infection. That's what's causing the fever, her jaundice and her listlessness."

A knot formed in Hadley's chest. She gripped Liam's forearm for stability. "Is it serious?"

"It can be. But Maggie is in good hands with us here at Royal Memorial. I'm sure she'll make a full recovery. The sooner she gets treatment the better the outcome. We've already started her on antibiotics, and we're going to monitor her for the next couple days while we run a battery of tests to determine what's causing the infection."

"How long will she be here?" Liam gave Hadley's fingers a gentle squeeze.

"Probably not more than three days. If there's bacteria in her blood, she'll be on antibiotics for three weeks and you'll be bringing her in for periodic checkups."

"Thank you, Dr. Davison." Liam extended his hand to the pediatrician and appeared less overwhelmed than he had before the doctor's arrival.

"Yes, thank you." Hadley summoned a smile.

Dr. Davison turned to the nurse. "Agnes, would you prepare Maggie for a lumbar puncture?"

"Certainly, Dr. Davison." She smiled at Liam and Hadley. "We have some paperwork at the nurses' station for you to fill out," she said. "We'll need just a few minutes for the spinal tap and then you can come back and be with Maggie."

Hadley tensed, intending to resist being evicted for the procedure, but then she remembered that she was the nanny, nothing more. She'd given up her rights when she'd given Liam back his ring.

When they stepped into the hallway, Hadley turned to Liam. "I should go."

"Go?" he echoed, his expression blank, eyes unfocused. "Go where?"

"I don't really belong here." As much as that was true in a practical sense, she couldn't shake a feeling of responsibility to Maggie and to him.

Foolishness. If anyone besides Liam had hired her, she wouldn't have let herself get personally involved. She'd never slept with any of her other clients, either. Even with Noah she hadn't stepped across that line. They'd been close, but something about sleeping with him with his children down the hall hadn't sat well with her. And right before the weekend they were supposed to go away and be together for the first time was when Noah decided to go back to his ex-wife.

"Maggie needs you," Liam countered. "You can't leave her now."

"I'm her nanny." It hurt to admit it, but Hadley knew that after what had happened between her and Liam, she needed to start pulling back. "What she needs is her family. Why don't you call her grandmother?"

"You mean the woman who left her with me and hasn't demonstrated any grandmotherly concern since?"

Hadley was torn. Her presence wasn't needed while Maggie was at the hospital. The nurses would see to it that the baby was well tended. Liam could give her all the love and snuggling she required.

"I'm sorry that Maggie's mother died and her grandmother is so far away, but I can't be here for you and for her in this way. She's in good hands with the nurses and with you. I've already gotten too involved. I can't keep pretending like nothing has changed." Hadley turned in the direction of the elevator so Liam wouldn't see her tears.

He caught her arm before she could take a step. "I'm sorry, too," he murmured in her ear, his breath warm against her temple. "I never meant for any of this to hurt you."

And then he set her free. Gutted and empty, she walked away without glancing back.

Liam sat on the couch in Maggie's hospital room. A nurse had appeared half an hour ago to take Maggie's temperature and change her diaper. When she'd completed her tasks, she'd dimmed the lights and left Liam in semidarkness. It was a little past six. He'd skipped both lunch and dinner but couldn't bring himself to leave the room. He felt empty, but it wasn't because he was hungry. The hollowness was centralized in his chest. Loneliness engulfed him unlike anything he'd known before.

He hadn't felt this lost when Kyle left for the navy or when his grandfather had died. The ranch had provided abundant distractions to occupy him, and he'd thrown himself into building the business. That wasn't going to work this time.

He rarely felt sorry for himself, but in the eight hours since Hadley had taken off, he'd begun to realize the wrong turn his life had taken. The arrival of Maggie and Hadley had been the best thing that had ever happened to him. Acting as Maggie's caretaker had taught him the true meaning of the word *responsibility*. Up until now, he'd had people who did things for him. Staff, his grandfather, even the women he dated. While he didn't think of himself as selfish, he'd never had to put anyone's needs above his own.

But even as he'd patted himself on the back for championing Maggie's welfare, hadn't he ignored his brother's needs when he'd decided to seek custody of his niece? And Hadley's? How had he believed that being married to him was any sort of reward for her love and the sacrifice to her career that staying in Royal would require?

He'd played it safe, offered her an expensive ring and explained that he needed her and wanted her in his life. But he'd never once told her he was madly, passionately in love with her and that if she didn't marry him, he'd be heartbroken. Of course she'd felt underappreciated.

Liam thought about the nightmare he'd had after returning from Colorado. Sleeping alone for the first time in three nights had dragged powerful emotions from his subconscious. He could still recall the sharp pain in his chest left over by the dream, a child's hysterical panic as he'd chased his mother out of the house, pleading with her not to go.

By the time he'd awakened the next morning, there'd been nothing left of the disturbing dream but a lingering sense of uneasiness. He'd shoved the genie back into the bottle. Craving love only to have it denied him was not something he ever wanted to experience again. And so he'd only shown Hadley physical desire and made a superficial commitment without risking his heart.

She'd been right to leave him. He'd pushed her to ride again, knowing how devastated she'd been by her friend's accident. He'd badgered her to forgive herself for mistakes she'd made in the past without truly understanding how difficult that was for her. But worst of all, he'd taken her love and given nothing back.

Liam reached into his pocket and drew out the engagement ring. The diamonds winked in the dim artificial light. How many of his former girlfriends would have given it back? Probably none. But they would've been more interested in the expensive jewelry than the man who gifted it. Which explained why he'd chosen them in the first place. With women who wanted nothing more from him than pretty things and a good time, he never had to give of himself.

What an idiot he'd been. He'd stopped dating so his head would be clear when the right girl came along. And when she had, he'd thought to impress her with a trip to Vail and a big engagement ring. But Hadley was smart as well as stubborn. She was going to hold out for what really mattered: a man who loved her with all his heart and convinced her with words as well as deeds just how important she was to him.

Up until now, he hadn't been that man. And he'd lost her. But while she remained in Royal, he had a chance to show her how he truly felt. And that's exactly what he was going to do.

Thirteen

After abandoning Liam and Maggie at the hospital, Hadley took a cab home and spent the rest of the day on the couch watching a reality TV marathon. The ridiculous drama of overindulged, pampered women was a poor distraction from the guilt clawing at her for leaving Liam alone to cope with Maggie. Worry ate at her and she chided herself for not staying, but offering Liam comfort was a slippery slope. Already her emotions were far too invested.

At seven she sent Kori a text about getting a ride to Wade Ranch in the morning to pick up her car. She probably should have gone tonight, but felt too lethargic and even had a hard time getting off the couch to answer the door for the pizza delivery guy.

It took her friend an hour to respond to the text. Hadley forgot she hadn't told Kori yet about her broken engagement. Leave it to her to have the world's shortest engagement. It hadn't even lasted three days. With a resigned sigh, Hadley dialed Kori's number.

"So, what's going on that you left your car at Liam's?"

Kori's question unleashed the floodgates. Hadley began to sob. She rambled incoherently about Maggie being in the hospital and how she'd turned her back on Liam right when he needed her the most.

"I'm coming over."

"No. It's okay." Hadley blew her nose and dabbed at her eyes. "I'm fine."

"You are so not fine. Why didn't you tell me about this last night?"

"Because I wasn't ready to admit that I'd screwed up and fallen in love with the wrong man again. Honestly, why do I keep doing this to myself?"

"You didn't know he was the wrong guy until too late."

"It's because I jump in too fast. I get all caught up in his life and fall in love with the idea of being a family."

"I thought you said Liam hadn't told you that he planned to fight for custody of Maggie."

"Well…no."

"Then technically, you weren't planning on being a family with Liam and Maggie, but a couple with Liam."

"And eventually a family."

"Since eventually is in the future, I don't think that counts." Kori's voice was gentle but firm. "You love Liam. You told me you had a crush on him when you were a teenager. Isn't it possible that what you feel for him has nothing to do with seeing yourself as part of a family and everything to do with the fact that you're in love with him?"

"Sure." Did that make things better or worse? "But what about the fact that he asked me to marry him because he thought he would have a better chance to get custody if he was engaged?"

"I'm not really sure it's that straightforward," Kori said. "Liam Wade is a major catch. He's probably got dozens of women on speed dial that he's known a lot longer than you. Don't you wonder why he didn't ask one of them to marry him? I think he fell for you and is too afraid to admit it."

As tempting as it was to believe her friend's interpretation, Hadley knew it would just lead to more heartache. She couldn't spend the rest of her life wondering what if.

Kori's sigh filled Hadley's ear. "I can tell from your

silence that you don't agree. I'm sorry all this happened. You are such a wonderful person. You deserve the best guy in the world."

"And he's out there somewhere," Hadley said with what she hoped was a convincing amount of enthusiasm.

"What time do you want me to come get you tomorrow?"

"It doesn't matter." She figured Liam would stay at the hospital with Maggie until she was ready to go home, and that would give Hadley a chance to collect her things from the house without the risk of running into him.

"I'm meeting a client at eight. We can either go before or after."

"I guess I'd rather go early." The sooner she collected all her things, the sooner she could put all her mistakes behind her.

Maggie's new nanny was set to start the day after tomorrow, and Hadley doubted Dr. Davison would release her before that, so she didn't have to worry about seeing Liam ever again. The thought sent a stabbing pain through her.

"How about seven?"

"That would be perfect," Hadley said and then switched to the less emotionally charged topic of their upcoming girls' night out.

After a few more minutes, Hadley hung up. It took about ten seconds to go back to thinking about Liam. How was Maggie doing? Had her test results come back yet? Liam must be frantic waiting to hear something.

She brought up the messaging app on her phone, but stopped as she realized what she was doing. Contacting Liam would undo what little peace she'd found during the afternoon. It might be agonizing to cut ties with Liam and Maggie, but in the long run it would be better for all of them.

Yet no matter how many times she reminded herself of that fact as the evening dragged on, she wasn't able to put the baby or Liam out of her mind. Finally, she broke down and sent Liam a text around ten thirty, then shut off her phone and went to bed. But sleep eluded her. Despite having reached out to Liam, she couldn't put concern aside.

Around six, Hadley awoke. Feeling sluggish, her thoughts a jittery mess, she dragged herself out of bed and climbed into the shower. The closer it got to Kori's arrival, the more out of sorts Hadley became. Despite how unlikely it was that she'd run into Liam, she couldn't stop the anxiety that crept up her spine and sent a rush of goose bumps down her arm. By the time Hadley eased into Kori's passenger seat, she was a ball of nerves.

"You okay?" Kori asked, steering the car away from Hadley's apartment building.

"Fine. I didn't sleep very well. I couldn't stop thinking about Maggie and wondering how she's doing."

"You should call or text Liam and find out. I don't think he would have a problem with you letting him know you're worried."

"I did last night. He never got back to me." Hadley sounded as deflated as she felt. What had she expected? That Liam would fall all over himself telling her how much he missed her and that he regretted letting her go?

"Oh," Kori said, obviously stumped for an answer. "Well, then to hell with him."

That made Hadley smile. "Yeah," she agreed with fake bravado. "To hell with him."

But she didn't really mean it. She didn't even know if Liam had received her text. His focus was 100 percent fixed on Maggie, as was right. He'd answer in due time.

Twenty minutes later, Kori dropped her off at Wade Ranch. Hadley was relieved that her car was the only one in the driveway. She wouldn't have to run into Liam and make awkward conversation.

As soon as Hadley opened the front door she was assailed by the mouthwatering scent of cinnamon and sugar. She followed her nose to the kitchen and found Candace putting caramel rolls into a plastic container. Forgetting her intention had been to pack her suitcase with the few belongings she'd brought to the ranch house and get out as soon as possible, Hadley succumbed to the lure of Candace's incomparable pastries and sat down on one of the stools next to the island, fixing the housekeeper with a hopeful gaze.

"Those smell incredible."

"I thought I'd take them over to Liam at the hospital and give him a break so he could come home and clean up."

"That's really nice of you."

"But now that you're here, maybe you could take them to him instead." Candace caught Hadley's grimace and frowned. "What's wrong?"

"I don't know that Liam is going to want to see me." At Candace's puzzled expression, Hadley explained, "We broke off our engagement and I left him all alone at the hospital yesterday." *After freaking out on him*, she finished silently.

"I don't understand. Did you have a fight?"

"Not exactly. It's more that we rushed into things. I mean, we've only known each other a short time, and who gets engaged after three weeks?"

"But you two were so much in love. And it is an engagement, after all. You'll have plenty of time to get to know each other while you plan your wedding."

Hadley couldn't bring herself to explain to Candace that Liam didn't love her and only proposed so he could improve his chances of gaining custody of Maggie. "It was all just too fast," she murmured.

"But what about Maggie? I'm sure that Liam would appreciate your support with her being in the hospital."

Nothing Hadley could say would be good enough to rationalize abandoning a sick baby, so she merely hung her head and stared at the veins of silver glinting in the granite countertop. "I'll take the caramel rolls to Liam," she said at last. "And maybe some coffee as well. He's sure to be exhausted."

Candace nodded in approval. "He'll like that."

While Candace sealed up the rolls, Hadley poured coffee into a thermos, wondering how she'd let herself get talked into returning to the hospital. Then she sighed. It hadn't taken much prompting from Candace. In fact, Hadley was happy for an excuse to visit.

"If you're afraid because things between you have happened too fast," Candace began, turning away to carry the empty caramel roll pan to the sink, "I think you should know that I've never seen Liam as happy as he is with you."

"He makes me happy, as well." Had she let a past hurt blind her to everything that was true and loving about Liam?

"Whatever stands between you two can't possibly be insurmountable if you choose to work together to beat it."

What if fear of being hurt again had led to her overreacting to Liam's desire to seek custody of Maggie? Was it possible that she'd misjudged him? Attributed motives to him that didn't exist, all because she couldn't trust her own judgment?

"You're probably right."

"Then maybe you two should consider being open with each other about what it is you want and how you can achieve it."

Hadley offered Candace a wry smile. "It sounds so easy when you say it."

"Being in love isn't always easy, but in my experience, it's totally worth the ride."

"And Liam is totally worth taking that ride with," Hadley agreed. "Perhaps it's time I stopped being afraid of telling him that."

"Perhaps it is."

* * *

Liam hovered over Maggie's bassinet as the nurse took her temperature. "Her appetite was better this morning," he said.

The nurse hadn't missed his anxious tone and gave him a reassuring smile. "Her temperature is down a couple degrees. Looks like the antibiotics are doing what they're supposed to."

While it wasn't a clean bill of health, at least Maggie's situation was trending in the right direction. "That's great news." He wished he could share the update with Hadley, but she'd made it clear yesterday that she needed distance. It cut deep that he'd driven her away.

"She's sleeping now," the nurse said. "Why don't you take the opportunity to get something to eat? From what I hear, you skipped dinner last night."

"I wasn't hungry."

"Well, you're not going to do your little girl any good if you get run-down and can't take care of her once she's ready to go home." The nurse gave him a stern look.

"Sure, you're right." But he couldn't bring himself to leave Maggie alone. "I'll go down to the cafeteria in a little while."

Once the nurse left, Liam brushed a hand through his hair, suddenly aware he was practically asleep on his feet. He hadn't been able to do more than snatch a couple naps during the night and could really use a cup of coffee. It occurred to him that he wasn't going to be able to keep this pace up for long, but he would never be able to forgive himself if Maggie got worse while he was gone.

A soft female voice spoke from the doorway. "How's she doing?"

Blinking back exhaustion, Liam glanced up and spied Hadley hovering in the hallway. From her apprehensive expression, she obviously expected him to throw her out.

"A little better."

"That's great. I hope it's okay that I came by."

"Sure." After yesterday, he could barely believe she'd come back. "Of course."

"I wasn't sure…" She looked around the room as if in search of somewhere to hide. "You didn't answer my text last night."

He rubbed his face to clear some of the blurriness from his mind. "You sent a text? I didn't get it."

"Oh." She held up a rectangular container and a silver thermos. "I brought you coffee and some of Candace's caramel rolls. She was going to come herself, but I had to pick up my car and was heading back this way…" She trailed off as if unnerved by his silence. "I can just leave them and go. Or I can stay with Maggie while you go home and shower or sleep. You don't look like you got any last night."

She didn't look all that refreshed, either. Of course she'd worried. He imagined her tossing and turning in her bed, plagued by concern for Maggie. It was in her nature to care even when it wasn't in her best interest to do so.

"I'm so sorry," he told her, his voice a dry rasp. "I should never have let you leave yesterday. We should have talked."

"No." She shook her head and took two steps toward him. "I should apologize. The way I acted yesterday was unforgivable. I should never have been thinking of myself when Maggie was so sick."

Liam caught her upper arms and pulled her close. He barely noticed the container of rolls bump against his stomach as he bent his head and kissed her firmly on the lips, letting his emotions overwhelm him. The aching tightness in his chest released as she gave a little moan before yielding her lips to his demand.

He let go of her arms and stroked his palms up her shoulders and beneath her hair, cupping her head so he could feast on her mouth. Time stood still. The hospital room fell away as he showed her the emotions he'd been keeping hidden. His fear, his need, his joy. Everything she made him feel. He gave it all to her.

"Liam." She breathed his name in wonder as he nuzzled his face into her neck.

"I love you." The words came so easily to him now. Gone were his defenses, stripped away by an endless, lonely night and his elation that she'd returned. He wasn't going to let her question his devotion ever again. "No, I adore you. And will do whatever it takes for as long as it takes for you to believe you are the only woman for me."

A smile of happiness transformed her. He gazed down into her overly bright eyes and couldn't believe how close he'd come to losing her.

"I love you, too," she replied, lifting on tiptoe to kiss him lightly on the lips.

"I rushed you because I was afraid your career would take you away, and I couldn't bear to lose you." Suddenly it was easy to share his fears with her, and from the way she regarded him, she understood what he'd been going through. "This time we'll take it slow," he promised. "I'm determined that you won't feel rushed into making up your mind about spending the rest of your life with me."

She gave a light laugh. "I don't need any time. I love you and I want to marry you. Together we are going to be a family. No matter what happens with Kyle, Maggie will always be like a daughter to us and a big sister to our future children."

"In that case." He fished the ring out of his pocket and dropped to one knee. "Hadley Stratton, love of my life, would you do me the honor of becoming my wife?"

She shifted the thermos beneath her arm and held out her left hand. "Liam Wade, loving you is the most wonderful thing that has ever happened to me. I can't wait for us to get married and live happily ever after."

He slipped the ring onto her finger and got to his feet. Bending down, he kissed her reverently on the lips. One kiss turned into half a dozen and both of them were out of breath and smiling foolishly when they drew apart.

"Kissing you is always delightful," she said, handing him the coffee. "And we really must do much more of that later, but right now my mouth has been watering over these caramel rolls for the last hour."

"You're choosing food over kissing me?"

"These are Candace's caramel rolls," she reminded him, popping the top on the container and letting the sugary, cinnamon smell fill the room.

"I get your point." He nodded, his appetite returning in a flash. "Let's eat."

The morning of her wedding dawned clear and mild. The winds that had buffeted the Texas landscape for the last week had calmed, and the weather forecasters were promising nothing but pleasant temperatures for several days to come.

Today at eleven o'clock she was marrying Liam in an intimate ceremony at the Texas Cattleman's Club. Naturally Kori was her matron of honor while Liam's best man would be Mac McCallum. Because the wedding was happening so fast, Hadley had opted for a white tulle skirt and sleeveless white lace top that showed a glimpse of her midriff. Since she was marrying a man she'd reconnected with less than a month earlier, Hadley decided to kick conventional to the curb and wear something trendy rather than a traditional gown.

Kori had lent her the white silk flower and crystal headpiece she'd worn at her wedding. Her something borrowed. She wore a pair of pearl-and-diamond earrings once owned by Liam's grandmother. Her something old. For her something blue and new, Hadley purchased a pair of bright blue cowboy boots.

The shock on her mother's face validated Hadley's choice, but it was the possessive gleam in Liam's eyes as she walked down the aisle at the start of the ceremony that assured her she'd been absolutely right to break the mold and let her true self shine.

"You look gorgeous," he told her as she took the hand he held out to her.

She stepped beside him and tucked her hand into the crook of his arm. "I'm glad you think so. I thought of you when I bought everything."

He led her toward the white arch where the minister waited. A harp played in the corner, the tune something familiar to weddings, but Hadley was conscious only of the tall man at her side and the sense of peace that filled her as the minister began to speak.

Swearing to love, honor and be true to Liam until the day she died was the easiest promise she'd ever had to make. And from the sparkle in his eyes as he slid the wedding ring onto her finger, he appeared just as willing to pledge himself completely to her.

At last the minister introduced them as husband and wife, and they led their guests into the banquet room that had been set up for the reception. Draped with white lights and tulle, the room had a romantic atmosphere that stopped Hadley's breath.

Flowers of every color filled the centerpieces on the tables. Because of the limited time for the preparations, Hadley had told the florist to pull together whatever he had. She'd carried a bouquet of orange roses and pink lilies, and Liam wore a hot-pink rose on his lapel.

"I had no idea it was going to be this gorgeous," she murmured.

"The only gorgeous thing in the room is you."

Hadley lifted onto her toes and kissed him. "And that's why I love you. You always know what makes me smile."

And so ended their last intimate moment as newlyweds for the next three hours as social demands kept them occupied with their guests. At long last they collected Maggie from her circle of admirers and headed back to Wade Ranch. Together they put her to bed and stood beside the crib watching her sleep.

"I meant to give this to you earlier but didn't get the chance." Liam extended a small flat box to her.

"What is it?"

"Open it and see."

Hadley raised the lid and peered down at the engraved heart-shaped pendant in white gold. She read the inscription, "Follow your heart. Mine always leads to the barn." She laughed. "I used to have a T-shirt with that on it."

"I remember." Liam lifted the necklace from the bed of black velvet and slipped it over her head. "You were wearing it the first time I saw you."

"That was more than ten years ago." Hadley was stunned. "How could you possibly remember that?"

"You'd be surprised what I remember about you."

She threaded her fingers through his hair and pulled him down for a kiss. "It's a lovely gift, but it no longer pertains."

"I thought you'd gotten past your guilt about your friend."

"I have." She smiled up at him. "But my heart no longer leads me to the barn. It leads me to you."

He bent down and swept her off her feet. "And that, Mrs. Wade, is the way it should be."

* * * * *

LET'S TALK

Romance

For exclusive extracts, competitions
and special offers, find us online:

- facebook.com/millsandboon
- @MillsandBoon
- @MillsandBoonUK

Get in touch on 01413 063232

MILLS & BOON

THE HEART OF ROMANCE

A ROMANCE FOR EVERY READER

ODERN
Prepare to be swept off your feet by sophisticated, sexy and seductive heroes, in some of the world's most glamourous and romantic locations, where power and passion collide.

STORICAL
Escape with historical heroes from time gone by. Whether your passion is for wicked Regency Rakes, muscled Vikings or rugged Highlanders, awaken the romance of the past.

EDICAL
Set your pulse racing with dedicated, delectable doctors in the high-pressure world of medicine, where emotions run high and passion, comfort and love are the best medicine.

rue Love
Celebrate true love with tender stories of heartfelt romance, from the rush of falling in love to the joy a new baby can bring, and a focus on the emotional heart of a relationship.

Desire
Indulge in secrets and scandal, intense drama and plenty of sizzling hot action with powerful and passionate heroes who have it all: wealth, status, good looks…everything but the right woman.

EROES
Experience all the excitement of a gripping thriller, with an intense romance at its heart. Resourceful, true-to-life women and strong, fearless men face danger and desire - a killer combination!

To see which titles are coming soon, please visit

millsandboon.co.uk/nextmonth

JOIN US ON SOCIAL MEDIA!

Stay up to date with our latest releases, author news and gossip, special offers and discounts, and all the behind-the-scenes action from Mills & Boon...

 millsandboon

 millsandboonuk

 millsandboon

It might just be true love...

MILLS & BOON
MEDICAL
Pulse-Racing Passion

Set your pulse racing with dedicated, delectable doctors in the high-pressure world of medicine, where emotions run high and passion, comfort and love are the best medicine.